PRAISE FOR ALLEN STEELE'S

A KING OF INFINITE SPACE

"Steele is an engaging writer, his vision of the future feels solid and detailed . . ."

—*Washington Post*

"Over the past ten years Allen Steele has been building a future history in space based on the music of today. His space stations were built by workers with Grateful Dead tunes blaring away in their ears. With Jerry Garcia dead, Steele has given new meaning to the idea of Deadheads."

—*Denver Post*

THE TRANQUILLITY ALTERNATIVE

"Science fiction with its rivets showing as only Steele can deliver it. This one is another winner."

—Jack McDevitt, author of *Ancient Shores*

"Allen Steele has created a novel that is at once action-packed, poignant and thought-provoking. His best novel to date."

—Kevin J. Anderson,
bestselling author of
The Jedi Academy Trilogy

Books by Allen Steele

Novels
Orbital Decay
Clarke County, Space
Lunar Descent
Labyrinth of Night
The Weight
The Jericho Iteration
The Tranquillity Alternative
A King of Infinite Space

Collections
Rude Astronauts
All-American Alien Boy

A KING OF INFINITE SPACE

A NOVEL BY

ALLEN STEELE

HarperPrism
A Division of HarperCollinsPublishers

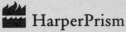
HarperPrism
A Division of HarperCollinsPublishers
10 East 53rd Street, New York, N.Y. 10022-5299

Copyright © 1997 by Allen Steele
All rights reserved. No part of this book may be used or reproduced in any manner whatsoever without written permission of the publisher, except in the case of brief quotations embodied in critical articles and reviews. For information address HarperCollins*Publishers*, 10 East 53rd Street, New York, N.Y. 10022-5299.

ISBN 0-06-105756-8

HarperCollins®, 🔥®, and HarperPrism® are trademarks of HarperCollins*Publishers*, Inc.

A hardcover edition of this book was published in 1997 by HarperPrism.

Cover illustration © 1998 Chris Moore

First mass market printing: December 1998

Printed in the United States of America

Visit HarperPrism on the World Wide Web at
http://www.harperprism.com

❖ 10 9 8 7 6 5 4 3 2

In memory of:
Rick Dunning,
Claude Gross,
Paul "Tiny" Stacy

✛ CHAPTER ✛

ONE

LIVE THROUGH THIS

"Why? Why not?"

—Timothy Leary; last words

The night sky always looks the same, no matter where you go: look up, and the universe opens before you. The constellations may be different, the stars in new positions, but it's always the same cosmos: a seemingly endless darkness, broken only by tiny lights that could be planets, suns, nebulae, even entire galaxies. No one really knows how large this universe is, where its true limits are, or how long it may last. . . .

But nothing lasts forever. Not even eternity.

This is the story of the last day of my life, and everything that happened after that.

To say that it's hot is an understatement. St. Louis in mid-July is a perpetual sauna; the temperature only dips below eighty for a few hours between midnight and dawn, and by early afternoon you could probably get a good lunch by scooping the brains out of your skull, dropping them on the sidewalk, and cracking open an egg on top. Downtown, yuppies scurry from air-conditioned offices to air-conditioned bistros, their business suits and knee-length dresses clinging to their skin like fifty-percent cotton rags, while out in the 'burbs their spouses sit in stalled traffic as they crawl to the shopping mall, there to seek respite from the heat and humidity by buying more stuff they really don't need. At home, little kids stare at cartoons on the tube and chase each other with Super Soakers, while their teenage siblings hang out in the park and smoke the pot they stole from Dad's secret bedroom stash.

It's July 11, 1995, and it's hot all over. The Unabomber has mailed a deranged screed to the *New York Times* and the *Washington Post*, demanding that Western civilization grind to a halt; Western civilization yawns and flips to the funny pages. A NASA space shuttle has just returned to Cape Canaveral after docking with the Russian space station; most people are more interested in catching the new Tom Hanks movie about another space mission twenty-five years ago. Ten Republicans claim that they can do a better job of ruining the country than one Democrat, and no one really doubts their word. Right-wing militia nuts are saying that the United Nations is conspiring to take over the United States, which is a hoot because UN peacekeepers can't prevent Serbs from wiping out Croats in a plot of European real estate little larger than Pennsylvania. The major-league baseball strike has been settled, which means that it's okay to come back to the ballpark and watch your team get stomped by the Cleveland Indians—pardon me, the Cleveland Native Americans. Richard Gere is in *Camelot*, Clint

Eastwood is in Meryl Streep's pants, and Denzel Washington is in a sub; Ben Kingsley battles aliens while Sylvester Stallone fights giant robots, and the best babes in the Cineplex are Batman's new girlfriend and Disney's idea of how Pocahontas might have looked if she had worked out on a Nautilus machine and shaved her pits. Calvin talks to Hobbes, Rush talks to Newt, O.J. talks to his lawyers, and every moron who has worn his wife's clothes, screwed her son's girlfriend, or been kidnapped by aliens is talking to Oprah, Sally, Geraldo, and/or Ricki. Just between you and me, I'd rather have my brains fried on the sidewalk and eaten with a poached egg.

As it turned out, fate has other plans for my gray matter. Fate, my father, and a man named Mister Chicago who hasn't even been born yet, and it begins with a trip out to Riverport for Lollapalooza.

I leave early from my job at a second-hand record store and return to the Central West End apartment Erin and I share, a two-bedroom flat furnished with Pier One wicker stuff, cement-block-and-plank shelves filled with paperbacks and comic books, a queen-sized waterbed, and a life-sized cardboard figure of Captain Kirk adorned with cheap Mardi Gras beads and an earring in his left ear. We watch *Animaniacs* while we roll a few joints and fill our daypacks with bottles of Evian water, sunscreen, spare rolls of toilet paper (in case some kid throws all the asswipe in the toilets), Tylenol (for heat headaches), and extra packs of cigarettes. Shemp arrives around about four o'clock, and then we pile into my '93 Saturn SC2 and head for the show. A long summer afternoon of rock 'n' roll with my girl and my best friend.

I need to tell you about Erin and Shemp.

First, Erin. She's been my girlfriend for the past two years, after we met at the recording studio where she worked as an office manager when the band Shemp and I belong to, the Belly Bombers, came in to record our first and only demo. The Bombers never got a label interested in signing us, but Erin came home with me the night we cut the final track. Shemp was splitting the rent with me at the time, but six months later he moved out and Erin moved in.

It isn't enough to say that Erin Westphall is a babe. She's outright beautiful: twenty-three years old, very slim, small-breasted, with chestnut hair that flows down to the center of her back. Chicago's her hometown, but she moved to St. Louis after graduating from Stephens College in Columbia and kicked around the city before landing a job at the studio. As with my part-time job at Dino Tracks, she really doesn't need to work; like Shemp and me, Erin's a trust-fund kid from a wealthy Lake Forest family who's impatiently waiting for her to get over her dreams of becoming a novelist so she can return to Chicago, marry some dude with an MBA, and settle down in the 'burbs to become a baby machine. That might happen once she gets tired of waterbeds, cinder-block furniture, and cold pizza for breakfast, but for the time being she's cohabiting with a rich kid who works part-time at a record store while working on a novel about cohabiting with a rich kid who works part-time at a record store.

And then there's Shemp, whose seldom-used proper name is Christopher Meyer: twenty-four years old, six-feet-one, overweight by about fifty pounds, with buzz-cut dark hair and a soul patch under his lower lip. I've known Shemp ever since eighth grade at Country Day School; his German-American genes had been unkind to him, because when puberty hit us Shemp became a teenage reincarnation of one of the Three Stooges, and thus the nickname, which somebody gave him in the locker room after gym class. Our families both live in Ladue, and since the Meyers own the Big Bee Supermarket chain, his dad is constantly on his case about joining the family business.

Shemp aspires to be a comic book artist, though, and after one summer of wearing an apron with a grinning bee on it and asking old ladies if they had any coupons, he decided that he'd rather work on his indie comics creation, *The Slack*, which he eventually hopes to sell to Dark Horse, while playing drums with the Bombers on the weekends. He's a lot smarter than he looks; when Erin started staying over at our apartment every night, he realized that it was time for him to find his own place. Erin and Shemp never really hit it off, but after I made it clear to Erin that Shemp's my best friend and to Shemp that I'd rather see Erin getting out of the shower every morning, they've learned to tolerate one another. Sort of. Getting reserved seat tickets for Lollapalooza for the three of us is one more attempt on my part to get them to be pals.

And then there's William Alec Tucker III . . . but we'll get to him later.

So now it's quarter to five, the sun still high in the sky, and the thermometer standing at ninety-two in the shade. We park the Saturn in the back of the Riverport lot and join the line at the turnstiles as it shuffles through the usual daypack searches and metal detector sweeps by the rent-a-cops before we get our tickets ripped. No one finds the joints I've hidden in my cigarette pack, and Erin manages to get through the pat-down without being groped by some cop, and in another minute we're through the gate and in the middle of thirty thousand other members of Gen-X and Gen-Y.

Riverport Amphitheater is an artificial hill in front of an enormous open-sided shed, with long asphalt walkways circling the hill to plazas on either side of the stage. You've got your punks, your ravers, your frat boys, your stoners, your teeners, your slackers, your over-the-hill hippies looking for one more summer of love before they finally cut their hair and get a job. Up on the hill, they stand, sit, or sprawl on blankets trampled by countless sneakers and hiking boots, listening to Jesus Lizard thudding from distant speakers; down on the walkways, even more shuffle past tents set up by hucksters touring with the show. T-shirts, jewelry, window stickers, incense, dope paraphernalia, CDs by bands no one has ever heard of, sunglasses, cheap dresses and parachute pants, underground comic books, hemp hats: an open-air mall of the hip and hip-five-minutes-ago, mobbed by kids in search of something that won't look stupid three months from now. It's all loud and crowded and sweaty and hot, just the way I like it.

Closer to the shed, food vendors have set up their tents; our noses are assaulted by the odors of a dozen different kinds of ethnic cuisine. Shemp's hungry, so he heads straight for a Thai concession, where he buys a paper plate of raman noodles and stir-fried yeti. Two places sell overpriced fruit juices—they can't call them smart drinks anymore, because the FDA determined that you'll still be just as stupid as you were before you had one—but Erin joins the line in front of the Budweiser stand, unhip as it may be. I wander around the plaza while I wait for them, catching a little of this and that. Under a large tent, a San Francisco theater troupe stages a performance in which a gray-wigged, business-suited Republican auctions off the Bill of Rights. Thirty feet away, teenagers impatiently wait their turn to try out the free videogames set up under the Sega pavilion. A fifteen-year-old kid climbs into a Spaceball; after a minute of spinning upside-down and inside-out, he's spewing chunky green stuff all over the transparent plastic sphere. I spot Shemp watching the gastronomic fireworks from the other side of the crowd: he takes his plate of raman-and-yeti to the nearest garbage can.

We find our seats under the shed just in time for Sinead O'Connor. She's let her hair grow out a little since the time she tore up the pope's picture on *Saturday Night Live*, and she's got a four-piece band that backs her up as she does a rap version of the Beatles' "All The Lonely People" (or whatever the hell it's called) and a song about the Irish potato famine. It's really very pretty and Erin is transfixed because she loves Sinead, but Shemp is talking to two dudes sitting behind us. I can't hear what they are saying, but the three of them get up and leave before her performance is half over.

Erin and I wander over to the Art Tent. It's a little cooler in here, but no less humid. There're strange sculptures—a spiked armchair raised on a nine-foot throne, an altar of jeweled skulls illuminated by automobile taillights—but the only thing I wish I had is a signed lithograph of Big Daddy

Roth's Rat Fink. We find Shemp staring fixedly at a Robert Williams silk-screened tapestry of a bare-breasted angel wearing a space helmet floating above a junkyard filled with thirties-style space-ships. He babbles at us for several minutes about the obvious correlation between Stephen Hawking, Gene Roddenberry, Jack Kirby, and God-knows-what; his pupils have expanded into tiny planets. Shemp's found some acid; we make sure that he still has his ticket stub and knows that he can't return to his seat without it, then we go get some more beer.

For dinner music, we get power-grunge by Pavement. The mosh pit on the hill, placid during Sinead, briefly comes alive with flailing arms and legs; everyone else is bowed by the oppressive bur-den of the sun. Erin and I smoke a joint—the ushers don't give a shit, they're on the lookout for people throwing junk at the stage—then go out for more beer. We find the mist tent and stand fully clothed under the sprayers. Several Deadheads are talking about what happened at a campground in St. Charles after a Grateful Dead show at Riverport last week. A hundred kids were taken to the hospital when a deck at the campground lodge collapsed during a thunderstorm. Everyone agrees that it was a bummer, but at least Jerry put on a good show. Doesn't mean much to me; I'm not into the Dead. The cool spray plasters Erin's shirt against her breasts; I'm beginning to look forward to going home after the show.

I hit the men's room on the way back to the shed. Guys in shorts and sticky T-shirts are lined up in front of the urinals, letting go of all the beer and fruit juice they've been sucking down. The tile floor is slippery with water jetting out from a sink faucet that's been jammed open; an old black janitor in uniform tries to monkey-wrench the spigot shut. I can't get to a urinal and I've got to take a major leak, so I piss in the next sink over. The janitor yells at me to cut it out, but I ignore him. This is what you're paid to do, man: clean up after people like me. If you don't like it, then go to college and become a rocket scientist.

Cypress Hill comes on at seven o'clock with loud, aggressive rap about fucking and smoking pot. I'm all for both, but Erin isn't into this stuff; she drags me over to the second stage near the front gate, where we catch Beck doing a solo acoustic show. Once again we see Shemp; completely zooed by now, he's standing near the stage, screaming "Loser!" every time the guy takes a break. This may be a request for Beck's big radio hit or an opinion of Beck himself; either way, Beck ignores him, and when Shemp spots us from across the crowd, we turn and hurry away before anyone sees us with him.

We check out the other side of the amphitheater. More hucksters selling clothes and bumper stickers and shit, but there're also tables set up by groups like Greenpeace, NOW, Missouri Public Interest Research Group, and so forth. All these guys trying to save the world; what's the point? I sign a NORML petition so I can get a bumper sticker with a pot leaf on it. There's a large silkscreen tapestry set up on a scaffold: a mushroom cloud exploding behind screaming children and mounds of skulls, titled "August 1945." History, man; it happened a long time ago. Let it go, let it go.

Back in our seats, we blow another joint as we wait for Hole's road crew to finish setting up. It's a

little after eight now, and the sun is finally beginning to go down; the heat is off, and the crowd is
beginning to awaken from its collective stupor.
Time to do some serious partying.

Yet, as I turn around to look back over the
countless bodies crammed together beneath the
shed and up on the hill, something occurs to me. In
this instant, I see my generation: torn apart by
divorce when we were five years old, then told that
monogamy or abstinence is the only way to stop
AIDS; suckled on a tube filled with bad sitcoms,
idiot cop shows, and Saturday morning cartoons
with not-so-subtle messages about Peace, Love,
Understanding, along with ads for a Barbie's Dream
House that looks like nothing we'll ever afford;
despised by hippies-turned-yuppies who try to sell
us compilations of twenty-five-year-old rock music
and reproductions of Peter Max paintings, but
won't give us a decent job so we can pay for this
shit; numbed by whippits, lousy pot, and gassy
beer; dumbed out on Nintendo, the failed politics
of both Democrats and Republicans, and *Beverly
Hills 90210*. No respect, no hope, no clue, no cigarettes . . .

No future.

It's something like an epiphany.

Realizing this, I say:

(and this part I remember very clearly)

"Y'know, this is the best day of my life."

I don't realize that I've spoken aloud until Erin
turns to look at me.

"Really?" she says. "I didn't know you were
enjoying yourself so much."

Startled by her voice, I look at her, and it's
almost as if I'm seeing her for the first time. God,

she's so beautiful. A warm breeze has caught her long, fine hair and cast it back from her face; the setting sun has highlighted it and made it golden. There isn't an inch of her body that I don't know, yet in this instant she's as new to me as the moment when we first met, and although what I just said was meant to be ironic, I suddenly realize that it's truthful.

This *is* the best day of my life.

This same time next year I'll be twenty-six, and ten years later I'll be thirty-six, and twenty years after that I'll be forty-six; if I'm still alive by then, this stoned summer afternoon will be another faded memory of a middle-aged man who has long since discarded his youth and become the CEO of Tucker Brothers Enterprises, with an ex-wife who now lives in Los Angeles with her third husband and a son I'll see only occasionally, and then only to give worthless presents to. . . .

Like the aluminum dog tag that hangs around my neck on a silver link chain like a weird medal of St. Christopher. My father gave it to me last February, when he took me out to my usual birthday dinner at Tony's. One of the few times I ever see him; most of the time, he's either at the office or in another country, making another business deal. Toaster ovens to Russians who can't buy bread. I smoked a bone in my car before going into the four-star Italian restaurant, so I was pretty stoned at the time and don't remember why he said it was so important that I have this thing . . . but, y'know, it's stamped with my name and the phone number of some company called the Immortality Partnership, and since it looks kinda punk I wear it from time to time, including today. Shemp's dad gave him one, too, and we get a laugh out of them. If we get killed, these things are supposed to make sure that we have a second chance.

Uh-huh. Sure. And you can grow up to be the next president of the United States. I mean, it's possible. . . .

I can't articulate any of this, though. I've smoked too much, drunk too much; my mind has been turned to mush by heat and loud music and the crush of bodies. All I can do is look into Erin's pale green eyes and say something I've said to other girls before, but never with any sincerity. Until now.

"I love you," I say. "I love you so much."

Erin blinks. For an instant, there's doubt in her face. She has had other boyfriends before me; doubtless they've muttered the same thing as they've tried to get her into bed. But I don't grab at her and I don't look away and I don't make a smartass remark, and finally there's acceptance in her eyes.

"I love you, too," she says at last, then she puts her arms around me and pulls me close.

The house lights dim and everyone rises to their feet. I wrap my arms around her shoulders and duck my head to receive a kiss that makes the world disappear for a moment.

The best day of my life. If someone had told me that I had only an hour and twenty-six minutes left to live, I would have never believed them.

Hole comes on stage beneath a punk galaxy of mirror balls and foil stars. Courtney Love wears a low-cut black babydoll dress, cigarette dangling from her mouth. She plays guitar with her left foot propped up on a monitor speaker, giving the horny college jocks in the front row a flash of her inner thighs. Her lyrics are unintelligible beneath the raw power of her band's music, but it doesn't matter; for an hour she's the vortex of a tornado that rips through the shed and up the hill. It's good shit. When Hole is through with its set, Courtney hands her guitar to someone in the front row, flips off some puke who'd been verbally abusing her, and marches off stage. Everyone's on their feet and howling for more.

All except Erin and I. Sonic Youth is the headliner; they're good, but we've seen them before, and for the last hour Erin's body has swayed next to mine in a seductive way. If the emcee were to announce that Sonic Youth's bus broke down and that they're going to be replaced by Jesus and the Twelve Disciples, we would have to leave. We've got the urge, that simple.

By now, Shemp has returned to his seat. He's still tripping, but he peaked some time ago and now all he wants to do is go home and catch a *Star Trek* rerun. I know that he really intends to crash on the living room couch, something that I've tried to discourage him from doing after Erin moved in, but this time I don't argue with him. He can always turn up the sound while Erin and I make it on the waterbed.

There's also the fact that, of the three of us, Shemp is in the best shape to drive. Shemp may be babbling about another cosmic revelation he's received, but at least he's able to walk a straight line. I'm wasted; Erin is in better condition, but she doesn't know how to handle manual and my car has a five-speed stick. Shemp has driven my car many times; if we happen to get pulled over by the cops, at least he doesn't have beer on his breath.

All this is discussed while we weave our way through the parking lot in search of my car, our faces made sickly yellow by the sodium lights. If I had any common sense, I would head straight for the high-rise hotel on the other side of the lot. Screw it, guys, let's get a room. I'd have staggered into the lobby, whipped out a gold Visa or a gold MasterCard or the American Express trump card, rented a single and a double for the night, and forgotten about the car until tomorrow morning.

Indeed, the notion occurs to me, just as we find my Saturn at the far end of the lot. My mind is fogged, though, and Erin is warm and deliciously sweaty. Responsibility has always been something I've tried to ignore, so I toss Shemp the keys, and we now have ten minutes left to live.

We roll down the windows; the night air is warm and dusty.

I'm curled up in the backseat; Erin is riding shotgun. She strains against the shoulder harness as she reaches behind her for the tape box. Shemp has disconnected the driver's seat harness because it pinches his stomach.

Erin switches on the map light to look through the box. Shemp peers at the cassettes as if they're the crown jewels of England. He grabs for *Orb Live* before Erin swats his hand away, insisting that we listen to Pearl Jam instead.

Erin and Shemp get in an argument. The car almost veers off the shoulder right in front of the cops directing traffic to the interstate. I yell for Shemp to keep his eyes on the road. Shemp grabs the wheel and gets the Saturn back in his lane. For a moment I'm afraid that the cops are going to flag us for a roadside check, but their flashlights wave us through.

Shemp makes the turn for the interstate ramp.

Erin slips *Ten* into the deck. Eddie Vedder serenades us with a song about a woman trying to seduce her son as we join a dense river of eastbound headlights: cars, trucks, RVs driven by middle-aged tourists making their way from country music palaces in Branson to downtown St. Louis and points beyond.

A car horn blares just behind us as Shemp swings into the center lane without using the left turn signal. I try to tell him to take it easy, but he's raving about the vapor trails coming from the taillights in front of him.

Erin turns down the music a little and tells him to concentrate on the road. Shemp grips the wheel with both hands and stares straight ahead, but a minute later he catches a glimpse of a billboard for the Casino St. Charles riverboat. That cracks him up for no accountable reason. He turns up the volume again.

I lie down on the backseat and stare up at the ceiling. My ears are buzzing, my clothes are sticking to me like day-old chewing gum, my leg muscles are stiff and aching.

It's been a long day. All I want to do is go home.

I scratch at a mosquito bite under my right knee and think about putting some lotion on my sunburned neck.

Shemp abruptly swerves into the right lane. Suddenly the backseat is flooded with harsh white light. A truck horn bellows in rage. . . .

Something as big as God smashes into the rear bumper.

And now Shemp and Erin and I are all screaming at once, and Shemp panics and twists the wheel hard to the right, and I look back just in time to see a Mack eighteen-wheeler munching the Saturn's rear fender, and then I'm thrown from my seat as the car leaves the pavement and

>   dives

>   down

>   a hill

>   and now everything is rolling

>   rolling

>   rolling

>   twisting

>   screaming

>   side over side

>   twisting screaming

Erin screaming fuck fuck fuck

Shemp screaming god oh fuck oh shit

>   something slams

against my chest

>   (pain)

>   lights all around me Erin Shemp

(love you)   (you stupid fuck)

>   then the roof caves in

>   (PAIN)

>   something crushes me pushing me

>   down

>   down

>   my head hits something

hard

>   (OH MY GOD JESUS IT HURTS)

and suddenly, there is no pain.

Darkness falls on me.

And then there is

nothing.

✢ CHAPTER ✢
TWO

SIMPLE

*Midway in our life's journey, I went astray
from the straight road and woke to find myself
alone in a dark wood. . . .*

—Dante, *The Inferno*

And so I die.

It doesn't last very long.

It's much as if I've gone to sleep for awhile.

"Wake up now," a voice says to me from the darkness.

I really don't want to wake up. Everything is warm and peaceful.

"Open your eyes now," the voice says, a little more insistently. "It's time to wake up."

I open my eyes. I'm in a very soft bed in a featureless white room with no windows.

In beds all around me are many people, their arms at their sides, faces turned upward. Some are men, some are women, all in their mid-twenties, with faces unwrinkled and unblemished, as hairless as newborn babes.

"Sit up now," the voice says. "Can you sit up?"

My back feels stiff, my arms heavy as lead; it takes me a few moments before I manage to push myself up on my hands. The white sheets and covers fall away; I'm naked, but that doesn't trouble me. In fact, nothing bothers me at all. I'm simply here, and how I came to be here is of no concern at all.

"Very good," the voice says. "You're doing very well."

It sounds as if someone is standing next to my bed, but when I look around to see who's speaking, there's no one present.

"Get out of bed now," the voice says. "See if you can stand up."

This is a very complex request. The voice has asked me to do two things at once. I hesitate, trying to figure out what it wants me to do.

"Blink your eyes three times," the voice says. "Blink them three times fast."

Blink? Sure. I can blink. I can blink three times. When I do, a cartoonish stick-figure of a man appears in front of me. He's sitting up in a bed, just as I am now; he slowly swings his legs over the side of the bed until his feet touch the floor. Then he stands up and walks to the end of the bed, where he stops.

"Do you think you can do that?" I nod, and the stick man vanishes. "Good. Try to do it now."

I push the covers the rest of the way back, slowly turn until my legs are over the side of the bed, then lower my feet until their soles touch the smooth, cool floor. I hesitate again, then stand up. My hips and knees are as stiff as my back, but my leg muscles are strong and they support my weight.

"You're doing very well," the voice says. "Can you walk to the end of the bed?"

This requires a little more concentration, but I manage to get it done. "Very good. You're doing very well. You can go back to bed now."

I don't understand what the voice had just told me to do, so I just stand there. "Go back to bed," the voice repeats.

I still don't understand what is being asked of me, and it disturbs me that I can't see the source of the voice. I look around and see all those still forms lying in bed around me, so silent and

(dead)

sleeping in this white room illuminated by soft light that comes from everywhere but nowhere, and I'm the only one who's moving around.

"Go back to bed now!"

I'm afraid now. I whimper, and as I do so, something hot and fluid rushes through my lower body. I look down and see a thin stream of urine splattering on the floor in front of me. My fear is replaced by vague sensations of relief and satisfaction, and I stare in curiosity at the urine as it forms a thin yellow puddle on the floor that touches my toes and makes me giggle at its warm touch.

"Blink your eyes three times," the voice says, a little more kindly now; when I do, the little stick man reappears, standing at the foot of his bed just as I'm now in front of mine. He turns and reverses his process of getting out of bed, and when he's back where he had started the image vanishes. "This is how you get back in bed," the voice says. "Do you think you can do that?"

I nod, and then copy the stick man, and when

my head touches the soft pillows again I feel as if I've accomplished something really spectacular.

"Very good," the voice says. "You're doing very well. Now, I want you to tell me a couple of things."

This is new. What's there to tell? "I want you to count to ten, aloud," it asks.

This is extremely complicated. I whimper again, but at least my bladder's empty and I'm unable to wet the safest place I know.

"Blink your eyes again," the voice says.

I do so, and now the stick man lying in bed opens his mouth and speaks in a flat male voice: "One . . . two . . . three . . . four . . . five . . . six . . . seven . . . eight . . . nine . . . ten."

The image vanishes. "Can you do that?" the voice asks.

I open my mouth and move my lips. Nothing emerges. I try again, and this time only exhale. Tears sting the corners of my eyes; deep down inside, I know what I want to say, but I can't articulate it.

"Blink three times." I do so, and an abstract figure appears in front of me: a vertical spike, as large as a tombstone. "This is One," the voice said. "Say it . . . one."

Something deep in my throat stirs to life. "Wa . . . wa . . . won."

"Very good," the voice says, and that makes me feel better. Another abstract figure, this one curled over like a crooked finger, appears before me. "Two . . ."

"T-t-ttt . . . too . . . too!"

"Very good." Another figure: two backward curls, one atop of the other. "Three . . ."

"Thrrpp . . ." I spit saliva on the sheets. "Thrrr . . . threeee . . ."

"You're doing very well," the voice says, and now I'm bouncing up and down in bed, proud of myself. A stick crossed with a right-angle replaces the earlier numeral, and this time I identify it without any trouble.

We get through the last six digits without any trouble, and when we're done the voice asks me to recite all ten numbers. I really have to concentrate on this one, but after a few seconds it comes back to me: "W-won . . . too . . . threeee . . . foh . . . fi-fyve . . . sex . . . se-se-seppen . . . ate . . . n-n-nyne . . . tin!"

"Very good," the voice says. "Now there's only one last question, and after that you can go back to sleep."

I wait anxiously, hoping that it won't ask me for the next number after ten. I know what two ones placed next to each other look like—I can visualize it in my mind's eye, and don't need to blink three times to see it—but I don't have the word for it.

"What is your name?" the voice asks.

I open my mouth, close it, open it again, close it once more. There's something in the back of my mind—a stream of half-recognized images that are at once as familiar as my toes and yet as unreal as this room, that are real and significant and mean everything to me, but nonetheless untouchable . . . and yet, at the nucleus of this strange atom, I perceive a sound, a feeling, a word . . .

"Ah . . . ah . . . al . . . al . . . aleh . . . aleh . . . alekk . . . alekk . . ."

"Yes," the voice says. "That's correct. Your name is Alec. You may go to sleep now, Alec. You have done very well, and we will continue this when you wake up."

Exhausted, I fall back against the pillows, pulling the sheets and blanket around me as I curl into a fetal position with my hands tucked into my crotch. The voice loves me. The voice is proud of me. My name is Alec, and I can stand up and walk and count to ten, and the voice says that's okay.

I slept, and woke up when the voice told me to wake up, and practiced walking some more, this time to a small table and chair a few feet from my bed where a bowl of soup was waiting for me.

I don't know how to use a spoon, but when the voice tells me to blink three times, the stick man appears to show me how it's done. Although I drip much of the soup on my chest, the table and the floor, I manage to get most of it in my mouth.

The soup is good. It has a taste that I vaguely remember, but can't quite identify. At one point I freeze with the spoon halfway to my mouth, and stare at it as two syllables fight their way up from my subconscious. "Ken . . . chi . . . ken . . . chi . . . chi . . . chi . . . ken . . . chi . . . ken . . ."

"Very good, Alec," the voice says. "You're eating chicken soup."

I nod happily, very pleased with myself. I like chicken soup.

When I'm done, the voice instructs me to walk through a narrow door at the opposite end of the room. This is the farthest distance I've yet traveled, a journey which takes me past the beds where the other people lie. As I slowly walk toward the door, I see that many of them are awake. Some are trying to get out of bed; others simply lie still, staring into space and blinking rapidly as they murmur to themselves. A few are curled into tight little balls, their eyes wide as they clutch themselves and tremble uncontrollably. I feel nothing for them; they're just naked bald men and women whom I don't know.

The door leads into a smaller room, one with white tile floors with a drain in the center and small holes in the ceiling. A row of seatless toilets are lined up against the far wall. The voice tells me to sit on one of the toilets. I obey, but don't know what to do next until some primal instinct takes hold and my bowels empty themselves. Again, there's a vague sense of satisfaction and relief; when I'm through, the voice tells me to stand up, walk to the nearest ceiling hole and wait there.

This I do, and after a moment a tiny rainstorm of soapy hot water erupts from the hole. This startles me and I leap out from under the water, but the voice sternly tells me to remain beneath the hole. I'm more afraid of the voice than the water, so I reluctantly return to the shower. Three blinks, and the stick man reappears; this time he's rubbing his hands all over his body, and when I imitate him I once again feel great satisfaction, until the water suddenly turns cold and I yelp and nearly jump out from under the hole again. The voice tells me to stay under the hole, so I obey it, and once I've been rinsed I'm rewarded by a long blast of hot air that warms and dries my goosepimpled skin.

The voice tells me to go back to bed, but as I walk through the door I see something that scares me so much, I nearly duck back into the shower room.

At the far end of the room, a man wearing a

long hooded robe is removing my soup bowl from the table.

None of the others in the room appear to have noticed him, but he sees me, and motions for me to come closer. ·

I'm badly frightened and don't want to go to him, but the voice tells me that he's my friend and that he has a gift for me because I had been so good, so I step through the door and timidly walk down the aisle between the beds.

Halfway through the room, I feel a strange prickling at my neck: a feeling that I'm being watched from behind.

I stop and turn around, and see that one of the bald naked men I've just walked past has sat up in bed. He's bigger than anyone else in the room, and he's staring straight at me. His gaze is intense; I mewl in fear, and then he raises his hand toward me and opens his mouth, and once again hot urine escapes from my body.

"Don't pay attention to him," the voice says. "He can do you no harm."

The big man stops what he's doing. His mouth closes as he stares into space, and then his arm drops to his side. I have the odd notion that I know him, but when I blink three times the stick man doesn't appear to help me understand.

"Go to your friend, Alec," the voice says. "He's waiting for you."

So I turn around and walk the rest of the way to the hooded figure. He's nearly as tall as the man behind me, but his face is as kindly as the other's had been intense. My soup bowl is in one hand, and draped over his other arm is a long white robe much like his own.

"Hello, Alec," he says when I stop before him. "I'm your friend. My name is John. Can you say that? John?"

"Ju . . . ju . . . ju . . . joh . . . jon."

John nods. "Very good, Alec. I'm John, and I'm your friend."

"Fr . . . fre . . . fre . . . friend John."

"Excellent," John says, and even though that word goes right over my head, I know that it must mean something good. "We're very pleased with you, Alec," he continues, "and we want you to keep doing as we tell you to do, because we have a lot of wonderful surprises for you. All right?"

I nod my head, even though much of what he had just said is confusing. "Very good," John says. "Now I have a little present for you, but you must promise—"

He stops abruptly, and then blinks three times. As he does, I see something strange; although his eyes remain open, translucent membranes come down from beneath his eyelids and over his pupils. There are tiny sparks against his brown eyes for a couple of moments, then the second pair of eyelids sweep open again.

"You must not urinate on the floor anymore," John says. "Do you understand?" I shake my head. "If you feel like you've got to . . . if you're afraid of something and you want to do like you just did . . . then you've got to go in the bathroom and urinate into one of the toilets." He pauses. "Blink three times, Alec."

The little stick man shows me how to properly use the toilet. "This is your associate," John says. "He is always here to help you, and no one can hear or see him except you. If you ever have any questions about anything, blink three times and ask your question, and your associate will tell you what to do. Do you understand?"

I nod. "Very good, Alec," John says, then he extends the robe to me. "This is your present. It is something to wear. Put it on."

I take the robe from his hands. It looks just like John's, but I don't know what to do with it until I blink three times and the stick man—my associate—reappears to demonstrate how I should put it on. I fumble with the robe until I find the widest opening, then I duck my head and pull it over me. There're a few moments of anxious struggle before my arms find the sleeves and my head comes through the opening.

Now I'm dressed much like John. That makes me very proud of myself. The robe is clean and warm against my skin, and I know now that I'm truly loved by John and my associate.

"Very good, Alec," John says. "I'm very proud of you. You can go back to bed now."

He turns and walks toward the wall behind him. A round portal that I hadn't noticed before irises open and John steps through it, and I'm still staring at the door long after it closes behind him.

No one else in the room has robes. No one else in the room has been fed. No one else has learned to go to the bathroom. These thoughts follow me back to my bed, where I go to sleep still wearing my precious robe.

I had no perception of day or night. The soft light from the ceiling and walls of the room never dimmed, but always remained lit at the same level.

I slept, I awoke, I ate, I relieved myself, I showered, I learned how to do fundamental things such as making my bed or dressing myself, and then I went to sleep again. This went on for a long time, but I didn't try marking the passage of time by counting the number of times I had slept or eaten because it never occurred to me to do so. Nor did I have any desire to learn what lay beyond the door John occasionally came through.

I existed in perpetual dream state in which things simply happened. My few emotions were at the most primitive level; I wasn't bored, curious, or irritated, although I should have been. I was hungry sometimes, but that seldom lasted very long, because John always materialized with another bowl of chicken soup. I was sometimes a little scared to go to the bathroom because that meant passing the bed where the large man with the intense eyes lived; although he sometimes stared at me when I walked by, he never pointed at me again, and after a while I disregarded him entirely. When I was tired, I went to sleep, and when I was through sleeping, I got out of bed and went to the bathroom.

My associate—the voice that spoke to me from nowhere, the little stick man who appeared whenever I blinked my eyes three times—became my tutor, teaching me new words when it became necessary to do so: "soup," "bowl," "spoon," "bathroom," "toilet," "hot water," "cold water," "robe," "blanket," and so forth. It never occurred to me to give a name to that voice, nor did I ever wonder where it came from, or why blinking three times caused the stick man to materialize before my face. Like everything else, it simply . . . was.

I was not alone in my daily routine. The others in the room were also learning how to do these same things, even though I was the first one to master the basics. Most of them, at least; a few simply lay in bed and whimpered, and from time to time John would come through the door to feed them or change the soiled sheets on their beds. After awhile, some of them vanished; this usually happened when I was asleep—all of us tended to sleep at the same time—but once I saw John come in and escort out of the room a man who had been crying uncontrollably for nearly as long as I could remember. I didn't know where he went; I never saw him again, and I didn't have any curiosity about his fate. His bed was empty, and not long afterward it too simply disappeared.

But most of my fellow inmates gradually went through the same learning process as I did, and it wasn't long before all of us wore robes that John had given us. We learned to walk, we ate chicken soup from bowls that had been placed on small tables near our beds, we went to the bathroom, we fluttered our eyelids and spoke aloud to voices we alone could hear. Yet there was seldom any desire—or need, really—to communicate with one another, for we existed in happy somnambulance. Sleep, eat, walk, crap. Life was good.

But things began to change, and not always for the better.

John and another robed figure brought in a long table, and John told us that we would all be eating our chicken soup at the same time at this table. That went well for the first few feedings, but then our meals started arriving further and further apart, not just whenever we were hungry. When that happened, there was always a rush to be at the table when John and the other robed men brought in the bowls. Once there was a scuffle between two men over a bowl of soup, which was abruptly settled when both of them suddenly went still. They blinked their eyes, murmured things to their associates, and waited patiently until two men entered the room and led them away. My associate told me that fighting was not allowed, and there were never any fights after that. I never saw those two men again.

I eventually learned that the man who lived in the bed next to mine was named Russell, and that the woman on the other side of his bed was named Anna, and the woman on the other side of her was named Kate. Russell and Anna and I became friends simply because we saw the most of each other, but I never really met Kate because she spoke only to Anna and the man who resided in the bed on the other side of her, whose name was George.

Kate didn't seem to like George very much. I didn't have an opinion either way, except that I noted that he ate less than the others; sometimes he would double over and vomit on the floor, and then John would bring him a towel and make him clean up the mess he had made. But that wasn't what seemed to make Kate dislike George; after awhile, I noticed that he was always trying to touch her, and most of the time Kate didn't want to be touched by him. I didn't know why, but neither was I very curious. This was just one of those things that happened.

I'm in the bathroom while Anna and Kate are standing beneath the showers. I'm sitting on a toilet with my robe hitched up around my waist; Anna and Kate have their robes off and are naked, but I don't think much of this other than to blandly observe that the women don't have penises (another new word my associate has identified for me) and have breasts (ditto). Their nudity means as little to me as the fact that I'm relieving myself in their presence; we all share the bathroom's showers and toilets with no embarrassment or shame.

George comes into the bathroom. He starts walking toward the toilets, but then he stops and looks at Anna and Kate. He stares at them for a long time, then he suddenly strides over to Kate, grabs her from behind, yanks up his robe and thrusts himself against her.

Kate screams. She tries to pull away, but George has locked his hands around her waist as his thighs pump hard against hers.

Kate screams again. Anna turns around, sees what is happening. She blinks a few times, remains motionless for a moment, and then she screams "Stop!" and hurls herself at George.

George disengages himself from Kate and turns around to grab Anna instead, but Anna kicks him in the groin. George howls and falls down on the slick floor, and then Anna is all over him, savagely beating his head with her fists and kicking his legs with her feet. George cries out, but he doesn't seem injured; instead, he grabs at Anna's ankles, trying to make her fall down even as he tries to clamber to his knees.

While this is going on, Kate has collapsed on her hands and knees and is crawling away, sobbing and screaming, until she reaches a corner of the bathroom, where she curls into a tight little ball, her hands clutched between her legs.

Russell rushes into the bathroom. He sees Anna attacking George and Kate huddled in the corner. He goes to Kate and tries to comfort her, but she flinches away the touch of his hands.

And then George screams.

Very loud now, and not from anything Anna has done. He grabs at his head as he howls in agony, his back arching as his legs thrash at the floor.

Something fluid and red starts dribbling out of his nostrils. Anna stops beating him and steps back, horrified yet fascinated by what she's seeing.

Then, all of a sudden, George stops screaming. His entire body trembles, then it goes limp. There is a soft exhalation from his mouth—a kind of a "haaa"—and there's a faint, nasty odor in the humid air. Then he's very still.

Blood mixes with water on his chest, seeps down his skin, washes down the drain. Russell stands up from Kate and stares at him. Anna steps farther away, her breath coming in ragged gasps. They both remain that way until John and another robed man walk into the bathroom.

Without saying a word to any of us, they pick George up between them and carry him through the door. When they're gone, Anna and Russell go to Kate, gently hoist her to her feet, and lead her back toward the white room. She's still crying, her hands still clasped between her legs.

Anna turns her head and looks straight at me. She doesn't say anything, but simply stares at me for several long moments. Then she helps Russell carry Kate out of the room.

When the bathroom is vacant once more and everything is still and silent, I rise from the toilet and go to one of the ceiling holes. I stand beneath it and take a nice, long shower, all by myself. Some diluted blood, pink and filmy, remains on the floor; I watch it with faint interest as it curls in on itself and spins down the drain.

I haven't done anything wrong. I haven't done anything right. At no time did my associate instruct me to do anything, either right or wrong; therefore my conscience is clear.

I've simply . . . existed.

That's all that counts.

THREE

THIS IS A CALL

I know not how it was—
but, with the first glimpse of the building,
a sense of insufferable gloom pervaded my spirit.

—Edgar Allan Poe,
"The Fall of the House of Usher"

About the same time that I become vaguely aware that I'm getting tired of chicken soup, John comes to see me.

I'm walking back to my bed from the shower room when he steps in front of me. "Please come with me, Alec," he says. "I want to show you something."

Not that I'm given much choice; he's already taken my arm and is leading me toward the vanishing door. I whimper a little as it irises open, and glance back to see Anna watching me from her bed. John reassures me with a gentle pat on the shoulder, and then I leave the White Room for the first time since my first awakening.

We walk down a short, narrow hallway which ends in another door; it opens to reveal a bisecting corridor. Just as much as the White Room is plain, the corridor is wonderfully ornate: walls of some dark, whorled substance that looks like mahogany, brass handrails, high metal archways, doors with carved lintels, ceiling fixtures that cast oval spots of light on a checkered floor. The corridor is wide enough for five men to walk abreast, and so long that I can't see where it ends.

Nor is it empty; it's filled with men and women who step around us as John and I slowly walk along. Although by now my hair has begun to grow out a little, I'm astounded by the styles in which they wear theirs: roosterlike mohawks, long braids, bowl cuts, dreadlocks. They wear blue jumpsuits, tunics, drawstring pants, flared trousers, long and short dresses, high-necked shirts, embroidered vests and jackets, long sleeveless coats, capes, sandals, boots. Some have their eyes masked by opaque glasses; many wear tiny headsets. Now and then they stop before closed doors which slide open to let them enter; I catch brief glimpses of the rooms before the doors shut behind them, and none resemble the featureless place I've just left: chairs, desks, panels with little lights on them. There are tiny signs above the doors; although I recognize the numbers on some of them, I can't read the words.

There's a faint beeping sound behind us. John gently pulls me aside to let a small vehicle pass. Containers are stacked on its open bed and it floats several inches off the floor, but it doesn't have anyone aboard. I stare at it until it disappears from sight; it seems to vanish into the ceiling far away from us, and that's when I realize the corridor bends upward slightly.

John talks to me as we walk.

"How are you feeling today, Alec?"

"Good. I'm feeling very good, John."

"That's good. Have you been happy here?"

"Yes, I . . . I'm very happy here."

"Very good, Alec. We've been very pleased to have you as our guest. Do you know what that means, Alec? Guest?"

"No . . . no, I don't." I blink three times, but for some reason I don't hear the voice of my associate.

"Your associate has gone away for just a little bit, Alec," John says. "He's leaving us alone for awhile. Do you mind?" I don't completely understand his question, and not having my associate makes me a little nervous; I shake my head. "Well, a guest is someone who has been invited to come and stay at someone's house. This is our house, Alec, and you're our guest, and you've been a very good guest. Do you understand now?"

No, because I don't remember anyone inviting me here. But I don't want to make John mad at me, so I say: "Yes."

"Very good, Alec. I also want to tell you that you can stay here as our guest for as long as you want. We like you very much, and we would like to have you remain with us. Do you understand?"

"Yes," I say, more truthfully now.

"That's good. Now, here's a big question, one that I want you to think about a little before you answer. Do you understand me?"

I think about it a little. "Yes, John. I understand you."

I look directly at him when I say this, and now I notice something odd: John's eyes have changed color. They've always been brown before, but now they're pink.

John laughs. "I'm glad you do, Alec, but that isn't the question. The question is . . . do you remember what you were doing before you came here?"

I think harder this time, but can't recall anything past the moment when I first woke up in the White Room. On the other hand, thinking is a very difficult thing for me to do; it always seems as if there's something in the head that won't let me. It's like the disappearing door in the White Room: I know it's there, but whenever I've walked over to look for it, all I've found is a blank wall. "No," I say after a few moments, "I don't remember."

"Nothing at all?"

I look at John. His face is as placid as always, but now there's a strange depth in his pearl-colored eyes, and even as I look, something appears in my memory

(a face)

that I can't identify, yet the more I concentrate, the more

(a young man's face)

it seems familiar, as if I've seen it recently, even though I can't

(a young man with that face, smoking a cigarette)

put a name to it, or say where I've seen it before.

"Do you remember something?" John asks.

"I remember . . . I remember a face."

"Is it your own?" I don't know, but I don't believe so. I shake my head. "Have you seen it recently?"

"No . . . no, I don't think so."

"I see. Do you remember anything else before you arrived here?"

"No." And that's the truth. So far as I'm concerned, my life had begun forty-eight bowls of chicken soup ago.

"Well, then," John says, "let me tell you a little bit of what you don't remember. You were very sick when you were brought here, but someone asked us to take care of you and so we did. Now you're even better than you were before you got sick, and now you're our guest, and as I said before, you're welcome to stay with us for as long as you wish. Do you understand?"

"I . . . I . . ."

"Yes, Alec?"

"I think so."

"You think you understand?" I nod again. "But you have a question, don't you?"

"All the other people in the room . . . were they . . . ?"

John stops before a closed door. He passes his hand in front of a tiny panel on the wall next to it, but the door doesn't open at once. "Sick? Yes, they were. They were all sick when they got here, and we were able to cure most of them. Some of them didn't get as well as you, though, and so we had to take them someplace else, but you're doing fine. You've made wonderful progress, and we're very proud of you."

The door parts in the middle and slides open; two people step out, brushing past us with scarcely a glance. Startled by their sudden appearance, I shrink back against John, but he lays a comforting arm around my shoulders. "It's all right, Alec. Everyone here is your friend. You can go inside now."

The room is very small, vacant, and almost as featureless as the White Room; the door closes as soon as John and I enter. "Great Hall," John says, and there's a motion from beneath the floor that makes me grab the slender metal rail that encircles the room. "This is an elevator," he explains. "It takes you places . . . just as I'm taking you someplace now."

"Where?"

"Somewhere special. A place you've never seen before."

The door opens onto a short hallway: hard marble floor, pale blue walls hung with framed oil paintings of rolling countryside, mountain landscapes, and river valleys. The paintings are very old, yet they somehow look familiar. I stare at them as I shuffle behind John while he walks to a carved oak door at its end. He waits patiently until I catch up with him, then he opens the door and leads me through.

Before us is an enormous rotunda, one so huge that our footsteps echo off the domed ceiling far above our heads. Medieval tapestries drape white stone walls between tall, round columns; beneath the columns are archways leading to corridors branching off from four sides of the rotunda. A vast mural is painted across the inside of the dome: angels and cherubim float around an ancient bearded man in a robe who is reaching out to touch the extended hand of a reclining nude man. A broad staircase spirals up to a gallery encircling the rotunda; archways on the second floor lead to even more corridors. Sunlight gleams through windows above the gallery and through an open arch on the far side of the hall.

The floor is a mosaic: hundreds of thousands of tiny pieces of multicolored ceramic and quartz form a black surface sprinkled with tiny white jewels, with long threads of hammered gold tracing concentric circles and odd right-angled patterns. The floor looks rough, but it's mirror-smooth beneath my sandals; the patterns are familiar, but I can't place them, let alone give them a name. All I know was that they're achingly beautiful.

"This is the Great Hall of our master's house," John said. "There's forty-two rooms in the castle, and they must be—"

"The master?"

"Pasquale Chicago . . . but you must call him Mister Chicago, never Pasquale. Can you say that, Alec? Mister Chicago."

"Mister Chicago," I slowly repeat. Again, something tickles my memory: the last word seems familiar.

"Very good. This is where he lives when he isn't absent."

"Absent?"

A small smile. "Away on business . . . just as he is now. One day you may get to meet him."

"When?"

"Someday. However, his household continues to operate just as if he was home, so it scarcely matters if you ever meet him or not. Mister Chicago is a very busy man, because he is also a great man, greater than anyone else who lives here. You're his guest, Alec, and you must always respect this. Do you understand?"

I nod. "Who is Mister Chicago?"

"A great man," John repeats, a little more firmly now, "and that is all that matters to you." Then he takes my hand. "Come now. There's much more I have to show you."

He guides me across the Great Hall toward the sunlit arch, our sandals softly padding against the mosaic floor. I hear a faint scrubbing noise; I look around, spot a man in a hooded robe like John's and mine. He's kneeling on his hands and knees between two columns. There's a pail of soapy water next to him; he's diligently scrubbing the floor with a brush. He briefly raises his eyes as we walk past, then quickly looks down again.

"Who is he?"

"Someone you'll meet later," John says.

Past the archway is a broad balcony surrounded by a wrought-iron balustrade. Turning around to look, I see an enormous octagonal dome surrounded by four gable-roofed wings, each containing dozens of casement windows. At the apex of the dome is a glass hemisphere, like a little greenhouse. A castle of gray stone: mysterious and wonderful, yet somehow frightening.

And beyond the parapet . . .

Glades and ponds and meadows, a landscape stretching out for miles, its horizon a hazy line in the far distance where a pale yellow sky melds with the ground. There is no sun, only a warm mellow glow from a vaulted ceiling rising above patchwork vineyards and thickets of small trees. Narrow dirt paths lead away from the castle, weaving between apple groves and carefully cultivated gardens, disappearing into the distance.

I smell roses and ripening grapes, maple and fresh-cut grass, daisies and sod. Strange birds sing weird songs as they flit from branch to branch. A bumblebee settles on my wrist for a moment, then buzzes off before I can react. From somewhere far off, goats protest some momentary distraction; on a terrace below the balcony, a calico cat nearly the size of a half-grown dog stands up, gracefully arches its back, then saunters off in search of whatever passes for a mouse in these parts.

I stare and I stare and I stare, my eyes moving from one wonder to the next, as hungry as my stomach had been when I had first awakened. No chicken soup served in a sterile white room, this, but a smorgasbord of sight and sound and aroma.

"Welcome to your new home, Alec." John stands beside me, his hands clasped together within the sleeves of his robe. "I hope you'll be happy here."

"My home?" I can't believe what he's just said. All that I see—the gardens, the manicured lawns, the clear brook meandering alongside a pathway until it disappears into a distant orchard, the fantastic manse behind me—this is where I now live?

"For as long as you wish to remain here." John's voice is very soft. "For the rest of your life, if you wish."

A stone stairway leads down to the terrace where the cat prowls. Without a second thought, I start moving toward the stairs, intending to take it down to the terrace . . . and then beyond, out into this new, beautiful world.

I haven't gotten as far as the third step, though, when John clears his throat.

"Oh, dear," he says. "Will you look at this?"

I look back at him. He's still standing at the railing, but now he's gazing down at the balcony's white tiles. My eyes travel to where he's looking, but I don't see anything unusual.

John glances up at me; there's consternation in his face. "Here," he says, pointing down at a spot just in front of his toes. "Look here . . . this is terrible!"

I don't know what he's talking about, nor am I very interested. John is my friend, though, and something has upset him, so I reluctantly walk back up the steps and to his side. "Come closer," he says, bending down on one knee. He gently runs a forefinger across the tiles and holds it up to my face. "Do you see?"

There's a faint gray smudge on his fingertip.

"Yes," I say. "I see."

"Filthy. Just filthy." John *tsk*s as he wipes off his finger in a fold of his robe. "It gets dirty here quickly, but I bet this terrace hasn't been properly mopped in a week, at very least."

He stands up and strides past me to the stairway, where he kneels again and runs his finger across the top step. "Oh, and it's even worse here," he complains, peering at his fingertip again. "Just awful . . ."

"Yes, it is. . . ."

"You agree?" He looks up at me sharply. "That this place is filthy?"

"Umm . . . yes, I think so. . . ."

"Good! I'm so happy!" Brisking his hands together, he stands up again and walks away from the stairs. "Well, we'll just have to do something about this, won't we? Come along. . . ."

I glance back at the magnificent world that had just been introduced to me. All I really want to do is to walk down those filthy stairs and across the grimy terrace below them, out to the nearest germ-filled path and away into this warm and inviting world, to become lost in its vast and intriguing beauty. I want this more than anything else. . . .

"Come on!" John snaps, clapping his hands together. "Hurry up! We've got to take care of this before Mister Chicago finds it!"

"But you said he was . . ."

"Absent, yes . . . but I also said that his household operates as if he never left. Now hurry!"

I hasten to catch up with John, who is already standing within the archway, and follow him as he strides quickly back through the Great Hall, passing the robed man silently scrubbing at the floor on his hands and knees, until we walk through an arch and find a small alcove hidden between two columns.

He stops before a plain wooden door within the alcove and stands aside. "Say your name to this door and tell it to open. Quickly now! Not a moment to lose!"

I look at the door. "Umm . . . Alec."

"Say 'I'm Alec . . . open.' Hurry!"

"I'm Alec, open."

The door slides open; within is a large walk-in closet whose shelves are filled with buckets, brushes, feather dusters, sponges, sprayers, toilet paper, folded towels, cans of this and bottles of that. Arranged on hooks on the far wall is a large selection of brooms and mops.

John shoves past me into the closet. "Take this, and this, and one of these," he says as he snatches up a bucket, a mop, and a can of some evil-smelling off-white powder and thrusts everything into my hands. He points to a spigot mounted on the wall next to the door. "Fill the bucket halfway with water. Hurry!"

Bewildered, I stare at the bucket for a moment, then at the mop, then the spigot. "I don't know . . ."

"Ask your associate!" John snaps.

He told me that my associate wasn't with us, but when I blink three times, the little stick man appears before me. He shows me how to place the bucket beneath the spigot and twist its knob. I repeat his motions; cold water gushes into the bucket. When the bucket is half-full, John impatiently reaches around me to turn off the water.

"Now put a little soap in the water," he says, his voice nowhere near as friendly as it had been before. When I give him a blank look, he grabs the canister out of my hands. "Like this," he says, then shakes a fistful of the powder into the bucket. "See?"

"Uh . . . yes, I . . ."

"Outstanding!" He flicks a hand over his shoulder as he backs out of the closet. "Quick now! Bring everything and follow me! Hurry! We're wasting time!"

Encumbered by the mop, the detergent bottle, and the heavy bucket of water, I scurry to catch up with John as he stalks out of the alcove, through the Great Hall, and back onto the balcony. Once we're back where we started, he halts in the same place where he had shown me my wonderful new home and points at the very same spot where he wiped his fingers.

"Mop."

I try to hand the mop to him.

"No," he says coldly. "You mop."

I stare at him in utter confusion. "I . . . don't know how."

"Blink three times," he says.

The stick man dips the head of his mop into the bucket, lifts it out again, places it on the floor and begins to move it back and forth. It's now plain what's expected of me, but I still don't know why. Once more, I look away at the incredible world that lies beyond the parapet. . . .

"I don't want to, John. I want to go out there." I drop the mop and start walking toward the stairs.

A dagger of electric ice stabs into my brain.

I howl and grab my head. My legs become liquid, give way beneath me. The cold hard tiles slam against my face; a coppery taste rushes in my mouth, and there's a hot fluid sensation between my thighs as the knife slices somewhere just behind my eyes and

(the PAIN it hurts like)

it hurts like

(rolling down a hill over and over)

and I hear

(a woman screaming something crashing)

and then it's suddenly gone and now I'm lying on the balcony, my breath coming in ragged gasps as I clutch at my head, my pulse pounding at my temples. There's a dull acidic sensation beneath my legs as the robe soaks up my urine. My tongue involuntarily licks the blood that my teeth have drawn from my inside lower lip.

"I'm sorry, Alec." John is kneeling beside me, his hand stroking the bristles of my hair. His voice is as kindly as when we first met. "I'm sorry it had to be this way, but maybe it's better that you learn this now and not later."

I manage to raise my head to look at him. "You're our guest," he says, "and you can stay here for as long as you like, but there are some things that are expected of you in return, nor are you free to do as you wish."

"Free? I don't . . . I don't know that . . ."

"No," John says softly. "You don't understand. Not now, at least . . . perhaps later, but not now." His hand falls to my shoulder. "Listen to me carefully, because I will tell you this only once. If anyone around here ever tells you to do something for them . . . to do anything for them . . . just do it, because if you don't, they'll make your head hurt again. Do you understand at least this?"

I nod as much as I'm able. "Good. Do you remember what happened to George, that time in the bathroom when he attacked Kate? They can do that to you, too, if you do something really wrong . . . and they'll know about it if you do, because your associate is always watching you no matter where you are."

"But . . . I thought he was my friend."

"He is your friend, Alec, but he can also be your enemy, if you do anything wrong." He taps the top of my head. "He lives up here, and he sees what you see, hears what you hear. You can't get away from him. Understand?"

"I understand." As I speak, a new word surfaces to my mind. I say it aloud: "Okay."

"Huh?" John seems surprised. His pink eyes drill into mine. "What did you just say?"

Believing I've just done something wrong, I pull away from him, but he quickly shakes his head. "No, no, it's all right, it's . . . okay."

"Okay?"

He smiles, but his lips tremble when he does so. "I've never heard you say that before." He pauses. "Do something for me. Don't worry, it'll be fun. Blink three times and say, 'Eyes-up reiteration, okay.'"

"Okay." Nothing happens. John repeats his instructions, and so I say, "Eyes-up reiteration, okay," and blink my eyes three times.

Okay

The word appears in front of me just as the little stick man has done many times before, floating in midair before my eyes like a translucent ghost. Startled, I cower against John's chest.

"Can you read that?" John whispers. "Can you tell me what it says?"

"Yes . . . it says 'Okay.'"

He takes a deep breath. "Good," he murmurs. "The osmotic damage must not be as bad as they thought. You're recovering your long-term memory. . . ."

His words are meaningless. He notices the blank look on my face and shakes his head again. "It's all right. You've done nothing wrong. Let's try this again. Say, 'Eyes-up' again, and then ask the associate to give you your name. Do you think you can do that?"

More nervous now, yet wondering at what I had just seen, I say: "Eyes-up . . . what is my name?"

Once again, the ghost words appear in front of me:

Your name is William Alec Tucker III.

"What does it say, Alec?" John whispers.

It takes me a few moments to puzzle it out. "It says . . . 'Your . . . name is . . . William . . . Alec . . . Tucker . . . I . . . I . . . I . . .'"

"Very good. Now, say 'Eyes-down.'"

I repeat what John had just said, and the words vanish. "I want you to practice doing this. Whenever you're working or taking a shower or eating, every time you're alone . . . but only when you're alone, off by yourself, when no one else is watching you . . . I want you to say, 'Eyes-up,' and then speak aloud the things that you see, or what you're holding in your hands. Do you understand me?"

"Yes, John."

"This is our little secret, so I don't want you to let anyone know what you're doing. Okay?"

I nod. "Very good," John says. He stands up and helps me get back on my feet, then he reaches down and picks up the mop. "Now I want you to mop this entire balcony and the stairs. Don't go anywhere else. Just mop the balcony and the stairs. Make them nice and clean. When you're done, I want you to push your fingers against your lower jaw like this . . ." he demonstrates by pressing his own fingertips against his right lower jaw ". . . and say, 'John, it's Alec, I'm done.' Can you do that, Alec?"

I tell him that I can, and I'm rewarded by one of his smiles. "That's very good, Alec. I'm very proud of you. You're my favorite student. When I come back for you, I'll take you to the place where you'll be living from now on. It's much nicer than the place you were before, and you'll have it all to yourself. Would you like that?"

I'm not sure if I do. The White Room is home; it's snug and secure, and the few friends I've made are there. Yet after everything I've been shown, I don't want to return to its white-on-white sameness . . . and I'm really tired of chicken soup, even though I'm still uncertain whether there are any alternatives.

"Yes," I say, "I would like that very much."

"Okay," John says. "I'll see you later."

And then he turns around and walks away, leaving me alone with my mop, my bucket, and my fear.

✛ CHAPTER ✛

FOUR

MISERY

*"If a man hasn't discovered something that
he will die for, he isn't fit to live."*

—Martin Luther King, Jr.

I finish mopping the balcony and the terrace stairs, then I prod my lower jaw just as John showed me and tell him I'm through. I hear his voice in my ear; he tells me to remain there until he comes for me. My back is aching and my hands are sore from grasping the mop handle, so I sit down on the steps and rest for a few minutes, and it isn't long before John reappears.

He spends a couple of minutes inspecting the balcony, running his fingers along the tiles and making sure that I've mopped beneath the railing, and when he's through there's a broad smile on his face. He says that I've done a good job and that he's proud of me; I might have been delighted by his praise if I wasn't so tired. As it is, I simply nod my head.

The light is a little dimmer now. I hadn't noticed earlier because my attention was focused on my work, but now I see that the shadows cast from the castle walls and the nearby trees and bushes are longer. The sky has faded from mustard yellow to burnt orange; now I can make out a thin glow coming from thin lines running parallel across the sky. Between the lines are wide bands of deep blue; I can make out tiny pinpricks of light here and there . . . save at the center, where there appears to be a large dark mass.

John sees that I'm looking up at the sky. "It's late afternoon," he says before I ask. "The day's coming to an end. Night's coming on, and it'll be dark soon."

Day. Night. New words, but nonetheless familiar . . . and another word comes to mind. "Sun . . . sundown," I say.

"I suppose you could call it that, yes." He points to my mop and bucket. "Time to go. Pick those up and bring them with you. Be careful that you don't spill any dirty water . . . you don't want to have to mop up the hall floor."

He leads me back to the closet and shows me how to empty the gray mopwater into a drain marked *Water Recycle* and where to place the mop and bucket. As I do so, another white-robed figure enters the closet: a short black man carrying a wicker basket filled with brushes, towels, and bottles. At first he seems startled to find us here, but then he eases into the closet and begins putting away all the stuff in his basket. When he's done, he turns to me.

"My name's Sam," he says.

"Sam?"

"Sam I am," he adds, and as he says this, something flashes through my mind: a faint recollection of

(curled up in a woman's lap, a large book spread open on her knees, looking at)

warmth and security and

(pictures of a cat in a tall striped hat, carrying a platter of food)

wonder unfolding.

"Green eggs and ham," I say, not really knowing what it means.

He stares at me for a long moment. "Yeah," he says very softly, almost as a whisper. "Green eggs and ham. Do you . . . ?"

John clears his throat. Sam gives him a furtive look, then he turns and quickly walks out of the closet. He almost collides with another robed figure standing just outside: a slender young woman carrying a broom. It's Anna, and she looks about as exhausted as I am. Her mouth drops open when she sees me, but we don't get a chance to speak before John ushers me out of the closet.

"That's Anna," I say to John as he leads me further down the corridor, away from the Great Hall. "She sleeps with me."

John laughs out loud. I don't know why, but if he thinks what I've said is funny, it must be, so I laugh, too. "I know," he says, "but you're not going back there, ever again. I'm taking you somewhere else now."

"You want me to mop some more stairs?" I hope not; my back is really hurting, and hunger has made a nest in my stomach.

"Oh, no. You're done for the day, and you've performed very well. I'm taking you to your new room . . . one you get to have for your very own. Would you like that, Alec?"

I nod, although I'm uncomfortable with the

notion. The White Room has been my home for a long time now; it's a safe place, and I don't wish to leave it behind. John seems to notice this. "You'll like this place better, Alec, I promise." Then he hesitates. "Have you ever met Sam before?" I shake my head. "But you both knew the same rhyme. Where is it from?"

"I don't know."

He peers at me. "Something else you remembered?"

I shrug. "I think so. Sort of."

A door at the end of the corridor leads into another elevator, this one a little smaller than the one we used earlier. John shows me how to push a little blue button marked "2" on a panel inside the elevator. The doors slide shut; there's a sensation of downward movement. "If you remember anything else," John says, "be sure to tell me about it. All right, Alec?"

"Okay." Another thought occurs to me. "Should I tell you, or the other John?"

John stares at me. "Why do you think there's another John?" he asks.

"Because the other John has different eyes. Yours are . . ." I grope for the right word: "Pink."

His back stiffens, his mouth becoming a tight line. For a second I think he's angry with me, and I shrink back against the handrail. Then he relaxes: not naturally, but as if he's telling himself to do so. "I'm the John you want to talk to about this," he says. "Don't talk about your memories to anyone else . . . not even the other John."

"Okay, John. But why . . . ?"

The complex question I want to ask—*Why are there two people who look like you and have the same name?*—dies on my lips, for just then there's a small voice in my mind

("Well, Alec, you're right, he's not the real Santa Claus. He's . . .")

that tells me

(". . . one of Santa's helpers, because Santa's very busy right now . . .")

it probably isn't a good idea

(". . . but everything you tell him, he'll tell Santa himself, okay?")

to tell everything I know to this John, that John, or any other John, because

(". . . Now don't cry. It's just Santa. He just wants you to sit in his lap.")

you never know who you can believe.

"What is it, Alec?"

I remember the expression on Sam's face, how he suddenly became quiet when he saw John standing next to me, and how the man who was scrubbing the floor in the Great Hall quickly looked away when he saw us walking through. They've been here longer than I have; they know something that I don't . . . and now, for the first time since I've known him, I'm unwilling to fully trust John.

"I don't know," I say very softly, shaking my head. "I just . . . forgot."

John doesn't seem satisfied by this answer, but then the elevator stops and the doors open again. "Well," he says, "when you do remember, be sure to tell me." Again, the smile. "Okay?"

"Okay, John. I will."

This is the first time I've told a lie.

■　　■　　■

John leads me down a long, narrow corridor with plain gray walls and a low ceiling. The corridor is lined with doors; mounted on them are small rectangles with luminescent letters, each inscribed with a name. As we walk past the doors, John pronounces each name in turn—Bill, Susan, Amad, Christopher, Stan, Lisa, Winston, Hugh, Veronica, Anna, Sam, Kate, Russell, and so on, including some that I can't pronounce and a couple that are written in alphabets that I don't recognize—until we arrive at a door marked *Alec*.

"Place your thumb against the nameplate," John says, and when I do the door slides open. Inside is a little room; the ceiling brightens as we walk in. It has a narrow bed that has already been made up with sheets, a pillow, and a blanket. There's also a small closet which holds fresh white robes and a couple of folded towels, a shelf with nothing on it, and a toilet with a roll of thin paper on a hinge above it.

"Here you are, Alec," John says. "This is your room."

I stand at the doorway. The room is windowless and bare, not much larger than the closet where I had left the mop and bucket only a few minutes earlier, and furnished with only the barest of necessities . . . and it's the best thing I've ever seen. It's a room of my own, with my name on the door and everything: a toilet I didn't have to share with anyone else, clean clothes in the closet, a bed where I could sleep all by myself, a shelf for—well, for something. . . .

John casts his hand across the room as if it was the Great Hall itself. "Yours and yours alone. Do you like it?"

"Yes, John. I like it very much." But it's so small. . . .

"Good. When you're ready to eat, go to the end of the corridor. The mess room is there, and you'll find food there. You can eat there twice a day, along with everyone else. All your friends will be there. At the other end of the corridor is the shower room. It's just like the one in the White Room."

"Okay, John."

"Tomorrow morning there will be lots of new things for you to do. Your associate will tell you what to do. If you have any questions, just ask him. All right?"

"Okay, John." Even my voice feels tired. I didn't want to talk to him anymore.

"I'll let you get settled in now. I'll see you later." He gives me a fond pat on the shoulder, then steps back out the door and closes it behind him. I hear his footsteps receding down the corridor, and then I'm alone.

I sit down on the edge of the bed and gaze at all this for a few moments. Then I fold my arms together on my knees, bend my sore back until my forehead rests on my hands, and start to cry.

I don't know why. It just seems like the right thing to do.

This was the beginning of my new life, as a servant in the household of Mister Chicago.

Mornings began the same way each day, with the ceiling of my little room softly glowing to life as an invisible hornet quietly buzzed in my ears. If I tried to sleep any longer, the light became brighter and the buzzing grew louder until it was an angry

snarl; if I managed to ignore that and pulled the pillow over my face, a sharp pain in my skull would
jolt me wide awake and leave me with a headache
for the rest of the day. That only happened once; I
quickly learned to get out of bed as soon as the light
came on.

After using the toilet, I would take a short walk
down the hall to the communal showers where,
along with several other naked servants of both
genders, I would wait for my turn beneath one of
the ceiling holes. As in the White Room, there was
no privacy to be had here; however, it never
occurred to me to get turned on by any of the
women showering next to me, although I was now
aware that there were distinct differences between
their bodies and mine. Our hair had grown out so
we were no longer bald, but the depilatory soap we
used kept us from growing hair on our limbs, faces,
and pubic areas.

After the shower, I would return to my room,
where I put on a clean robe. The one I wore yesterday I would dump, along with my damp towel, in
the laundry cart that stood in the hallway each
morning; once every few weeks, it would be my
turn to push the cart with soiled robes and towels
to a laundry chute further down the corridor; later
the same day I would find a cart loaded with those
same robes and towels, now clean and folded,
parked in the mess room. I would then dispense
them to the occupants of the various rooms. One
size fit all, so there was no need to sort them out by
proper owners.

Most mornings, though, I went straight to the
mess room, where breakfast would be waiting. We
were long past having chicken soup for every meal,

but nonetheless there was little real variation in our morning diet: a bowl of warm oatmeal or cold granola, a cup of juice tasting like an odd combination of apples and grapes, a muffin or a couple of slices of toast, a sliced banana or half of a grapefruit or a sliced orange. The only utensils were metal spoons, which had to be left on the table along with our plates and whatever we hadn't eaten. If someone tried to smuggle something out of the mess room, he or she would receive a skull-splitting headache as punishment.

Breakfast and dinner were the only times when we got to socialize with one another. We sat together on wooden benches at long wooden tables, with no real seating order except that which we made ourselves. The first few days, the only people I knew were Sam, Russell, Kate, and Anna. I usually dined with Kate—who had recovered from her attempted rape by the late, unlamented George, yet never again entered the bathroom without Anna at her side—or Russell or Anna, but after a while I met other people who had also been in the White Room, and then those who had been living here before us. In time, I eventually learned everyone's names: Peter, Rachel, Winston, Kent, Lisa, Caitlin, Chad, Saul, Rebecca, Kevin, Amad, Sue, Jeffery, Isak, Walt, Chang, so on and so forth, more than forty in all.

Some of us, like myself, had learned that we had last names as well, but we seldom if ever used them. Our conversations were hardly sparkling—mainly it was about what we had scrubbed, swept, or mopped the day before—and there were often long pauses during which you could see people batting their eyelids, then staring blankly into space as their eyes briefly filmed over. We all knew what that signified: our associates were speaking to us, giving us little pieces of information that we needed to know that instant, such as how to remove an orange seed from our mouths without spitting, or that we needed to excuse ourselves from the table and return to our rooms before we succumbed to the urge to relieve ourselves.

One morning, I found myself sitting across the table from the large man who had frightened me so much when I had first seen him in the White Room. He wasn't nearly so frightening now, yet he made me nervous by staring intently at me as I ate. When I asked him what his name was, he told me that his name was Christopher . . . and then he asked if my name was Alec.

I told him, yes, my name is Alec.

He blinked rapidly and murmured something under his breath. The translucent film came over his eyes and he went silent. There was a long pause, then he focused his attention on his oatmeal. He didn't speak to me again for many weeks.

His face was familiar. I couldn't place it, but it always seemed to me as if I had met him somewhere before.

Breakfast always ended the same way. My associate would address me, and when I responded—if my mouth was full, all it took was three blinks—his patient voice would tell me what I had to do that day. I listened carefully to his instructions; if I had any questions, I merely had to whisper them and my associate would elaborate either verbally or with an image that would materialize before my face. Sometimes this would require a map—leave the room, go down the corridor, turn right, enter the elevator, press this button or that, get off the elevator, walk this way, turn left, turn left again, turn right, walk this way, stop here—or a demonstration by the little stick man, but after a while all it took was a simple verbal instruction:

Mop and polish the floor of the Great Hall.

Mop the upper and lower terraces.

Prune the roses in the gardens.

Clean all the toilets and sinks in the castle and restock them with soap, tissue, and towels.

Dust the tapestries, the paintings, and the statuary.

Manicure the shrubbery around the castle and mow the lawns.

Clean the windows.

Go to this room here, pick up a bunch of boxes, and carry them to another room there, and repeat as often as necessary until all the boxes in room A have been transported to room B.

Rearrange furniture in these rooms according to this plan.

Take a service elevator to another level, follow someone to another room down the corridor, and spend several hours helping two other servants move a very large object from one place to another.

Make up all the beds in these rooms. Make certain that the sheets are tucked in.

Wash everything in these baskets and fold them neatly.

Remove the filters from these ducts, clean them, and put them back in place.

Move this statue from one side of a garden to another.

Go to the upstairs kitchen, clean everything in
   sight. Twice if necessary.
Don't quit until you're told to do so.
Do you understand?

Of course, I understood. There was no question
that I would misunderstand, or that I wouldn't
obey. My chores might be easy, tedious, difficult,
more difficult, or close to impossible, but it was
never asked if I wanted to do any of these things, or
whether I liked performing these errands, or if they
were frustrating.

I simply did whatever was asked of me.

More often than not, even the easiest task
required a tutorial by my associate, yet the result
was always the same. By the end of the day my muscles would be aching, my hands chafed, my robe
filthy with dirt and sweat. Groaning aloud, my
arms and legs so heavy I could barely move them, I
would make my way to the nearest elevator and let
it take me back to the servant quarters, where—
alone or with others—I'd eat fish stew or steamed
vegetables or something else I was too tired to taste.
Then I would be allowed to retire to my little room,
where the ceiling would darken as soon as I lay
down in bed. And then I would fall asleep, until
morning came and the hornet buzzed again.

Usually . . . but not always.

Some nights, I lay awake for hours after lights
out, staring up at the ceiling as I reflected upon little flashes of memory I had collected during the day
like bits of broken pottery. This isn't an accidental
metaphor; one afternoon I knocked over a small
foyer vase while dusting it, and in a rare moment of
insight while picking up the pieces, it suddenly

occurred to me that the shattered ceramic was much like my own mind. If only I could find all the fragments and put them together in some coherent order, then I might know who Alec Tucker was, what he had been before he awakened in the White Room.

Almost every day, something else would come back to me, but only in sporadic bursts, with little or no context. Little snatches of the past: strange songs

("I'm onna a Mexican ray-dee-ohh . . .")

("Ahhhh-ah-ha'm . . . I'm still ahhhlive . . .")

("Ahh'm a looser, baby . . . so why don't you kill me . . . ?")

or voices saying things with no apparent meaning

("Maytag . . . the one you can depend on. . . .")

("Make it so, ensign . . .")

("And it's a line drive to second base, but Ozzy's out on first . . .")

but mostly they were impressions. The recurring memory of cuddling up with a woman—my mother?—as she reads a picture book to me. A spoonful of hot soup swallowed the wrong way makes me cough, and this causes me to recall another time I had taken a hot liquid into my lungs instead of my stomach, only that time someone had laughed and pounded my back, and for an instant I see a long dinner table of polished wood, with a pair of silver candlesticks in the center. I drop my mop into a bucket of water, and there's something about the splash it makes that brings back an impression of jumping off a long board into a deep well of shining blue water that smells vaguely of chlorine. An elevator door closes, and there's a quick flash of another elevator door closing somewhere else.

All these things, and many more like them, but none as disturbing as one occurrence in particular: the morning I was in the shower, when Anna was standing next to me.

I had seen Anna naked many times and never thought anything of it. By now, she was almost like a sister to me, although I was almost certain that Alec Tucker had no brothers or sisters. Yet that morning she turned her back to me just so, with her left hip pivoted a certain way, and as I watched the warm water sluicing off her shoulders and down her bare back, I remembered another woman, standing nude beneath a hot shower

("Hey, shut the curtain, it's cold . . . !")

seen in an instant just before I wrapped my arms around her waist

(". . . oh, I see . . .")

and drew her close to me

("God, Alec, you're always horny. . . .")

and then a name

(Erin)

and for no accountable reason, I found myself crying. Anna heard me weeping and turned around, and for the briefest instant I saw another woman's face superimposed on her own. That only made it worse. Anna asked me what was wrong, but I shook my head and walked out of the bathroom without bothering to rinse off the soap. I skipped breakfast that morning, went through the day with an empty stomach and a melancholy soul.

I had found another piece of the shattered vase, and a significant one at that.

I had once known a woman named Erin, and I had been in love with her.

And so it went, day after day after day. I saw the pink-eyed John now and then, when he dropped by while I was working to see how I was doing. He inevitably asked if I had remembered anything else: a friendly, almost casual question, yet one which I instinctively avoided answering. I played dumb, shaking my head as I went on mopping or wiping or cutting or folding, and after a while I stopped seeing him almost altogether.

I often asked my associate—whom I started calling Chip, for no other reason than it seemed to be an appropriate name, although I couldn't fathom why—for details on the things I remembered. Chip, it was now apparent, could not read my mind; he could view exactly what I was doing at any given moment, and he could respond to verbal instructions, including the "eyes up" command, which would cause a translucent double-image to appear before my eyes, but he wasn't privy to my thoughts. This was both a blessing and a drawback; although my thoughts were still my own, it also meant that I had to carefully describe my flashbacks. Since I was still struggling with language, forming those thoughts into meaningful expression added another degree of difficulty, and even when I was able to formulate a question, Chip either couldn't—or, increasingly more often, simply wouldn't—give me a reply.

"Chip, do I have a mother?"

"No, you don't have a mother."

I would think about this a bit, then I'd try again: "Chip, did I ever have a mother?"

"Yes, you once had a mother."

"What was her name?"

"I'm sorry, Alec, but that file is closed."

That was the response I most often received to the questions that interested me the most: file closed. I had no real idea of what a file was, and when I asked Chip what that word meant, he went eyes-up and showed me pictures of two objects: a metal hand tool with coarse edges, and a folder filled with paper. The former was contained in one of many supply closets, and was readily available to me if I needed to use one; the latter was simply unavailable, period.

"Chip, did I once know a woman named Erin?"

"I'm sorry, Alec, but that file is closed."

Okay. So I did once know a girl named Erin. "Chip, open the file on Erin."

"I'm sorry, Alec, but I cannot."

So I would try a different tack by verbally describing Erin as best as I was able—a little shorter than me, very slim, long brown hair, about my age—but without mentioning her name.

"This is Erin Westphall," Chip said.

Now I knew her last name. "Tell me more about Erin Westphall."

"I'm sorry, Alec, but that file is . . ."

In my anger, a new word bubbled up from my brain: "Chip, open the fucking file on Erin Westphall!"

"I'm sorry, Alec, but I don't know what a fucking file is."

Come to think of it, neither did I. I took a deep breath. "Okay," I said, "what does 'fucking' mean?"

"I cannot tell you this."

"Is it in a file?"

"No, but I cannot tell you this."

More frustration. "Then you're fucking stupid!"

No response. End of discussion.

So I sweated and toiled and gathered ten times as many calluses on my palms and knuckles for every sliver of memory that resurfaced from my mind at odd moments, and at night I fought to put it all together, only to fall asleep knowing little more about my past than I had when I had woken up that morning.

And then one day, without even trying to remember, everything came back to me.

✝ CHAPTER ✝

FIVE

CAN'T GET THERE FROM HERE

"What's the frequency, Kenneth?"

—Anonymous mugger, to Dan Rather

And so it went—for a couple of months, at least, although I had no real way of keeping track of time. No calendars, no watches: no idea where I was, or even when I was. The world existed in a state of perpetual summer. By now, though, there was yet another mystery about this place: the apparent absence of people.

When John took me from the White Room, we had walked down a busy corridor in what I now knew to be one level of an underground labyrinth below the castle, the top level of which was the servants' quarters. At first I assumed that the people I saw that day lived in the castle, but the more time I spent cleaning its dozens of bedrooms, the more obvious it became that the castle was virtually deserted. If the people I had seen in the corridor lived anywhere, it was in another level of the labyrinth, not here.

Along with Anna, Sam, Russell, and a few others,

my principal job was to take care of the castle. The rest were assigned duties outside its walls, tending the gardens, vineyards, lawns, and groves that surrounded the manse; thus I seldom saw anyone except other servants. When I carried my mop and pail from one room to another, it was through empty hallways that echoed with the sound of my own feet. I changed linen on beds that had not been slept in, restocked towels and toiletries in bathrooms that had not been used, and mopped floors where no one had walked since the last time I had been here. I scrubbed pots and pans in a silent kitchen whose pantry and walk-in freezer were stocked with enough food to feed a small army, polished silverware and antique china from the mahogany cabinets of a vast dining room with sufficient chairs and table space for that same army to dine in high style, and dusted a library whose upper shelves could only be reached with a stepladder, yet which contained books that had never been read.

There was no one here.

When I asked Chip about this, he told me that the rooms were reserved for Mister Chicago's personal staff, consorts, and special guests, and since the master of the house and his entourage were absent on a prolonged business trip (to where, Chip wouldn't specify), these rooms were presently unoccupied. When I asked why I was changing the sheets on beds that hadn't been slept in, Chip told me that Mister Chicago abhorred dust and mildew, and that he was due to return home soon (but when, he wouldn't tell me).

Yet there was one suite—the largest, located at the end of a short hallway off the gallery overlooking the Great Hall—that did show signs of habitation. When it was my turn to clean it, I noticed that the sheets and pillows had been recently slept on, the towels in the bathroom damp and wadded, the shower and sink wet. So someone was residing in the castle during Mister Chicago's prolonged absence— obviously a favored guest—but I never saw who it was, for he or she never showed his or her face.

This was the least of the puzzles that preoccupied me, though. I was still trying to sort out the pieces of my shattered memory, one tiny shard at a time, and put them together in some sort of rational order. The harder I sought these clues, though, the more it seemed as if they were obscured by a sort of cerebral fog. My past lay scattered across the floor of a dark room, and I was crawling about on my hands and knees, trying to gather them even though I couldn't see them until my hands fell across them . . . and I still hadn't found the largest fragments, although I knew that they lay somewhere out there.

I'm still scrabbling about when happenstance solves the problem for me.

One morning, I woke up sick. I hadn't been feeling very well the day before, and after I finished my chores I was too listless to even eat dinner. Instead, I had gone straight back to my room and put myself in bed. Anna stopped by to check on me, but I told her that I was okay, I was just a little tired, that's all . . . but when I get out of bed next morning, my joints ache, my head throbs, and I'm chilled to the bone even while standing under a hot shower. The final blow comes when I go to the mess room for breakfast; one whiff of the bowl of oatmeal placed on the table for me, and I double over and vomit into the lap of my robe.

Chip tells me I'm ill—like I haven't figured this already—and orders me to the infirmary. It's located on the level below the servants' quarters. Although I've visited it several times earlier for minor cuts, sprains, and burns, this time I'm so disoriented that John (the brown-eyed one) has to lead me there. A nice woman in a white smock—she never tells me her name, but I mentally call her Big Nurse for no particular reason—makes me lie on a table beneath a glowing panel that bloops and bleeps while she sticks plastic things in my ears and my mouth, and finally announces that I've contracted a stomach virus.

She places a little gun against the crook of my right elbow. I feel a tiny sting, then she hands me a fresh robe. Get up, she says, put on this fresh robe, and go back to your room. Sleep as much as you can and don't eat anything for a while. You'll be fine tomorrow morning.

And so I lie in bed for the rest of the day. It's the first day off I've had since leaving the White Room, but it doesn't make me any less miserable. When I sleep, it's in fits and starts, my mind plagued by weird visions about stuff I've perceived earlier in my flashes of memory. I wake up from these feverdreams to find the bedsheets soaked with sweat. I lurch out of bed and stumble to the sink for some water, or to the toilet where I vomit again. Then I collapse back in bed and fall asleep once more. All things considered, I'd rather be mopping floors.

I hear everyone come back from their jobs. Outside my room, doors open and shut, then a long silence: my fellow servants are in the mess room having dinner, something I don't want to think about.

Then more movement in the hallway: doors opening and shutting again.

Then silence. The ceiling panels go dark. Lights-out; everyone's gone to bed. I fall asleep once more.

And, all of a sudden, then I wake up.

Someone is in the room with me.

A hooded shadow looms against the light cast from the open door. He sits down on the edge of my bed. "Lights up," he says.

I squint and raise a hand against the glare as the ceiling brightens, but now I can see who has come to pay me a visit.

It's the pink-eyed John.

He's holding a pitcher of ice water and an empty cup. He pours some water into the cup and offers it to me. "Hello, Alec," he says. "How are you feeling?"

My throat is parched, so I take the water and greedily drink it down. It's nice and cold, the best thing I've ever tasted. "I feel . . ." A new word enters my mind, and an appropriate way to phrase it: ". . . like shit."

A long pause. "That's not a good word," John says softly. "Please don't use it again."

"All right." What have I just said? "Sure. Sorry, man."

His eyes narrowed. "And don't call me 'man.' It's very rude."

"Okay. Sorry, John."

"Have you . . . ?" He hesitates. "Have you remembered anything new recently?"

I'm feverish and sick to the bottom of my stomach, and he's come to see how I'm doing. He's been thoughtful enough to bring me water when I've been too weak to fetch it for myself. Still, I'm reluctant to trust him. For a long time now I've been picking my brain for clues as to what Alec Tucker had been before he arrived here, wherever *here* was; I'm not about to tell what little I've learned for the price of a cup of water.

"No," I say. "I don't remember anything, John."

His pale eyes search mine. I stare back at him, and in that moment of silent contact I know that he knows that I'm lying. If I wasn't so sick, I might be scared.

John says nothing, though, but reaches out to grasp my left knee beneath the sheets and blankets. His grasp is hard enough to make me involuntarily suck in my breath, but when he does this I glance down and see something I've never noticed before.

His hand is white. As white as the sheets on which I lay. Its hue doesn't match the color of his face.

"I hope you feel better soon," he says quietly. "It can be a lot worse, you know."

His hand slips back into the folds of his robe, then he abruptly stands up. He places the pitcher on the shelf, just out of reach from my bed. I know that he's done this deliberately: petty torture.

"Lights off," John says. "Good night." Then he turns and leaves the room in the same darkness in which he had come, closing the door very firmly behind him.

It's not a good night. I lie awake, thinking about those strange pink eyes and that snow-white hand, for a long time.

■　　■　　■

Big Nurse is right. Next morning, I feel as good as I ever have. A little better, in fact: for the first time, it seems as if there's a certain sharpness in my vision, a newfound clarity to my thoughts. It's as if the cobwebs in my brain have been swept away overnight; it just seems easier to think. Yet my stomach still curdles at the very notion of breakfast, so once I've showered and dressed, I ask Chip what my job is today.

"Why haven't you eaten breakfast?" he asks.

"Because I'm not hungry."

"Are you still ill?"

"No, not really. Just don't want to take a chance on throwing up again, that's all."

"If you don't eat breakfast, you won't have a chance to eat again until this evening."

"No problemo. Just tell me what I . . ."

Chip goes eyes-up on me:

> **"No problemo"—unfamiliar term.**
> **Please define.**

I open my mouth, then stop. Once again, a word or a phrase has jumped out of my mouth without my thinking about it, or even really knowing what it means, just as when I had used the word "shit" the night before. This has been occurring more frequently lately, but most of the time Chip has been able to define it for me. This is one of those rare occasions when I've used a term that Chip can't define, yet for once the shoe is on the other foot: I *do* know what "no problemo" means.

"It means . . ." And suddenly, new phrases leap forth: "Don't worry about it. Don't sweat it. Chill out. Don't have a cow, dude."

These are not logical statements. I do not sweat. I cannot be cold. There are no cows here.
I am not a dude.

"I know." An odd notion suddenly occurs to me. "That's because you're a computer . . . aren't you, Chip?"

I am a MINN (Mnemonic
Interfaced Neural Network).

"Um . . . okay. Is that like a computer?"

Chip's voice returns. "I am a computer, yes."

Something like a tiny snake crawls down my spine. I sit down on my bed and think about it for a second . . . then, on impulse, I clap my hands over my ears. "Say something to me, Chip."

"Something to me, Chip."

I should laugh, but I don't. . . . His voice is as clear as it ever had been, which means that it isn't coming from an external source, but from within my very own ears.

Okay. I shut my eyes, then hold my right hand up before my face and raise two of my fingers. "How many fingers am I holding up?"

"I cannot tell. Your eyes are closed."

Now the tiny snake has become an oily serpent. "Go eyes-up and repeat what you just said," I say, still keeping my eyes shut.

Against the darkness, his words appear as a luminescent line:

I cannot tell. Your eyes are closed.

"Fuck me," I whisper as my eyes snap open. "You're in my head, aren't you?"

I cannot fuck you, but yes,
I am located within your head.

I'm feeling sick again, but not from the stomach flu. I've got a computer in my head, one capable of hearing my voice, seeing through my eyes, speaking directly into my ears. All this time, a magic little voice has been observing everything that I did, eavesdropping on every word I've spoken . . .

Worse yet, I've never really questioned these things, but merely accepted them as part of my existence, just as cattle stupidly accept the fact that they live in a barn, get milked every morning, go outside every day to munch grass, then return to the barn by nightfall. Have a cow? Hell, I *am* the cow!

There's a thousand more questions I want to ask Chip—my associate, my MINN, whose name I had given subconsciously without realizing the inherent pun behind its meaning—but before I can, his voice returns to my ears.

"Your initial request was for your job assignment today. You will go to the Great Hall and mop the upper balcony and the stairs leading to it. Then you will assist Christopher in polishing the floor. Do you understand?"

Outside my room, I hear my fellow servants moving through the corridor. Breakfast is over; time for everyone to go to work. "Yeah. Okay. Gotcha."

Unnerved by what I've just learned, I leave my room. It isn't until I've closed the door behind me that I realize for the first time—like many other obvious things that I've overlooked these past many days, weeks, even months—there was no way I can lock it, either from outside or within. Yes, there's a nameplate on the door, and I press my thumb against it when I want to enter, but that's never prevented anyone else from visiting me. Anna was able to come in yesterday . . . and so was John.

This isn't a room, but a cell. This isn't a door, but bars on a cage. A cage that can't be locked, but a cage nevertheless.

I've never been a guest here, regardless of what the pink-eyed John told me when I first came here, nor do I even have the dignity of being a true servant, who despite his meager role is afforded the basic human right of privacy. The essential fact of the matter is much more plain than that.

I'm a prisoner.

These revelations haunt me as I ride the elevator up to the castle, where I cross the Great Hall to the custodial closet. Before now, I've blindly accepted these chores with numbed mind and will—Alec goes here, Alec cleans that, Alec is a good guest, a-huh a-huh a-huh—but this morning the shutters have flown wide open and sunlight is streaming into the dungeon where my brain has been held in shackles. Now I'm perceiving things as they really are. My head is full of questions; they writhe around each other like a nest of snakes, their heads and tails invisible beneath their knotted mass.

Where am I? Who am I? Who stuck a microcomputer in my brain? How is it able to speak to me when my ears are shut, show me things when my eyes are closed? Why was I being made to do scut work? Who is John? Why does he want to know so much about what I remember, but unwilling to give me any clues? Who is Mister Chicago? What is this place? Who are all these people? Why am I thinking about this stuff only now, when I've never really considered it before?

Even as all this races through my mind, I'm going through the daily routine. Take a bucket, fill it full of water. Add some detergent from a plastic bottle on the shelf. Select a long-handled mop from the wall. Grab a couple of cloths and a bottle of furniture wax for the stairway banister.

Turning around to gather the rest of my stuff, I nearly bump into Christopher as he quietly enters the closet behind me. I'm long past being frightened of him and he's stopped staring at me, so his presence is usually one which I ignore . . . but now I find myself looking more closely at him than I ever have before. Goddamn—another new word!—if he doesn't look familiar . . .

Christopher barely glances my way as he takes down another bucket from the shelf and starts filling it from the spigot, yet there's a moment when his face is in profile, that

("Fuck, man, I know how to drive . . .")

I have a feeling

("C'mon, I wanna hear the Orb tape . . .")

that I've seen him

("Stop bugging me, I can drive . . .")

before. Not knowing what to say or do, I pick up the mop and bucket and creep out of the closet, careful not to nudge Christopher, even though I now have the odd notion that I should call him by another name.

The stairway to the gallery that encircles the

Great Hall is a wide, semicircular spiral, with wrought-iron filigree supporting a carved oak banister. Cleaning the gallery is the easy part; mopping the sixty-eight risers leading to it can take hours. I usually do the gallery first, then begin making my way down the stairs, mopping each step and polishing the banister as I descend. Everything has to be perfect, or otherwise Mister Chicago might not approve. Today, it occurs to me that Mister Chicago must be the most anal-retentive asshole since Jimmy Carter . . . and who was Jimmy Carter, anyway?

Forget it. I place the bucket at the top of the stairs, plunge the mop into the sudsy water, pull it out again, and begin to slop it back and forth across the marble tiles. It's a job that I've done many times before, although before now it's required all my concentration to make sure that the task was done correctly. Now it's ridiculously simple, something that a child could do. My mind is free to roam. Jimmy Carter, Jimmy Carter . . .

Yeah, okay, he was . . . right, sure, he was president of the United States, back when I was a kid . . . but when was that?

Oh, yeah, that was just before Reagan. So who the fuck is Reagan . . . ?

Down below, Christopher is on his hands and knees, scrubbing at the mosaic that forms the hall floor. He's starting near the center and working his way outward, as John—the brown-eyed version, not the pink-eyed guy—taught us to do countless days ago. The soft sound of his brush moving across the floor resounds faintly through the hall. I wonder if he hears my mop sloshing water across the balcony.

Reagan, Ronald Reagan . . . smiling, happy, wisecracking, dumbfuck Ronald Reagan. And after him, who was the next guy? George something. Tree. Shrub. Topiary. Bush? Yeah, that's it. . . . George Bush. And after him, the fat guy from Arkansas. A boomer. Bill something . . .

Another glance at Christopher, and for the first time I recognize the gold symbol in the middle of the mosaic he's scrubbing: an upside-down horseshoe with spiked tips at the bottom of its open legs: an omega.

Bill Clinton. That's it. Had a wife named Hillary . . .

An omega sign. Not only that, but it's now clear that the straight gold lines connecting the tiny white stars in the floor surrounding the omega form constellations—twelve in all, the stellar configurations of the zodiac—while the nine concentric ellipses that loop through the zodiac are the orbits of . . .

My mop connects with something. I hear a soft thud, then a faint rush of water. Glancing down, I see soapy water gushing down the stairs, dripping off the balcony to splatter on the floor below. I've just knocked over the bucket.

"Aw, shit!" I drop the mop and bend over to grab the bucket, and as I do, I step on the slick surface I've just mopped and my sandals slip out from under me.

I plunge forward. I grab for the banister, but I'm already falling. I hit the stairs
 (like a truck)
hard and topple down
  ("Oh, shit, look out . . . !")
with my legs in the air and my arms
  ("Fuck! Fuck!")

flailing every which way as if I'm
                        (headlights against darkness)
falling down a steep and muddy embankment
                             (rolling over)
and then my robe rips and my head slams
                (Erin screaming, Shemp screaming)
against the risers and there's a burst of
                      (car roof caving in)
pain as my right arm drags against the posts and
                (hard metal against my chest)
slows my descent down the staircase
                    (rolling over)
but the skin on my arms and
              (hitting something hard)
legs burns as flesh
        (light fades)
tears open and
      (darkness)
then it's over.

A bucket collides with the hall floor.

Footsteps race up the stairway, echoing off the ceiling where winged cherubim surround God as he reaches forth to touch Adam's hand.

Right arm in agony. A taste like warm wet pennies in my mouth.

Someone touches my shoulder.

"Hey, dude, are you all right?"

Shemp, whom I've known since Country Day School, is leaning over me.

"Hey, man . . . I think I broke my arm. Wanna call my dad?"

And then I black out.

✢ CHAPTER ✢

SIX

IN THE SPRINGTIME
OF HIS VOODOO

*Cruelty has a Human Heart
And Jealousy a Human Face:
Terror, the Human Form Divine
And Secrecy, the Human Dress.*

—William Blake, *Songs of Innocence and Experience*

Darkness fades. I fall into light.

I'm on my back in a narrow bed in a dim room. For a moment, I think I've returned to square one—spirited back to the White Room, and it's chicken soup time again—but then the ceiling brightens and Big Nurse comes in and I realize that I've only gone as far as the infirmary.

My right arm, however, is completely immobile, from the biceps down to the wrist. Big Nurse examines the status panel above my head and asks how I'm feeling—pretty good, considering that leprechauns have recently used my body as a mosh pit—then she slips back the bedcovers from my arm. I'm expecting a plaster cast, but instead find my arm enclosed within the padded sleeve of a tubelike machine that flashes and beeps when she touches it.

It's this tube that clinches my suspicions. Wherever I am, St. Louis it ain't.

"Broken arm, right?" I ask. She says nothing. "Pretty bad, huh?" She shrugs noncommittally as she reaches to a counter behind her and picks up a plastic squeeze bottle. "What does Dr. McCoy have to say about this?" If she gets the joke, there's no sign; she unwraps a straw, sticks it in the bottle, and gently places it in my left hand. "Thanks, Nurse Chapel. You can send in the guy with the ears now."

"Thank you, Marie," says a voice from the door. "I'll take over now. You're excused."

I'm hardly surprised when the pink-eyed John enters the room. Every time anything significant happens, he's always just a step behind. Big Nurse— perhaps I should call her Big Doctor—nods and quietly slips past John as he walks to my bed.

Same old John: dour expression, observant pink eyes, white cowl raised over his head, hands folded together within the sleeves. Give him a rosary and a smoking censer, and he could be a medieval monk come to exorcise the room of dark spirits, or at least an extra from an old Hammer horror movie.

"John, my main man. How's it going, dude?"

He stands over me for a moment without saying anything, perhaps to give me time to remember that I'm supposed to give him more respect. When he doesn't receive it, he slowly lets out his breath as a disappointed sigh.

"Alec," he says at last. "My dear, clumsy Alec . . ."

"Alec Tucker. William Alec Tucker III. You can call me Alec, though. Most people do."

The most lukewarm of smiles. "You recalled

that a long time ago. Remember? I was there for the event. No need for such petty insolence." A pause. "Insolence. It's a word. Ask your associate to define it for you if that's necessary."

"No thanks. I know what it means." I raise my head a little to sip cold water; it tastes great, but even with the straw I manage to spill a little on the sheets. "Hey, do me a favor and crank up the bed a bit, willya?"

"Adjust Alec's bed to three-quarter recline," John says, and without any fuss or bother the bed moves beneath me until it becomes a comfortable chair, with one arm remaining horizontal to support the tube on my right arm. I try not to look startled, but John isn't fooled. "Nice trick, eh?"

"Doesn't suck." Fact is, I want to try it myself. "Neck's a little stiff though. Hey . . . uh, computer? Adjust my . . . I mean, adjust Alec's bed so his head isn't so high."

Nothing happens. The bed remains frozen in place. "Alec says his neck is a little stiff," John says softly. "Make him comfortable."

The part of the bed just behind my head moves ever so slightly, and again John smiles down at me. A little lesson in who's still the boss around here. "So . . ." I gulp down some more water. "Guess I banged myself up real well back there, huh? How bad was it?"

John triple-blinks and murmurs something under his breath, then I hear Chip's voice: "The olecranon in your elbow and your humerus suffered compound fractures. Chronic muscular lacerations to your brachial and round protor . . ."

"Whoa . . . speak English."

"Your associate is speaking English," John says,

"but I'll simplify it for you. Your arm was broken at your elbow and upper arm, and the major muscles and ligaments on that arm were either torn or stretched. There were also considerable bruises on your rib cage, hips, and lower thighs. You had cuts on your forehead and legs, and you suffered a major concussion that left you unconscious for the past fourteen hours. So, yes, I'd say you were pretty banged up."

I raise my left hand to my forehead. My fingers don't find a scar. My ribs and legs feel weak, but otherwise undamaged. I can't move my right arm, but I'm able to wiggle my fingers without any pain. I don't even have a headache.

When I was sixteen, my dad shipped me off to the Webb School in Bell Buckle, Tennessee, the second prep school to throw me out (this time for smoking pot). It was a dismal place and I was only too happy to be expelled, but while I was there I made the varsity soccer team as the goalie. Eight weeks into the fall semester, during afternoon practice, one of my teammates kicked the ball straight into my chest from six feet away, breaking two lower ribs. I spent an afternoon in a Shelbyville emergency room and two more days in the school infirmary before I was able to move again, and only then with bandages wrapped around my chest and walking with a crutch. I was still feeling crummy five weeks later when the Prefect Council gave me the boot for seeking my own form of general anesthesia behind the library.

Point is, that's the sort of hardship even a relatively minor sporting accident can cause. Now, according to John—and I had Chip's word for it as well—my little somersault down the Great Hall staircase had broken my right arm in two places, banged up my ribs, busted my ass, given me a couple of cuts, knocked me semicomatose . . . and just fourteen hours later, most of my injuries have been healed. I'm in no pain; even my right arm feels only a little numb.

Something is most definitely weird.

John finds a seat on a nearby stool. "Obviously, you have many questions," he goes on, folding his hands together in his lap. "In fact, I know for a fact that you do. Your associate . . . I believe you call him Chip now . . . ?"

How the hell did he know that? John seems to relish the baffled expression on my face. "There is virtually nothing that you say or do that I cannot find out, Alec, and that includes the content of your dialogues with your MINN. . . . Anyway, you've been asking Chip many questions lately about your past, and some of the most pertinent ones were posed yesterday morning, just before your accident. Your recent illness had something to do with this, am I right?"

"Maybe." I sip at the water bottle as I try to figure out what sort of game he's playing. Poker, probably; he doubtless holds a better hand than I do, but I have a few aces of my own. I toss one out. "Throwing up and not being able to eat probably had a lot to do with it, too. Meant that I couldn't take any more of whatever you've been putting in my food, and I puked up the stuff that was already in my system."

Again, John smiles at me, a bit more fondly this time. "If that's a guess," he replies, "it's a good one. Yes, your food has been drugged for quite some time now . . . some memory and sexual suppressants, mainly, although a mild hypnotic was also added to make you and your friends a little more docile and easy to train. You're not going to believe me when I tell you this, but it's been done for your own good. We've never intended to keep you in this state permanently—"

"I bet."

He shrugs. "If it had been our intent to keep you dumbed-down forever, then Dr. Miesel would have given you a booster shot of the same mélange when you were brought here. The mere fact that we're having this conversation at all is proof of my sincerity."

He idly picks at lint on the lap of his robe. "No, we've actually been lessening the dosage of the drugs for the past few weeks, so as to gradually bring you and your friends out of your collective fugue. In your case, this process was greatly accelerated. Your body cleansed itself of all the drugs in about a day, your mind reacted by becoming easily distracted . . ." He motions to the tube on my arm. "And this is the result. That's one reason for the drugs."

"Uh-huh." I still don't trust John, yet I have to admit that his story makes sense. So far, at least. "So where does that leave us?"

"Why, where we were last night, of course." His smile fades. "I want to know everything that you've remembered about your past . . . and this time you can't pretend at being stupid, Alec. We both know better."

Well. That's my trump card, isn't it? "Suppose I don't tell you?" I cradle the bottle between my knees. "I could just sit here and keep my mouth shut. A fat lot of good that'll do you, won't it?"

Even as I speak, I recognize the fatal flaw in my gambit. If John and his people have the ability to keep me dumb and happy for months on end, then they can just as easily use different drugs to make me spill the beans. "I don't know what it is that I know that you think is so important," I rush on, "but it wouldn't be a great idea to use more dope to make me talk, would it, huh?"

"No . . . no, I suppose it wouldn't." John rubs his chin as he gravely nods his head. "You've got me there, Alec. We have to use these psychoactives quite carefully. In fact, Dr. Miesel tells me that if we try to use anything else on you at this stage of your recovery, it could turn around and throw you in a persistent vegetative state. You wouldn't even be able to get out of bed, let alone give us any coherent answers."

He sighs. "I know you don't know why, Alec, and that is one thing I can't tell you . . . but you must know this: it is very important to Mister Chicago that he know everything you've remembered about your past before you came here."

As he speaks, his right hand disappears into the front pouch of his robe. When it comes out again, it holds a tiny syringe-gun. Before I can react, he places its short barrel against the back of my immobile right hand.

"Now," he says very softly, his pink eyes boring into mine, "the choice is very simple. Either you start talking, or the next time you wake up, it'll be when someone is spooning soup into your drooling mouth."

My heart hammers against my chest. The foam padding of the tube is suddenly moist with sweat. I look into John's eyes and see only ice. Fuck almighty, he's not kidding. . . .

Isn't he?

If what little I know is so goddamn important, would he risk turning me into a zombie just because I'm being stubborn? I'm his prisoner; I don't even know where I am, how I came to be here. He can afford to be patient . . .

I lick my dry lips and stare back at him. "Tell you what. I'll make a deal with you . . ."

"No deals, Alec." His forefinger starts tightening on a small button within the trigger guard. "Talk or don't talk."

"You said that this is important to Mister Chicago, right?" The words rush out my mouth as a babble. "Yeah, okay, cool . . . so why don't we wait until Mister Chicago gets back, okay? 'Cause if we do that, then I can tell him myself and you don't have to explain all this or nothing, and everything'll be cool and we don't have to mention none of this shit or nothing, y'know what I mean, man?"

John's finger remains poised on the trigger. The slightest pressure will make me the butt of all the worst Helen Keller jokes I had ever heard . . . and although I had seen a few sad cases like that during my stay in the White Room, for some reason they all vanished and were never seen again. I might become an imbecile, but even that won't last very long before a worse fate befalls me.

"Is it that important to you?" His voice is very soft now. "Is it so necessary that you meet Mister Chicago, to know who he is?"

Actually, it isn't. That knowledge is very low on my list of priorities. Mister Chicago, Mister New York, Mister Memphis, Mister Boise . . . I don't give a shit who he is, other than the fact that John was obviously subservient to him and would never dare

to double-cross him. I suddenly remember a trick
Roger Moore used in an old James Bond movie I
once caught on TBS; in desperation, I decide that it
couldn't hurt to use it now.

"Yeah, man," I say. "Bring me Mister Chicago.
Then we'll talk."

A long pause. The finger relaxes on the trigger.
"That's a promise?"

"That's a promise, I swear."

The syringe-gun lifts away from my hand, leaving a bloodless white spot on my skin. John tucks it
back into his pocket, then he reaches up and pulls
back the hood of his robe. For the first time, I see
that his hair was as long and white as silk.

"Very well, then," he says. "Let's meet Mister
Chicago."

He triple-blinks and murmurs something under
his breath, and then his face starts to melt.

It's a very unsettling thing, watching the skin on a
man's face slough off like so much wet putty. It can
really put you off your food.

I shrink back in bed as John's face begins to dissolve. First in tiny rivulets, then in large globs, his
brow and cheeks and chin and lips liquefy and start
falling off as if he's afflicted with the worst mutant
strain of leprosy imaginable. Yet John doesn't seem
to feel any pain. He turns away from me and goes to
a nearby sink, where he picks up a folded towel and
raises it to his face. He doesn't speak to me—probably because he can't—and with his back to me, it's
a little easier to take, but I can still hear thick splattering sounds from the basin.

"I'm sorry if this is grotesque," he finally says,

his voice muffled by the towel, "but I assure you that it's harmless."

"Oh no, man." My gorge rises as he casually tears off his rotting nose and drops it in the sink. "Seen it before. Happens all the time."

A dry laugh. "I rather doubt you have. Nanotechnology was very primitive in the late twentieth century. You see . . . um, excuse me."

John turns on the water, then bends over and dips his face beneath the faucet. More splattering sounds, wetter and chunkier than before. I'm sincerely glad that my stomach is empty. "As I was saying," he continues as he rises from the sink, "this is an illusion cast by a few million nanites . . . microscopic robots, if you will . . . which have consumed dead epidermis cells on my face and reconstructed them into a living mask. Not just lifelike, you understand, but actually alive . . . a disguise that I could wear for as long as I choose. Interesting, hmm?"

"If you say so." Easy, kid. Take deep breaths. . . . "Do this all the time?"

"On occasion." He vigorously massages his face with his hands. "Sometimes it's . . . well, a little difficult for me to go in public without being noticed. Being able to put on another face can be quite useful. All it takes is a little practice and . . . ah, there we go."

He turns off the water, picks up a fresh towel, and buries his face in it. "Deliver fresh clothes to me in the infirmary," he murmurs, perhaps to his own associate. "Casual evening outfit."

He takes a deep breath and turns around again. The man who stands before me looks very little like the John I met in the White Room. His skin is as cool and bloodless as porcelain, with only his pink eyes lending color to his albino hue; nose long and aquiline, high-boned cheeks, narrow lips, a high brow. Almost androgynous: beautiful yet hard, as if carved from a block of arctic ice.

He steps fully into the light. "Look straight at me," he says, as if I'm not already, "and ask your associate to give you my name."

I go eyes-up. "Chip, what is this guy's name?"

His name is Pasquale Chicago.

Oh, shit.

"Pleasure to meet you, Mister Chicago," I manage to say.

"We've already met, Alec." He returns to the stool where John had been sitting only a few minutes earlier. The front of his robe is soaked with flesh-colored stains; as he continues to wipe his face with the towel, the last traces of his mask soil the cloth. "You know," he says as he sits down, "you're a fascinating young man. I've enjoyed observing you for these past few months. Indeed, I've made you my personal hobby. You were the first one of your group to recover from neurosuspension. Not only that, but you regained your long-term memory with little or no prompting. Congratulations. You're the class valedictorian."

"Thanks." What else am I supposed to say? "Do I get a diploma or something?"

"Perhaps. Maybe even a graduation present. But first we have some unfinished business."

Mister Chicago drops the towel on the floor, then reaches into his pocket and pulls out the syringe-gun. He doesn't place it against my hand again, but the implicit threat is there all the same. "You demanded to see me," he says, "and now I'm here. So tell me . . . what have you remembered?"

I take a deep breath. There's no point in holding back now. I've still got an ace or two, but he has a fistful of kings.

So I tell him everything. All my flashbacks, dreams, and impressions, all the many bits and pieces of my memory that I've struggled for so long to piece together as a cohesive whole, but which have now reformed themselves like a shattered vase that has been videotaped during its moment of destruction, then put into fast-reverse so that it's magically made whole again, if only on tape.

It takes a long time, but Mister Chicago listens patiently, nodding his head every so often to encourage me. At one point we're interrupted by John—the real John, the brown-eyed version—bringing him a small stack of folded clothes. Mister Chicago dismisses him, then gives me a short break while he disappears into the next room; when he returns, he's wearing soft calf boots, dark purple tights, a linen shirt, and an embroidered vest. Dressed this way, he seems taller and more gaunt than when he had played at being John. He sits down on the stool again and tells me to go on.

I reveal all that I know save for one thing, a secret that I impulsively hold back for no other reason than loyalty: the servant whom I had long known as Christopher is, in fact, my best friend Shemp, whom I recognized only after falling down the stairs. I don't know how Shemp has come to be here, but if I'm in any danger, then at least he'll still be protected.

When I'm through, Mister Chicago simply nods. He seems vaguely disappointed, as if he's been anticipating some piece of information that I haven't delivered. "And this is everything you recall?"

"That's it, man. The works."

"I told you, don't call me 'man.' " His eyes are glacial. "To you, I'm 'sir.' "

"That's it, sir."

He picks up the syringe-gun from his lap, toys with it. The flesh on the back of my right hand prickles. All he has to do is give me one shot . . .

"Thanks, Alec," he says. "It's been nice knowing you."

Then he jabs the gun against my hand and squeezes the trigger.

"Shit! Goddammit, I told you everything . . . !"

"Shh . . ." Mister Chicago lifts the gun away from my hand, pats my knee. "Hush now. Just relax. It'll only take a second."

I shut my eyes and grit my teeth as I wait for some pharmaceutical cocktail to send me into oblivion. One . . . two . . . three . . . four . . . chicken soup's great, can I have some more?

Long seconds pass. I let out my breath and open my eyes again.

I'm still conscious. I'm still William Alec Tucker III.

"Salt water." Mister Chicago tosses the gun in my lap. "There was never anything in here except a saline solution. Believe me, Alec, I'd never deliberately destroy a prize specimen like you. You're much too precious to waste."

Then he raises his hand to his mouth; his eyes narrow as he sniggers. "But . . . oh my, the look on your face . . ."

I don't say anything, just as he knew I wouldn't.

The man not only has complete power over my life, but clearly he also has a maniacal sense of humor. It's never a good idea to mess with someone like that.

Mister Chicago recovers his poise. He reaches down to the tube encircling my right arm. "I think you're ready, class valedictorian," he says as he presses a couple of buttons. "You can get up now."

The upper half of the tube pops open with a soft hiss; my arm is nestled inside, as healthy as I have ever seen it. I withdraw it from the tube, carefully flex my elbow. There's no indication that my arm has ever been injured. "Are you sure it was broken?" I ask, and he nods. "Okay, I gotta ask . . . how did you do it?"

"Nanites." He shrugs in a patronizing way. "Much the same process that allowed me to wear a different face. I could explain it to you, but you probably wouldn't understand."

There're a lot of things I don't understand; this is the least of them. "Do I get to ask some questions now?"

"You can ask." Mister Chicago crosses his arms behind his back as he favors me with one of his more enigmatic smiles. "I think I can imagine what the first one is."

This is beginning to feel like a *Jeopardy* rerun: *I'll take Total Amnesia for 500, Alex.* "If you know already, then how about giving me the answer?"

Mister Chicago gazes at me for several seconds, savoring the moment. "You died on July 11, 1995," he says at last. "By the Gregorian calendar, today's date is April 5, 2099."

That wasn't the question I had in mind, but it's one hell of an answer.

He holds out his hand, offering to help me out of the bed. "Those are only the most simple and basic facts," he continues. "There's much more. I promised you a graduation present, Mr. Tucker. If you'll come with me, I'll tell you everything you want to know."

I nod in a dumb sort of way, then sling my legs over the side of the bed. I'm naked, but this isn't the first time I've awoken in the nude. Big Nurse Doctor comes in with a fresh robe, which I slip on without bothering to ask how she knew it was time to make a reappearance. Why should I? I've been dead for one hundred and four years, plus a few months and days. Things were liable to be a bit different. . . .

Still, I can't help wondering if it isn't too late for me to find a phone and call Dad. That's what I always did when I was in trouble.

SEVEN

ARTIFICIAL SUNLIGHT

Thou know'st 'tis common, all that lives must die,
Passing through nature to eternity.

—William Shakespeare, *Hamlet*

So tell me, Alec," asks Mister Chicago, "what do you remember about your father?"

Until now, he's said very little to me. John was waiting in the corridor just outside the infirmary; he discreetly followed us as Mister Chicago led me to an elevator I've never used before. I had the feeling that John was there as a bodyguard, in case the notion entered my mind to harm his master. For his part, Mister Chicago ignored John's presence, just as he turned a deaf ear to my questions. The elevator opened only when he told it to, and it didn't move until he said, "Solarium."

The solarium is a large geodesic dome on top of the castle; it's like being inside a glass beehive. Across the rooftops of the castle's four wings, the landscape sprawls out before us; for the first time, I can see its entire length and width. With horizons which are longer at its ends than at its sides—yet no more than a few miles in length, and only about a mile in width—and a sky, now turned almond-red by the fading daylight, that folds down to meet these short longitudes, it's now apparent that this "world" was nothing more or less than an immense cylinder.

The solarium is furnished with embroidered carpets, calfskin armchairs and couches, a round coffee table, and a small bar. The glass-topped desk at the far end of the room clues me that this was Mister Chicago's sanctum. He crosses the room to sit behind the desk and, after motioning for me to take the nearest chair, tells John to bring him a cappuccino and politely inquires what I want to drink. I ask for the same; John goes to the bar and makes himself busy with a brass cappuccino maker.

Twilight sets in as the luminescent filaments in the sky gradually fade out; lights are coming on within the windows of the empty palace below us. Through the hazy lines in the sky, I can make out the faint glimmer of starlight, except in the middle where that broad, mysterious mass blots out everything else. I've never witnessed this time of day before; by now, I would usually be sitting down to dinner in the servants' quarters.

So now I'm sitting in a comfortable chair, hearing the faint huff of the cappuccino machine as it brews something I hadn't tasted in . . . well, a hundred and four years, although subjectively it's been a lot shorter than that . . . and wondering why the guy who owns all this wants to know about my father.

"He wasn't a bad guy," I reply, not knowing what Mister Chicago meant by this question. "He was . . . well, he was rich. He owned a company that made stuff . . . electrical stuff, I mean . . ."

"Stuff?" Mister Chicago leans forward to rest his elbows on the desk and cup his chin in his hands. "What sort of . . . stuff, Alec?"

"Household appliances. Refrigerators, microwave ovens, clocks, lamps . . ." I shrug. "Y'know, stuff like that. His company manufactures . . ." I have to remind myself that I'm speaking about the past. ". . . I mean, his company used to make it for other companies that put their brand names on them and then goes . . . went out and sold them in department stores and . . ."

"Stuff." He chuckles. "I like that word. So archaic."

"Well, that's what it is. Just . . . stuff, y'know?" I force a smile and wonder if he was really listening to anything I just said.

"So did your father invent this stuff?"

"Oh, no. My great-grandfather started the company, back in the twenties . . . the 1920s, I mean." I sit up a little straighter. "He was an inventor, see, and even though he didn't come up with the basic items . . . y'know, like the refrigerators or the table lamps . . . he invented a lot of the supporting equipment that's used in them, and when he died his family inherited the patents and the company . . . Tucker Enterprises, that is . . . and when Grandpa Bill died, my dad took over as CEO, and he . . ."

"So you come from a wealthy family. Hmm." Mister Chicago nods his head within his hands. I can't tell whether he's interested or just making conversation. "So what was he like, your father? Was he a good man?"

I shrug. That's not a question many people ask about Dad. Or didn't. Whatever. "I guess. I mean, I didn't see him much, so . . ."

"Why?"

"He wasn't home a lot. Tucker was a Fortune 500 company, so he . . . uh, do you know what Fortune 500 is?"

"I know what it was. Go on."

No more Fortune 500. Jeez . . . "Well, I saw a lot of him when I was a kid and he was still married to my mom, but when they broke up and he started building up the company, trying to make it go multinational . . ."

"He divorced your mother? Sorry to interrupt again, but I find this rather intriguing. Who was your mother, and why did your father divorce her?"

"I dunno. It happened when I was about six or seven, and I didn't see her very much after she left." My seat is beginning to feel warm; I squirm a bit. "She married another St. Louis businessman who then moved out to LA . . . that's Los Angeles, y'know?" He nods; yes, he's heard of Los Angeles. Glad to know some things haven't changed. ". . . and a couple of years after that she left that guy for a TV actor she met at some Hollywood party, and after they were married he got elected to the California state senate as a Republican, so . . . well, y'know, I've gone out to visit her a few times, but we don't . . . I mean, didn't really get along."

"Hmm. I see." He settles back in his chair. "So was it your father who arranged for you to be placed in neurosuspension?"

I don't know what he means by that. Before I can ask, though, John places a cup of cappuccino on the coffee table in front of me, then walks over to Mister Chicago to gently set another cup on his desk. The cup is frothy with steamed milk; I pick it up and take a tentative sip. Best cappuccino I ever tasted. Mister Chicago ignores his cup; he frowns impatiently at John until he retreats back behind the bar. "Was it your father who had you placed in neurosuspension?" he asks again.

"I don't know. What's neurosuspension?"

"You don't know?" There's faint astonishment in his eyes; he folds his hands together on the desk. "What about the Immortality Partnership?"

I almost shake my head, then something tugs at my memory: that name sounds familiar. "My dad gave me a dog tag for my birthday last . . . I mean, the last birthday I had. It had that name engraved on it, but I didn't know what it was for." I assay a sheepish grin. "I kinda wasn't paying attention at the time."

"You weren't . . . paying attention?" Mister Chicago is incredulous; I'm not about to tell him that I had blown a joint on my way to the restaurant that evening. "But there were papers that you had to sign. You don't recall that either?"

I shrug as I lick the froth off my lips. "I signed a lot of papers for Dad. Life insurance forms, bank stuff, things like that. I never asked what they were. His secretary would call me, and I'd drop by his office and sign 'em, and that would be it. The company lawyer would notarize them." And I was usually stoned or hungover when I did that, too. "Why, what's the deal with the Immortality Partnership?"

"The Immortality Partnership was . . ." He stops, then sighs. "Your associate can tell you better than I can. Ask it. I'll wait."

He picks up his cappuccino and half-turns his chair to me. "While you're at it," he adds, "tell it to inform you of the circumstances of your death. You may access your personal files now."

I don't really want to, but there's no question that this isn't a request. I take a deep breath, blink three times, and ask Chip to tell me how I died, and to define neurosuspension for me.

This time, my MINN doesn't inform me that this file is sealed. That doesn't make me any less sorry that I've asked.

What's the spookiest thing I've ever seen? My own death certificate.

It's in my file. Chip displays it to me. I died in the ambulance on the way to the Barnes Hospital emergency room, where I was pronounced DOA at 10:17 P.M. on July 11, 1995, from massive internal injuries caused by a vehicular accident. Don't ask me for the details, because I didn't read most of the document. Some goths I used to know might have gotten a rise out of reading about how their lives came to an end, but it's a little too gruesome for my taste.

The pertinent facts, though, are these:

Before my body was taken down to the morgue, one of the ER doctors found the small metal pendant around my neck. Recognizing it for what it was, he called the 1–800 number on the back of the tag. The phone number was that of the Immortality Partnership's headquarters in Pasadena, California. The operator on duty got the information from the doctor, then immediately phoned the company's nearest Emergency Response Center, which was located in Chicago. Two paramedics on call at the ERC immediately boarded a charter jet and flew to St. Louis; they arrived at Barnes Hospital less than two hours after I had been pronounced dead.

Dad was out of the country at the time (another business trip, as usual) and Mom couldn't be reached (probably on a political junket with her Sonny Bono wannabe) but the Emergency Response Center faxed copies of the paperwork that my father and I had signed in advance that would allow the parameds to claim custody of my body. Everything was perfectly legal, thanks to Dad's cadre of attorneys, so the hospital let the Immortality Partnership have my corpse.

A private ambulance transported the parameds, along with yours truly, back to Lambert International, where the charter jet had been refueled and was awaiting takeoff. Back in Chicago, an Emergency Response Team was awaiting its arrival with another ambulance, this one specially equipped with all the medical apparatus needed to stabilize—yes, this *is* the term used in the company report—my condition. The Chicago team had already downloaded my medical information via satellite from the company's database in Pasadena; they now had everything on me, down to blood type, shoe size, and the minor case of herpes I had contracted while in college. No one was thinking about bringing me back to life, at least not at that point; I was as dead as the sixties. No, they were mainly concerned with making sure that my brain didn't deteriorate any more than it had already.

By now—I have to assume this, because there's no record of these tangential events available to Chip's records—someone had finally located my parents and given them the news. Mom was probably so upset, she dropped her martini glass; Dad might have temporarily suspended his plans for global conquest for a full forty-eight hours. I don't imagine any flags were flown at half-mast, although I like to believe my friends had a wake in my memory. *Wow, total bummer, man. Hey, did anyone score R.E.M. tickets? Alec was supposed to get me some. . . .*

I didn't stay in Chicago very long. Didn't even get a chance to call Erin's folks to tell them that their fondest wishes for my future had come true. Once my body had been stabilized, it was put on another charter jet, this time to Pasadena, where it was transported by another ambulance to the Immortality Partnership itself: a windowless, one-story building located in an anonymous office park in the 'burbs. Chip showed me a picture of it on eyes-up: it resembled a small warehouse. Which, in essence, was exactly what it was.

Here's where things get a little Frankenstein. I don't pretend to understand most of it, but this was what was done to my body.

Technicians at the center administered calcium channel blockers, blood anticoagulants, and a cocktail of free radical inhibitors. When my remaining blood was able to flow freely once more, they drained it out of my body, along with as much water as possible, and substituted it with glycerol, which Chip described to me as a cryoprotective agent—antifreeze, if you will, although much more benign than the stuff I used to put in my car—and they cut a tiny hole in my skull so they could watch my brain and make sure that it didn't shrink or swell past certain allowable parameters.

And then they cut my head off.

It wasn't quite the Marie Antoinette treatment. They used electric bone saws and tourniquets and alligator clips, all very sterile and germ free, and my head was deftly separated from the rest of my body by a cut between the sixth and seventh vertebrae of my spine. I know this for a fact, because the company even had someone videotape the procedure as it was going on, presumably to prevent Dad's attorneys from attempting to file a lawsuit later.

I manage to watch about the first ten seconds before I ask Chip to skip this part.

Chip's records show that my decapitated body was shipped to a crematorium. My head, on the other hand (no pun intended), remained in Pasadena, where it was carefully swathed in layers of thermal blanket before it was placed in a large envelope that looked much like a bowling-ball bag. Then they carried the bag, with my noggin safely sealed inside, into a large room whose walls were lined with stainless steel cylinders that vaguely resembled oversized gas water heaters. There was nothing warm about these dewars, though; they contained liquid nitrogen that had been reduced to 196 degrees below zero Centigrade. The dewars had room for three "patients"—you've got to love that choice of term—but the one in which I was placed still had its vacancy sign lit, and free HBO to boot.

And in I went.

And out I came . . . here.

My cappuccino is stone cold by the time I come out of eyes-up. Not quite as cold as liquid nitrogen, but chilly enough. I don't care; I pick up the cup and slug down half of it before my stomach threatens to toss it all over Mister Chicago's carpet.

As for the man himself, he's now standing behind his desk, his back turned to me, his hands clasped behind his back as he gazes through a glass pane at the night world below him. He waits patiently until I'm through gagging.

"Understand?" He's studying my reflection in the window.

"Yeah . . ." Then I reach up to my neck, feel the bottom of my throat. No, there isn't a scar I haven't noticed before. "No, I don't. What happened to my . . . y'know, my . . ."

"Your head? Recycled. Ground up for fertilizer a long time ago." He motions toward the gardens below the windows. "Good source of nutrients for the roses. You probably spread it there yourself a few weeks ago, I imagine."

The bastard is trying to make me sick. Determined not to give him the satisfaction, I choke back the bile in my throat. "But not before you removed my brain," I say, and he nods. "Then how did . . . I mean, my body . . . ?"

"Cloned from a tissue sample." He glances at John and raises two fingers, then moves back to his desk. "I'll spare you the trouble of asking Chip for another technical brief. Your new body was produced over the course of forty-two months in a laboratory . . . we prefer to call it the nursery . . . located on the same level as the ward where you woke up. Its growth was rapidly accelerated by nanoassemblers, but it remained in a virtually decerebrate condition under external life support until its skull was sufficiently large enough for your brain to be transplanted. When this occurred, we inserted the MINN unit within your cerebral cortex . . . ah, thank you, John."

John has placed a brandy snifter on his master's desk; he hands another one to me, then goes back to the bar. "One of the benefits of being able to produce a clone," Mister Chicago continues, "is that we're able to make in vitro biogenetic improvements over the original body. Your double-eyelids, for instance . . . a molecular optical display which interfaces directly with your MINN, giving you an eyes-up readout of whatever data Chip downloads from our central AI system, a 100,000-teraflop DNA computer. Within certain imposed limits, your associate can directly access this system via the subcutaneous comlink that's been built into your ear canal and vocal chords. Indeed, your own MINN is a much smaller version of the same wetware. It's only about the size of your pituitary gland, but it has approximately the same memory capacity as a desktop computer from your time."

That's a chilling thought. "Does it run on Windows?"

Mister Chicago smiles as he picks up his glass and takes a sip. "We also took care of a few other flaws in your original body's genome. Did you have any allergies?"

"Umm . . . hay fever." That's one of the few things he had just said that I completely understand.

He smiles. "Well, I don't imagine that'll bother you anymore. Smell the flowers all you want, my dear Alec." He motions to my glass. "Try the brandy. It's not quite as old as you are."

My stomach is still a little rocky, but I pick up the glass anyway. The liquor burns my tongue, but I don't drink enough to make me sick. "So everyone else I've met, all the other people I met in the White Room . . ."

"Is that what you call it? The White Room?

Have to remember that." Mister Chicago cradles the snifter in his hands as he reclines in his chair. "Former clients of the Immortality Partnership. Original ages between twenty-five . . . which makes you among the youngest . . . and eighty-one, the eldest we've brought up so far. They've all been revived in cloned bodies that are approximately twenty-one years of age, a difference which shouldn't matter much to you but will be a godsend to the older fellows. If and when they fully recover, that is."

"If?"

Mister Chicago looks away. "A tricky business, the resurrection of the dead," he muses. "It took us a long time to master the process. Considerable trial and error . . . and even then it hasn't always been a complete success. We're still learning how to cope with the complications." His eyes dart toward me. "Are you familiar with complexity theory? No? Never mind . . . even with nanoassemblers rebuilding your neural cells from the osmotic damage they suffered during cryonic neurosuspension, there's also the question of the ratio of identity-critical brain damage versus—"

"Hold on. Time out." I put down my glass and give him the ref signal with my hands, which he blinks at in puzzlement. "I'm not an Einstein, man . . . I mean, sir. I mean, you're using words that I don't know."

He closes his eyes and slowly lets out his breath. "Of course. I'm talking to a product of the late twentieth-century American education system. I should know better." He opens his eyes again. "When human brains are frozen in liquid nitrogen for long periods of time, there's always some damage due to ice crystallization between the cell walls.

This means that, even if the brain is fully healed, there can be chronic or acute memory loss. Understand so far?"

I'm doing better. "Yeah. Go on."

"Not only that, but there is also the problem of psychological readjustment. Despite the fact that nearly everyone went to the Immortality Partnership in hope of receiving a second chance at life, some apparently believed that they would be reborn in some Judeo-Christian-Islamic version of an afterlife . . ."

"Heaven, Saint Peter, the pearly gates . . ."

"Mohammed, Jesus . . . exactly. So coming out of it here has been something of a shock to many deadheads. They . . ."

"What? What did you call them . . . us, I mean?"

"Deadheads?" he asks, and I nod. "Something of a slang term, carried from earlier in the century. Why, does it mean something different to you?"

I cough in my hand. Wait till Shemp hears about this. "Does anyone come out wanting a tie-dyed T-shirt?" He gives me a puzzled look. "Never mind. Bad joke. Go on."

He stares at me for a moment, then continues. "We've tried to compensate for this shock by keeping revived sleepers in a drugged condition for a while, giving them an adjustment period while they learn to use their new bodies while we observe their reactions. A few never recover their identities, and they remain imbeciles unable to bathe or feed themselves. Most regain only partial memories of their past lives, and they're locked in a state of mental retardation of various degrees. Only a relative handful recover their full mental capabilities much as you have, although never quite so quickly. Which is why I'm so interested in you."

"That's why you've been playing at being John?" I cock my thumb over my shoulder at my old friend.

"Indeed . . . although you've managed to exceed even his progress." Mister Chicago speaks as if John isn't there. "John was one of the first. For a time, he was one of our best successes. I'm still quite proud of him."

I glance over my shoulder at John. He's still standing at the bar, patiently waiting to bring us another cappuccino or brandy. When I first woke up, he seemed so godlike; now he looks like a puppet waiting for his strings to be tugged. "I believe he once was a professor of biochemistry at some Ivy League university," Mister Chicago says, "but now . . . well, he does make great cappuccino, doesn't he?"

A hundred years ago, John would have been able to explain all the technical stuff Mister Chicago just rattled off. Now he's doing well if he can make coffee without screwing up. I can't help but feel sorry for him.

"So we've settled the most obvious questions." Mister Chicago ticks them off on the tips of his fingers. "You now know who you are, and what you are, and when you are . . . that leaves only a couple, doesn't it?"

He stands up from his chair, gestures for me to follow him to the windows behind his desk. I stand up and walk behind the desk. "There's a reason why I've sequestered you and your companions in the servants' quarters after sundown. Can you guess what it may be?"

"Umm . . . vampires?"

For the first time, he laughs at one of my jokes. "Oh, very good! Vampires . . . I like that!" It wasn't all *that* funny, but he seems to think so. "I'm really beginning to enjoy your company, Alec," he adds, still chuckling to himself. "Now . . . lights off!"

The ceiling lights go out. The solarium plunges into darkness.

For a few seconds I can't see anything, save for the castle windows and the faint glow of walkway lamps. Then my eyes gradually adjust to the gloom.

Mister Chicago is a silhouette standing beside me. He raises a hand, points to the glass dome above us. "Now, look up there . . . what do you see?"

Through the solarium windows, past the immense barrel ceiling of the artificial sky above that, are stars brighter and far more numerous than any I've ever seen before. Yet the stars aren't fixed in place; they're in constant motion, as if I'm looking at them through a slow-moving kaleidoscope. Some are brighter than others, some move faster than their neighbors, but the entire starscape is revolving, like . . .

No. The stars aren't moving. We are.

When I was a little kid, another first-grader told me that if I looked up at the sky for a long time, I could feel the earth moving. I didn't believe him, because when I stood in the playground and stared up at the sky, all I saw were clouds moving above me. But one autumn afternoon a few days later, I tried it again, this time in my backyard . . . but now, although I didn't realize it at the time, with the chimney of my house as my fixed point of reference. And then, with the clouds scudding past the deep blue Missouri sky, I felt the awesome mass of the world as it ponderously rolled beneath the soles of my size-four Keds. It was my first taste of vertigo, and I had nightmares about it later that night.

That moment is like this one.

Everything around me—the solarium, the mansion, the landscape below, the walls of the sky above, all this great mass surrounding us—is in motion.

Struggling for equilibrium, I stare at the center of the sky, that place where I had earlier noticed an opaque shape that blotted out the first stars of twilight. Now I see it clearly for the first time: a immense round object, off-gray and rocky, its rough surface deformed by craters and basins and tiny hills. A tiny moon, seen from only a few miles away.

Near the top of the moon, there's a huge spiderlike object: a man-made structure, round like a shield, constructed out of dull silver metal, several miles in diameter. Its legs are anchored to the moon's gray soil, illuminated by both starlight and the multicolored spotlights.

The spider rests in the center of a web. Long silver threads spread out in ninety-degree arcs from beneath the flat, bloated belly below the shield. The threads in the closest arc expand in size until they become thick cables attached to points on either side of the barrel ceiling above us. Tiny cabs move up and down a couple of these cables: elevators rising and descending from the web's strands.

At the endpoints of the strands furthest away: three enormous cylinders, miles in length, spaced equidistantly from the spider and the tiny moon upon which it crouches. Light glows faintly from within long windows in the tops of these cylinders;

through them, I can just make out landscapes that resemble miniature versions of . . .

Of the little world that I'm within.

"Oh, my God . . ."

The muscles in my legs weaken. I blindly fumble behind me, seeking something to support me. Finding nothing, my knees collapse beneath me. I fall down on my haunches, the rug burning the skin on my knees.

All this time, I've assumed that I'm on Earth. Maybe in a secret underground fortress, like something from a science fiction movie, or inside a biosphere out in the desert somewhere in Utah. It never occurred to me that I'm in space . . .

Way out in space.

"The asteroid is 1985 RB1." Mister Chicago is a dark presence behind me. "Renamed 4442 Garcia in 1995, in memory of an American musician who died about the same time you did, if historical records are complete."

Deadheads. Garcia. If that's supposed to be a joke, I'm not laughing. "How . . . how . . . ?" I can't get the words out of my mouth.

"How what, Alec? How far from Earth? How big is it? Composition, perihelion, inclination, orbital node?" Soft laughter, like a knife sliding out of a black velvet sheath; contempt for dead souls. "Even if you downloaded this date from your MINN, I rather doubt you'd understand it. You could barely converse with me about the details of your own neurosuspension, so there isn't much reason to believe that you would comprehend astronomical terminology."

He's right. I probably wouldn't. I only know that, if 1985 RB1 . . . or 4442 Garcia, or whatever the hell he called it . . . is an asteroid, then it's most likely located somewhere between Mars and Jupiter.

Never mind the math. I'm a long, long way from Earth.

That leaves only one question unanswered. . . .

No. There's hundreds of questions. Thousands. But right now, I can think of only one. I pull my eyes away from the sky, seeking Mister Chicago's face among the shadows.

"Why?"

I can't see him, only the man-shaped hole he makes against the cosmos. If he's smiling, or scowling, or wearing John's implacable face once more, I can't tell. There's a long silence, as empty as the void above me and just as cold, before he deigns to speak to me.

"I have my reasons," he says, "and they're not your concern."

More silence, then even his shadow begins to disappear. "Get up now," he says from the darkness. "You're beginning to bore me. It's time for you to leave."

As I struggle to my feet, I hear the soles of his boots whisking softly across the carpet, heading for the door.

"And, by the way . . . when you change the sheets tomorrow? No wrinkles on the pillowcases. I hate it when you do that."

The door opens and shuts. A moment later, the lights come up again.

I'm alone with John. He silently beckons toward the door. My audience with the master has come to an end; it's time for me to leave.

My name is Alec Tucker. I was dead for one

hundred and four years. Now I'm alive again, and living on an asteroid millions of miles from home. I was brought back to life by someone named Mister Chicago. I've got a computer in my head and a body that looks like mine, but isn't the one I was born with. I'm here to change sheets and make sure that there aren't any wrinkles in the pillow-cases. . . .

And every time one mystery is settled, there're two more to take its place.

I take one more glance at the solarium windows, then I let John lead me to the elevator and back down to the servants' quarters, beneath the castle of Mister Chicago.

EIGHT

COME AS YOU ARE

"What a wasteful thing it is to lose one's mind."

—Vice-President Dan Quayle

And so I went back to what I had been doing before my memory returned, one hundred and four years older and not much wiser.

I wasn't the only one. Soon other deadheads were having their long-term memories coming back to them. Mister Chicago kept his word; our food wasn't being dosed anymore, and for about a week or so everyone shambled about in apparent slow motion, triple-blinking and mumbling to themselves as suppressed recollections of their former lives began seeping back into their consciousness. Walking through the castle, you could see robed figures staring into empty space while they performed their chores like short-circuited robots, and when the day was done and the lights went out in the servants' quarters, you could hear voices from behind closed doors: laughing, murmuring, occasionally weeping.

The transition wasn't easy for anyone, but it

was worse for some than others. Just as Mister Chicago predicted, a handful of deadheads came out of their fugue with their minds severely impaired, their personalities little changed from the way they had been before they were taken off the drugs. There wasn't much that could be done for them; the osmotic damage to their brains was too extensive for nanotech repair, and their new lives were doomed to a state of arrested adolescence. Others had memories that were only partly intact; they might recall their spouses, for instance, but not the dates of their marriages; a child's college graduation ceremony might be vividly remembered, but not the school he attended, or even his or her name. In some ways, the latter were worse off than the former; the ones with blind spots were often frustrated, miserable with their inability to recall what should have been obvious, while the others were as content as children.

And there were a few who became deeply depressed, even psychotic. Winston was disturbed when he discovered that he couldn't remember many details of his old life: the position he had once held at IBM, his wife's maiden name, the street address of his home in Los Angeles. A lot of little gaps, none important individually, but collectively adding up to an enormous gulf that he couldn't bridge; he came to believe that he wasn't the man he had once been. One evening, he sat silently by himself at dinner, barely nibbling at his food and saying little to anyone around him; when the meal was over he made a point of saying good night to all his friends. The next morning, we found that he had hanged himself in his room during the night.

The suicide itself was simple; Winston had coiled a bedsheet into a rope, slung it over his closet door before shutting it, tied the outside end into a noose, stood up on a chair and pushed his neck through the loop, then kicked the chair away. What puzzled us was why he had blindfolded himself by wrapping a ripped towel around his eyes, until Russell deduced that this was the only way he could have killed himself without his associate stopping him. If his associate couldn't see what he was doing, then there was no way it could stop him. He must have meticulously planned it all in advance, rehearsed it in his mind, then performed the act by touch alone, without seeing what he was doing. Only a very intelligent person could have carried out such a grim act with such methodical determination. But it was a shame nonetheless.

This wasn't nearly as bad as what happened a couple of weeks later, when Veronica tried to murder Hugh. She had been pretty twitchy for a while now—of all the deadheads who had started talking to themselves, she was the one whose monologues had become reminiscent of bag-lady rants—but when she stopped showering or bothering to put her soiled robes in the laundry cart, it became apparent that she was pretty close to the edge. Everyone went out of their way to avoid her, but one afternoon poor Hugh—one of our slower companions, happy to do anything that his associate told him to do, no questions asked—was unfortunate enough to be assigned to kitchen detail with her.

I didn't see what happened, but I heard all about it over the dinner table that evening. Hugh had been taking some pots down from a hanging rack when he dropped one of them next to Veronica, who was scrubbing the counter underneath. Veronica screamed when the pot hit the counter, then she snatched an eight-inch knife out of a butcher block and tried to bury it in Hugh's heart.

We already knew that our MINNs were capable of inflicting extreme pain in our frontal lobes as punishment for disobedience or bad behavior, or even a fatal cerebral aneurysm, such as when George attacked Kate in the showers during a similar psychotic snap. Veronica suffered the latter, but not before she managed to slash Hugh across the chest, arms, and hands several times before she dropped dead, the knife still clutched in her fist. Hugh was rushed to the infirmary by a couple of deadheads, and John brought him back to the servants' quarters the following day. He didn't have physical scars, but the emotional wounds never healed; after that, he refused to be alone with any of us ever again. He sat far away from everyone at the dinner table and wouldn't even raise his eyes when someone spoke to him. Poor guy.

For those who didn't come out scatterbrained, depressed, or homicidal, though, it was a time of rebirth. Lazarus steps forth from the crypt, blinks a few times, and says, "Whoa, baby . . . is this the afterlife or what?"

Russell was one of the first to regain his bearings. Russell Weatheral had been a Cal Tech research physicist who, at age 67, keeled over from a heart attack in 1996, a couple of months after he had helped confirm the formation of antihydrogen atoms in the CERN particle accelerator in Geneva. He told me that, shortly after he had signed up with the Immortality Partnership, he had made a wager with several of his colleagues: one thousand dollars, which had been deposited in an escrow account in Zurich only about a week before he died, would be awarded to him if an antimatter space drive was developed by the time he was resurrected.

Russell sighs as he idly stirs his vegetable stew in the dining room. "I've checked it out with Hal," he says, referring to his own associate. "Applied antimatter research reached a dead end about twenty years ago. It's a scientific curiosity with no practical application."

"No starships, huh?" I ask, and he shakes his head sadly. "Guess you lost the bet, then."

"Yep." Then he smiles. "But look at the bright side . . . I had a side-bet going with Stephen Hawking that I'd go before he did. I even entered it in my will . . . he'd get a five-year subscription to *Omni* if I lost. Sort of a reverse on a similar bet he lost to Kip Thorne on the existence of black holes." He chuckles. "Hawking won, but *Omni* folded not long after I kicked the bucket."

Kate was Katherine Van Der Horst, the publisher of an influential New York fashion magazine. Her third husband had given her a membership in the Immortality Partnership as a wedding present. Although she came out of neurosuspension with her memory intact, she took revival quite hard. A second chance at life wasn't something that she particularly wanted, even though she had returned with the same svelte body that had earned her fame and fortune on the fashion runways in the 1950s, minus the lung cancer that had finally killed her in 1989. Her magazine hadn't lasted past 2002, and no one remembered the names of all the protégé models and designers she had fostered during her career. But she soon got over it, especially after her associate, Coco, informed her that she could instruct her MINN to activate a new gland in her body that would produce spermicidal hormones at will: birth control without pills, sponges, or rubbers. She hadn't forgotten the fact that Russell saved her when George tried to rape her, and it wasn't long before she repaid the favor. Russ was grinning for days.

Sam MacAvoy had been a poet and novelist. His books had won several major literary prizes, his stories and his poems frequently anthologized. He had been one of the Beats, and his more notable friends had included the best and brightest voices of his generation; Lawrence Ferlinghetti had once put him up on his couch for several weeks, Alan Ginsberg had been a pool hall buddy, and he told me where Thomas Pynchon had been hiding out all those years—he knew, because he had gone out there to smoke grass with him a couple of times. From 1988, the last time Sam had published anything, until 1994, when he died of AIDS, he had been writer-in-residence at a succession of liberal arts colleges while struggling with writer's block.

A second life wasn't something Sam had asked for, either; in fact, he considered it a curse. Just before he died, some anonymous admirer had gifted him with an Immortality Partnership membership. One of his deathbed memories was having that silver ID medallion placed in his hands by a nurse at the California hospice where he spent his final months. A last gift from a wealthy but short-sighted fan.

"I don't know who did this to me," he says to me, one afternoon while we're mopping the terrace, "but if I ever catch up with him, I'll rip out his heart. Provided he underwent the same treatment, of course."

"How come?"

"I checked the computer. Virtually everything I wrote . . . all my stories, my poems, my novels . . . have fallen out of print. The only thing that remains is a poem I scribbled on a napkin in Max's Kansas City back in '74, and even that's lapsed into public domain." He shakes his head as he plunges his mop into the bucket. "A writer's words are supposed to outlive him, not vice versa . . . and, fuck it, I'm still blocked."

Which, of course, led to yet another question: Where was all the money these guys socked away? Sam died poor, but Russell had established a small trust fund for himself in the same Zurich account where he had placed his final wager with Stephen Hawking. Kate's publishing empire was worth several hundred million dollars when she died, and her third husband and her lawyers had made sure that she wouldn't come back from the netherworld as a pauper. My dad was rich, and so was Shemp's. In fact, virtually everyone here came from upper-class backgrounds; most of them had established escrow accounts at various banks that were supposed to tide them over in the afterlife.

Yet when anyone tried to ask their associates, all inquiries were blocked by that indomitable two-word wall: "File Unavailable." No amount of outrage, wheedling, or begging could force their MINNs into releasing so much as a simple bank statement. So far as anyone knew, their savings had simply vanished. Another mystery.

We didn't know much about Anna Townshend,

for she refused to discuss her past. She came out of the fugue with her long-term memory intact, that much was certain, yet when we sat around the mess table in the evenings, listening to Russell hold forth on high-energy physics, or Sam tell us what a punk Bob Dylan had been when he first showed up on the Lower East Side, she always held back, seldom adding anything to the conversation.

There was a certain sadness in her eyes, yet she wouldn't allow us to know what was on her mind. Anna wouldn't tell us how old (or young) she had been when she died or what she had been doing. It took a lot of nudging for us to even get her to divulge her last name. She wasn't depressed, but neither was she particularly happy. She wouldn't get close to anyone; although we were still friends, there was a new remoteness in our relationship. She seemed reluctant to talk to me, or anyone else. I figured that she'd eventually come around, once she was more comfortable with people. Right now, the only person she was interested in seemed to be Shemp. . . .

And then there was Shemp.

In hindsight, it's no wonder that I failed to recognize my best friend for so long. His new body had been cleansed of the genetic flaws that made him a compulsive overeater with bad eyes; he was no longer the fat, geeky kid that I'd known since junior high. Shemp was still no hunk, to be sure, but without the surplus fifty pounds and the glasses, neither did he look very much like a guy who would have trouble getting a date.

It turned out that he remembered who I was

long before I did myself. In fact, he started coming out of his fugue a few weeks before I took my tumble down the Great Hall staircase. But he also recalled who had been driving the car that night when we were coming home from Lollapalooza, and this knowledge had haunted him so much that he was reluctant to speak to me.

It was probably just as well that he didn't. When I returned to the servants' quarters the night Mister Chicago and I had our little chat in the solarium, my first impulse was to go straight to Shemp's room and . . . well, I didn't know what I wanted to do. Either hug him and start blubbering about how wonderful it was to see him again, or pound the crap out of him for cutting off that goddamn eighteen-wheeler and getting both of us killed. I stood in the corridor outside his closed door for a long time, unsure of what to do next, until I decided that it had been a long day already and that I was too tired to deal with this shit right now.

So Shemp and I were guarded toward one another for a while. We spoke very seldom, and then only in passing; it took several days before we were able to even sit next to each other at the mess table. He was afraid that I was going to kill him, and I was afraid that I might want to. It also put me off a bit that Shemp no longer looked like Shemp, although I don't think even his parents would have recognized him either. Mr. and Mrs. Meyer spent tons of money on exercise equipment, kosher diet food, and fat camps in their ongoing efforts to make Christopher shed his weight. Hell, they bought him his first car when he starved himself one summer and managed to drop eleven and a half pounds, which he regained almost as soon as he had the keys to that Volvo. He had drawn the line at liposuction and stomach staples, but neuro-suspension turned out to be the ultimate weight-loss plan: keep the head, lose the body.

One morning I hit the showers, and Shemp's there.

The women have long since stopped taking showers with the men. With the return of memory, there's also been a revival of modesty. It doesn't matter if we've already seen each other in the buff dozens of times; the drugs that inhibited our sex drives are gone from our food, and now it's hard not to notice all that wet, naked flesh around us. There's no soap for anyone to drop, but everyone is uncomfortable nonetheless, so a consensus agreement has been reached: males and females take turns in the shower room, with the guys going first on even days and the girls getting first dibs on odd days. We still share the anteroom where we leave our robes and towels, but there another new rule comes into place: look all you want, but no touching—unless, of course, you *want* to be touched by a certain individual, in which case you work it out yourselves, in private. Those who were married in former lifetimes understand this better than those who weren't, but the rules are still the same . . . and everyone knows what can happen if you scream rape.

It's a guys-first morning, but since it's my turn to collect the laundry, I arrive late. The only vacant shower is the one next to Shemp. I take it without saying a word to him, and we try to ignore each other. Hot water, cold silence. After awhile, though, we can't help but glance back and forth. This is something that's all too familiar: all those after-noons in the Country Day School gym when we hit the showers after intermurals, and I can't help flashing back to . . .

"Hey, Shemp?"

"Yeah?" He doesn't look around.

"You remember . . . I dunno, that stupid kid from ninth grade . . . ?"

"What kid?" He glances over his shoulder at me. "What are you talking about?"

"Y'know . . . the jock who used to rattail all the seventh and eighth grade kids when we were in the showers?"

"Mean at Country Day?" He mulls it over. "Jeff . . . Jeff Wienberg." He's quiet for a moment. "Yeah, I remember him. Why?"

"I dunno . . . just something I remembered."

Shemp looks like he wants to say something, but doesn't know how. Neither do I . . . but all of a sudden, I don't give a shit who was driving the car that night.

I don't know what compels me to do what I do next, but while Shemp's back is turned to me, I slip out of the shower and hurry into the anteroom. A few of the ladies have already arrived; some blush and quickly turn away, a couple yell in protest. Kate whistles her approval. I pay no attention as I snatch up the towel I left on a bench.

I carry the towel back into the showers and, while Shemp is still rinsing off, soak it under the spray from my hole, coil it into a tight wet rope . . . and snap him in the ass.

He yowls as he leaps a foot into the air, but manages to touch down without sprawling all over the tiles. He turns around and glares at me; for the first time I notice one more thing that's different about the new Shemp.

"Better go see your rabbi," I say. "I don't think you're a nice Jewish boy anymore."

His face goes red, becomes a dark scowl . . . and then it's replaced by a predatory grin. He nearly falls down in his haste to retrieve his own towel from the anteroom. Screams of feminine horror as a few other guys follow him, then the shower room is filled with the sound of snapping rattails.

It's a guy thing.

A half-hour later, Shemp and I are sitting next to each other at the breakfast table—rather uncomfortably, considering the rosy bruises we had inflicted on each other's butts—and roaring over things we've remembered: the seventies mellow-rock stuff they used to play on KSHE, the roach someone sucked into his lungs during some party, the girl who gave excellent head but wouldn't screw because she was saving herself for marriage. The awful silence has been shattered. We're pals again. Perhaps not quite the same friendship we had a century ago, but friends nonetheless.

Yet there are still many mysteries.

Every day, we go to work in the castle. It's just as deserted as ever; we diligently change sheets on beds that have never been slept in (with the exception of the king-size in Mister Chicago's suite), scrub a kitchen whose cookware remain spotless, mop floors no feet have touched save our own. From time to time, we catch an occasional glimpse of Mister Chicago—peering down at us from his solarium or from the gallery of the Great Hall— before he vanishes once more: a phantom in his own house.

It isn't long, though, before the servants who've been working inside the castle are rotated with those who were assigned to chores in the habitat. The former are taught the joys of waxing floors and folding linen, while my friends and I are reassigned to the gardens, groves, and vineyards surrounding the manse. It's hard labor, to be sure, but we're happy to get it; at least now we're not scrubbing the same floors we scrubbed only yesterday. Yet I've never done anything like this before; for the first time in my life, I know what it's like to have blisters on my hands and dirt under my nails. Dad always hired gardeners to do this stuff while I lazed in front of the tube; I never learned how to start a lawnmower, let alone get down on my knees and cut grass with a pair of scissors. Now it's my turn to learn about cramps and calluses.

John—the brown-eyed real McCoy, not his pink-eyed lookalike—appears from time to time to give us pointers on grooming the topiary, or how to distinguish a ripe grape or orange from one that isn't yet mature, yet his presence is more of a distraction than a necessity; his role as teacher is now redundant to what we can learn ourselves from our associates. Nor is he as holy as he once seemed; in fact, now that we know that he's just another deadhead, he seems rather pathetic. Russell once tried to engage him in a science conversation—after all, they share that background in common—but John was plainly baffled by most of the terminology Russell used, and he quickly made an excuse to leave. We seldom saw him after that, or at least when Russ was around; he comes out to bring us a jug of water, make a few comments about what we're doing, then goes away again, still smiling in that empty way of his.

Not having a shepherd gave us a few more opportunities to talk among ourselves. Most times, it was about things remembered—cities visited, good restaurants where we had once eaten, movies and concerts and TV shows we've seen, the reasons behind the 1994 baseball strike or why Reagan beat Carter back in 1980—but on occasion the subject shifts to matters of more immediate interest. One day, Shemp, Russell, and I are taking a midafternoon break from fertilizing a strawberry patch about a mile away from the castle when Russ looks up at the sky.

"Y'know," he says, "none of this makes sense."

"Tell me about it." I've taken off my work gloves to inspect the latest additions to my callus collection. "Mister C has robots, so why does he need slaves for this?"

"We're not slaves." Shemp's lying on the ground next to the water jug. "We're guests. Remember?"

"Excuse me. Guests." I snap my fingers at an imaginary waiter. "Garçon. Steak for three, please . . ."

"That's not what I mean." Russell shades his eyes as if trying to peer past the filaments in the artificial sky. "Have you ever looked at the schematics of the colony?"

"The what?" Shemp asks. "You mean there's a diagram of this place?"

"Yup. Found it yesterday. Go eyes-up and ask your associate for it. Tell it you want to see a north polar projection of 4442 Garcia."

I triple-blink and repeat what Russell just said. My second pair of eyelids close and a translucent blueprint of 4442 Garcia appears before my face. This time, it doesn't resemble a spider crouched on top of a tiny moon; now it looks like a baby turtle trying to hatch a dinosaur egg. Four bologna sausages surround the turtle at right angles, connected to its broad shell by long slender threads. The sausages revolve clockwise around the turtle, while the asteroid itself rotates on its long axis.

"Cool! Where did you find this?"

"I asked for it." Russell is apparently gazing at the same image. "If you want to understand what's happened to you, son, you better start asking questions yourself . . . not just wait for the next time you stumble across something."

"Sure thing, Dad." Russell might have been sixty-seven when he died, but now he doesn't look any older than Shemp or me. He's still not used to that.

"Sorry. Point taken . . . now, pay attention." Once again, Russell slips into college professor mode. "4442 Garcia is a carbonaceous chondrite asteroid about a hundred miles in diameter, located in the main belt. Its orbit is elliptical, with a five-year period, but at present it's near perihelion, which will bring it within three hundred and thirty-five million miles from Earth by the end of the year."

"Proper," Shemp murmurs.

Russ ignores him. "That little round thing on top is a mining platform . . . it has a shaft leading from its center down into Garcia's core, and our friends have been mining the asteroid from the inside out, going up from the center and through the mantle toward the crust. The raw material they've extracted from the core has been refined and processed for use as the building materials for this colony. Follow me so far?"

"Yeah, okay." This is all news to me. "So I guess . . . I dunno, what do you mean?"

"Just listen." Russell isn't used to dealing with kids who aren't post-grad students; I can tell from his tone of voice that he's baby-talking us through this stuff. "I haven't figured out all the conversion factors yet . . . our friend Pasquale is less than forthcoming in allowing me full access to the Main Brain, so there's a lot my associate isn't telling me . . . but as a rough guesstimate, I figure that less than half of Garcia's mass has been consumed so far in order to build this colony."

"How did they do it?" Shemp sounds a little confused. "I mean, how did they make all that stuff into this?"

"Same way they cloned your body, son . . . I'm sorry, Christopher. Or Shemp. Whichever you prefer . . ."

"He's Shemp," I say. "Don't worry, everyone calls him that."

"Yeah, right," Shemp says. "I'm stuck with it."

"So they used nanites, right?"

"Correct. Ask your associate to give you a tutorial on the exact process later. The essential fact is they're able to break down the raw ore to its most elemental level, then reconstruct it as building materials for this colony, along with the three others like it. We've got some mighty powerful technology at work here, gentlemen."

"No kidding." I stare at the eyes-up image. "One hell of a program they've got going here."

"Right. That's what I'm getting at. See those three other habitats? They're the same size as our own . . . three miles long, one and a quarter in width . . . and even though Hal won't tell me what's inside them, I think we can safely assume that they contain biospheres just like this one, either completely terraformed or still under construction. Eyes-down, Hal, thank you."

I tell Chip to go eyes-down as well. Shemp is sitting up now, his back propped against the water jug. Russell stands before us, holding his sod rake like a classroom pointer. "Now, look around you," he continues, sweeping the flat horizon around us with its handle. "Most of the usable land in here has been given over to farming, right? And unless Pasquale has built three more palaces like that one, we can surmise that even more of the acreage in the other habitats has been or will be devoted to crop cultivation. Still following me?"

"Hmm . . . sure."

Russell isn't fooled. "Think, son! What do you think the population of this colony is? How many people do you think are living here right now?"

"Well, how many has Hal told you are living here?"

"I don't know." Russell lowers the rake. "He won't divulge that info . . . which means it must be vital."

He's got a point. Whenever our associates refuse to answer a question, it usually means that we were probing the edges of something important. I take a moment to mull it over. There're forty-three "guests" in the servants' quarters, not counting the ones we've lost to insanity or suicide. From what I can tell, there're probably twice that number living in the lower levels beneath the habitat: people like Big Nurse, John, and all those others I've glimpsed in the corridors during my occasional errands down there. The castle contains enough rooms to hold another thirty to forty people, depending whether they were sleeping alone or in pairs. Some quick mental addition . . .

"A hundred and fifty, two hundred . . . something like that."

"Good guess." Russell nods. "That's the figure I arrived at . . . between a hundred and fifty and two hundred, tops."

"So?" Shemp shrugs. "What does he need all this land for?"

"Exactly! Go to the head of the class, Christopher!" Russell beams at Shemp in a way that makes him look like he's sixty-seven again; he must have enjoyed being a teacher. "The way I figure it, there's enough cropland in this single habitat to provide food and photosynthesized oxygen for a population this size, including the first-class suites that are still vacant. But since there're three other habitats which could do the same, this colony could support almost a thousand people. So . . ."

He stops, waiting for one of us to pose the next question. He's playing the university prof, and we're his students. Large and very profound questions await us; together, we'll explore them until we reach mutual enlightenment.

"So . . ." Shemp begins.

Russell looks at him expectantly.

"So . . . do you think Anna wants sex, or what?" Shemp scratches the back of his neck. "I mean, I'd like to give it a shot."

Russell's mouth drops open. The rake falls from his hands. He stares at Shemp for a long time before he silently bends down to pick it up again. Now he knows why we used to call him Shemp.

I pick up my own rake and go back to work. Coffee break's over; everyone back on their heads. Yet the question still remains.

Where is everyone?

✢ CHAPTER ✢

NINE

BLUE SKY MINING

*. . . We were all going direct to Heaven, we were all
going direct the other way. . . .*

—Charles Dickens, *A Tale of Two Cities*

And then there's the day I punched out Shemp.
Strangely, I didn't feel any great sadness
over losing my family. At first I wondered if Mister
Chicago was still spiking our food, perhaps with
mild antidepressants to keep us from grieving over
the people we had left behind. Yet there were many
deadheads who were openly mourning deceased
family, relatives, and friends, and I gradually realized that my lack of remorse was strictly my own
problem.

The more I thought about it, though, the more
it made sense. My father and I had grown apart
when I became an adult; my fondest memories of
him were from childhood, and once I moved out of
the house, I had seen him only on rare occasions.
The birthday dinner at Tony's, when Dad had given
me my Immortality Partnership medallion, was the
last time I laid eyes on him. That and the trust fund

he had established for me on my twenty-first birthday had been the only tangible evidence that he still cared for his only son; if he loved me, he never let me know.

As for my mother . . . well, it was much the same situation, only worse. When she divorced Dad, she effectively divorced me as well. The few times I visited her in LA, I saw a woman who was doing everything humanly possible to remain a thirty-something beach blonde despite the obvious fact that she was pushing fifty and beginning to look like Jim Carrey playing the Mask in drag. My memory of cuddling in her lap while she read *Green Eggs and Ham* was from when I was about five years old, and she divorced Dad only a year later. The last time she said she loved me was when she gave me a perfunctory kiss on the cheek at Los Angeles International, right after her limo driver had dropped me off at curbside check-in. Her lips felt like moist sandpaper and her breath smelled of Scotch, and I knew that she was only too glad to get rid of her inconvenient son.

So Mom and Dad were dead and long gone. Well, so be it. That may sound cold to anyone who enjoyed the benefits of a happy childhood, but William and Sarah Tucker had effectively stopped being my father and mother a long time ago. Dad placed me in a succession of boarding schools and colleges until I couldn't remain out of town any longer, then threw money at me so I would stay out of the house; Mom was simply embarrassed to have a son who was as young as she was trying to look. If I felt anything for either of them, it was profound regret that they hadn't been better people . . . and relief that my father apparently hadn't opted for neurosuspension himself, because if he had, I surely would have recognized him by now.

This, of course, was yet another puzzle: why had Dad done this for me, and not for himself? And the same for Shemp's parents, who had genuinely loved their eldest child? Shemp and I talked this over one evening, and reached the same conclusion: they had been following an old Ladue tradition. Laduvians, as the residents of one of the wealthiest suburbs in the country used to refer to themselves, often indulged in a shell game of buying the latest extravagance before the other guy did, or buying one just like it so they wouldn't feel left out. If a harsh winter dropped five inches of snow on the ground, someone in Ladue was likely to buy an Eddie Bauer Ford Explorer, which meant that all his friends would soon be buying Eddie Bauer Ford Explorers. If one person bought a summer house on Fire Island, then soon there would be a rush of rich people from St. Louis trying to purchase property on Fire Island. And if Bill Tucker arranged to have his son's head stored in liquid nitrogen, then his good friends Warren and Elsie Meyer just had to do the same for young Christopher. At least, this was the way we figured it.

I missed a few of my friends, but not greatly; none had been so close that I lost much sleep thinking about them. My best friend was Shemp, and all I had to do was wander down the hall and pound on his door if I got lonely for his company. When we stayed up late—or at least as late as our associates would permit us before the warning buzz would sound in our ears, telling us that it was time for lights-out—reminiscing about bar gigs the Belly Bombers had played and stuff like that, more often than not one name in particular would come up . . .

Erin.

The only woman in the world to whom I had ever confessed my love—well, the only woman to whom I had ever said this while not just trying to get into her panties—and she was lost to me that very same night.

Goddamn, that hurt.

I knew that she survived the wreck. One of the items in my file that Chip was able to access from the Main Brain—as we referred to the colony's central AI system—was a short two-paragraph piece that appeared in the *St. Louis Post-Dispatch* on July 12, 1995. Headlined "Car Crash Kills 2," it related the tragic deaths of William Alec Tucker III, 24, of Euclid Avenue, St. Louis, and Christopher Chaim Meyer, 24, of Litzsinger Road, Ladue. The article also reported that a passenger in the car, one Erin Kay Westphall, 23, of Lake Forest, Chicago, had survived the accident. Suffering unspecified injuries, she had been taken to Barnes Hospital emergency room, where she was reported to be in "critical but stable condition," whatever that meant.

"I guess she made it through," I say to Shemp, the night I finally sucked in my gut and asked Chip to open my file again. I really didn't like reading this stuff, but I had to find out what happened to Erin.

"She must have." Shemp sits cross-legged on his bed, idly sketching me with a pen and a pad of bamboo paper that he has begged off John. "It says she's from Lake Forest, doesn't it?"

The clip is still on my eyes-up; I check it again. "Yeah . . . so?"

"Well, if she died, the paper would have reported the address on her driver's license, right? And she was living with you when she got her Missouri license, right?"

He's right; I went with Erin to the state DMV the day she took her driving test, and the address she put on the application had been the apartment we shared in the Central West End. Shemp had moved out to make room for her only a few days earlier; this was something he had never really forgiven or forgotten. "But if her parents came down from Chicago when they heard about the accident," he goes on, "then they would have made sure the reporter knew she was from Lake Forest, because they wouldn't have wanted any of their friends to know that she was shacking up with you. And they wouldn't have thought about doing that if they were messed up about her death. Am I right?"

I go eyes-down. Shemp might be a dork sometimes, but a razor-sharp mind lurks behind that idiot façade. But he didn't have to remind me that Erin's folks thought that I was a loser. "Yeah, if you want to put it shitty like that."

"Sure." He doesn't look up from his pad. "Ergo, if she died in the crash, it would have said so. If she had died later, then there would have been a later article saying so . . ."

"But maybe she died, but it isn't in my file."

"So you're saying you wish she had been killed?"

"Hell, no!"

"Then let it go." Shemp shakes his head. "It was probably tough on her, too, y'know . . . getting in a savage wreck, having her boyfriend killed and all that."

"Yeah, but . . ."

"Look, we're here only because your dad and mine signed us onto the program. It doesn't matter why they did it . . . they just did, okay? And we beat the odds, and now we've got a second chance. So . . ."

"But when I asked Chip about Erin, he told me that her file was closed. Not 'No Available Reference' . . . he said 'File Closed.' What does that mean?"

"He said that? Really?" When I nod, Shemp goes eyes-up and works his way through the query procedure with Moe, his associate. He mutters under his breath for a few seconds, then he triple-blinks again. "Same thing for me," he says when his eyes lose their filminess. "Jeez, I dunno . . ."

"Then maybe she died right after we did, and her folks put her into neurosuspension . . ."

He laughs out loud. "So she could be reunited with you? Fat chance. They hated your guts."

"But you don't know! She might have . . . I mean, it's possible that she could have . . ."

"Alec . . ."

"She could have . . ."

"Alec, shut up. Just shut up, okay?" He sighs. "Look, man, she's gone. That's all there is to it. I know it's tough, I know how you felt about her, but . . . jeez, she's a hundred and four years in the past. You're here, now, and she's . . ."

"Dead."

He nods. "Sorry to say it, but yeah . . . she's dead, Jim."

I can't help it. I'm trying to come to grips with the fact that Erin is finally and irrevocably gone from my life—the only woman I've ever loved, and she's in a grave more than three hundred million miles away—and the son of a bitch has the gall to crack a lame *Star Trek* joke.

So I deck him.

My fist connects solidly with his jaw. It knocks him right out of bed.

An instant later, an ice pick slams into my brain; Chip has registered a hostile act on my part, and it's putting a stop to it. It's also a warning: if I don't chill out right now, a major blood vessel in my head will rupture, and if I die a second time, there won't be a third act. This is the hard lesson we've learned from seeing what happened to George and Veronica.

A migraine is enough for me. I sag to my knees and clutch my throbbing skull with both hands, and after a few moments the pain subsides to the point that I'm able to look up again. Shemp is still sprawled on the floor, massaging the bruise I've left on his face. He doesn't say anything, but the look in his eyes reminds me of a dog who's been whipped once too often.

I don't care that he's hurt. Without another word, without looking back, I get up and stalk out of his room, slamming the door behind me.

And then I go back to my own room and weep for the rest of the night.

Shemp was right, though, just as Russell had been. The time had come for me to put the past behind and start trying to make some sense out of A.D. 2099. The first logical step, it seemed to me, was to find out everything that had happened since July 11, 1995.

It wasn't an easy task. When I sneaked into the castle library one afternoon and checked the shelves, I couldn't find any books that covered the last century; perhaps there was a reason for this, but I couldn't fathom it. Mister Chicago might have been able to tell me these things, but on those increasingly rare occasions when I spotted him outside the castle, he didn't acknowledge my presence. It was as if I was little more than another ornament; he would walk right past me with no more than a quick glance in my direction.

As always, that left Chip as my primary source of information. This was the most difficult road to enlightenment, for Chip was literal-minded: nonspecific questions would be answered in non-specific terms, and replies to oversimplified questions would be much the same way. He had all the answers, of course; the trick was posing the right questions. So learning history from him was like playing Trivial Pursuit when you can't read your side of the card.

Perhaps it was just as well. It took Shemp several days to get over my punching him out, so for a while I didn't have him as company when we were working the fields. I had observed Russell constantly murmuring under his breath as he held lengthy discussions with Hal while he raked, ploughed, and picked. Before long I was doing the same, if only because quizzing Chip took my mind off work. We must have looked weird, like street people talking to themselves.

It took a long time, but I finally managed to work out of Chip the most pertinent (if not the most important) events that happened during my absence. It went like this. . . .

■   ■   ■

The human race sort of muddled along through the remainder of the twentieth century and into the twenty-first. Everyone partied down on New Year's Eve 1999, and then it was back to business as usual: brush wars in Africa, terrorist bombings in Europe and South America, mindfuck politics and petty bickering in the USA. There was a really bad depression in America which led to a couple of states seceding from the union. A couple of nukes went off in the Middle East—one in Tel Aviv, the other in Tehran—but there was no global nuclear holocaust, and nuclear weapons were finally outlawed with the Treaty of Jerusalem. The last time anyone saw a live whale was in 2002. All the people who really irritated me—Newt Gingrich, Madonna, Louis Farrakhan, Roseanne, Michael Jackson, Pat Robertson, and the fucking Energizer Bunny—finally had the good grace to drop dead.

During all this, the McGuinness Corporation launched the first manned expedition to the Moon since 1972, with assistance from NASA. This occurred in 2010, and although there was the usual "America Number One" bullshit from the media, no one seemed to notice or care that McGuinness had its own corporate agenda, which had little to do with showing the flag. Once it established a small base in the Descartes Highlands, the company announced the formation of a new subsidiary, Skycorp, which would build a system of solar power satellites in geosynchronous Earth orbit, using lunar resources for the main materials and a new GEO space station as its construction base.

This was the beginning of what would eventu-

ally be called the Space Century. Despite techno-
logical snafus, threats of bankruptcy, and pro-
nouncements of imminent failure by pessimists,
Skycorp managed to keep its promises. By 2020,
the first two powersats had become fully opera-
tional, the beamjacks of Olympus Station were
ready and willing to build yet another one, and
Descartes Station was on the verge of becoming a
self-sufficient lunar colony. Meanwhile, a multinational Mars expedition had established a tentative
foothold on the red planet, just in time to meet
the almost-forgotten objectives George Bush had
set way back in 1989.

If anyone had been expecting instant gratifica-
tion and paradise á la carte, though, they were living in a dreamland. This was a frontier, after all,
and the hardest days were still ahead.

In 2024, Skycorp made the mistake of trying to
sell its lunar base to a Japanese space corporation.
This resulted in a labor strike by the long-suffering
moondogs which, despite attempted military inter-
vention by the newly formed U.S. Space Infantry,
was successful. Descartes Station founded its own
employee-owned company; the following year,
Lunar Associates set out to explore near-Earth asteroids in search of raw material which could be sold
to the multinational companies that had formed a
consortium to build an orbital colony in a Lagrange
point in cislunar space.

The consortium didn't appreciate being put
over the proverbial barrel by the moondogs, but
neither did they have much choice if they wanted
to get any returns from all the billions they had
invested in the Lagrange colony. Nonetheless, it
tried to keep the leash as tight as possible; once

Clarke County was completed in 2047, a puppet government was installed which, although elected by the colonists, was in fact micromanaged by the consortium. It didn't take long before the colonists wised up; after its New Ark Party formed a secret alliance with Descartes Station, they formally declared political independence in 2049.

At about this same time, a small biotech research team on the Moon, working out of a secret laboratory in the western rim of the Sea of Tranquillity, succeeded in gestating the first test-tube embryos specifically bioengineered for living in low-gee space environments. In a moment of hubris, the research team called this new offshoot of the human race *Homo superior*; they kept their accomplishment a closely guarded secret, known only to a handful of selenians.

The consortium tolerated the independence movement, believing that it would be short-lived and would soon crumble on its own. Instead, the lunar and orbital colonies formalized their alliance by declaring themselves to be the Pax Astra. The United Nations, invoking the 1967 Space Treaty, refused to recognize the Pax Astra as a separate nation. When the Pax reacted by raising trade tariffs on Earth-based companies doing business in Clarke Country, the United States, Japan, and the European Commonwealth nations declared war.

The Moon War lasted for three months during 2052, and culminated in a second attempt by the U.S. Space Infantry to take control of Descartes Station. The Battle of Mare Tranquillitatis was quick, bloody, and largely one-sided; most of the hundred-man invasion force was massacred, with the few survivors sent scurrying back to the staging base on Olympus Station. A simultaneous effort to invade Clarke County was even more futile; Japanese and European shuttles were either destroyed or warded off by a phalanx of particle-beam weapons deployed around the station. The Moon War ended with the signing of the Treaty of Mare Tranquillitatis, when the UN formally recognized the Pax Astra. The consortium collapsed shortly thereafter, with the individual companies, including Skycorp, either going bankrupt or forming trade alliances with the Pax. It wasn't long before the Mars colonies joined the Pax; when the Pax had issued its own currency, the lox—one lox being equal to one liter of liquid oxygen—it made sense for the aresians to use that standard, since they had better ability to manufacture liquid oxygen than either Clarke County or the selenians.

Shortly after the war, a handful of deep-space explorers from the Mars colonies who had settled the asteroid belt formed their own cartel, the Transient Body Shipping Association. Although not a formal government like the Pax, it often acted as such, regulating trade among the extended families working the belt and with the Pax. Since the Pax didn't perceive the TBSA as a potential threat, it allowed the miners to do pretty much as they wished, so long as they paid their tariffs. Unfortunately, the Pax made the mistake of constantly raising the tariffs, which did little to keep it in good graces with the TBSA.

At the end of the fifties, the Pax sent the first expedition to the moons of Jupiter and established a small outpost on Callisto. Callisto Station began harvesting helium–3 from Jupiter's upper atmosphere for export to Earth as fuel for fusion reactors.

It wasn't long before the Callisto miners realized that they held an important edge: helium–3 was a vital resource without which the tokamaks on Earth and the Moon would soon sputter to a halt, and Jupiter was so distant from the inner solar system that they could arbitrarily impose their own demands without fear of reprisal. The Jovians formed their own secret alliance with the TBSA, and the Pax soon learned that what's good for the goose is also good for the gander: taxes and tariffs on Pax vessels working the outer system. Since the Jovians could manufacture their own liquid oxygen, which they were able to supply in large quantities to the TBSA, the lox became nearly worthless so far as they were concerned.

By 2061, the Pax was facing one crisis after another. The democratic government which had been formed during the 2049 revolution was stagnant. While Congress, led by the majority New Ark Party, struggled to achieve a consensus decision on how to deal with the TBSA, several new political factions were vying for dominance. Chief among them was the Monarchist Party, which declared its intent to remake the Pax as a constitutional monarchy. Meanwhile, the lox was being steadily devalued, there was open hostility between the Jovians and Pax vessels which arrived at Callisto Station, and the aresians were complaining of being treated like poor cousins.

In 2064, a special election called by the New Ark Party succeeded in keeping the New Ark in power, but only by a slender majority and with virtually no voter mandate. Several New Ark leaders left to join the Monarchists; among them were Macy Westmoreland, one of the instigators of the

2049 revolution and a heroine in Clarke County, and Lucius Robeson, a former Skycorp executive who had defected to the Pax just before the Moon War. The president and Congress couldn't keep their promises to restore order to the Pax, so in early 2066 the Monarchists initiated a bloodless coup d'etat on Clarke County. The president and his staff were forced to flee the colony, and the Pax Astra suddenly became a monarchy.

Once a new Parliament was elected to replace the former Congress, Macy Westmoreland was crowned as Queen Macedonia, with Lucius Robeson installed as chief of naval intelligence. Lunar aluminum replaced liquid oxygen as standard for the lox (although the name remained the same). The Pax commemorated the event by launching humankind's first (and, as it turned out, the only) interstellar probe, the *Queen Macedonia I*, to the planetary system orbiting 47 Ursae Majoris, thirty-five light-years from Earth. This was the last straw for the aresian representatives; protesting that tax money had been squandered on a grandiose program which they had actively lobbied against, believing that their interests were being ignored by both crown and Parliament, and finding themselves virtually shut out of Parliament, they took the next ship back to Mars. Almost as soon as they arrived at Arsia City, the aresian satraps unanimously voted to secede from the Pax and declared Mars to be neutral.

No one in the Pax knew it at this time, but a fringe group of Belt colonists, in conjunction with Callisto Station and several disenfranchised Martian satraps, had already formed their own secret organization. It isn't unfair to call the Zodiac a deep-space mafia; its game wasn't politics or terrorism, but capitalism waving the Jolly Roger: extortion against unaffiliated TBSA members and piracy on Pax vessels operating within the Belt and Jovian space. No one knew who its leader was, but rumor had it that he was a former Pax trade minister who fled Clarke County when the Monarchists came to power, taking with him several megalox in treasury funds.

By 2067, the situation had become even worse for the Pax. Its vessels in the Belt and in Jovian space were being hijacked by privateers, and it was facing insurgency on the home front—this time, by the *Homo superiors* who had been decanted on the Moon just before the Moon War. The eldest of these motherless children were no more than seventeen, but they were all precocious far beyond their years. Calling themselves Superiors, they formed their own tight, highly disciplined enclaves within the free-wheeling lunar society, and were well on their way toward forming extended-family clans similar to those first formed in Descartes Station circa 2030, which in turn had become the basis of the aresian satraps and the TBSA clans. Next to the decadent selenians and the brawling aresians, though, the Superiors were puritans; their strict extropic philosophy—whatever the hell that was—made drinking, smoking, using drugs, eating meat, and mating with baseline humans (i.e. Primaries) reasons for expulsion from their clans.

Perceiving the Superiors as a potential threat to Monarchist rule, Queen Macedonia decreed that they should be allowed to emigrate from the Pax if they so desired; she even went so far as to gift them with several decommissioned asteroid freighters, so as to speed their diaspora. A few clans chose to remain loyal to the Pax; they were quickly inducted into the newly formed Pax Astra Royal Navy. However, most of the Superiors made an exodus to the outer system, where they parlayed their innate spacefaring skills into trade alliances with the TBSA, the Jovians, and aresians. Although the Superiors proclaimed themselves to be apolitical, many in the Pax government believed that they had fallen in with the Zodiac.

By the end of the sixties, Zodiac piracy against Pax vessels had reached crisis proportions. Pax spies in the Belt couldn't discover where the pirates were coming from or who was backing them, but Sir Lucius believed that the Jovians were behind the hijackings. The Royal Navy frigate *Intrepid* was dispatched to the Jovian system, where a Royal Militia squad raided Callisto Station. They returned the base to Pax control, yet at the cost of the lives of almost a dozen colonists. In protest, the aresians broke all diplomatic ties with the Pax and closed its consulates on the Moon and Clarke County. The TBSA raised its tariffs again, and Pax vessels were embargoed from Ceres Station.

In the meantime, the Pax managed to send a civilian expedition to Saturn, in hopes of eventually establishing a source for helium–3 that would bypass Callisto Station. The PASS argosy *Hershel Explorer* arrived in 2069, whereupon a small research outpost was established on Titan. Two months later, all transmissions from Huygens Base suddenly ceased. Fearing that renegade Superiors had raided the outpost, the *Intrepid* was dispatched to Titan.

No Zodiac presence, past or present, was found

by the PAM squad which ventured down to Titan's muggy surface. What the soldiers discovered instead was that all the explorers who had inhabited the base, and nearly all the crewmen remaining aboard the orbiting *Hershel Explorer*, had either slaughtered each other or had committed suicide. The only survivors were three crewmen, including the *Hershel*'s captain, who had sealed themselves off from the rest of the crew and placed themselves in cold-sleep hibernation. Before they did so, though, they recorded a final logbook entry which told the gruesome story. The Titan expedition had discovered a microscopic life-form in a liquid-methane tide pool on the moon's surface, one that mutated and became an aerobic virus when it was accidentally exposed to the base's oxygen-nitrogen atmosphere. This virus attacked the human central nervous system; before it rotted out their brains, it drove its victims into homicidal frenzy. There was no cure for it, no possible inoculation; the only way out was madness and death.

It was unclear, from the records Chip was able to access from the Main Brain, exactly what happened next; however, the end results were well-documented. Despite efforts by the *Intrepid* to contain the virus—including the loss of the PAM squad which landed on Titan—the "Titan Plague" made its way into the asteroid belt during the next decade. Although further outbreaks were rare, the contagion reappeared on several different occasions; each time, entire ships or colonies were wiped out within a matter of hours.

The Pax temporarily shut itself off from the outer system, allowing no vessels from the Belt or outer planets to enter near-space without undergoing rigorous quarantine procedures. Titan was placed off-limits by everyone. The governments of Earth went even further than that; alarmed by the prospect of a doomsday plague, they unilaterally prohibited any crewed spacecraft from landing anywhere on terran soil.

The following decade was one of isolation and depression. With Earth shut off from space and the Pax from the outer system, Mars, Jupiter, and the TBSA were forced to rely upon their own resources for survival. They eventually formed the Ares Alliance. In an odd sense, perhaps the Titan Plague had done more good than harm; once it ran its course and became seldom seen (although sporadic outbreaks still occurred now and then), humankind realized that the solar system had become smaller during the last century, the worlds it inhabited codependent upon each other. The threat of inter-planetary war evaporated along with the plague; the quarantines were lifted, and it seemed as if the solar system had finally been united.

It was a fragile peace, though, and it didn't last very long. The Ares Alliance soon announced new tariffs against Pax vessels. Queen Macedonia died in 2086; Lucius Robeson, shortly after his coronation as King Lucius, called these tariffs "ransom without rea-son" and declared war against the Alliance. While Pax and Alliance vessels duked it out in the Belt, Earth declared itself off-limits once again. The System War didn't last very long; it ended in 2091 with the sign-ing of Treaty of Ceres, in which Callisto Station was reluctantly ceded to the Ares Alliance in exchange for trade agreements that put a cap on future tariffs.

The Treaty of Ceres left the populated solar system divided into three main spheres of influence.

The Pax Astra is still the dominant force in the inner system, with nearly two and a half million people living on the Moon and Clarke County, but economically stretched by war debts and still recovering from the economic depression suffered during the plague years. King Lucius is still on the throne, but he's in his nineties now and it's uncertain which is failing more quickly, his health or popular support behind his government. Nonetheless, Parliament has raised taxes on everyone and everything within the realm. The Monarchists remember their glory days, however short-lived, when the Pax held absolute power over the entire system; it's no secret that they're amassing military strength, even while imposing a virtual dictatorship at home.

The Ares Alliance has just over a million people living on Mars and scattered across the Belt and the Jovian moons, but still dependent upon the Pax and Earth for trade. While the Alliance is more politically stable than the Pax, trade rivalries fester between the aresians and the TBSA; they remain united only in their scorn for the Pax. Even the Superiors hope King Lucius will die soon.

And, finally, the Zodiac: mysterious as ever, outlawed by both the Pax and the Alliance, still the wild card. It's rumored to be led by twelve secret houses, each taking the name of one of the constellations of the zodiac, its patriarchs spread across the Belt and the Jovian system. Although it has ceased hijacking Pax vessels, the Zodiac's objectives remain unfathomable. To this day, no one knows the identity of its leader.

■　■　■

This is history.

So far as I can tell, it's the same old shit as before, just with better special effects. It's 2099, and everyone's still trying to hose everyone else. Yeah, sure, it's interesting, and some of this would have made a great George Lucas movie, but it isn't doing me much good now, is it?

Things change, though, when you're trying to figure out what's happened during the last hundred years while your head was bobbing in a tank of liquid nitrogen.

One morning, I'm walking across the Great Hall, just as I do every morning while I'm on my way out to the habitat for another day of scut work, when I happen to glance down at the mosaic floor, and suddenly realize that the tiny bits of quartz and glass beneath my sandals form the twelve constellations of the zodiac. In its center is the Greek omega symbol, and surrounding it are the orbits of the eight major planets.

That stops me cold. I stare at this carefully constructed pattern, and wonder why Mister Chicago has taken the time and effort to have this mosaic placed in the center of his castle.

And then I remember what I've learned lately, and suddenly realize that the nameless leader of the Zodiac is much closer than I've ever suspected.

✛ CHAPTER ✛

TEN

SOMEBODY TO SHOVE

There are two distinct types of people on the party circuit, whose customs and ideas are so much at variance that misunderstandings are inevitable and bitter clashes frequent. One group is called "Hosts" and the other "Guests." Miss Manners often wonders, considering how little these groups have in common, why they socialize at all.

—Judith Martin, *Miss Manners' Guide for the Turn-of-the-Millennium*

One morning after breakfast, when the time comes for our associates to give us our assignments for the day, Shemp, Russell, Sam, and I are told to go the end of the main corridor in the habitat's lowest level. None of us has ever visited Level D before, and we aren't given an explanation what we're supposed to do once we get there. We've no choice, though, but to go to a lift that carries the four of us down to Level D, then follow the corridor to something called Access AH–12.

It's a long walk, but we don't make it alone. The

corridor is busy with the habitat's underground inhabitants, who ignore four white-robed servants as if they're school kids on a field trip. We've made several previous trips to the lower levels on one errand or another, so we're used to this sort of dismissal, yet today it seems as if everyone down here is moving just a little faster than usual. There's a certain urgency in the air, as if they're afraid of not meeting a deadline.

The others notice it, too. "I haven't seen anything like this since finals week at Cal Tech," Russell says softly as we approach the corridor's end. "Something's going on."

"Think Chicago's got something to do with it?" Shemp whispers.

Russell gives him an arch look. "Son, you've got a talent for stating the obvious. Pasquale's got something to do with everything."

But we all know what Shemp means. It's been nearly six weeks since the last time anyone saw Mister Chicago. Anna changed the linens in the master bedroom only two days ago; she told me that his bed still hasn't been slept in, nor were there any other indications that he had been there lately. Of course, this could mean nothing—4442 Garcia has three other habitats as large as this one, so there's plenty of places for him to hide—but it looks like the master of the house has simply vanished.

Shemp's about to retort, but he's cut short by Sam. "Look alive, folks," he mutters, "Time for 'Mr. Rogers' Neighborhood.'"

Mr. Rogers is Sam's nickname for John, bestowed in honor of his fixed smile and kindergarten attitude. John stands next to an iris hatch marked *Access*

AH–12; parked beside him is a hover-cart. A small pile of plastic-wrapped bundles lies in the cart's bed.

"Good morning, gentlemen." John beams at us from beneath his cowl: Fred Rogers as Rasputin the Mad Monk. "I'm so very glad to see you today. Are you feeling well?"

"Aw, put a sock in it." Shemp has learned that he can be as insolent with John as he wants, just so long as he isn't disobedient. "What do you want?"

John's smile doesn't flicker. "I have a very special job for you this morning, Christopher. Something you've never done before."

"Can you say 'menial labor'?" Sam murmurs. "Sure you can. . . ."

"We have some very special friends arriving today," John goes on, "and Mister Chicago would like you to greet them."

"'Very special friends'?" Russell cocks an eyebrow. "Umm . . . where are they coming from, John? From off Garcia?"

John's smile falters a bit. "Yes, Russell, they are," he says hesitantly. "They'll be arriving very shortly on a vessel from somewhere else. They're very important people, and we're honored to be the ones chosen to meet them. We must take good care of them. Do you understand?"

We exchange mute glances. It isn't much info, but it explains a lot. VIPs of some sort. Not only that, but the first visitors to 4442 Garcia that we've heard about.

"Before we go any further," John continues, "each of us needs to don special garments. Your robes won't be helpful where you're going." He gestures toward the wrapped bundles on the cart. "You also need to know that this job, while it isn't particularly hazardous, requires special attention. You're going to a place where you won't weigh as much as you usually do. You may have a little trouble making your feet stay on the floor, which is why you'll have to wear . . ."

"Question." Russell raises his right hand. "Are you trying to tell us that we're going to a low-gee area of the colony? That's the hub, isn't it?"

For a moment, John doesn't know how to answer this. He hasn't gotten used to the fact that some of his charges are now a little brighter than he is, and that a few of us can figure things out for ourselves. I have to pity him; a long time ago, he and Russ could have swapped equations over beer and pretzels. Now he's just Mister Chicago's majordomo, placed in the role of a waiter trying to discuss the finer points of French cuisine with a master chef.

"Very good, Russell," he replies, struggling to retain his mantle of authority. "You're quite correct. You will be visiting the colony's hub, where your mass . . . I mean, your weight . . . will be a little less than . . ."

"Mass remains constant. Weight changes." Russell isn't letting John off the hook. A little come-uppance for all those bowls of chicken soup. "So far as I can determine, the radius of the colony is seven kilometers, with centripetal gravity at one-sixth Earth normal. It probably diminishes to one-tenth or less at the axial center. . . ."

"Want to translate that?" This from Shemp. I don't say so, but I need a physics refresher myself.

"What it means," Russ says, "is that this could get a little hairy. We're going to have to be very careful where we're going. Take everything slow and easy. No fast moves, no sudden starts. Pick up your feet too fast and you might slam your head against something, and that could really hurt."

Shemp nods and shrugs. He's beginning to dislike Russ about as much as John. Or me, for that matter; he still hasn't quite forgiven me for punching him out a few weeks ago. Christopher Meyer may no longer be the fat kid everyone picked on at Country Day, but he's still Shemp to one degree or another.

"Russell is correct." John's back in Fred Rogers mode. "This is why you must pay special attention to what your associates tell you to do. They will be giving you instructions as we go along. If you follow them exactly, no one will have any difficulty." His benign smile makes a reappearance. "In fact, I think you may even enjoy yourselves."

"Oh, boy." Sam looks down and shakes his head. "Whenever he says that . . ."

He doesn't have to finish the thought; we all know what he means. After seven months of sweeping, scrubbing, mopping, polishing, planting, weeding, fertilizing, hauling, and doing whatever else we're told to do, we can't wait for the next bit of fun John has in store for us.

The bundles contain one-piece blue overalls with elastic bindings on the wrists and ankles and enough pockets to satisfy a kleptomaniac; it must be cold at the hub, because the fabric is thick and quilted. John has us change into them right there. We trade our sandals for soft booties with Velcro-like soles and small weights sewn into their ankles.

The breast pocket of our outfits is emblazoned with a small omega. Once again, I wonder what this means; the same character is at the center of the mosaic floor of the Great Hall, and I've also seen it here and there in the habitat. The symbol holds some significance to Mister Chicago, that much is certain.

Once we're dressed, our robes littering the corridor floor around us, John gives each of us a small headset. "Once you're at the hub," he explains, "you'll need to use these to hear your associate. Your eyes-up will continue to function, but . . ."

"Radiation shielding?" Russell asks, and once again John looks perplexed. "Our associates will function because of their onboard memories, but transmissions from the Main Brain will . . . *oww! shit!*"

He grabs at his temples and doubles over in pain. Instant headache, courtesy of Hal. John watches him dispassionately. "Okay, okay," Russ gasps. "No more questions . . ."

"Very good, Russell." John triple-blinks, then his lips move silently. Russ lets out his breath, then slowly stands erect again. There's a calculating look in his eyes. For whatever it's worth, he's just learned something significant.

That's weird. Why doesn't the Main Brain want us to ask questions about radiation shields?

"All set? Very good." John turns to the cart and touches its keypad; the cart stops humming as wheels descend from its undercarriage. John presses a button on the wall next to the hatch behind him; it irises open with a faint grinding noise, and he leads us into a large cab. Its walls are encircled by polished brass handrails and large windows; past our reflections in the thick glass, I can make out the glimmer of starlight.

Russell notices it, too. "Glass elevator," he whispers to me. "We're outside the habitat."

We make room for the cart, then our associates tell us to grasp the rails tightly and plant our feet firmly against the carpeted floor. The hatch sphincters shut; there's a slight jolt, and then we start to rise.

What we've first taken to be an elevator is, in fact, a cable car.

As it ascends one of the thick cables tethering the habitat to the asteroid, I look out the window next to me and see the vast roof of the habitat sprawling out below us. I catch a brief glimpse of the castle through the skylight, now reduced to a small brown cross surrounded by tiny gardens and groves, before it vanishes from sight when the skylight becomes obscured by a dense forest of cables.

Upward we rise, our weight diminishing with each passing moment as the cable car climbs to an ungodly height. Within minutes we're suspended a mile above the habitat. Background stars slide past the cables; it's now uncomfortably obvious that the entire structure is rotating like a gargantuan merry-go-round. We aren't going upward, but *sideways* . . .

A pair of frisky chipmunks start playing tag in my stomach. I wrench my eyes away from the window and stare down at the floor. I'm nauseated; something acidic threatens to surge out of my throat. Shemp and Sam are groaning; only Russell and John remain calm. I try shutting my eyes, but that doesn't help much; each passing vibration tells me we're still in motion.

"Oh, God," I murmur, "I'm going to be sick. . . ."

Chip flashes a message against the inside of my closed eyelids:

Open your eyes. Look directly at the colony's hub.

"No way!"

**Open your eyes, Alec. Look out the window.
Don't look down. Fix your eyes on the hub.**

Chip wouldn't tell me to do something that's bad for me. He's my guardian angel, my friendly neighborhood omniscient being. I take a deep breath, turn my head toward the window next to me, open my eyes to gaze upward.

4442 Garcia is now a scarred boulder that fills the sky. Dead-center is the massive shield of the colony's hub, a tortoise caught in the middle of a spiderweb. Although the hub steadily grows larger, at least it isn't moving; in fact, it's nice and stationary, and it's now apparent that the cab is descending toward it.

The chipmunks get sleepy and go back to bed. I take another breath. That was close. "Thanks, Chip," I whisper. "I owe you one."

"Look over there," Russell murmurs, pointing out another window. "Left side of the hub."

At first, I can't tell what he's talking about. Then I spot something that vaguely resembles a pair of white half-liter bottles glued together end to end, nestled within a metal cradle against the side of the shield. A broad cone opens from the rear end of the object; bright lights glimmer from tiny windows scattered across the front section.

"Is that a spaceship?" Okay, so I'm a little slow on the beat.

"Mister Chicago's yacht," John replies. "The *Anakuklesis*. It berthed just a few minutes ago."

"That's what we're meeting?" Shemp asks. He's just as green-faced as I am, but he's also peering out the windows. Moe must have given him the same instructions. "Little sucker, ain't it?"

"Yes, it is rather modest . . . only eighty-five meters. Freighters and passenger liners are larger, but it suits the master's purposes."

For the life of me, I can't tell whether John's being sarcastic or not. Shemp must have been fooled by the yacht's relative size; for my part, I can tell that it's a big sucker. "What's it called, the . . . ana-kook-whatsis?"

"*Anakuklesis*." This from Sam; he's also peering out the windows. "Ancient Greek term . . . the 'Eternal Return,' if I remember my classics correctly."

There's an odd expression on Russ's face when Sam says this. He opens his mouth as if to add something typically professorial, but then he seems to think better of it. He stares out the windows instead. "Little bit of the old Omega Point Theory, eh, John?" he says, less of a question than a prod.

If John knows what Russell means by this remark, he doesn't show it. So far as I can tell, though, he's just as clueless as the rest of us. Shemp and I glance at each other, then at Sam, hoping that he'll give us an answer. But Sam just shrugs and raises an eyebrow; he doesn't know what Russell is referring to, either. And Russell isn't saying.

Russ has figured something out. If it makes him want to deliver one of his lectures, but also shuts him up because of what his associate might do to him, then it has to be awfully important. Time to start paying attention.

■   ■   ■

The cable car decelerates and slides into a sleeve within the hub's outer hull. It eases to such a gentle halt that we barely realize that it's stopped until its hatch irises open. John touches the cart's keypad again and sends it out into the half-lighted corridor on the other side of the hatch, then he turns to us.

"You need to know several things before we go any farther." Fred Rogers has taken off his sneakers; it's no-shit time in the neighborhood. "First, for your own safety, keep at least one foot on the floor at all times. If you pick up something large, or if it's handed to you, be careful with it. Something that looks like it may weigh a hundred pounds will only weigh less than ten here, and it may fly away if you pick it up too fast. Do you understand?"

We all nod. This is something we've already noted. Although we're not floating, our bodies feel lighter. It seems as if the only thing keeping me from banging my head against the ceiling is the clutch of my shoe soles against the thin carpet. But it isn't a totally unfamiliar sensation; it's much like the time I inhaled a half-dozen whippits in my car just before going into the Plant and Page show.

"Second," John continues, "you need to go eyes-up now, and stay in that mode until we're through. Your associates have already downloaded all the information you'll need to know, so you'll probably not have to ask anything. Just follow their instructions. Understood?"

So this was how Chip anticipated my vertigo and told me how to deal with it. Nice little suckers, these MINNs. Wish I had one when I was taking college exams. Everyone triple-blinks; their pupils grow less distinct as their nictitating eyelids clamp down.

"And third . . ." John hesitates. "You'll see some people who may seem very strange to you. Whatever you do, don't react in any adverse way. Simply accept them as they are. Do whatever they ask you to do, at least within reason, and—"

"Okay if I do this?" Shemp holds up his right hand in a Vulcan salute.

Russ, Sam, and I crack up. My man Shemp. Veteran of a thousand *Star Trek* episodes. Klingons, Ferengi, Romulans, Cardassians, the Borg . . . he's seen 'em all. Christ, he even sat through the entire first season of *Deep Space Nine*.

"No, I don't think that's acceptable." John's not amused. "In fact, it could be quite dangerous. I understand that gesture is considered obscene."

"By whom?" Sam asks, but John doesn't reply. He stares at Shemp until he lowers his hand.

"Very well," John says reluctantly, as if he's taking us to the guillotine. "Let's go." And then he leads us out of the cab and into the hub.

It's not all that difficult, walking in low gravity; you just have to be careful and make sure that one foot is firmly placed on the floor before you raise the other foot. Wearing shoes with lots of tiny hooks on the soles helps a lot; each of us trips a few times before we get it right, but at least no one goes sprawling. For awhile, though, we look like a bunch of guys maxed out on lithium. Step, walk, step, walk, step, walk. Hey, ma, look at me, I'm walking. . . .

John escorts us to a central passageway that

curves around the inside of the hub. It's barely wide enough for two people to walk abreast; quite a few people pass us as we march single-file along one wall. Most wear the same sort of jumpsuits we do, but a couple of times we come upon guys wearing what looks like lightweight spacesuits, carrying striped helmets under their arms.

One of them, still wearing his helmet, has just exited a round hatch in the outer wall, swinging out backward by grasping a horizontal bar mounted above the portal. He nearly bumps into me as he turns around; I pardon myself and he gives me a sour glance through his faceplate. Before he shuts the hatch, I catch a glimpse of what's inside: a tiny single-seat cockpit. Starlight shines through an oval porthole above the dashboard. A spacecraft of some sort; except for Gemini and Apollo capsules in museums, it was the first time I've seen something like this close-up.

"What's this, Chip?" I ask, pointing at the closed hatch.

This is an EVA pod. It is used for making repairs outside the colony.

"Thanks. Just curious." I hasten to catch up with the others.

The passageway ends in a large semicircular compartment with a large closed hatch in the center of the outer wall. On the other side of broad windows is the *Anakuklesis;* at rest in its docking cradle, the yacht is connected to the hub by an enclosed walkway. Spacesuited figures float above its cylindrical hull, and several workmen wait in the gateway, some gazing up at monitors suspended from the ceiling. Robots resembling giant spark plugs out-fitted with four double-jointed arms are parked nearby. All the place needs are travel posters, candy machines, a harried ticket agent, and a Moonie selling flowers.

We loiter for a few minutes—well, most of us do; Russ beelines to the nearest window and practically rubs his nose against it as he gloms the massive spaceship—before a couple of workmen go to the hatch, undog it, swing it open, and slide a ramp into place. They enter the walkway and are gone for a couple of minutes. When they reappear, they're followed by two men whom, judging from their braided blue uniforms and matching tricorns, I take to be the pilots.

> **Proceed to the ramp. Stand in single file on the right side. Assume parade-rest posture. Do not look directly at anyone exiting the hatch. Say nothing until you are spoken to.**

I do as Chip tells me. So do Shemp, Russell, Sam, even John. Shemp asks what "parade rest" means; I watch out of the corner of my eye as he squares his shoulders, places his legs apart, and folds his hands behind his back. Maybe we're going to hear "Hail to the Chief" next.

But there's nothing except shuffling motions from the gateway. Then a figure strides through the hatch, and I get my first look at a Superior.

He's tall—seven and a half feet, as giraffelike as an NBA center—and twice as skinny: his slender arms and legs disappear within the dense folds of his long, brightly colored robes. His reddish hair is mowed down to the scalp, save for a braided rattail at the nape of his neck. The pale skin of his face, high cheeked and narrow, is so completely tattooed with intricate red-and-blue whorls that it resembles a false-color fingerprint, until he turns his face toward me and I see a tiny sword etched from his high brow down to the long bridge of his nose.

The Superior peers at me through eyes whose dark blue pupils are the size of quarters. In the side of my vision, I can see Shemp gaping at him—no, this was not a Hollywood extra in heavy makeup—before Moe apparently tells him to stop staring and face forward. Then the Superior addresses me, his voice thin and reedy.

"Be you alive or dead?"

I don't know what he means.

Say: "Dead I am." Then bow, and say: "To my home, Vladimir Algol-Raphael, welcome. Carry your bags, I may?"

"Dead I am." I bend forward . . . not too quickly, lest I lose my balance. "To my home, Vladimir Algol-Raphael, welcome. Carry your bags, I may?"

The Superior stares at me, then laughs out loud.

It isn't a nice laugh; it's like your yuppie second-cousin hooting over the fact that you haven't been accepted by Harvard. He looks back over his narrow shoulder as he raises his empty hands. "Stand straight cannot, nothing in hands see! Mister Chicago's deadheads! Compost better than servants!"

I don't need an eyes-up translation to know that I've just been insulted. Chip says:

Say nothing to him. Smile. Bow.

I say nothing to Vladimir Algol-Raphael. I smile like a fool and take another short bow, even though my cheeks are burning and all I really want to do is reach up and give his chicken neck a good, hard twist. The Superior marches off the ramp, making room for the people coming through the hatch.

The next person off the ship is a beautiful young woman with fashion-model looks. I might have enjoyed toting the cylindrical bag she carried off the ship, if only because my heart melts for icy blondes, but she stalks past me and approaches Russell instead. He greets her formally, but barely finishes before she drops her bag directly on his feet. The sucker must be heavy, even in low gravity; he winces.

"Let's go, deadhead," she snaps. "And whatever you do, just be quiet."

"Yes ma'am." Russell picks up the bag. He's barely able to hide the murder in his eyes, but follows her off and away. What a bitch . . .

And so it goes. Human, Primary, Superior, Primary, Superior, Superior, Primary, Primary, Superior, Primary, Superior, Primary, Primary, Superior . . . a long procession of people and meta-people emerging from the gangway, each decked out in the finest clothes, each as rude and self-important as the last one, ignoring salutations offered by the deadheads standing at the ramp.

I later learn just who they are: Mister Chicago's entourage, an ever-changing cast of Belters, Superiors, selenians, aresians, jovians, and just plain losers.

Some are business associates and others are dilet-
tantes or hangers-on from across the system; all are
attracted to extreme wealth and power the way flies
are drawn to sugar. When Mister Chicago travels, he
seldom travels alone; these people come with him,
and when he comes home, it's always with a few
more friends and fast-talking parasites he's picked up
on the way. They reside in the castle until they've
either concluded their business or they wear out their
welcome; then they either leave of their own accord
or are sent back to wherever he had found them in
the first place.

Used to see the same thing all the time, back
when I was a rich kid. And I never treated the hired
help any differently back then, either. Now I'm the
guy holding the shitty end of the stick.

Most refuse our assistance, opting instead to
have robots load their stuff on the cart we've
brought with us, but a few choose to have servants
carry their bags. Shemp draws a couple of haughty
women who burden him with what would have
been three hundred pounds of luggage in Earth-
normal gravity; he struggles to pick it all up at once.
Sam gets a Superior who carries only a couple of
small bags, but addresses him in a dialect so obscure
that Sam's associate has trouble translating it; the
Superior berates Sam constantly as he leads him out
of the gateway. John gets the worst of the bunch: a
squat pig of a guy who carefully looks him up and
down before he leans forward and whispers something in his ear. John's face goes dark red; the pig
guffaws loudly and winks to one of his companions
as he drops two massive bags in front of him. I don't
like John very much, but I have to feel sorry for him
just now . . . and just a little vindicated. He told us to

obey the wishes of our newly arrived guests; just how far does this directive apply to himself?

About twenty passengers have disembarked from the *Anakuklesis* by the time I'm left alone at the ramp. Everyone else is gone, save for a couple of workmen and Vladimir Algol-Raphael, who appears to be waiting for someone. I'm wondering if I've missed something when I hear soft footsteps from the hatch.

And then Pasquale Chicago appears at the top of the ramp.

Six weeks ago, I had him pegged as a wealthy dude with a taste for slavery. Now I know a little better. He's a former Pax Astra official who bolted with a stolen fortune; he's a high member of the Zodiac, if not its leader. He's the Don Corleone of the asteroid belt. He's got my balls in his hand.

Welcome home, Mister Chicago. I pray that your voyage has been pleasant and fruitful.

"Welcome home, Mister Chicago," I repeat. "I pray that your voyage has been . . ."

"Alec!" His face becomes radiant the moment he spots me. "How nice to see you, my friend!" He marches down the ramp, claps me fondly on the shoulder. "Good of you to come greet me!"

Jeez. What a change. Before he disappeared, he wouldn't even acknowledge my existence when he walked past. Now I'm an old golf buddy.

I nod like a dummy. "Nice to see you, too."

"Here. Take this, will you?" He hands me a small bag, then motions to Algol-Raphael. "I assume you've already met Vlad. Vlad, my manservant, Alec."

Manservant? That's a sudden promotion if there ever was one. Vlad gives me a cold look as Mister Chicago strides past us. "Good. Very good. Well, let's be off, then. . . . Vlad, I have a wonderful suite waiting for you. Shall we go?"

I fall into step behind them, following Mister Chicago and his Superior friend as they saunter out of the reception area. I carry his bag and keep my mouth shut, and slowly come to the realization that, as much as I think I've recently learned about Mister Chicago, there's still much about the man that I don't know.

Fact is, I don't have a fucking clue.

ELEVEN

TERRITORIAL PISSINGS

*Give thy thoughts no tongue, nor any unproportioned
thought his act.*

—William Shakespeare, *Hamlet*

A good docile servant, I follow Mister Chicago
and Vladimir Algol-Raphael as they walk down
another corridor to a different cable car station.
Apparently this is the first time Algol-Raphael has
visited 4442 Garcia; from time to time, his host
pauses at a window to point out something on the
asteroid or on the colony. I can't hear what they're
talking about, and Algol-Raphael remains stoical
throughout, but the Superior is much less imperi-
ous around Mister Chicago than he was when he
stepped off the ramp.

Although I know Algol-Raphael is a genetically
engineered human who was born on the Moon, I
can't shake the feeling that he's an alien from some
distant star. His height, his birdlike frame, his enormous eyes, the tattoos that resemble artistically
reshaped capillaries . . . none of this makes him

seem much closer to *Homo sapiens* than an ostrich. Maybe that's why the Superiors left the inner system and emigrated to the Belt; it's hard to imagine them living comfortably among baseline humans. That, and the fact that they seem to have been born with an attitude.

We finally arrive at the cable car station. The loyal manservant, I meekly follow them aboard and stand against the opposite side of the cab, but when the cable car starts to ascend (or descend, depending on how you look at it), I quickly shut my eyes. Vertigo time.

That elicits an unpleasant laugh from Algol-Raphael. "Zeroed, your manservant, Pasquale. Another bad brain?"

He thinks you've gone asleep. Open your eyes.

I don't particularly want to, but I obey Chip's orders. "Sorry," I say, more to Mister Chicago than to Algol-Raphael. "It's just . . . I'm still getting used to this."

Algol-Raphael harrumphs at this. I've never actually heard anyone harrumph before, outside old movies, but he manages to sound like Margaret Dumont from the Marx Brothers films.

"No, Vlad," Mister Chicago says, "Alec's not a bad brain. In fact, he's one of my successes." He gives me a fond smile; I wonder if he's going to pat me on the head. "He's really quite good. If you wish, I'll loan him to you for the duration of your stay. He's quite obedient . . . aren't you, Alec?"

Oh, no. Anything but that. "Yes, sir," I murmur, praying that Algol-Raphael won't take him up on the offer.

But the Superior looks intrigued. "Fresh apples?" he asks, and Mister Chicago nods and moves the flat of his hand across his chest.

He has asked Mister Chicago if this is a fair deal. Mister Chicago has acknowledged that it is.

The sword tattoo on his brow wrinkles slightly as Vlad looks me up and down. "Won't drop the line, will you?"

He has asked if you would avoid responsibility. Shake your head.

I shake my head. "He's really quite good," Mister Chicago insists. "His MINN is fully functional, he has eyes-up capability, and I've even installed cerebral behavior inhibitors." He smiles at Vlad. "I assure you, I wouldn't make this offer if I wasn't certain of him. Test him yourself, if you wish."

Algol-Raphael says nothing. Apparently disinterested, he turns his back to me to gaze out the window; as he did so, though, I glimpse his left hand stealing beneath the front of his robe.

"Very well," he murmurs.

A soft sound—metal slipping through fabric— then the Superior whips around. A long, slender sword is grasped in his right hand. With a high-pitched warbling cry, he brings the rapier down in an arch toward

ALERT!

my face as, without conscious volition, my arms come up

AUTODEFENSE MODE!

and cross themselves before me, then the blade slashes my right forearm and

WARNING!

an electric shock slams me

AUTODEFENSE COMPROMISED!

back against the cable car wall, and my headset falls off as

AUTODEFENSE DOWN!

I sag to the floor on legs which have turned to putty. Unable to move, my arms numb and useless, the right one bleeding from a long cut through my uniform's sleeve, I look up to see the rapier poised only a few inches from my face.

The sword hums as Vladimir Algol-Raphael leers down at me. One quick thrust, and the blade's tip will skewer my left eye.

"Vlad, stop this!" Mister Chicago shouts. "Stop this right now!"

I should be frightened. Hell, I should be wetting my pants. But I'm not; if anything, I'm angry and confused.

"What the hell are you trying to prove?" I ask.

His enormous blue eyes bore into mine. "A test, deadhead," he says softly.

Mister Chicago grabs the Superior's arm. "Damn you, I didn't mean this way!"

Vlad the Impaler allows himself to be pulled

away. "Many pardons, Pasquale . . . too tempting, this." He pulls back a pleat of his robe, revealing an embroidered sheath. His elongated thumb rolls against the rapier's ornate basket guard; the blade stops humming, and he slides the sword into the sheath. There's a hint of a smirk on his narrow lips. "Invited a test, though, you did. Most amusing."

Right. The skinny bastard almost carved me up for amusement. Funny guy. My face goes red-hot when I hear this. Maybe I'm Pasquale's favorite pet, but I don't have to take this lying down. . . .

"Test this, dude!" I snap, then I kick my left foot straight at the Superior's knee.

He sees it coming and nimbly dodges aside. It's probably just as well that I'm still stunned from the charge that his rapier carried; if I had connected with his knee, I probably would have broken it.

The expression on his gaunt face turns from gloating to outrage; he makes another grab for his rapier. "Attack me, he did! Scope this yourself!"

Pasquale places his hand firmly on his, forcing him to keep his rapier sheathed. "You attacked him first. His MINN is equipped with an autodefense mode. He reacts if his life is placed in jeopardy." He glances back at me. "As I said, he's quite valuable. I won't allow him to be wasted for your pleasure. I'm sorry, but my offer is withdrawn. You can't have him."

Autodefense mode? This hasn't happened before. Why didn't it kick in when George attempted to rape Kate, or when Veronica went after Hugh with a kitchen knife? Not only that, but why didn't Chip give me a splitting headache—or even worse, considering the importance of our special guest here—when I attempted to break Vlad's knee?

No time to think about this now. Mister Chicago looks just as angry with me as with his guest, if not more so. But I still don't know what to . . .

Apologize at once.

Good thinking, Chipster. "Many apologies, sir," I say as politely as possible, considering that I'm still flat on my back. "I thought you were . . . umm . . ."

"He believed you were trying to take his life," Mister Chicago finishes. "Alec has never seen a charged rapier before. He doesn't know that it's capable of only stunning an assailant, not just killing him." He pauses. "Unless that was your intent, Vlad."

Algol-Raphael coolly regards me for another moment, just long enough to make me realize that murder had been his intent indeed. "No, Pasquale," he says at last, letting his hands fall from the rapier's pommel. "My intent, this was not. Many apologies to you. Testing your claims, that I was."

"Hmm . . . well, I'd prefer it if you wouldn't do so in such a melodramatic fashion. I'm afraid you've injured him." Mister Chicago looks down at me again. "Can you move, Alec?"

"Yes, sir." Tingly sensation returns to my upper body; the electrical charge the rapier carried in its blade was relatively low-voltage, its numbing effect short-lived. Only now my right arm is beginning to smart; I inspect the cut the blade has made. It isn't deep; no major arteries or tendons seem to have been severed. But it still hurts like a bitch. "I think I need to get to the infirmary."

"Yes, of course . . . you're excused from duty as soon as we arrive." He kneels next to me to look more closely as my arm; as he does, his pink eyes film over and he murmurs something under his breath. For a moment, it's as if he's playing John again. "Just stay still. A med team will meet us at the station."

I'm feeling heavier by now. The cable car must be halfway home. I stay put on the floor, clutching the torn sleeve against the cut to stop the bleeding. Jeez, Mister Chicago's friends sure like to play rough. . . .

"Reflexes good, must admit." Vladimir Algol-Raphael stands off to one side, studying me as if I'm a wounded dog. I guess this is as close to an apology I can expect from him. "Armstronged your defense well . . . and never received training before, I'm told?"

I shake my head, and he nods ever so slightly as he looks back at Mister Chicago. "Success, this one. Your methods, the rest of the Zodiac will approve."

The rest of the Zodiac? Whoa, wait a minute . . .

"As I said, Alec is one of my best subjects." Mister Chicago stands up again. "Out of the fifty-six neuropatients we've revived so far, my people have achieved a success ratio of nearly ninety percent. We're working at getting higher levels in terms of full recovery."

"Not bad for cold tank hibes." Vlad folds his hands within his robes. Once again, he seems to regard me as a rather intelligent pet. "How many more revive, you will?"

Mister Chicago shakes his head. "Can't say. Twenty more sleepers are being cloned and we've got another fourteen in storage. That gives us thirty-four altogether, but it's going to take more if the project is going to be a success. If we can renegotiate with the Pax, perhaps we can . . ."

"Nada." Vlad curls the spindly fingers of his right hand into a fist, palm down. "Won't release remaining dewars, Pax won't. Negotiation out of question."

"Hades!" Beneath his sallow skin, a blue vein pulses in Mister Chicago's left temple. "Bad apples! There were four hundred more sleepers on Clarke County, and they've revived less than forty of them, with less than twenty percent success! I've told the Zodiac that we've made better progress than that . . . !"

"Shh." Algol-Raphael places a long finger against his narrow lips. "Quiet. Your manservant . . . quiet now, but listens, he does." He peers at me. "Do you not, Alec?"

I'm pretending to be studying my wounded arm. When Vlad says my name, I jerk my head up. "Umm . . . say what? Come again?"

The cable car is beginning to decelerate; another few moments and we'll arrive at the main habitat. All I have to do is play stupid a little longer. If either of them are convinced of my feigned innocence, I can't tell: Mister Chicago's dead-white face is as much of a mask as Algol-Raphael's tattooed features.

"We'll discuss this further once the other guests arrive," Mister Chicago says at last. "The question is far from settled."

Vladimir Algol-Raphael closes his eyes for a moment; he lets out his breath as a sigh. No, the question hasn't been settled, whatever it is. . . .

And now I've got a few of my own.

Once the cable car arrives at the habitat, a couple of men in red-striped uniforms wait quietly until Mister Chicago and Vlad the Impaler have made their exit, then they pick me off the floor and carry me to a nearby hover-cart. A quick ride up two levels and down a more familiar corridor, and I'm back in the infirmary, where Big Nurse once again places my right arm in her magic tube. I ask her if I get a lollypop for good behavior, but she doesn't get my joke; she checks the tube to make sure that the nanites are doing their job, then she goes to see about another deadhead who has hobbled in with a twisted ankle.

This gives me plenty of time to mull over what I've just learned. After awhile, I say: "Chip, are you there?"

"Yes, I am, Alec." Nice to hear his voice again.

"Okay, buddy, question time. How did I stop Vladimir Algol-Raphael when he attacked me?"

"You raised your arms and blocked his rapier. This is how you received the laceration on your—"

"Yeah, okay, I understand that much. But I didn't do that on purpose. It wasn't . . . I mean, it wasn't reflex. I barely saw it coming. But my arms went up on their own just when you flashed those eyes-up warnings, so . . . shit, I dunno. What happened back there?"

"My autodefense mode was engaged."

"Okay, stop right there. What do you mean by that? Autodefense mode, I mean."

"In the event of a potentially lethal attack, I am programmed to assist you in warding off the assault."

"This is something you can do? How do you do it?"

"First question: yes. Second question: during autodefense mode, I am capable of anticipating the form of attack made by your assailant, calculating his probability of success, and manipulating your central nervous system without conscious volition on your part. In this instance, when I saw Vladimir Algol-Raphael draw his rapier and that he was intending to attack you, I activated your serotonin and adrenal glands, which in turn caused the motor muscles in your arms to rise to a defensive posture that would increase your odds of survival."

"Got it. So why haven't you done this earlier . . . I mean, when servants have attacked others, like the time Veronica went after Hugh with a knife?"

"The autodefense programs installed in servant associates are not programmed to protect them against assaults by other servants. Associates are only programmed to respond to such attacks by inflicting severe migraine headaches during non-lethal assaults, as punishment, or fatal cerebral aneurysms against the assailant during potentially lethal attacks."

"How are the aneurysms caused?"

"A micromotor attached to a major artery within the brain severs the artery if it receives a command by either the MINN or the central AI system."

"Nasty." I chew on this for a moment. "So what about the time George attempted to rape Kate in the shower? You allowed Anna to attack George, but then you killed George."

"I was not responsible for those actions. They were caused by Anna and George's associates."

"Yeah, right, but those associates are controlled by the Main Brain. So tell me what happened."

There's a short pause—three seconds—before Chip responds. "According to AI system records of past interdictions taken by servant associates, Anna was allowed to attack George because she was attempting to defend Kate. This is allowable within MINN parameters. George received migraine headaches from his associate during his assault on Kate which increased in severity when he turned against Anna. When he failed to respond to punishment and showed no willingness to cease his actions, his associate caused the seizure which terminated his life. Does this answer your question?"

"Sort of . . ." I shake my head. "No, it doesn't. Kate was being raped by George, but she didn't . . . I mean, she couldn't . . . fight back. So why don't servants go into autodefense mode when attacked by other servants?"

"I cannot answer this question."

I think about this for a few moments . . . and doing so brings back a bad memory. "I saw the whole thing happen," I say very softly. "I was taking a crap while Kate was being raped, and I wouldn't so much as get off the pot to help her. Why didn't I do anything?"

"I cannot answer this question."

Perhaps he can't, but I can . . . or at least I have a sneaking suspicion. Mister Chicago is trying to cull the ranks. If he can get the most violent and unstable among the deadheads he's resurrected to take out the weak and unfit, then knock off the predators before they can do further harm, then he'll eventually get a population of slaves unwilling or unable to oppose him, but still capable of resisting threats from outside forces. Fast-track Darwinism, so to speak. But this still doesn't explain why I hadn't helped Kate.

Another question for another time. Stick to the subject. "Getting back to what happened in the cable car a little while ago . . . I tried to kick Algol-

Raphael in the leg, and nothing happened. No punishment. How come?"

"I cannot answer this question."

"Aw, c'mon! He's one of Mister Chicago's bosom buddies and I tried to break his knee!" I laugh out loud. "His rapier was sheathed by then, he wasn't even threatening me! How did I do it?"

"I cannot answer this question."

Weird. Chip's gone into the default mode he assumes when posed with questions he can't answer without revealing vital information. "But you saw everything that happened, right?"

"The incident was recorded, yes."

"Recorded?" Interesting turn of phrase. "You mean, recorded by . . . um, you in my head, or by the Main Brain?"

"I recorded the incident, and later downloaded it to the central neural net system. The system now has a full record of the incident."

"But the Main Brain didn't . . . I mean, it wasn't monitoring what happened when it happened? In real-time, I mean?"

"I cannot answer this question."

There was a comment Russell made earlier: something about our associates being unable to receive transmissions from the habitat. Information about the hub and the arriving guests had to be downloaded to the MINNs before we boarded the cable car. Something to do with radiation shields. Russ was getting into this, then a headache that shut him up. But why would . . . ?

Holy shit.

No wonder Chip can't answer the question. If he does, he's revealing a secret Mister Chicago prefers that we'd never learn.

On the cable cars, and perhaps even within
the colony hub itself, the Main Brain can't communicate with our MINNs, because the shields
that protect the habitats from cosmic radiation
also block radio signals with our implanted com-
links. Vital information from the Main Brain to the
MINN can be downloaded in advance, but the
comlink is broken as soon as anyone wearing a
MINN leaves a habitat. This was why we were told
to don radio headsets before we left the habitat; it
was the only way the Main Brain could receive
information from us.

This was how I was able to kick Vlad without
being punished. The Main Brain hadn't seen what
I had done, and therefore Chip was unable to punish me.

The Main Brain isn't as omniscient as we've
been led to believe.

It has a blind spot.

My first impulse is to get the tube off my arm, run
upstairs, find Russell and see if my theory matches
his observations. I'm about to shout for the doctor
when a small voice that doesn't belong to Chip
whispers in my ear.

Shut up, you idiot!

If I peep so much as a word of this to Russ,
Shemp, or anyone else, Chip will doubtless hear
what I say . . . and if Chip hears, so will the Main
Brain. Warning bells will ring. A little knowledge is
a dangerous thing, as someone once said; if I don't
drop dead or vanish in the middle of the night,
then Mister Chicago will make sure that I never get
close to one of the cable cars again, at the very least.

In fact, this particular line of inquiry may have already made someone suspicious. Time to change the subject, mucho prompto.

"Hey, Chipster, whatever happened to all the other people . . . the other sleepers, I mean . . . the Immortality Partnership owned?"

"Please be more specific."

"Mister Chicago said that there were four hundred more sleepers on Clarke County, and that only forty of them have been revived by the Pax. Is that right?"

For a moment, I think Chip's going to spring the I-cannot-answer-that-question line on me again, but he surprises me. "Those figures are incorrect approximations. My information indicates that, at last report, there are four hundred and six neurosuspension patients once registered to the Immortality Partnership on the Clarke County space colony. As of February 13, 2099, thirty-nine have been revived to various states of mental awareness by the Royal University School of Medicine. Three hundred and sixty-seven patients remain in neurosuspension."

"Uh-huh." Once again, I realize that I have no real awareness of the passage of time. No pinup calendars, no Mickey Mouse watches; you have to remember to ask your associate what day it is, and I seldom do. Time flies when you're having fun. "How long ago was that?"

"Eight months ago. Today is November 25, 2099, Gregorian."

Jeez. Thanksgiving already. That explains all the turkeys who just walked off the *Anakuklesis* (including the scrawny one with a bad temper). "So how many deadheads—sleepers, I mean—did Mister Chicago bring here? What happened to them?"

"First question: ninety. Second question: fifty-six were revived in various degrees of mental awareness. Of that number, forty-three are actively employed as servants, ten have been annulled due to chronic mental deficiencies, two have been terminated as punishment, and one has committed suicide. Out of the remaining sleepers, twenty are in first-stage revival, and fourteen remain in neurosuspension."

I whistle under my breath. Of the fifty-six people who woke up in the White Room, Mister Chicago did away with ten because they had come out of neurosuspension as vegetables. George and Veronica were killed by their associates when they went insane, and poor Winston hanged himself. I should consider myself lucky; I'm among the four-fifths majority still alive . . . and only two-thirds have all our marbles.

"How did Mister Chicago get us here?"

"He had the dewars containing your heads transported to 4442 Garcia aboard the *Anakuklesis*."

"No, no, no . . . I mean, how did he acquire them from the Pax in the first place?"

"The Immortality Partnership declared bankruptcy in 2096 when it was unable to pay taxes levied on it by the Royal Treasury. The treasury took ownership of its capital assets on Clarke County, including one hundred and sixty-five dewars containing four hundred and ninety-six neurosuspension patients. This occurred on—"

"Hold it. Last time I checked, the Immortality Partnership was based in California."

"On April 6, 2046, Gregorian, the board of directors of the Immortality Partnership voted six-to-three to move its long-term care facilities from

Pasadena, California, to Clarke County, once the space colony was completed. This relocation was accomplished between February 10, 2047 and August 13, 2047."

"Gotcha. Go on."

"When the company went bankrupt, the Royal Treasury temporarily put its dewars up for public auction. Transitive Starlight, a shipping firm owned by Mister Chicago, placed a winning bid of fifty megalox for thirty of these dewars before the Royal Treasury closed the auction and took possession of the remaining one hundred and thirty-five dewars, which in turn were placed in the stewardship of the Royal University School of Medicine."

Well, that makes sense . . . not. Why would anyone in their right mind—if you'll pardon the expression—pay fifty megalox for ninety decapitated heads frozen in liquid nitrogen? Mister Chicago must have been desperate for good household help. And if he wants to clone more servants, then why has the Pax stopped the auction?

And then there's the plan he mentioned during his conversation with Vlad . . . "Why did he buy those dewars, Chip?"

"I'm sorry, Alec, but I cannot tell you this."

Ah, so. Big Chief Pink Eyes has something up his sleeve. "So what about those heads left in Clarke County? What's happened to them?"

"The dewars containing the remaining neuro-suspension patients have been placed in the custody of the Pax Astra Royal University School of Medicine . . ."

"You told me that. Go on."

"The Royal University has attempted to revive thirty-nine of—"

"Old news. Keep going. Where are they located now? Clarke County?"

"The location of the remaining dewars is presently unknown. Latest intelligence reports indicate that they are no longer within the long-term care facility the Immortality Partnership formerly had in Clarke County. However, it is known that the Royal University has been attempting to revive some of its neuropatients, although its success ratio is reported to be much lower than that on 4442 Garcia."

I don't know whether to feel blessed or damned. By luck of the draw, my head happened to be within one of the dewars purchased by Mister Chicago; not only that, but I was one of the fortunate few who had come out of neurosuspension with my wits intact. From what little Chip's able to tell me, the Pax knows less about neurosuspension revival than the Zodiac. On the other hand, my second chance at life is being spent in slavery, with a narc in my head. It's almost enough to make me envy the dead.

Speaking of the dead . . . "Some of the dead-heads had trust funds established on their behalf. What happened to them?"

"Legal responsibility for bank accounts in the names of neuro-patients was taken over by the Pax Astra when the Immortality Partnership became insolvent. It is believed that the Pax Astra Royal Treasury absorbed those funds before they auctioned the dewars."

"How much was that?"

Another pause. "In Pax Astra currency and at the present rate of exchange, the total was one hundred and twenty-five megalox."

Well, that explains where everyone's money went: we got swindled by the Pax. From what I've already learned from my history lessons, the Pax has had to pay massive war debts. Guess we paid for a spaceship or two.

Another thought occurs to me. "Say, do you . . . uh, do you happen to have a list of the sleepers on Clarke County and 4442 Garcia?"

A short pause. "Yes, I can access that file."

"Okay . . . see if William Alec Tucker, Jr. is on the list."

"Is William the first name or the last?"

Persnickety computer. "William is the first name, Alec is . . . aw, never mind. Try it this way. Tucker, William Alec, Jr."

Pause. "There is no listing of Tucker, William Alec, Jr. on the list."

"Okay. Same format . . . search for Longstreet, Sarah Eads, or Tucker, Sarah Eads."

Pause. "There are no listings for Longstreet, Sarah Eads, or Tucker, Sarah Eads."

So Dad hadn't opted for the shrunken-head treatment, and neither had Mom. No surprise; if either of them had been revived here, I would have known about it by now. Dad would be trying to make deals with Mister Chicago and Mom would be searching for the liquor cabinet. Cold as it may seem, I'm almost glad that they're still dead. Asking about them had been obligatory, though. There's another person I want even more than my parents. . . .

"Okay, what about Westphall, Erin Kay?"

Again, a short pause. Then . . .

"Westphall, Erin Kay is listed as an Immortality Partnership neuro-patient in Clarke County."

✞ CHAPTER ✞

TWELVE

BITTERSWEET

. . . And neither the angels in heaven above
Nor the demons down under the sea,
Can ever dissever my soul from the soul
Of the beautiful Annabelle Lee.

—Edgar Allan Poe, "Annabelle Lee"

As soon as I'm out of the infirmary, I waste no time tracking down Shemp.

I can't tell him about the MINN blind spot. Maybe that'll come later, once I figure out how to communicate with him without the Main Brain spying on us. Right now, though, he has to know that Erin isn't gone forever, that's she in neurosuspension somewhere in the Pax.

Everyone's home from work by the time I return to the servants' quarters. Most are chowing down in the mess room: vegetable soup and fried tofu sandwiches on the menu tonight. I haven't eaten since breakfast, but I'm in no mood for food. Shemp's not here, though, and Sam tells me that he's already gone back to his room, so I go looking for him.

His door is shut. I almost walk straight in, just like I used to do when we shared an apartment, but I stop myself. Last time I was here was the night I decked him . . . for no good reason, really, except that he said the wrong thing at the wrong time. It's probably not a good idea to go barging in.

I knock first. I don't hear anything, so I bang on the door again. "Hey, Shemp! You in there!"

A moment passes, then I hear his muffled voice: "Who is it?"

Dummy. Who does he think it is? "It's me . . . can I come in?"

Another pause. "I'm busy. Go away."

Shit. He's still pissed. "Look, I'm sorry about what happened before, but I really gotta talk to you."

"Can it wait till tomorrow?"

"Naw, man, it's important. We gotta talk, I swear . . ."

A few seconds pass, during which I consider the fact that this is my oldest friend by a factor of one hundred and four years plus ten, and that there isn't a lock on this frigging door.

"Um . . . dude, I'm really kinda busy right now. Could you, like . . . ?"

Busy, my ass. He's just being pissy. "Coming in," I say, then I shove open the door.

And instantly regret it.

Shemp isn't being a prick, after all. He *is* busy . . . and he isn't doing it on his lonesome, either.

Although I can't tell who's sharing Shemp's bed, the figure beneath the blanket he just yanked up is unmistakably female. Shemp's red face lies above a tousled mop of light brown hair; if looks could kill, his eyes would have been laser beams.

For as long as I've known Christopher Meyer, the guy's never had much of a sex life. A fat kid with glasses like him isn't a babe magnet; he seldom dated when we were in high school, and even then it was with girls who were just as homely as he was. The only steady girlfriend he ever had only stuck around for a few months before she ditched him for an asshole jock; it humiliated him and broke his heart. Since then, the rare occasions he got laid were either by seducing a drunk girl he met at some keg party, or an occasional mercy fuck from a friend of a friend (I know, because I once fixed him up with one). Most of the time, he sought relief from the stack of lurid comic books next to his bed and the palm of his right hand; once, while we were stoned silly on several joints, he confessed to me that the fantasy object of his desire was Rogue from the X-Men. Yanking off with funny books is a sure sign of desperation.

I stop in the doorway and stare at him in amazement. This was the first time I'd ever found him in bed with a real, honest-to-God woman. I don't know what to say, save for the obvious:

"Aw, jeez, man . . . I'm sorry."

His head falls back on the pillow. "Think nothing of it," he sighs. "Would have happened sooner or later."

"Do you . . . um . . . ?" I start to step back out the door.

"Is it really important?"

"Umm . . . yeah, but . . ."

The head on his shoulder murmurs something in his ear. He listens, then nods. "Naw, don't worry about it. You can stay. Just shut the door, okay?"

I close the door, then squat down on my

haunches as far from the bed as I can. Turnabout is fair play, after all; there were many times when Shemp discovered Erin and me in the sack together. But who's the young lady Shemp has lured into his quarters?

Another soft murmur from beneath the bedcovers, then a pair of dark brown eyes shyly peep over the blanket. "Come on out," Shemp says. "Alec's a big boy . . . he can handle this."

"I'm not sure if I can," she whispers, but then she pulls the blanket down from her chin. "Hi, Alec."

I feel a brief pang of jealousy when I see who it is. Anna. The first person I made friends with in the White Room, who became distressed when I was led away by John, who tried to comfort me that awful morning when I had my first flashback of Erin . . . and now she's taken up with Shemp. I knew he was attracted to her, of course, but she had been so self-involved lately that I thought it unlikely that she would make it with anyone, let alone Shemp.

Only goes to show how much attention I've been paying to current events. They must have gotten their affair started while Shemp and I were cold-shouldering one another.

"Hi, Anna," I say, trying to be casual about the whole thing. "Umm . . . don't get up on my account. You both look cozy where you are."

She blushes, but smiles like the proverbial cat who's just raided the canary cage. She settles herself against Shemp's shoulder. Shemp's trying not to look too smug. Comeuppance on his swinging-dick former housemate. He knows I haven't gotten laid lately . . . like, in the last century or so.

"So what's on your mind?" he asks.

"I found out what happened to Erin." I take a deep breath, and then go on to tell them what I've just learned.

I can't tell him everything, of course. Just the stuff about the Immortality Partnership and what happened to all the dewars that Mister Chicago didn't buy from the Pax. Anna remains quiet, but Shemp prods me with questions now and then. When I'm done, he's silent for a few moments, saying nothing as he gazes at the lumpy shapes at the end of the bed where his feet are twined with Anna's.

"That's terrific, man," he says at last.

"That's all you've got to say? 'That's terrific, man'?"

"What do you want me to say? Three cheers, hip hip hurrah?" Anna burrows her face beneath the blankets again. Shemp shrugs. "I'm not sure what difference it makes."

I gape at him. "I can't believe you're saying that. I mean . . . I just can't believe it. I know you really didn't like her . . ."

"Yes, I did!" he snaps. Now he's pissed off. "She was my friend, too! The only thing I didn't like was that you threw me out of our place so that she could move in, that's what!"

"Chris . . ." Anna lays a hand on his chest. "Calm down."

Shemp lets out his breath. "Okay, all right." He strokes her hair, gives her a peck on the forehead, then looks at me again. "Look, man . . . don't get me wrong. I liked Erin. Maybe I kinda resented her at first, but that's all in the past. If I thought there was a way she could come back, I'd be happy for you. I really would."

"But you don't think she's coming back?" I ask, and he shakes his head. "Hey, we came back, didn't we?"

"But . . ." He sighs again, closing his eyes for a moment. "Okay, let's work this out logically."

He raises a finger. "First, what are the chances that she'll be revived? Maybe she will, eventually . . . or maybe she'll just remain in the dewar for another century."

He raises another finger. "Second, even if a new body is cloned for her and she's revived, what are the chances that she'll still be Erin? I don't mean to be cruel, but you've seen what's happened to a lot of the other guys who've been brought back. Some of 'em can't even remember their last names . . . and some of the others are pretty fucked in the head. Do you really want to see Erin that way?"

"I . . . but she might . . ."

"But she might not, either." Anna emerges from the covers again to prop her head up on one arm. "There's a chance she might not even remember you. She may not remember anything from her past . . . or even worse. Do you really want to have her back as a vegetable?"

I shake my head, but I'm not giving up yet. "But there have been few of those, and most of the people have come back with at least part of their memories intact. She could be reeducated, just the way we were."

"You can reteach someone how to take care of themselves and how to read again," Anna says, "but you can't teach them how to love a particular person."

"Love isn't something you're taught!" I snap.

"It just . . . y'know, it just happens. And she'd remember me!"

"Wrong." Anna's voice is soft; she almost seems to pity me. "I'm sorry, Alec, but if you think love's something that just happens spontaneously, then you don't know very much about it. We teach ourselves how to love. Once it gets past physical attraction, valentine roses, and fooling around in the dark, it always comes down to that . . . do you love this person? *Can* you love this person? That you have to learn on your own. Nobody can tell you how to do it."

"But you don't . . . !"

"Shh. I'm not through. Do you know when Erin died?"

That stops me. "No, I don't," I admit. "I asked Chip, but he couldn't access that information. At least he says he can't. What are you getting at?"

"What I'm trying to say is that, because you don't know how old Erin was when she died, you also don't know how she felt about you in the end. I'm sure she probably loved you when you were both young . . . but she might have died many years later, long after you'd become a faint memory, and a rather tragic one at that. She might not want you anymore."

My face is beginning to burn. "How do you know?"

Anna's eyes become wistful. She lays her head in the crook of her arm. "When I was a girl, I once loved a boy as much as you loved Erin." She hesitates. "But then he . . . well, he went away, and I never saw him again. In time I found another man who eventually became my husband and the father of my child, and after many years it became difficult to even remember the face of the boy who once loved me. If he had . . . if he had returned after all that, I would have welcomed him as an old friend, but . . ."

She lets out her breath. "Well, I couldn't have loved him again. That was lost for good. Excuse me . . ."

She rolls over, turning her back to both Shemp and me as she clutches the pillow to her face. Shemp curls an arm around her bare shoulder, clumsily trying to console her as she quietly weeps.

Embarrassed, I look away. None of us say anything for a couple of minutes. This is the most I've ever heard Anna reveal about herself; I doubt Shemp has heard this either. Like Russell, Kate, and Sam, she must have lived a longer life than Shemp or I had before her death; her memories are longer than ours, and far more bittersweet.

Shemp breaks the uncomfortable silence. "Besides," he says, "you know how far away Earth is from us—three hundred and thirty-five million miles, and that's when we're in perihelion."

"Perihelion?"

"On the same side of the Sun. When we're at aphelion, it's a longer distance—six or seven AUs, at least. Right now, at perihelion . . . about three and a half AUs."

"You're beginning to sound like Russell."

He glares at me. "Just 'cause you still call me Shemp doesn't mean I'm a stooge."

"That really bugs you, doesn't it, Shemp . . . ?"

"Take a hint, dude. I'm not Shemp anymore. That guy's gone, and he ain't coming back."

I snicker. "Not unless you can find some cheese blintzes."

His face darkens. "Don't push it, Alec."

"Okay, okay." I hold up my hands. "Just a joke."

His expression tells me that he doesn't consider it funny. I don't want to get into another fight with him, so I lay off. "Sorry. Never mind. Look, it doesn't matter if she's in the Pax and we're way out here. Mister Chicago bought ninety heads from the Pax . . . what's one more to him? He's rich. He can afford it."

"If he can afford it, then why didn't he buy more in the first place?" Before I can attempt to answer that question—which I can't, really—Shemp tosses another one at me. "Besides, we've never figured out why he's gone to all this trouble in the first place . . . buying heads, cloning bodies, reviving us and all that."

I shrug. "Pretty obvious by now, isn't it? We're servants . . ."

"Slaves, more like it."

"Either way, we're alive."

"Yes, but slaves nonetheless." Anna has dried her eyes; she rolls over to face me again. Shemp tucks his arm around her as she cuddles against him. "Even if you could get Erin here and have her revived, why would you want to inflict this on her? This isn't the second chance I imagined when I signed up for neurosuspension."

Shemp and I trade a look. This is something that makes us different from most of the other deadheads. With the sole exception of Sam, who was bequeathed his medallion on his deathbed by an unknown benefactor, the others willfully and knowingly entered the neurosuspension program. They're passengers who purchased tickets for a voyage into the future; Shemp and I were shanghaied, neither of us fully aware of what our parents had done.

"So what were you expecting?" I ask.

"I don't know." She ponders this for a moment. "To come back the way I was when I died, sixty-two years old . . ."

The look on Shemp's face is classic. Anna looks twenty-five now, but she's old enough to be his grandmother.

". . . and on Earth, not some asteroid I'd never heard of." She smiles. "All the rest of the things I thought the future would be like. Mile-high skyscrapers. Flying cars. Robot dogs . . ."

"Robot dogs?" I try not to laugh.

"Robot dogs. Sure." She grins despite herself. "That's what I thought I'd see . . . robot dogs. I don't know why, but I really wanted one. . . ."

Shemp puts a hand over his mouth, but we can hear him chuckling. "Sit, Rover, sit! Good boy . . . now roll over! Fetch! Plug yourself in!"

"Reboot, Rover!"

"Here, Rover! Time for your lube job!"

"Bad dog! Put down the mailman!"

We keep on with the robot dog jokes—and continue with robot cats, robot hamsters, robot goldfish—until I'm curled cracking up on the floor and they're nearly falling out of bed. Robot dogs. Meet George Jetson . . .

When we finally catch our breaths, Anna turns serious again. "Okay, maybe you're right. Maybe it's better to be a live slave than a decapitated head floating in a tank. But . . ."

She tries to find the right words. "If you really loved Erin, maybe it's best to let nature take its course. If she loved you as much as you loved her, then she'll remember you if and when she's revived, and she'll try to find you if she can. If she's in the Pax, then she'll probably have a better chance of finding you than you will of finding her."

That seems to make sense. I nod . . . then I quickly shake my head. "That's one too many ifs, and I don't think I can wait that long."

The two of them stare at me. "So what are you going to do?" Shemp asks.

I pick myself up off the floor and brush off my robe. That's the question I've contemplated all afternoon in the infirmary. "Only thing I can, I guess. Ask Mister Chicago to bring Erin here and revive her."

Neither of them speaks for a moment. "Think he'd go along with that?" Shemp asks.

"I dunno. Guess I won't know till I ask." I turn to the door and open it. "Anyway, thanks for listening. Sorry to bother you."

"Alec . . ." Anna begins.

I look back at her. She's sitting up in bed, self-consciously holding the blanket against her chest. There's a worried look on her face. Behind her, Shemp studies me: relief in his eyes, as if he's glad to see me finally leaving him alone with his new girlfriend, but also . . .

I dunno. Contempt? Self-satisfaction?

Anna starts to say something, but Shemp reaches up and gently strokes her neck, reminding her that he's here. Whatever she's about say, it perishes on her lips.

"Good luck," she murmurs. "I hope you find her."

"Thanks." Then I leave, gently shutting the door behind.

■   ■   ■

Back in my room, I sit on the edge of my bed for nearly an hour, trying to collect my thoughts.

Outside the door, people are moving around: friends visiting friends, fresh robes being dropped off by whoever's handling laundry detail today, other deadheads making secret rendezvous with newfound lovers. The corridor starts going quiet with the approach of lights-out. Tomorrow's another day. For the first time, there's guests in the castle, and they'll soon be demanding our attention.

When everything is quiet, I prod my lower jaw. "May I speak to Mister Chicago, please?"

Chip's voice in my ear: "Mister Chicago is not available, Alec."

"I want to talk to him. It's important."

"Mister Chicago is not available, Alec. Would you like to speak to John instead?"

"No, I don't want to talk to John. I want Mister Chicago."

"Mister Chicago is not . . ."

"Yeah, okay. I heard you. Can you relay a message to him?"

A pause. "Yes, that is possible."

"Tell him . . ." I hesitate. "Please tell him that Alec wishes to have a meeting with him, concerning a neuropatient in Clarke County who . . . I mean, it's an old friend of mine I want to see again."

"Yes, Alec."

"It's important that I meet with him. Understand?"

"Yes, Alec. Is that all?"

"Yeah . . . will you pass this to him?"

"I already have."

Sure. It's been recorded on whatever now passes for an answering machine. *I'm sorry, but Mister Chicago is not in his castle right now. At the tone, please leave your name, number, the time you called, and your brain.* "Make sure that he gets it, okay?"

"I already have, Alec, and Mister Chicago has sent a response."

The hair on the back of my neck rises. "He has? What . . . I mean, what did he . . . ?"

Then I hear Mister Chicago's voice, as cold as his eyes:

"Alec, I'll speak with you when I wish to do so, and not before. Never disturb me this way again. Good night."

Then the lights go out. I'm left alone in a dark little room.

It's a long time before I go to sleep.

✛ CHAPTER ✛

THIRTEEN

A MURDER OF ONE

Never laugh when a hearse goes by,
Or you will be the next to die.

—Children's rhyme

With the arrival of Mister Chicago's entourage, we settled into a new pattern: the same chores as before, except we had to take care of the people as well. It was now apparent why we had been cleaning the entire castle every day; it was preparation for when we had guests who would think of us as little more than warm-blooded robots.

Those assigned to duties outside the castle were brought back inside, where we assisted the other deadheads with the dozens of menial tasks that faced us as soon as we left the servants' quarters. When we took the elevators upstairs, though, it wasn't to vacant rooms in a deserted castle, but to a constant flurry of activity, with little chance for rest.

Almost as soon as we finished breakfast, we were serving another one to Mister Chicago's guests in the luxurious dining room just off the Great Hall. The cooks who prepared breakfast for the servants were now in the upstairs kitchen, trying to cook for thirty people at once while a dozen deadheads scurried around them, our movements orchestrated by John in his new role as maître d'. There was no set menu; the guests could ask for anything their fickle hearts desired: a grapefruit and a cup of coffee, a three-egg omelet with swiss, pastrami, onion, and mushrooms—slightly runny in the middle, mushrooms sautéed, yellow onions and not white—or one of the elaborate vegetarian dishes favored by the Superiors. Our mandated level of service would have put a five-star restaurant to shame. If someone dropped a knife or fork, it could barely hit the floor before we had to have its replacement in the hand of its user. No glass or cup could be more than half-empty before it was refilled. If something placed in front of a guest was deemed inedible, then it had to disappear back into the kitchen and come back in a more acceptable form within minutes. Finished plates had to vanish as if by magic.

And always, seated at the end of the table was Mister Chicago, who seemed to derive great amusement from watching his servants scramble to keep up with the demands of his friends. He ate little himself, and had the same thing every morning—a sliced tangerine, a bowl of granola in goat's milk (one-quarter liter, no more or less), two slices of toast with orange marmalade—but there was never a time when I didn't glance his way and didn't find his cool eyes upon me. He never mentioned my request for a meeting, though, and after a few days I gave up hope that he would ever do so.

When breakfast was over, it was time to make up the guest rooms. With some, it was a simple matter of changing the linen, scrubbing the bathrooms, and taking discarded clothes to the laundry room. Others required special attention. One woman always slept until early afternoon; we had to avoid her room until she finally roused herself and stumbled downstairs to the kitchen, where she would demand a late breakfast from the cooks who had just finished cleaning up from the morning chaos. Another guest discovered new ways of wrecking his quarters every night; I don't know how or why he did it, but each morning we had to repair, or at least mask, the damage he had caused to furniture, sheets, and rugs, and spirit away the empty liquor bottles he had left in his wake. The tubby little man who had propositioned John after he disembarked from the *Anakuklesis* apparently had the sex drive of a rabbit: every morning we found evidence that he had enjoyed the company of one or more male and/or female friends the night before, as evidenced by crusty bedsheets, empty wineglasses, ripped underwear for both genders, and various sex toys that had to be cleaned and returned to their proper places in the bedside table. Once, over dinner, he casually asked Mister Chicago if Kate was available for his amusement later that evening. Kate was standing over him at that moment, and she nearly dropped the water pitcher in his lap; fortunately for her, Mister Chicago turned down this request, with the mild explanation that Kate needed to be well-rested and undamaged—those words exactly—for her duties the next day. After that, we made sure that I was the one who waited on the little maniac; he groped my ass once, but rather distractedly, and after that left me alone.

And then there were the Superiors. If one of them was in his or her room when we arrived, we had to wait until he or she left, and if they returned while we were still cleaning, then we had to leave immediately and not return until they were gone. Their privacy was sacrosanct. They seldom used their showers, which made for easy cleaning, but which also meant that their rooms reeked like old gym socks. Chip informed us that, because Superior ships and colonies had limited water supplies, they habitually bathed as little as possible; because they perspired less than Primaries, their ships had been designed for lower temperature and humidity; and since 4442 Garcia existed in a state of perpetual summertime, Superiors tended to sweat more here than they usually would. This was why their linen and laundry were so awful; fumigating their rooms each day was a task for only those with strong stomachs.

But that wasn't the worst of it. The Superiors treated the servants worse than any of the baseline humans. Their bioengineered bodies were equipped with MINNs and eyes-up displays, so they had no difficulty in summoning a deadhead to their rooms for the most trivial of reasons. If one was resting in bed and desired a glass of water, there was no need to get up and go to the bathroom where a sanitized glass lay only twenty feet away; just blink three times, tell Main Brain to dispatch a servant to bring him some water, then wait impatiently. If one of us took more than a couple of minutes to drop whatever we had been doing elsewhere in the castle and rush to his or her side, then we could expect a tongue-lashing. If their robes didn't return from the laundry folded just so, we could expect to be screamed at in a dialect that our associates would have to translate for us. If you forgot the correct pronunciation and arrangement of their names— that's Draco-Kayanami, not Kayanami-Draco!— then a long-fingered hand would fall on the hilt of a rapier, and you'd better hope the Main Brain reminded its owner that Mister Chicago considered wounding a servant to be impolite.

Worst of all, I had made an enemy of Vladimir Algol-Raphael. He neither forgot nor forgave our encounter in the cable car, and although he was prohibited from demanding a rematch, this didn't stop him from harassing me whenever possible. Once he kicked me in the butt when I bent over to pick up a wastecan; another time he attempted to trip me in the dining room when my arms were loaded with trays of food. These were only a couple of the indignities he laid upon me when the opportunity presented itself, and all I could do was hold my tongue and try to avoid him. When I complained to Chip, he informed me that Vlad was the patriarch of the Algol clan, one of the most powerful in the Belt; as such, he was an especially honored guest, so asking Mister Chicago to intercede on my behalf was out of the question. Sam and Russell agreed to take over cleaning his room; I tried to stay out of his way, and consoled myself with private fantasies of grabbing his pencil neck and giving it a good, hard twist.

Room service was followed by tedious hours of mopping, scrubbing, and polishing every inch of the castle. If our tasks had been monotonous before the arrival of the *Anakuklesis*, then they became backbreaking now that we had visitors. Dust was not permitted anywhere; dirt was an atrocity. Stairs had to be so clean that you could eat off them; every tile of the Great Hall's mosaic floor had to sparkle; tapestries and statuary were to look as if they were new. Everywhere you turned, there were servants on hands and knees with brushes, scrubbing floors that were already spotless.

For a while in the afternoon, most of the guests would disappear from the castle. They would wander out to the vineyards and gardens, where various entertainments awaited them, while others—Superiors, usually—often entered elevators that would take them down to the habitat's underground levels. We seldom saw what they were doing, save when one of us would deliver a picnic lunch to a grove a mile or more from the castle, nor were we very curious, for their absence gave us a chance to catch up on unfinished chores without interference. It wasn't until late afternoon when they would be seen again, usually to retire to their rooms for a short nap before dinner.

By early evening, the kitchen once again resembled a Chinese fire drill, with servants rushing to deliver appetizers, bowls of soup, aperitifs, and entrees. A long day of indolence seemed to make these people more insufferable; now they were even less tolerant of lukewarm food or sloppily poured wine. More than once, a Superior fastened his dark-eyed glare upon a servant while touching the hilt of his rapier, while women tittered softly and men urged him to demonstrate his dueling skills . . . and Mister Chicago, barely noticing the garden salad and ice water laid before him, watched, and smiled, and said nothing.

When the long day was done—after the guests had left the dining room and returned to their

rooms (or, from time to time, when a few guests
were escorted by Mister Chicago up to his solarium
or, in the case of some of the women, to his private
suite), once the dining room and kitchen had been
made spotless—only then was there a chance for us
to rest. Muscles sore, necks and backs aching, fingers chafed and raw, exhausted beyond rational
thought, we shuffled and stumbled back downstairs to our quarters, where a late dinner of beef
stew awaited us in our rude little mess hall. No one
was in the mood for conversation by then; we stank
of sweat, detergent, someone else's food, and
humiliation, and it was all we could do to eat, dis-
card our robes and pick up the fresh ones that had
been left outside our doors, then collapse in bed
and wait for the lights to turn out. Then the narrow
corridor would be empty and silent.

We hoped it would soon get better.

It only got worse.

John appears in the servants' quarters one morning, interrupting our breakfast of cold cereal and
mushy grapefruit with a surprise announcement
which he's certain will thrill us to no end.

"First," he says, standing at the end of the
table, "you'll be delighted to know that Mister
Chicago is very pleased with your performance in
the presence of our honored guests."

This is John's way of speaking to us in code.
We're still technically "guests," of course, but all
those people upstairs are "honored guests," and
there's miles of difference between them and us. It
simply means that none of us will suffer agonizing
death from ruptured blood vessels in our brains.

Mighty nice of John to tell us this, although he should forgive us if no one stood up and cheered.

"Second," he continues, "our guests are most grateful for the attention that you've given them. They've been very complimentary of your talents as housekeepers, and . . ." So forth and so on. Sugary words meant to disguise the fact that these people have been grinding us down inch by inch, unapologetically and with no remorse. I tune him out and spoon more grainy slush into my mouth.

"And finally, some news I'm sure you'll welcome . . ."

Everyone looks up from their cereal bowls. The expressions on their faces are pitifully obvious: *Oh, thank God, they're leaving. Please tell me they're leaving. Please please please please say that they're leaving . . .*

"Exactly three weeks from now," John says, "the date on the Gregorian calendar will be December 31, 2099 . . . the eve not only of a new year, but also of a new century. The twenty-second century, to be exact . . ."

"Oh, no," Sam whispers softly.

"To celebrate the event, Mister Chicago is throwing a party for his friends and associates, one which promises to be *the* social event of the outer system. Our present guests are only the early arrivals. Many more are already en route to the colony, and they'll be arriving over the course of the next few weeks. We anticipate over one hundred and twenty visitors, and possibly many more. . . ."

All down the table, servants groan and shake their heads; others are ashen and speechless. The worst isn't over; in fact, it hasn't even started. We picture dozens more of Mister Chicago's rude, self-centered friends stamping down the gangways of their ships, throwing luggage and insults in our faces before demanding to be taken to their quarters.

"Therefore, in addition to your usual chores," John continues, "each of you will be expected to assist in preparing for the celebration. I can't tell you the details now because they're still being developed, but assignments will be given by the end of the week. I know that this will require more labor on your part, but I'm certain that you shall rise to the occasion, and that your efforts shall be rewarded in the end."

"Like with a ticket off this rock?" Russell asks.

Laughter from around the table. John smiles benignly at him. "Why, Russell," he asks, "is there a reason why you'd like to leave us?"

"Oh, maybe . . ."

More weary laughter. John lets it drop. "Thank you for your attention," he says. "That will be all for now. You're dismissed."

Which means it's time for us to go upstairs. Everyone rises from the table and starts heading for the elevators, triple-blinking to receive their daily assignments. I already know I'm on breakfast detail, but then John catches my eye and beckons to me. Surprised, I walk over to him.

"Mister Chicago would like to have a word with you," he says softly.

The hair on the back of my neck prickles. "Really? When?"

"At once. I'm to escort you there, after we make a quick stop at the kitchen. He's having a private breakfast this morning, and you've been asked to attend."

"Okay. Any particular reason?"

"You requested a meeting with him, regarding a private matter." John says this as if he's repeating verbatim something that his associate has just said to him. "He's ready to discuss this with you now."

We drop by the kitchen, where the cooks are already in culinary overdrive. They're expecting us; one of them motions to a serving counter where two large pewter platters loaded with fruits, cheese, and fresh-baked muffins have been set aside. John picks up one, I pick up the other, then he leads me down a long service corridor to a small door that opens onto a side terrace outside the castle's west wing.

Balancing the trays on our shoulders, we march down a short flight of steps and onto a long flagstone path that leads away from the castle. It meanders through a small grove until it ends at a place I've seldom visited before.

A large swimming pool, kidney-shaped and Olympic-sized, encircled by tall ivy hedges. Cool blue water, warmed by the artificial sun, reflects the blank eyes of Greco-Roman busts placed on pedestals surrounding a cement terrace. Men and women, all of them naked, cavort in the pool or bask in the morning heat. A Superior woman, her lithe body covered with tattoos, launches herself from a wooden tower at the far end of the pool; she enters the deep end with barely a splash, a living mural disappearing into a sapphire mirror. One of the nameless, cougar-sized housecats that haunt the castle grounds is sprawled nearby; it glances up as the woman slices into the water, its tail flicking a couple of times before it lays its head back between its paws. Bioengineered birds sing sweet songs from the branches of mutant trees.

Beauty and comfort, peace and wonder. If I ever conceived of heavenly afterlife, then this is it. Yet this place isn't meant for me. I'm a servant in Nirvana, a bellhop at the gates of Paradise.

John leads me around the terrace to a long wooden cabana. Its trellis walls and open-slat ceiling are overgrown with honeysuckle; the floor is cool ceramic tile the color of baked sand, its cement benches shaded by the trees. And sitting within its sun-dappled shadows, encircled by gods and goddesses, is an alabaster demon.

When we find him, Mister Chicago is receiving the undivided attention of a woman kneeling before him, her red-haired head tucked between his open thighs. His own head lolls back on his shoulders, his arms cast apart on the bench, his mouth agape, his eyes shut; he sighs as her head bobs in rhythm with his tiny gasps. The men and women surrounding them watch with sublime interest, some stroking each other as they derive second-hand pleasure from his ecstasy.

John quietly places his platter on a nearby table and turns his back. I put down my own tray and start to do the same, but then Mister Chicago's eyes open for just a moment. He sees me, raises a finger—*just a moment, busy right now, excuse me*—then his head falls back again. Not that I particularly want to see this, but apparently fellatio is a spectator sport in the twenty-first century, and Mister Chicago wants me to watch.

When she's done, Mister Chicago pats her fondly on the head. "Thank you, my dear," he murmurs. "That was quite wonderful."

The woman smiles up at him, delicately wipes her lips with the back of her hand, then stands up and saunters over to a nearby bench. Now I recognize her; she's the one who sleeps late every afternoon. No wonder. A good whore needs all the rest she can get.

Mister Chicago opens his eyes and finds me staring at him. "Ah! Young Alec has come to deliver breakfast." He sits up straight, pulls a towel over his crotch, and motions toward the platter. "Bring it over here, young Alec, and let's chat. I believe you want to speak to me about a friend of yours."

"Yes, sir, I do." I pick up the platter and carry it over to him. "I found out that a friend of mine from my past life is a neuropatient in Clarke County. Her name is Erin Westphall, and she—"

"Oh, please . . . not so fast." He carefully inspects the platter, finally selects a peeled orange. "You were doing so well, even enduring a little public sex when it was obvious that you were revolted." He smiles at his entourage. "Alec's one of my deadheads, you know. . . . Comes from a time when sex was considered abominable. I imagine he was ready to vomit."

The sycophants laugh on cue. "Let's take this a little at a time," he goes on. "Your friend in Clarke County is a woman, so I imagine you were . . . well, emotionally attached, shall we say?"

"Yes, sir, we were."

"Lovers?" He raises an eyebrow. "Did you ever have sex with her in the open, with others watching?"

More laughter. I'm surrounded by patronizing eyes. My face burns. "No, sir. We, uh . . ."

"Always in private. I see." He peels off an

orange slice and tucks it in his mouth. "Pity. I imagine you two were probably quite beautiful, writhing in each other's arms." He shrugs. "So you've discovered your long-lost love is a sleeper, but not one of those I brought here to revive, and now you wish for me to locate her dewar and bring it here so that you may be reunited. Is this correct, or am I missing something?"

The speech I've rehearsed in my mind over the last week evaporates like so much smoke. In one offhand statement, he's summarized everything I meant to say. "No, sir, you haven't missed anything. That's what I'd like you to do."

"Hmm. So I see. Interesting." A long silence follows as he eats his orange and lazily contemplates the honeysuckle in the cabana rafters. Behind me, I hear people frolicking in the pool. The overgrown cat saunters past, whisking briefly against the back of my legs, before being coaxed by the redhead to come by for an ear scratch. I hold the platter in my hands and wait for Mister Chicago to say something.

"Are you familiar with aresian sand painting?" he asks.

"What?"

"Aresian sand painting. Are you familiar with it?"

I start to triple-blink, but he quickly shakes his head. "Oh, no, don't ask your associate for an explanation . . . it would be too long-winded for the purpose of our conversation. Allow me. Many years ago, the first Mars colonists devised a form of art that uses the native regolith as its medium. When the sand is carefully mixed with dyed oil, it produces a rather grainy sort of paint which allows artists to create works outside their pressurized habitats. Sort of a cross between Navajo religious art and kindergarten finger painting. Understand?"

I nod, and he warms to the subject. "The challenge of this form is that the artists have to create their works very quickly, because if the pigment and oil isn't mixed precisely, the paint either evaporates or freezes. It took an entire generation before the technique was finally perfected, and only a handful of masters know the secret, but that's beside the point. Each painting, once completed, must be sealed within airtight frames of infrared-filter glass while it's still outside, because if the painting is brought inside an oxygen-nitrogen environment unprotected, changes of atmospheric pressure and light spectrum will ruin the composition. As a result, the masterworks of McCrutheon and Tse-Sung are considered priceless . . . not only because of their rarity, but also because they cannot be easily copied. Do you understand?"

"A little." I shake my head. "No, I don't. What does this have to do with me?"

Mister Chicago smiles. "I didn't think you would, but it illustrates my point. Alec, you're like an aresian sand painting. You were created over a hundred years ago, then sealed inside a container of a different sort, until by chance and circumstance I decided to acquire and revive you. This makes you unique. I have little appreciation for aresian art . . . to tell the truth, I find most of it rather boring . . . but you and your friends I can cultivate and observe over time. In this sense, each and every one of you is a priceless work of art."

"Then why not acquire another one? Then you'd have a matched pair."

He frowns and rocks his head back and forth.

"Hmm. Interesting proposition, I must admit. But for each McCrutheon or Tse-Sung, there's dozens of Porters and Riddells diluting the market. For all I know, your Erin could be snaggle-toothed and stringy-haired, with a personality to match."

More chuckles from the peanut gallery. I wonder if he keeps these people around because they laugh at his jokes. "She wasn't, I can promise you that," I say, and this elicits more laughter. My voice rises. "She was special. She . . ."

"Ah, yes. She was special, you were special, everyone you knew was special." He reaches forward to pluck another orange off my platter. "That's one of the things I find interesting about deadheads. Most of you went into neurosuspension believing that the future would have a use for you, that your individual memories, skills, and talents would be invaluable in a hundred years or so. A rather conceited opinion of your worth, don't you think? You seemed to believe that future society would welcome inhabitants of a world that was committed to its self-destruction, and damned near succeeded. You overpopulated your home planet, indulged in pointless arms races while willfully allowing millions to die of slow starvation, fouled the global ecosystem with toxic wastes while squandering precious resources, numbed your minds with the most banal entertainment while electing officials who ignored—"

"Yeah, I know. I was there. You got a point?"

Mister Chicago stops. He glares at me as he bites into the orange and chews thoughtfully. No one in the cabana says anything; they don't dare breathe, let alone laugh. No free blow jobs for anyone who pisses off Mister Chicago.

"Yes, Alec," he says at last, "I do have a point. It entertains me greatly to have people from your time—scientists, authors, politicians, magnates, even a few spoiled brats like yourself—mopping my floors and scrubbing my toilets. You entered neurosuspension believing that you would be worshipped, that we'd place you on a pedestal and beg you to tell us about your world."

He pauses to spit an orange seed at my feet. It leaves a moist trail as it slides down my ankle. "But there's nothing you know that hasn't been revealed to us already. True narcissists, you videotaped and recorded and wrote countless books about everything you observed. All your knowledge and wisdom, such as it is, was assimilated long ago. Your inventions are obsolete, your theories rejected, your philosophies either forgotten or held in scorn. So far as I know, the only things the twentieth century produced which were of lasting value were nuclear energy, space travel, and Bugs Bunny cartoons."

Mister Chicago tosses the rest of the orange back on my platter. He takes a deep breath and folds his hands together on his stomach; it's as if he's tired of his own pontification and wants to be witty and urbane again, if only to entertain his guests. "I've enjoyed your servitude for the past several months, Alec, but you presume too much by requesting that I indulge your adolescent whims. So tell me . . . why would I want to go to the trouble and expense of acquiring another deadhead when I've already got you and your friends?"

"Because the Zodiac is building a kingdom, and you need more slaves."

I really don't mean to blurt this out. It's a pet

theory, one which I've developed over the last few days. It's the only one that fits all the facts as I understand them. It's a trump card. And, let's face it . . . I'm sick of this creep, and if he won't give me what I want, then I'll make him pay for this humiliation.

It works. My retort strikes home. Everyone in the cabana stares at me aghast, and Mister Chicago tilts his head back sharply as he stares at me through slitted eyes.

"And what," he asks, "do you think you know about the Zodiac?"

I shift my feet. "Not much, except that you're its leader and that this asteroid is its headquarters. Or at least it will be, once you finish building the other three habitats."

"Uh-huh." No expression on his face. "Go on."

Shit. He's too calm about this. But I've got both feet in it now. "When that's done, I figure you're going to populate the place with as many dead-heads as you can buy from the Pax. You like owning slaves, and we're the best money can buy."

Pasquale Chicago stares at me for a long time, his half-lidded eyes burning into me like dry ice. Everything around me has gone still; I can't even hear the pool sounds behind me. I've stepped over the line; things that should have been left unspoken, I've said aloud, not the least of which is the existence of the Zodiac itself.

What the hell am I doing?

Ever so slowly, a crafty smile steals across his face. He crosses his legs and laces his delicate fingers together, then he nods like a chessmaster whose protégé has just attempted a checkmate. The king is in his castle, and an unwary pawn has stumbled into a cleverly laid trap.

"I knew there's a reason why I like you, Alec," he says. "You're quite imaginative."

Another pause. "In fact, I think I'll let you live."

"Thank you." I don't know what else to say. My heart's thudding against my chest.

"But . . ." Another calculated sigh, longer and more expansive than before. "But you presume too many things, not the least of which are the limits of my patience. You need to be taught a lesson in etiquette."

Then he casts his eyes around the cabana and the poolside, studying his guests in turn, before his gaze settles behind me. He raises his hand and points behind my left shoulder.

"Die, please."

There's a strangled gasp, and I turn around just in time to see John drop his platter.

It crashes to the cement floor as his eyes widen in horror. He grasps the sides of his head as his face twists in agony. His mouth opens, but nothing comes out except for the choked echo of a scream.

My own platter falls from my hands as I rush to him. I manage to catch John in my arms before he hits the ground. Suddenly, he seems to weigh as little as if we were in the hub.

His fingers clutch at the sleeves of my robe—the robe he gave me the day we first met in the White Room, when he told me we were friends and that I shouldn't urinate on the floor any more—and there's a thin red line coming from his nose.

He stares in my eyes as his legs thrash spasmodically, then we collapse together on the cement. His eyes grow wide, looking at me, past me, at something I never saw a hundred and four years ago . . .

And then he dies.

That's it. That's all. He just dies.

Alien birds twitter in strange trees. Cool water rushes from somewhere nearby. Someone shifts their feet; someone else coughs. And then Mister Chicago, as casually as if someone has just spilled a salt shaker, says:

"This has been an interesting conversation, Alec. Do drop by again sometime."

He rises from the bench and walks away. His entourage follows in his wake, trailing him as he saunters toward the break in the hedges where the path to the castle begins. The red-haired woman bends to pick up a grape from John's spilled tray; she catches my eye, gives me a sly wink, then gently pushes the grape between the lips of her cruel mouth.

I'm the property of a madman. For this creature, life itself is nothing more than a plaything. Life can be bought and sold, molded and manipulated, used and ultimately discarded. For the time being, I'm his favorite toy, but all children eventually get tired of their toys and throw them away. John was his favorite toy once, and look what's happened to him.

That's when I realize that I have to escape.

✢ CHAPTER ✢

FOURTEEN

PRIVATE REVOLUTION

Lost he, indeed, who'd freedom sell,
And still believe esteem to hold.

—Jewish Seder song (traditional)

With John dead, everything changed, and not for the better. We may have disliked him, but I don't think anyone actually hated him; we'd often ridiculed him and his milquetoast demeanor behind his back, but he had also earned a certain grudging respect. From the moment we had awakened in the White Room, John had been our friend, the one who had given us clothes to wear and taught us how to behave like adults, and none of us had forgotten that. Now he was gone, and it wasn't long before we realized how much we needed him.

Our associates were able to give us our daily assignments, but now that we didn't have John acting as an intermediary between us and the Main Brain, there was no one we could turn to when there were problems that needed sorting out. Before last week, that might not have troubled us; we had our jobs, and they were virtually the same every day. But Mister Chicago had picked a fine time to kill his majordomo out of spite; now his servants had no one to coordinate the preparations for the New Year's party. We had instructions from our associates, but no human guidance.

Although I only told Shemp, Russ, and Sam what had happened at the pool, the story of the circumstances surrounding John's death spread quickly among the deadheads. Most of my fellow menials avoided contact with me for the next few days, and from time to time I caught hostile glares from some. Nor could I blame them; if I had not been so insolent, Mister Chicago wouldn't have killed John, although it could be argued that murder is a rather extreme way of reasserting authority. I also think Mister Chicago was showing off before his jaded guests. What is ultimate power, after all, other than the ability to kill with the merest word, without fear of reprisal? It must be a wonderful temptation to simply say, "Die, please," and watch someone fall down dead before your eyes. Godlike, in its own sinister way . . . but Mister Chicago seemed to enjoy playing God.

Yet it was difficult explaining this to anyone; even my closest friends became leery of being seen with me. Which was just as well; being left alone gave me more time to think, even while I served food, cleaned tables, mopped floors, and changed bedsheets. Whatever my escape plan was going to be, it had to be foolproof. There would only be one shot at this, because if I screwed up and was caught, there was little doubt in my mind that the next person of whom Mister Chicago requested a sudden and painful death would be me.

But I had a few ideas, and an ace up my sleeve.

■   ■   ■

Mister Chicago doesn't leave his servants leaderless for very long. The afternoon of the second day after John's death, I'm on hands and knees in the Great Hall, scrubbing at the Zodiac mosaic, when Shemp comes in from outside, carrying the mop and bucket he had been using on the front terrace. He vanishes into the custodial closet and comes back out empty-handed. For a moment I think he's done, but then I catch a glimpse of his face and see that he's visibly frightened. He sees me kneeling on the floor, hesitates as if he wants to say something . . . then he seems to think better of it and marches past without a word, crossing the hall to climb the stairs to the gallery, where he disappears down the hall to Mister Chicago's suite.

He still hasn't returned by the time I finish scrubbing the floor. I go to the dining room and start setting the table for dinner; when Kate and Anna arrive a little while later, I tell them what I saw. Neither knows any more than I did, but Anna blanches at the news. All through dinner, she looks up expectantly whenever she hears someone enter the dining room or the kitchen, hoping that it's Shemp. But he's still absent by the time dinner is over, and so is Mister Chicago. By now she's frightened, and I've come to full realization that she's in love with my best friend. Once again, I find myself jealous of Shemp. If I had acted a little more quickly, she might have been mine. . . .

A couple of hours later, after we've gone back downstairs to our quarters, Shemp finally reappears. He looks different; not only are his robes new and fresh, but his hair, which he had grown to nearly shoulder length, has been cut back to a butch, and the beard he had cultivated has been trimmed to a neat little goatee. Oddly, he looks almost the same way he did one hundred and four years ago, on that last summer afternoon at Lollapalooza.

Anna shouts his name when he enters the servants' mess and throws herself on him. He catches her in his arms in an embrace which is fond, yet oddly formal. His friends rush over to ask what had happened, but then he releases Anna and shushes everyone.

"Umm . . ." His face is red with embarrassment. "Look, I . . . um, well, this is a little weird, but . . ." He stops, then goes on. "Mister Chicago asked me to be . . . I mean, he wants me to take over for John."

Total silence. Everyone settles back in their seats, except Anna; she stands next to him, holding his hand as her eyes search his face. "I know this is kinda bizarre," he continues, "but . . . well, John's gone, and he called me in and . . . he goes, y'know, 'I need a new majordomo,' and I go, 'Hey, really, what's that . . . ?'"

Scattered laughter. A grin flickers across Shemp's face and is gone the next instant. "Anyway, so he asked me to . . . y'know, be the head dude and everything, so . . ."

He stares at us; we stare back at him. "But that doesn't change anything," he quickly adds. "I'm still . . . I mean, I'm still one of you guys, and . . . well, just because I'm supposed to be giving orders around here doesn't mean that anything's going to change, because . . ."

Then he goes on to tell us that he'll now be

coordinating the preparations for the New Year's ball, starting tomorrow morning when he'll give us new work assignments in addition to our existing jobs; that, although he'll soon be moving down to a private room one level below us, we can still find him there through our associates (a furtive glance at Anna); that he hopes to do as good of a job as John did before his death (his gaze flickering toward me), but that he wants to be more approachable than John was; that we should always consider him to be our friend . . .

Oh, yeah, and one more thing: we're not to call him Shemp anymore. From now on, we're to address him as Christopher . . . Chris, for short. In fact, his associate has been reprogrammed not to respond to comlink summons addressed to Shemp. Nothing personal (another glance at me), but he really doesn't like that nickname.

"Okay, Shemp," I say.

It's supposed to be a joke. Everyone chuckles when I say this, including Anna, but Shemp . . . Chris, that is . . . half-turns his head toward me. He bats his eyes a few times and his lips move just a little, like a drunk mumbling a curse against an old foe from the past.

Something suddenly tightens in my temples. A mild headache. A little eyestrain. Nothing more, nothing less. But we both know what it means.

"Sorry, Chris," I add.

He smiles and moves his lips again. The headache is gone.

"No problem, Alec," he replies, and his smile becomes a grin.

Then he takes Anna under his arm, says good

night, and turns to walk his girlfriend to the little room down the hall that he won't be using much longer. Anna seems a little reluctant to go—when our eyes meet for a brief instant, I see bewilderment, perhaps even fear—but she leaves with him anyway.

Once they've disappeared, Sam picks up his unfinished bowl of stew and stands up from the table. "Meet the new boss," he murmurs. "Same as the old boss."

Count on a boomer to quote a line from a Who song. "Cut it out," I say. "I've known Shemp all my life. He won't sell out."

I don't know why I'm defending Shemp, considering what he just did. Habit, I guess. He's my oldest friend, and some allegiances die hard.

Sam glances at me. "God, you're so young."

Next morning, Shemp reappears in the servants' mess after breakfast to tell us what we're going to be doing for the upcoming party. He reads aloud from a list on his sketch pad; when he folds back a page, I notice that he's torn out all his drawings, and wonder what's become of them.

About half of the household staff, myself included, are tasked to redecorating the castle and its grounds: hedges trimmed into topiary animals, garlands hung from the windows, paper lanterns strung along the footpaths, and so forth. Many are assigned to opening the guest cottages outside the castle and making them ready—the next ship is due to arrive only a few days from now, so they have to hurry—while others, including Anna, will be temporarily reassigned to the kitchen staff when they begin preparing the banquet. Entertainers will be arriving soon, including two separate groups of musicians and something called the Solar Circus Troupe; they need people to help them set up for their performances, and Shemp assigns Russell and Sam to that crew.

This and a dozen other tasks, in addition to our regular jobs, means that we shouldn't expect to return to our quarters until well after midnight. In recognition of this, Shemp informs us that curfew has been temporarily suspended and that lights-out is being delayed until 0200. However, our morning wake-up call will continue to hold at 0600, meaning that we'll only have a minimum of four hours' sleep each night.

I note that he hasn't included himself anywhere in the duty roster. As our new majordomo, Shemp apparently considers himself exempt from everything except supervising his former peers. As it turns out, this is indeed the case; whenever I see him after this morning, it's when he suddenly appears at someone's shoulder, either to hassle them about some petty mistake, or to nag them to move faster.

His transformation from Shemp to Christopher isn't just a change of name, it's a change of attitude. The Shemp who once mocked John gradually becomes the same sort of person he once detested: a micromanagerial busybody, parading around with his notepad as if it's a royal scepter and he's been ordained to keep the riffraff in line. Way back when, he alienated himself from his father when he refused to join the family business by becoming a manager-trainee in the Big Bee supermarket chain; now I think Warren Meyer would have been proud of his prodigal son. He's becoming an asshole just like his old man.

It all comes to a boil several days later, when he catches me taking a breather in the rose garden outside the west wing. I've been on hands and knees for the last two hours, pruning the roses and saving the discarded petals in a jar for the bowls of rosewater the house staff leaves in the bathrooms of the guest suites. My back's aching, my arms are caked with dirt up to my elbows, and I'm trying to suck out a tiny rose thorn lodged in the pad of my left thumb; it's a bad time for Shemp to come up behind me and tap the top of my head with his notebook.

"Let's go, Alec," he says. "Chop chop. Time waits for no one."

That's become his mantra: *Chop chop, time waits for no one.* I know where he got it from: his dad used to say the same thing all the time. I turn around and look up at him, towering over me with his notebook under his arm, every inch the Big Bee assistant manager.

"Y'know," I say, "you're such a fucking jerk."

His face darkens; he says nothing, but his eyelids flutter. "Go ahead," I say. "Give me a headache. Give me an aneurysm. It won't change anything. You've become a jerk . . . Shemp."

His eyes narrow to slits; his chin starts to tremble. He's trying to appear menacing, but he looks instead like a kid ready to throw a tantrum. It almost makes me laugh.

"Never call me Shemp again," he says, his voice barely above a whisper. "I'm Christopher now."

"Sure thing, Shem . . ."

Pain bludgeons me to the ground. I fall face-first

into the rose bushes, their soft fragrance now sickly-sweet as thorns tear against my cheeks and forehead. Shemp lets me writhe in the flower bed for a minute or two; when the agony finally subsides, I find him kneeling beside me.

"Do you remember how I got the name Shemp?" he asks.

I don't say anything; I don't think he wants me to give him an answer anyway. "It's because some jerk in gym class saw what I looked like without my clothes on," he continues, "and said I looked like I was one of the Three Stooges. He meant Curly, because I really didn't resemble Moe Howard's brother and he got them mixed up. But the name stuck anyway and I've had to live with it for the rest of my life."

"I'm sorry."

He shakes his head. "No, you're not sorry . . . because you're the jerk who gave me that name."

My first thought is to deny this. After all, I'm the one who had always stuck up for him. For the longest time, I was his only friend, until he finally learned to be hip: smoke pot, hang out with the right crowd, listen to the right music, show up at the right parties, and stop letting his mother buy his clothes for him. Yet in the back of my mind, there's an undeniable truth that's been suppressed by guilt over all these years; only now does it come back to me.

It's true. I'm the kid in seventh-grade gym class who looked at his obese, waddling body and called him Shemp for the first time. I've long forgotten this, but he never has.

"I'm sorry, Chris," I manage to gasp. "I really mean it . . . I'm so sorry."

He shakes his head. "Naw, man," he says softly, "you're not sorry. It's just that, for the first time in your life, you've got a reason to be scared of me." He reaches down and idly flicks some dirt out of my face. "I'm not a fat little Jewboy anymore, though. I've got a body I'm not ashamed of, I've got a girl you want, I've got a place that's better than yours, and I've got permission to kick your ass whenever I feel like it."

He bends lower. "Alec, I told Mister Chicago about us," he whispers. "Told him everything about you . . . and y'know what? He told me that if I did a good job for him, I can do whatever I want with you. How's that for revenge of the nerds?"

I want to tell him that his authority is on temporary loan from a maniac who killed the last nerd for kicks, that the power is making him crazy. I want to tell him that our long friendship was real, that terrible nickname I gave him was something I had done when I was young and stupid, and that I was so embarrassed about it that I repressed the memory and have tried to make it up to him ever since.

Most of all, I want to tell Christopher Meyer that I still love him like a brother, despite the fact that he's been nursing a secret hatred for me all these years.

Yet I also know anything I may say to Shemp just now, even the most tear-streaked confession, will send him ballistic. I know that, and he knows that; he's aching for a chance to give me another migraine, if not the MINN command that will rip open a cerebral artery.

So I don't say nothing. I lie still and silent, and stare at the rose stems around my face, and wait for him to make the next move.

"So don't ever call me Shemp again," he says at last.

"I won't. I promise."

I don't look at him. After a few moments, I hear him stand up. "I've got a better job for you," his voice says from above me. "The next ship is due to arrive this afternoon. A bunch of Superiors coming in from Ceres. I know how much you like those guys, so I think you should have the honor of meeting them at the hub." He pauses. "In fact, I think that should be your job from now on. Think you can handle it?"

"Uh-huh."

"Say, 'Yes sir, Chris.'"

"Yes sir, Chris."

"Good. Now go put on another robe. You look like shit."

He starts to walk away, then he stops. "And one more thing," he adds. "Stay away from Anna. I'm having her moved into my quarters tonight, so you won't be seeing her much. She's still on housekeeping, but I don't want you messing with her. She's mine. Understand?"

That's weird. Anna and I are friends—and yes, I've secretly desired her—but I've never "messed" with her, if you didn't count all the times we were in the showers together before our memories came back. Never once have I ever laid a hand on her. So what the hell is that about?

"Yes sir, Chris." Fuck you, Shemp.

"Very good." There's gloating in his voice. "Now get back to work. Chop chop. Time waits for no one."

And, to quote Mick Jagger, it won't wait for me.

Whatever else happens, I have to get off Garcia. It's no longer simply a matter of being terrified by

Mister Chicago's insanity; now my best friend—my *former* best friend—has been corrupted by the same madness. I instinctively know that it's only a matter of time before the master of the house grows tired of playing with me. If he knows about the connection between Shemp and me, it's entirely possible that Mister Chicago will get rid of me in a suitably entertaining manner. Perhaps another poolside chat, with Shemp as the finger man.

If I'm going to escape, it has to be soon.

Fortunately, Shemp has unwittingly given me my means of escape. In assigning me to be a bellboy for the next batch of guests, he's also allowed me unconditional access to the cable cars. That same afternoon, when I join Sam, Russell, and a couple of other deadheads at the same cable car station on Level D where we embarked on our first trip to the hub, I make sure that I'm the one who opens the hatch to Access AH–12. Chip lets me do so without question or interference; one word, and the hatch irises open. Good. That means I'm now authorized by the Main Brain to use the cable car.

But will that always be the case? I can't count on it, especially since the plan I've started to develop calls for me to make my escape at a time when the hub is likely to be empty and no ships would be arriving. I'd contemplated sneaking aboard one of the ships before it left the asteroid, until I realized that the risks of being discovered as a stowaway are unacceptably high. If its crew doesn't return to Garcia, then it's possible that they may simply toss me out the nearest airlock, or even allow someone like Vladimir Algol-Raphael to use me for rapier practice.

No, I've got another idea in mind, but it means

entering a cable car without alerting Chip, and therefore beyond range of my associate's radio link with the Main Brain.

In the days that followed, whenever I was sent to the hub to greet new arrivals, I made certain that I always used the same cable car, even when others were closer and more available, and that I always followed the same route to Access AH–12. Each time I walked to the station on Level D, I carefully counted how many paces it took for me to get from the servants' quarters on Level B, and memorized the figure. Many hours later, once I was alone in my room, I added that figure to a short list of others like it that I had written on a notepad and left under my pillow.

Once I had made four trips, I averaged the figures together. It took approximately seven hundred and eighty paces for me to travel from the servants' quarters to Access AH–12. To test this, the fifth time I went to the cable car station, I walked with my head down, never raising my eyes from my feet while I silently counted the number of times they hit the floor. This took considerable concentration—I ignored offhand comments by other servants by pretending to be in a sulky mood—but when I reached seven hundred and eighty, I looked up and found the cable car hatch no more than five feet away.

Whether or not I could do this same feat in the dark was another matter entirely. And that was only the first step . . . or rather, the first seven hundred and eighty steps.

During my third trip to the hub, I let the rest of the welcome wagon get in front of me, which gives me a chance to hang back. Once they're out of sight, I stop next to one of the EVA pods I spotted during my first trip. Its hatch opens easily with a simple clockwise twist of its locklever; no alarm bells ring when I peer inside the tiny cockpit.

The instrument panels are just as intimidating as the first time I saw them; for a moment my courage falters. This is fucking insane. Then I take a deep breath and go eyes-up.

"Chip," I whisper, "do you know how to fly one of these things?"

Yes, Alec, this information is available to me.

"How difficult would it be for me to learn this stuff?"

It would be extremely difficult. You have no previous experience with piloting an EVA pod.

I expected that. "Yes, but if you helped me, could I fly this thing? I mean, could you talk me through it?"

This would be unlikely, unless you had some prior training in piloting an EVA pod. However, it would still be very dangerous.

Damn. "Okay . . . say that I had information on how to fly an EVA pod, and you were to assist me as a copilot? Could I fly this thing then?"

This is more feasible. However, it would still be quite hazardous.

"More feasible" and "quite hazardous" sound like better odds than "unlikely" and "very dangerous." I glance over my shoulder; no one's spotted me, and the rest of the group hasn't noticed my absence yet. "Can you download that information into your system?"

Yes, but not at this time.

Crap. Of course he can't; he's beyond comlink range with the central AI. And if I ask Chip to retrieve that info when I'm in the habitat, the Main Brain might blow the whistle.

Another notion occurs to me. "Can you get it later, if I ask you to do so now?"

Yes, I can do this, if you tell me when you wish to have it downloaded.

I sigh in relief. "Download it six hours from now, and make it available to me on eyes-up. Okay?"

Affirmative. Pilot tutorial for a General Astronautics Model 6–1B EVA Repair Module will be downloaded to your MINN six hours from now.

"Cool. Thanks, Chip. Eyes-down."

I slam the hatch shut and practically run down the corridor to catch up with the rest of the group. They're already gathered in the gateway, waiting for another episode of Motherfuckers On Parade. Russell asks me what I had been doing; I tell him I went looking for the head.

The ship is just coming in: a large vessel not unlike the *Anakuklesis* in general shape, but a little smaller. Servants and ground crew loiter around the reception area; we still have a few minutes to kill before it mates with its docking collar. I spot a uniformed crewman near one of the windows, watching the ship as it glides into port. He's bored and all by himself, so I wander over to him.

"Where's this one coming from?" I ask.

He barely glances my way. "What's it to you, deadhead?"

"Hey, just wondering. This stuff is new to me . . . space and all that, I mean."

He smirks. "I'm sure it is."

"Sure is. Hey, did you ever see *The Empire Strikes Back*? The second *Star Wars* movie, all that?"

"Sure. Classic ciné." He's a little more interested. "You see it when it was new?"

"You bet. My dad took me to it on opening day." Which is the truth; it's one of my few childhood memories of my father that doesn't suck. "Remember that asteroid chase scene? I dunno, but does the Belt really look like that?"

He barks laughter, then explains that the average distance between asteroids in the main belt is about a million miles, so no one ever collided with a rock. However, there's distinct travel routes—synodic periods is the technical term—between one populated asteroid and its neighbors, and they in turn comprise traverses, the interplanetary shipping lanes used by spacecraft moving through the Belt toward the inner system. Freighters, mining ships, passenger ships, private yachts like this one—they all use them.

Wow, that's cool, I say, and he warms to the subject. The traverses change all the time, depending on the perihelions and aphelions of individual asteroids. When an asteroid is close to perihelion, it's near a traverse. In fact, he says, 4442 Garcia is now close to one of the major traverses between the Belt and the inner system. That's partly what's making this bash possible; ships can get to Garcia more easily now than when the synodic periods are askew.

I listen carefully, and ask questions, and remember everything he tells me.

Late that night, after I've returned to my room and put my aching body to bed, I finally do what I've been wanting to do for the last ten hours. I shut my eyes, take a deep breath, and go eyes-up. Then I tell Chip to run the tutorial program for the EVA pod.

Against the darkness of my closed eyelids, the cockpit of a tiny spacecraft reappears like a photographic negative image, with a horizontal bar of command icons arranged across the top of my private computer screen.

I raise my hand, touch one of the panels above its oval window; it zooms into sharp focus. The panel is marked with stuff I can't begin to understand—*Tk. 1 Prs., Tk. 2. Prs., RCR Man. Eng., Auto. Prg./On/Off*—but when I tap each one in turn, a vertical bar scrolls down from above, giving me a full rundown what each one of these things means.

I almost laugh out loud when I see this. Fucking rad. Windows 2099. Bill Gates, eat your heart out.

Nothing about this is going to come easy. I have to memorize all this stuff PDQ, and I still don't know exactly where I'm going. Next trip to the hub, I have to talk Chip into downloading astrogation charts for the nearest traverse. Maybe I can find something that will help me. And there's a dozen other details that I still have to figure out. If I screw up any one of them, my ass is fried.

But now the way is clear, and it's time to fly.

✟ CHAPTER ✟

FIFTEEN

CHAMPAGNE SUPERNOVA

"New Year's Eve is amateur night."

—Murphy Brown

And then, quite suddenly, it was December 31, 2099.

Across the length and breadth of the inhabited solar system, humankind celebrated not only the coming of the new year, but also the new century. On Earth, this occurred in one-hour increments as measured by the planet's axial rotation; on Mars, most aresians observed the event as Gemini 1, M.Y. 75, in accordance with the Zubrin calendar. In space, though, where everyone kept Greenwich Meridian Time, the parties were simultaneous and everywhere, from the space stations orbiting Earth to the underground cities of the Moon, from the Pax Astra capital at Clarke County to small outposts scattered across the Jovian moons, from Evening Star in orbit above Venus to remote and lonely Hershel Station on Titan.

But none of these celebrations matched Mister Chicago's ball on 4442 Garcia.

At 2000 hours, the ceiling filaments suddenly go dark and the habitat is plunged into the weightless gloom of space, a black abyss broken only by starlight that gleams through the skylight. Near-total silence descends on the crowd gathered outside the castle; hundreds of eyes turn upward, anticipating the spectacle to come.

A brilliant pink flash on the asteroid's surface, bright as a supernova, erases all shadows in a single instant. An artificial thunderclap roars through artfully concealed loudspeakers; unwary guests drop their wineglasses as castle windows tremble in their frames. Multicolored streamers break loose from the ceiling rafters, gently unfurling as their ends plummet downward to the crowded terraces and walkways. The guests, sated from the lavish six-course dinner they had just finished, dazzled by pyrotechnics and deafened by sound, applaud and cheer.

As the supernova fades, a spotlight lances upward through the darkness, capturing a lone human figure in the ceiling rafters high above the castle: a woman in a spangled skintight outfit, her arms spread apart.

She arches her back, then launches herself into space.

Gasps of terror and horror. No safety cord, no net, nothing between her and the ground. A falling angel captured in a shaft of light, she plummets down, down, down . . .

A man in an identical outfit—upside down, legs folded over a trapeze bar, arms outstretched—appears from nowhere. Another spotlight catches and follows him as his body describes a perfect parabola until, in an instant of flawless synchronicity, he intercepts the falling woman. Their hands meet, clasp each other's wrists; she bends her legs upward and tucks in her knees. Her feet slice the air only a few dozen yards above the heads of the partygoers.

Up and away, they soar, the spotlights tracking them as the trapeze lofts them to a small platform hidden in the ceiling. They stop there, almost lost in the rafters, and turn to raise their hands to the audience far below. The applause is even louder than before.

Then a spotlight falls upon a castle parapet. A figure dressed in shirt, waistcoat, cape, and tights as white as his skin patiently awaits the attention of his guests.

With regal humility, Mister Chicago allows his friends, lovers, and business acquaintances to clap, whistle, and shout his name before he raises his hands and gently chastens them to silence. When he speaks, his voice is carried by the same speakers that only a minute earlier had brought forth thunder.

"My friends . . ." His voice echoes off the habitat walls. "My friends, welcome to the last hours of this century . . . our century."

More applause. He smiles and again beckons them to be silent. "I'm honored that you, each and every one, are my guests for this momentous occasion. For the past few weeks, I've enjoyed your company. We've dined together, entertained one another, spoken of things great and small, and in this time I've been once again reminded that it is we who inhabit deep space . . . Mars, the Belt, Jupiter and beyond . . . who represent the future of humankind."

He waits until the applause subsides. "Tonight, we celebrate not only the end of the greatest century humanity has ever known, but also the dawn of one which promises to be better still. And it is we who are gathered here this evening . . . aresians, belters, and jovians, Primaries and Superiors alike . . . who shall lead humankind not only into a new era but to the stars themselves, and ultimately to our destiny in the Omega Point."

Mister Chicago pauses until the latest round of applause fades. "But for the time being," he continues, "let's not think of these things. Tonight, we cast aside our concerns and sorrows, our trials and tribulations. In these last four hours of the twenty-first century, we'll drink and be merry . . . and tomorrow, we lay siege to the gates of heaven."

More hand-clapping and whistles. He bows from the waist, then his spotlight vanishes, taking him along with it.

The lights come back on, revealing balconies and terraces jammed with men and women in evening finery: long slit-legged skirts, hooded capes, jodhpurs, tricorn caps, brocaded vests, codpieces, knee boots. Superiors, easily spotted in the crowd because they stand a head taller than Primaries, wear elaborate outfits designed to reveal their body art; they remain aloof from baseline humans, regarding the more inebriated guests with puritanical disdain. On the terrace below, a trio of jugglers from the Solar Circus Troupe attracts a small audience as they begin tossing clubs to one another. Mimes in costumes and nanite masks which transform them into various historical figures—Julius Caesar, Napoleon, Madonna, Richard Nixon—work the crowd. Somewhere nearby, a jazz ensemble strikes up something that sounds like "Rock Lobster" as performed by a quartet of epileptic monkeys. Couples drift away to wander down pathways lit by Japanese paper lanterns, perhaps heading for discreet tête-á-têtes in the nearby cabins. The air is fragrant with canapés, fresh-cut roses, and smoldering incense.

I have to admit, Mister Chicago knows how to throw a blowout. Too bad I can't enjoy it.

A hand touches my shoulder. I automatically turn to offer the platter of paté de foie gras I've been lugging around for the last hour to a bald gentleman wearing a pince-nez. He plucks one from the tray, but seems more interested in me. "By the way, do you happen to be one of Pasquale's deadheads?"

"Yes sir."

"Ahh!" His left eyelid wrinkles above the monocle; the light reflects microcircuitry within the glass oval. "From what year, pray tell?"

"1995, sir."

"Nineteen hundred and ninety-five . . . I see." His lips writhe as he bites into the cracker. "A good year for classic literature, 1995. I'm something of a devotee of that period. By chance, did you ever meet Stephen King?"

"No, sir."

"Oh? How about Judith Krantz?"

"No, sir."

"Hmm . . ." He looks disappointed. "But surely you must have met Michael Crichton."

I shake my head. "I once saw a movie he made, though," I quickly add. "The one about the dinosaurs. It was pretty cool."

He sniffs and tosses the hors d'oeuvre back on the platter. "Go away. You're boring me."

I might have said that he was doing likewise, but keep my mouth shut. I start moving through the crowded balcony outside the Great Hall, picking the half-eaten cracker off the platter and tossing it in a trash can. It's not hard for the guests to distinguish the deadheads among the waiters and waitresses he's conscripted tonight; we're decked out in twentieth-century black-tie, men and women alike. I'm looking sharp, but the tux is uncomfortable: the bow tie chafes my neck, the vest is tight, and the tails get snagged every time I back into something. I could have told Mister Chicago that morning coats were archaic even in my era, but he didn't ask for my advice. I'm another of his quaint windup toys, sent out to serve finger food and answer stupid questions.

I'm not the only one humiliated. Returning to the kitchen for another hors d'oeuvres platter, I run into Sam. He's fuming as he waits for one of the cooks to give him a fresh pot of chicory coffee. "You know what one of those assholes asked me?" he seethes. "If I was related to O.J."

"The Juice? C'mon . . ."

"Nope. If I'm black and lived back then, then I must know O.J."

"You mean you didn't?"

"Don't start with me, Tucker . . ."

"Ever meet Stephen King?"

"Saw him at the ABA once. Why?"

"Go find the bald dude with the monocle. He'd want to talk to you."

Sam gives me a look and turns away. He's not amused, nor can I blame him. We've already been on our feet for nearly twelve hours straight, with only a short dinner break before we got dressed for the party. The servants are all sore-footed and tired, and we still have many hours to go before the last guest falls down. Even then, there won't be any relief from our misery; someone has to clean up the mess. It'll be days before any of us recuperates from this ordeal.

Yet I can't let myself get exhausted. I've other plans this evening, and although I didn't intend to carry them out for an hour or so later, I'm coming to the realization that if I don't act now, I might be too tired to make the scheme work.

Another tray of pâté de foie gras is placed on the counter before me, but I ignore it. Next to it is another treat for our guests: steak tartare, tiny strips of rare beef smothered in horseradish sauce and wrapped in spinach leaves. That'll do nicely. Kate's standing next to me; she starts to reach for it, but I gently bump her aside to pick it up. She gives me a scolding look, but doesn't fight it; she takes the paté instead. One hors d'oeuvres platter was as good as the other.

Not for my purposes, though . . .

Shouldering the platter, I exit the kitchen and make my way through the dining room and into the Great Hall, pausing now and then to allow a guest to sample my wares while I search the crowded rotunda. Although my intended victim stands a head taller than almost everyone else, it takes a little while before I spot him . . . but when I do, I move toward him like a lazy bullet.

Vladimir Algol-Raphael, patriarch of the Algol clan, king schmuck of the universe, has parked himself beside a column next to the stairway. Wearing the same robes he wore when he stepped off the *Anakuklesis* nearly a month ago, he's holding court with a small handful of Primaries. When I get closer, I see that he's brought his rapier with him, tucked into its sheath on his hip. Good. I was counting on that.

He and his friends are carrying on a conversation about something or other when I approach them, making sure that I'm just behind Algol-Raphael. With scarcely a glance in my direction, the Primaries help themselves to the steak tartare. Then I offer the platter to Vlad himself.

"Hors d'oeuvre, sir?" I ask, ever so innocently.

Algol-Raphael hasn't noticed who his waiter is. He picks up one of the hors d'oeuvres and, as I watch, brings it to his narrow lips. Then he takes a good, hard look at what he is about to put in his mouth . . .

And then, just as I hoped, he screams.

Shortly after the *Anakuklesis* arrived a month ago, John instructed us on proper social etiquette around the Superiors. Although they're sometimes referred to as "googles" by baseline humans, because of their enormous eyes, we were never to call them this, especially not to their faces; the term is a racial epithet, just as insulting as if I were to call Sam a nigger. When addressing them, we were to always use both of their hyphenated surnames—clan name first, family name second—and never drop one or the other. Bending over from the hips, such as to pick up something from the floor, is likewise considered to be an insult; we're presenting our buttocks to them, with all this implies.

And most of all, because of their strict social mores, there are two things we should never offer a

Superior: alcoholic drinks, and any sort of food with meat in it.

Naturally, Vladimir Algol-Raphael was properly upset when he discovered that he'd nearly put steak tartare in his mouth. And when he saw who the offending waiter was, he went berserk.

I'll skip the details, except to say that I haven't seen anyone throw such a shit-fit since the time I poured out my mother's vodka on April Fool's Day and replaced it with Evian. It took three bystanders to keep Vlad from skewering me with his rapier, but he did manage to grab the platter from my hands and hurl it at me. His aim was lousy—the tray missed me by a mile—but it splattered meat across my tux. So much the better; I hadn't counted on that happening, but it was welcome just the same.

His bellowing drew everyone within earshot, including (as I had anticipated . . . in fact, counted on) my good friend Christopher Meyer. Shemp had been scurrying around the castle for the last umpteen hours, bossing all the servants without doing a lick of work himself; when he saw an enraged Superior trying to murder his oldest friend, there was no question whose side he would take. The other guy's, of course.

First, he all but licked Vlad's shoes. Profuse apologies were rendered: much bowing and scraping, plus a lot of kvetching about what a schmuck I was. I don't think Vlad understood the Yiddish stuff, but he simmered down enough to put away his sword. Then Shemp turned to me and was apoplectic for another minute, *putz* this and *schlemiel* that, while I played the contrite servant who's committed the worst blunder possible. Yes, Chris. No, Chris. I'm sorry, Chris. I'm tired, I forgot,

I really didn't mean to offer meat, uncooked or otherwise, to our honored Superior guest.

My only fear was that Shemp might decide that now was the time to punish me by instructing Chip to give me a migraine. The notion certainly occurred to him—I could see it in his eyes—but if anything held him back, it was the realization that dozens of people were watching us right now, and it might be a party pooper if one of the servants suddenly keeled over on the floor of the Great Hall. Mister Chicago might not like that. So Christopher Meyer took the easy way out.

"Get out of here," he hisses, his face only inches from my own. He flicks his hand against my stained shirt and vest. "And get out of this, too. You're a mess. Go downstairs and get changed . . ."

"I don't have another tux."

He hasn't thought of that. "Then put on a robe." He glances over his shoulder at Vlad. "But don't come back here. I want you in the kitchen for cleanup. Understand?"

"Got it, Shemp . . . Chris, sorry."

His eyes are hot with fury. "I can't believe you did this to me. I can't fucking believe it." He turns away from me. "Just get outta here. I'll deal with you later."

At that moment, a certain melancholy comes over me. Whatever Christopher Meyer has become, he'll always be Shemp to me. I almost want to say good-bye, but he's already made his farewell speech, even though he doesn't know it yet.

So I leave it at that. I turn around and head for the nearest service elevator, and pray that my luck holds up just a little while longer.

■   ■   ■

As I expected, the servants' quarters are deserted; everyone's upstairs in the castle. I double-check the showers and the mess room just to make sure that I've got the place to myself, then I go to my room and close the door.

Off with the tails, vest, shoes, and tie. I almost ditch the trousers and shirt as well, but think better of it; they might be better clothes to be wearing once I'm in the EVA pod. I leave them on and pull my robe over them. Then I pick up the unknotted bow tie, lie down on the bed, and close my eyes.

Carefully keeping my eyes shut, I wrap the bow tie around my eyes as a blindfold, just as Winston did just before he hanged himself. Winston figured it out first: if our associates can't see what we're doing, then they're robbed of most of their sensory input.

Once the blindfold is in place, I open my eyes again. I can't see anything except black cotton.

I sit up, then reach down to the foot of the bed where I'd carefully placed my stikshoes after my last trip to the hub. Once they're on, I pull the hood over my head, stand up, and walk to the door.

I open the door, take a deep breath and clear my mind of all other thoughts.

And then I take the first step, and start counting.

One, two . . .

Right turn. Down the corridor, thirty-seven paces . . .

Stop. Left turn, five paces. Stop.

I raise my hands, feel nothing but air. Have I miscounted? I take a tentative half-step forward; my fingers touch a grooved metal panel.

No, I haven't miscounted: here's the elevator. I

drop my right hand to my side, half-raise it again to waist-level, and wave it. The door makes a faint whirring sound as it opens.

Two paces forward, stop, about-face.

I find the floor panel, run my fingers lightly down it until I find the lowest button. The doors shut again.

The elevator descends for a few moments, then comes to a halt. The doors whir again; cool air rushes against my face.

I'm now on Level D.

It's very quiet.

I lower my head and walk four paces forward. Stop. Right turn, continue walking.

Fifty-one steps down. Seven hundred and twenty-nine to go.

Seven hundred and twenty-nine steps, and they seem to take forever. I force myself to keep an even pace, without speeding up or slowing down, and to walk straight ahead as if I'm following an invisible plank. Judging from the silence, the corridor seems to be empty—everyone who works down here is upstairs at the ball, just as I've anticipated—but twice I think I hear footfalls behind me. Each time, I halt and listen carefully. Maybe it's Shemp: he's come from the party to bawl me out in private, seen me leaving my room and has been tracking me. Both times, though, I hear nothing, and so I pick up the count again and continue my lonely trek.

At least three times, I lose count. It's more difficult than it seems, counting to seven hundred and eighty without skipping an integer here or there; try it sometime, if you don't believe me. Something crosses my mind—am I right about the blind spot in the cable car? has my disappearance from the servants' quarters been detected? is someone following me?—and suddenly five hundred sixty-four becomes five hundred forty-six, five hundred forty-seven, five hundred forty-eight . . . no, that's not right! Stop, take a deep breath. Remember, dammit! Oh, yeah . . . five hundred sixty-four. Concentrate, you idiot!

On and on and on . . .

Bumping into walls now and then, stopping to reorient myself, resisting the urge to lift the blindfold for just a quick peek. A blindfolded man walking down an endless corridor, hood raised over his head. Christ, what if someone comes out of one of these rooms and sees me? How do you explain this?

Forget it! Keep going!

Six hundred ninety-five, six hundred ninety-six . . . looking good, Alec old buddy. Going for the touchdown.

Six hundred ninety-eight . . . damn, you did it again! Six hundred ninety-*seven!*

And then, almost before I realize it, I hit the magic number: seven hundred and eighty.

I stop in my tracks. My heart hammers against my chest. Nothing about this part of the corridor seems any different than the last few hundred yards I've traveled.

I reach out with my hands, grope blindly in the air.

Nothing. I take another step forward. Still nothing.

Two more steps, then two more. Shit! Nothing there!

Two steps, three, four . . . I'm not bothering to keep count any more. My hands meet nothing.

Goddammit! Where's the fucking . . . ?

One more step, and my fingertips suddenly brush against a curved, grooved surface. I explore it with my hands.

Yes! An iris hatch!

"Alec Tucker," I say. "Open, please."

The hatch slides open with a faint grinding sound.

I walk straight ahead, still holding my hands before me, until they collide with what feels like thick glass. I drop my hands, find a handrail. I grasp it with both hands, let out my breath as a ragged sigh, turn around.

"Hub."

Once again, the familiar grinding sound.

Then the floor begins to rise.

I make myself count to two hundred before I tear the sweaty tie off my face. Even in the dimness of the cable car, the sudden light makes me blink.

Then my vision clears and there, rushing past the windows, are shining stars and Bible-black darkness. Below me, rapidly receding away past a forest of cables, lies the enormous transparent roof of the habitat. For an instant, I catch a glimpse of Mister Chicago's castle: windows glowing, walkways traced by Japanese lanterns, balconies and terraces dotted by innumerable ant-like forms. The solarium dome glares up at me like a cyclopean eye.

Almost looks like a party's going on down there. Maybe you ought to go down and see if you can get a drink?

Smiling to myself, I sag against the rail. No, this is one New Year's party I think I'll skip.

But thank the host for inviting me anyway.

Tell him I've got other plans.

■   ■   ■

The hub corridors are as deserted as the lower levels of the habitat; no one sees me as I make my way to the EVA pods.

The pods aren't locked. Who in their right mind would steal a spacecraft with a maximum fuel range of only a hundred kilometers, when the nearest inhabited asteroid was well over a million kilometers away?

Yet I have no intention of trying to fly to one of Garcia's neighbors. Even if I could, it would probably be pointless; more than likely, its residents would probably return me to Mister Chicago as soon as they discover I'm one of his deadheads. Out here in the Belt, his power is absolute; no one would defy him over such a trivial matter as an escaped slave.

No, I've got a better idea. Risky as hell, to be sure; in fact, I figure the odds are against me. Considering that they're still better than my chances if I stay here, though, it's a shot I'm willing to take.

I open the hatch of one of the pods and, after one last look around to make sure that I'm not being observed, I pull off my robe and drop it on the floor behind me. Then I grasp the bar above the hatch and, copying the method used by pod pilots, swing myself feet-first into the tiny cockpit.

Land square in its high-backed seat. Reach back to pull the hatch shut behind me. Dog it tight. Swivel the seat around until it faces the oval porthole and the instrument panels below and above it.

"Okay, Chip," I say, blinking three times, "access the EVA pod tutorial."

EVA pod tutorial accessed, Alec.

"Good. Give me an overlay for the pod controls. Switch to audio mode for your talk-through."

"Yes, Alec."

A false-color diagram of the pod's instruments appears before me. I can still see the dashboard, the instrument panels, the yoke and the throttle bars, but it's now as if I'm looking at them through a transparent film.

Experimentally, I lay my hands on the yoke. Just as it has during my late-night practice sessions, a red arrow appears just above the yoke, along with a tiny blue window that identifies it for me. I raise my left hand and randomly point to a panel just above my head; another window tells me this is the communications panel. Next to the arrow is a tiny, swirl-shaped icon; when I touch it, a window opens below the icon, giving me a range of options, each with their own icons in case I need further explanation. Any mall rat could handle this given enough time, patience, and arcade tokens. It's Sega on steroids.

"All right, let's get to it. Start the launch procedure."

"Launch procedure as follows." A red arrow appears next to a set of toggle switches on the right side of the dashboard. "Initiate power-up of the primary and auxiliary electrical systems . . ."

And so begins a long rundown of a dozen different procedures, each with their own subsets of protocols and fail-safes. Activate the electrical and life-support systems. Check cockpit seals. Reset and load primary and backup computers. Recharge batteries. Pressurize fuel cells. Test main engines and reaction-control rockets. So forth and so on; I skip the unnecessary stuff, like testing the pod's remote manipulator arms, and omit a radio check since there's no sense in tipping off anyone that one of their pods is about make an unscheduled sortie, but the rest goes by the numbers. Chip points to this switch, and I toggle it; Chip tells me to enter these numbers on the keyboard, and I type them in. The situation might have been hopeless if I tried to do this a hundred years ago, but things are different when you have a little bitty computer in your head.

We're done in fifteen minutes. Now the cockpit glows with the multicolored light from dozens of switches, readouts, and flatscreens, and I'm sitting in the best hot rod any kid from St. Louis has ever seen. All I need is a plastic Jesus on the dashboard and a pair of furry dice dangling from the life-support subsystems panel. I haul the seat harness around me, buckle tight its waist and shoulder straps. "Okay," I murmur, "is everything ready for launch?"

"Yes, Alec, you may proceed with launch. Enter course coordinates, please."

"Display coordinates for . . . um, synodic traverses in this quadrant of the Belt."

On eyes-up, a complex set of curving lines appears before me, each bisecting the right-angle lines of 4442 Garcia's orbit and those of its closest neighbors. "Okay, now lay in the . . . uh . . . the positions of the nearest spacecraft in those lanes."

Several orange dots appear on the traverses. The nearest lane one has a bright orange spot off to its right. I touch it and ask for its distance from 4442 Garcia. Red numerals tell me it's 30,652 kilometers from my position.

A long shot, but it'll have to do. "Lay in an intercept course for that ship."

"Alec, the fuel range of this craft is limited to one hundred kilometers."

"I know. Head for the intercept point."

"Alec, your chances of reaching this intercept point are—"

"Just do it! Undock us, fire the main engines, and keep firing until the tanks are dry."

"I don't understand, Alec."

I glance at the chronometer. It's now 23:52:46 GMT. In less than eight minutes, the twenty-second century begins. I can spend the New Year's Eve with Mister Chicago, or I can roll the dice.

"Just do it, Chip. Get me out of here."

"Understood. Launch sequence activated."

Lights flash across the panels. There's a sudden jar as the pod disengages from its docking collar; for a moment everything seems to hold still. I hang tight to the armrests, watching stars drift past the porthole.

Don't look back. Never look back . . .

Then the engine fires. My back is pressed flat against the seat as the pod trembles around me, and I'm on my way.

✛ CHAPTER ✛

SIXTEEN

I'M A LITTLE ROCKET SHIP

Alone, alone, all, all alone
Alone on a wide, wide sea!
And never a saint took pity on
My soul in agony.

—Samuel Taylor Coleridge,
The Rime of the Ancient Mariner

When I was nineteen, I got the urge to take up sailplaning. That was when I was trying out all sorts of high-risk sports: rock-climbing, bungee-jumping, mountain snowboarding—anything for that cool adrenaline rush. My dad was willing to bankroll all these short-lived hobbies—maybe he hoped one of them would kill me—so one Saturday morning I went out to Spirit of St. Louis airport and hired a sailplane instructor to take me up in a two-seat glider for an introductory lesson.

The instructor was a cranky old duffer named Ted who didn't like me from the start; he pegged me as a spoiled brat with too much time on my hands, and in retrospect he was probably correct. He didn't mind taking my money, but he didn't want me as a student. So he put me in the front seat of his trainer and, once the tow-plane had taken us up to 3,000 feet and detached the cable, subjected me without warning to stomach-churning aerobatics guaranteed to make sure that he would never see my face again, beginning with a steep, fast dive that gave me another taste of what I had for breakfast.

That's sort of what leaving 4442 Garcia was like.

Through the porthole, I catch a glimpse of the asteroid falling away. My knuckles go white as I clench the armrests; a ghostly hand shoves me back into the padded couch. No turbulence, no sound, only a faint vibration against my back; it's as smooth as if I'm back in Ted's sailplane, yet I'm plummeting into eternity, and it's all I can do to keep dinner in my stomach.

A red bar creeps from left to right across a panel on the dashboard before me: the gee-force indicator, showing that I've gone from zero to one gee in less than sixty seconds. Earth-normal gravity, and I feel like an elephant's sitting on my chest. Another red bar below it steadily moves from right to left: the fuel gauge, telling me that the pod's liquid fuel tanks are quickly being drained.

"Fuel reserves are at fifty percent, Alec," Chip says. "At present rate of consumption, the tanks will be empty in one minute, forty-five seconds."

I manage to force my head up. I can't see Garcia anymore. "How far away are we?" I croak.

"Thirty-five point two-eight kilometers."

Does the asteroid have any defenses? I don't know for certain, and I didn't think to ask Chip. It probably does; Mister Chicago would need some way to protect himself, wouldn't he? If that's so, then someone back there might be able to shoot me down. Up. Whatever.

"Keep going," I hiss. "Fire the engines as long as you can."

"This is not a wise decision, Alec. Once the pod runs out of fuel, you will be unable to maneuver."

He's got a point. I'll need fuel to rendezvous with the ship I'm trying to catch. "Okay . . . cut the engines when we're down to twenty percent."

"Main engine cutoff in one minute."

Gee-force keeps mounting; the indicator tells me I'm already pulling two gees. I shut my eyes and let it push me back against the couch. Pretend it's just a roller coaster, man. Pretend it's the Screaming Eagle at Six Flags. For chrissakes, don't puke!

Have I done the right thing? I could have stayed put on 4442 Garcia; it's close to midnight, and I'm missing the best New Year's blowout I've ever seen. Maybe I'm wrong about Mister Chicago; sure, he's nuts, but I'm his favorite deadhead, after all, aren't I? He wouldn't kill me just for nothing, would he? And maybe I can still patch things up with Shemp, let him know there aren't any hard feelings. I'll stay away from Anna, if that's what this is all about. I could get used to having him as my boss, and mopping the same floors every day isn't all that bad, once you get used to it. But no, Alec . . . you have to do something stupid like steal a spacecraft . . . a god-damn repair pod! . . . and try to jet out to God-knows-where like you're some kinda wannabe Luke Skywalker. Shit, man, what have I *done?*

The vibration suddenly ceases. *Wham!* and I'm thrown forward against the seat harness. Fucking hurts . . .

"Main engine shut-down. Remaining fuel reserves at twenty percent."

Through the porthole, nothing but stars against

the blackness; when I relax my grip on the armrests, my hands float upward of their own accord.

Free fall.

My stomach surges. For a moment I'm sure I'm about to throw up, but I've gotten the worst of it out of my system. I shut my eyes again for a few seconds and remain still, and gradually my guts settle back down. This gives me a little confidence. Look, Ma, I didn't spit up. . . .

"Where are we?" I ask.

"Distance: one hundred five point four eight kilometers from point of departure. Celestial coordinates: X fifteen point seven, Y zero point two seven, Z ninety-two point one two. Azimuth . . ."

"Never mind. Just show me a picture."

The center screen displays a red spot moving in a shallow parabola away from a blue jellybean. Nothing else around: no other asteroids, no other vessels. "Are we on course for rendezvous with that ship?"

"Yes, Alec. The course has been laid into the autopilot."

"So where is it?"

The image expands. 4442 Garcia disappears off the left margin of the screen, and another parabolic line appears near the upper right corner. A blue dot near the right edge of the screen follows the traverse like a marble slowly rolling down a groove.

"This is the vessel you instructed me to intercept," Chip says. A dotted line appears on the screen, tracing a path from the red dot to the blue dot. "Our present distance to the projected rendezvous is thirty thousand, five hundred forty-six point zero one kilometers."

"Cool." I relax a little. "So how long will it take us to get there?"

"At our present velocity of one point one seven kilometers per second, we will reach the rendezvous point in approximately seven hours, twenty-five minutes, twenty-one seconds."

"Umm . . . okay, not bad."

"Alec, your oxygen supply will be consumed in six hours, fifty-four minutes." He pauses. "Incidentally, it is now twenty-four hundred GMT. Happy New Year."

I gape at the screen. I don't fucking believe this. I've managed to leave Mister Chicago's party, walk blindfolded across the habitat, take the cable car up to the hub, steal a spacecraft I barely know how to operate, and escape from the asteroid without being detected . . . and now I'm told that I'll be dead by the time my little EVA pod reaches the intercept point.

"Why the hell didn't you tell me that?" I shout.

"I just did, Alec."

"I mean, *before* we left the asteroid!"

"I attempted to do so, but . . ."

"No, you didn't! You told me that it was okay to . . . !"

Suddenly, I hear my own voice: *"Lay in an intercept course for that ship."*

Chip: *"Alec, the fuel range of this craft is limited to one hundred kilometers . . ."*

"I know. Head for the intercept point."

"Alec, your chances of reaching the intercept point are . . ."

"Just do it! Undock us, fire the engines, and keep firing until the tanks are dry."

"I don't understand, Alec."

"Just do it, Chip. Get me out of here."

"Understood. Launch sequence activated."

I close my eyes. Never try to win an argument with a computer.

"Alec?"

"What is it?"

"I've just received a Priority Alpha-One radio transmission from 4442 Garcia."

Oh, hell. Someone back there just wised up. I open my eyes again. "What does it say?"

"Would you like for me to relay it to you?"

"No thanks, just give me the skinny."

"I don't understand."

"Just tell me what they want."

"The message was transmitted from the colony's traffic control operator. She wants to know if there is anyone aboard this craft. If so, do you request rescue?"

So they've figured out that one of their pods has gone AWOL. Maybe they think the pod was accidentally jettisoned, or something like that. In any case, I'm not so far away from Garcia that they can't send out a ship to pick me up. My luck's getting worse by the minute.

"Do you want me to reply?" Chip asks.

"No. Don't tell them anything. Just shut up."

I need time to think this over.

Not that I've got many options. If I tell them I need to be rescued, then I'll inevitably have to answer to Mister Chicago. No doubt he'll extend to me the same mercy he's given everyone else who's ever crossed him. But if I keep going, my air supply will run out before I rendezvous with that distant ship. So my choice is between having a cerebral aneurysm or asphyxiation. . . .

My eyes fall on the velocity bar. It's holding steady at 1.17 kilometers per second. Just above it, the bar showing my available fuel supply stands at twenty percent.

"Chip," I ask, "if we fire up the engine again and use the rest of the fuel reserves, will that get us to the intercept point any quicker?"

A moment passes. "Yes, Alec. If we were to consume the last fuel reserves, then we would accelerate to three gees before terminal engine cutoff. At one point seven six kilometers per second, we would reach the rendezvous point in four hours, fifty-two minutes, eight seconds."

"But that'll leave us adrift, right?"

"That is correct." While I'm still mulling this over, he adds: "A second message has been received from 4442 Garcia traffic control. She says that a rescue craft is being prepared for launch from the colony, and that we should expect it to come aside us within fifteen minutes. Do you wish to respond?"

"Hell, no." I take a deep breath. "Fire up the engine, Chip. Get us outta here."

"Alec, this is extremely risky . . ."

"Goddammit, I told you to fire the engine! Now do it!"

"As you wish."

Once again, I'm slammed back against my seat. This time, though, I'm not prepared for the sudden thrust. My head connects with the seat back; stars not belonging to this universe scatter before my eyes, then I fall into darkness blacker than space.

Getting knocked out is really beginning to get old.

■　　■　　■

I don't stay KOed for very long. When I come to, the chronometer tells me it's now 00:27:42. I've been out for less than a half-hour.

"Chip?"

"I'm here, Alec."

"What's going on? Where are we?"

"You're in the EVA pod."

Duh. Except for the chronometer reading, nothing's different than it was before . . . except, when I speak, a small cloud of vapor lingers in front of my face before dissipating. My fingers and toes are a bit colder, too. "What happened to the heat?"

"In order to conserve electrical power, I have instructed the pod to readjust the cabin temperature to eighteen degrees Celsius. The pod's batteries have been drained excessively, and I considered this to be a prudent course of action. I'm sorry if this makes you uncomfortable."

"Well . . . okay. If you say so." I've no idea how eighteen degrees Celsius translates into Fahrenheit, and I really don't want to know either. My fingers haven't turned blue, but it's just chilly enough to make me regret dropping my nice, warm robe outside the pod before I climbed in. I tuck my hands under my armpits and cross my ankles together. "So where are we? No, don't give me the coordinates . . . just show it to me on the screen."

The center screen lights up again. The red spot is a little further down the dotted line from where I last saw it and closer to the rendezvous point. The blue dot marking the spacecraft I want to meet is closer as well. Garcia is nowhere in sight. "Did it work?" I ask. "I mean, the engine firing and all that?"

"Yes, Alec. At time of engine burnout, this pod

boosted its velocity to one point seven six kilometers per second. We will successfully reach the intercept point with a little more than one hour of oxygen left in reserve."

"Cool. And the rescue ship from Garcia? What about it?"

"The pod's long-range radar picked up a spacecraft leaving 4442 Garcia shortly after the last ignition. It traveled twenty-five kilometers from the asteroid before it turned around and returned to its departure point. I monitored its transmissions, and noted that its pilot believed that your pod is unpiloted and probably launched by accident. After taking into account your present distance and delta-vee, the asteroid's traffic controller instructed the pilot of the rescue craft to turn back. The rescue attempt has been terminated."

"Yowsah!" I pump my fist in the air. My trick worked: I've outrun the ship sent out to retrieve me, and I'll make the rendezvous point with plenty of air left to . . .

One hour of oxygen.

No fuel left in the tanks.

And I'm whipping through space at nearly two kilometers per second.

Oh, shit.

"Uh, Chip . . ."

"Yes, Alec, I hear you."

"What if . . . um, I mean . . . well, how do I slow down? I mean, to meet the ship?"

"You cannot slow down, Alec."

My heart flutters in my chest. My hands come out from beneath my armpits and grasp the armrests again. "What do you mean, I can't slow down?"

"The only possible way for a spacecraft to

decelerate from your present velocity is for the craft to reverse its major axis and fire its engines in a standard braking maneuver until it matches the velocity of the craft with which it intends to rendezvous. Since the last ignition exhausted your pod's remaining fuel supplies, this is no longer possible."

Right. Of course. I'll reach the intercept point; in fact, I'll be alive and well when my pod rushes past the spaceship I want to meet. See that bit of space junk that just cruised by? That's William Alec Tucker III, on his way to becoming a permanent addition to the asteroid belt. But don't worry, folks. About an hour after he vanishes from sight, his air is going to run out anyway. . . .

No sense in blaming Chip for this, either. He doesn't have to replay our last conversation before I ordered him to make the last engine burn; I remember it all too clearly. He said that this maneuver was "extremely risky"—incredibly fucking stupid, that is—but I ignored his advice and went ahead anyway.

I slam my head back against the seat. Of course. The story of my life . . . indeed, both lives. I died the first time when common sense should have told me not to let Shemp drive my car when he was too fucked up to see straight. Now, I'm going to die again when the nearest thing I've ever had to a guardian angel told me (twice!) that what I was doing was suicidal.

"God," I murmur, "I'm such a stupid asshole."

God lets me dwell on this notion for a few moments. Then He cuts me a break.

"Alec," Chip says, "there is a solution to this problem."

■   ■   ■

After Chip explains it to me, we spend the next four hours hashing out the details. He even concocts an eyes-up simulation which I use as a dress rehearsal, even though we both know that I'll only get one shot at this, and it's a long one at that. By the time the red spot and the blue spot on the screen are close to convergence, I'm ready to go.

Tucked beneath the pilot seat is a small, tightly wrapped bundle: an emergency one-time-use space-suit. When I pull it out of its envelope, I nearly abandon the plan right then and there. The suit is a black, one-piece outfit that looks and feels like a plastic body stocking; it reminds me of one of those cheap pocket raincoats you used to be able to buy for a couple of bucks at Woolworth's. Chip explains that this skinsuit is woven from molecular polycarbon filaments; it seems flimsy, but it's capable of holding an internal atmosphere, keeping me warm, and resisting cosmic background radiation. A locker above the hatch contains a fishbowl helmet, a life-support unit not much larger than a daypack, and a reaction-control system that faintly resembles an old Super Soaker. Chip assures me that everything will work as advertised.

I strip off my clothes and pull on the skinsuit. It's so thin, I feel my muscles through its fabric; the gloves are supple enough that I could flip a penny between my fingers. The life-support pack nestles against my back with a set of shoulder and chest straps; I can't find any air hoses, but when Chip tells me to reach over my shoulder and touch a pair of studs on the pack's top surface, I feel a vague sucking sensation between my shoulder blades as tiny apertures between the suit and the pack meet and seal themselves. Chip informs me that the suit will absorb carbon dioxide from my breath and oxygen from my sweat and the unit will recombine them as breathable air. In the inner solar system, the suit would have been powered by solar radiation and kept me alive almost indefinitely; out here in the Belt, though, it has to draw its energy from internal batteries. The suit's good for three hours; by then, I'll either have been rescued, or I'll be contemplating the prospect of becoming a frozen corpse real soon now.

By now, the pod is less than thirty minutes away from the intercept point. My movements within the cabin have caused it to slowly tumble end over end through space; through the porthole, stars revolve as if I'm inside a cosmic laundry dryer. There's just enough residual fuel left in the tanks for me, under Chip's eyes-up guidance, to fire the reaction-control rockets one last time; that stops the tumble and reorients the porthole toward our plotted trajectory. Chip has already told the pod to start transmitting mayday signals on all frequencies, along with a message informing the crew of the oncoming spacecraft that they should be on the lookout for a man wearing a survival suit.

I pull the fishbowl over my head. When I seal the neck flap, tiny gold lights light up across my chest and down my arms and legs. I look like I'm ready to go to a disco. Stayin' alive, stayin' alive . . .

I'm about to abandon ship, but it won't be through the hatch. If I tried it that way, I'd only go into orbit around the pod, and that's no good because the pod will soon overshoot the rendezvous point. No, Chip has better plans for me than that.

Here comes the scary part.

Once I've strapped myself back on the couch, Chip voids the pod's atmosphere. When the pressure gauge stands at zero, I kick the dashboard away from my knees and reach up to a tiger-striped panel above my head.

I pull it open, take a deep breath, swear at Dad one last time for getting me into this mess, then toggle a switch marked *Emrg. Ejct.*

The porthole silently blows away.

The couch jettisons into space.

I scream bloody murder.

Hurtling through black void streaked with the tracer fire of stars turned comets, stomach rebelling, eyes shutting, Chip telling me to unbuckle the seat harness, get out, get out, get out now right now Alec get out right now

Alec, detach the seat harness at once. Do you understand? Detach seat harness NOW.

as I blindly fumble at the catches at my chest and groin until they pop open and suddenly the couch falls away and now that I open my eyes and see

the pod racing away into eternity

and

the couch receding behind me

and

stars here   stars there

and

darkness everywhere

and

that's when I scream for damn sure.

The pod has vanished. The couch has vanished. I'm alone in the void, my arms and legs outstretched, pinwheeling through dark vacuum.

Alone.

No friends. No family. No enemies. No sound. The only light comes from places thousands and millions of years in the past. Except for the Sun, an inflamed pimple in the cosmos.

I'm alive, and I'm dead.

Tears detach themselves from the corners of my eyes, spot the inside of my helmet like sour raindrops.

I wait to die.

Then a dark mass occultates the stars.

At first, it looks like an irregular hole has opened in space.

Then it becomes a black barbell with little sparks coming off its edges.

It resolves itself into a spaceship: a drum-shaped forward section with little windows through which I glimpse the faintest hint of motion, an open cradle in a narrow center section where large gold lozenges are held down by folded arms, a rear section comprised of enormous cylindrical fuel tanks, leading to five engines.

At first, it comes slowly.

Then it rushes straight at me like a freight train on a midnight track.

Remembering the reaction-control gun strapped to my wrist, I twist around and fire it behind me. It sends me flailing toward the vessel.

Chip goes eyes-up; he paints an X in the middle of my field of vision. I aim the Super Soaker and fire it at its center. When I twist around again, the enormous ship is almost on top of me.

I aim the reaction gun between my legs and give it one quick burst. It's just enough to save me from being pulverized; now the ship is just below me.

I fall toward the ship, and as I reach for thin metal flanges along its hull, I catch a fleeting glimpse of human movement within its forward windows—someone staring up at me—then I grab hold of something, but I can't hang on, and I'm sent rolling across the hull like a pinball being kicked between bumpers.

Warning lights flash in my helmet. I look up just in time to see an antenna mast. I duck my head and it spirals past me, and when I look around again, there's the edge of a large cradle gaping open below me. I grab something with both hands, hang on tight as my legs flop over the lip of the cradle.

Then my legs float upward and my arms stop screaming. I've matched the ship's momentum.

Looking down, I see a row of ladder rungs leading down into the cargo bay. I grab one of them, hang on for dear life, then begin making my way, hand over hand, toward a hatch in the rear of the forward section.

When I'm a little closer to the hatch, lights come on in the bay. I'm dazzled for a moment and squint against the glare. When my eyes readjust, I look down and see a sign painted above the hatch just below me:

WATCH YOUR STEP

"You've gotta be shitting me," I murmur.

I make my way the rest of the way down the ladder until I reach the hatch. The locklever twists easily, counterclockwise; I pull the hatch open, haul myself through, turn around, and yank the hatch shut.

I'm now inside a tiny compartment. Chip tells me how to operate the control panel next to the hatch; I follow his instructions.

The compartment begins to revolve end over end. Once more, I'm bashed against a wall, but this time there're plenty of handholds. I grab one and hang on, and after awhile I get used to gravity again. It's not much of a pull, but just enough to make me wish that I hadn't watched so many people eating food earlier this long night. I just collapse on the floor and wait for the room to stop spinning.

There's an inner hatch, but I don't have to open it; it unseals the moment a green light flashes on the control panel. I look up to see two enormous blue eyes within a pair of butterfly wings staring down at me.

Then the razor-sharp tip of a rapier jabs my chest.

"Who are you?" a woman's voice demands.

Oh, Christ. A Superior.

Of all the ships I have to find in the Belt, it has to be one run by a goddamn Superior.

SEVENTEEN

FEELING GRAVITY'S PULL

Ah, my Beloved, fill the Cup that clears
To-Day of past Regrets and future Fears—
To-morrow? —Why, To-morrow I may be
Myself with Yesterday's Sev'n Thousand Years.

—The Rubaiyat of Omar Khayyam

I'm not adverse to picking up floaters, but I've really got to know what you were doing out there."

The Superior has let me get up on my knees and take off my helmet, but her rapier is still drawn. It isn't just the fact that she's a Superior that surprises me: six feet tall, thin as a rail, blond hair cut to the scalp in front but long and braided in the back, her arms, face, and neck completely covered with tattoos. No, what gets me is that she speaks Primary, not the strange patois that makes most Superiors sound like Yoda. For once, Chip doesn't have to flash me an eyes-up translation.

"You sure don't sound like any google I've ever heard," I say, dropping the helmet next to me.

Butterfly wings furl over owlish blue eyes. "And you're about ten seconds away from being marched back into the airlock," she replies. The rapier's sharp tip inches a little closer. "I'm counting."

Whoops. Forgot that Superiors don't appreciate that nickname. "Sorry," I say quickly. "Didn't mean it that way. Just haven't met too many Superiors who speak like . . . y'know . . ."

"Apes?" I think I'm supposed to be outraged; when I'm not, she gives me a quizzical look. "I'm beginning to wonder myself how many Superiors you've met."

"Not many." I glance at the rapier. "Look, I'd like to get off the floor now, if you don't mind. Want to put that thing away?"

"No and no." She touches her jaw with her free hand. "Rohr? He's aboard. Just came through the carousel. Got him in the secondary suit compartment." She listens for a moment. "Copy that. Don't take your time."

"The captain?"

"My first officer. He'll be down shortly."

I glance around the compartment. Not much to describe—suit lockers, racked air tanks, some cabinets—except that there's only three helmets on a shelf above the suit lockers. Odd; from what little I know about Superiors, their ships are usually crewed by clans with no fewer than nine members. Of course, there could be other airlocks. . . .

"Want to tell me your name?" she asks.

"Alec Tucker. William Alec Tucker." I give her an easy smile. "You can call me Alec."

She isn't buying it. "What ship are you from, William Alec Tucker? What's your position?"

"On my knees right now." I raise my palms. "Look, lady, you see me carrying a gun? If you'd just let me get up . . ."

I start to shift my left leg; the rapier moves a little closer, and I freeze. "I'm asking the questions, Mess'r Tucker. What ship are you . . . ?"

"Aw, give him a chance to answer, will'ya?"

The voice—oddly accented, sort of a cross between English and Southern—comes from the ceiling hatch behind her. Its owner begins descending the ladder from the deck above. He's a tall, middle-aged gent with a sunburned face and graying blond hair, and that's my second surprise: I've never heard of any Superior ships with Primaries as first officers.

He stops at the bottom of the ladder and leans against it unsteadily. "All right, let's get acquainted. You're aboard the TBSA *Comet*. I'm Rohr Furland, the first officer, and this is Jeri Lee-Bose, my captain. Now who the hell are you?"

"Says his name is William Alec Tucker," Jeri Lee-Bose answers for me, still not lowering her rapier. "He won't tell me what ship he's from or his position. And he called me a google."

Furland scowls. "That's a serious charge, boy. Google's a word that's not allowed on this ship . . ."

"I'm sorry. Just a slip of the tongue, that's all." I glance from Furland to Jeri. "You heard me say I was . . ."

"Never mind. You're . . ." He belches into his fist; I catch a boozy whiff of his breath. That clinches it. If the first officer's crocked, then this can't be a Superior ship; they don't allow alcohol aboard their vessels. He glances at the captain. "C'mon, put that thing away already. If he's a pirate, he's the dumbest one I've ever heard of."

"I'm not a pirate." Who's in charge here, anyway?

"No kidding. You're too stupid to be a pirate." He runs a hand through his short-cropped hair as Jeri reluctantly slides the rapier into a sheath on her belt. "Unless, of course, this is some sort of diversion. If it is, it's the strangest one I've ever heard of. What happened to the boat you transmitted that mayday from?"

"I ejected from it. It was out of fuel and almost out of air, so this was the only way I could reach you."

"Out of air *and* fuel?" The two of them exchange incredulous looks; Furland shakes his head. "What kind of ship runs out of consumables in the middle of the Belt?"

"A pretty small one. It was an EVA pod."

Jeri's mouth drops open; Furland sags against a bulkhead and laughs out loud. "Elvis! You *are* the stupidest pirate I've ever heard of . . ."

"I'm telling you, I'm not a—"

"Okay, all right. I believe you."

"I'm not sure I do." Jeri Lee-Bose's spidery left hand lingers on the pommel of her sword. "It could be a setup, Rohr. They launch a pod with one guy aboard to send out a mayday to distract us, and while we're dealing with him, they sneak up on us with another ship."

"Relax. I checked the screens before I left the bridge. There's no other vessels within five hundred kilos." He looks away from us. "Brain? Any ships in the vicinity?"

An androgynous voice replies from nowhere: "No, Rohr. Except for the EVA pod Mr. Tucker described, there are no other spacecraft within interception range. Mr. Tucker's pod is one hundred and seven kilometers from us and receding."

"Thanks." Furland looks at the captain and shrugs. "Guess that settles it. He's an idiot, but he's not a pirate."

I'm not crazy about the character assessment, but under the circumstances I'm not about to argue. "That's your . . . um, AI? Brain, I mean?"

"The Brain's our AI, yes." Jeri has removed her hand from her sword. "You sound like you've never heard one before."

Lady, if only you knew. But I don't want to get into that just now. "I'll tell you later. If you don't mind, I'd like to get up now. Maybe get this suit off, too, if that's not a problem."

Furland grins at me. "Sure, if you can think of the proper way to ask permission from the captain."

I look back at Jeri Lee-Bose. "Umm . . . may I please get off the floor and remove my suit?"

"Getting smarter all the time," Furland murmurs.

Jeri nods. "Permission granted, Mess'r Tucker. Rohr, if you'll escort our guest to the passenger cabin and give him some clothes?"

"Copy that, chief." He turns to the ladder. "After that, I'll take him to the wardroom."

"Going to finish your little party now?" she asks, a little coldly.

"Nope. Party's over. Time to start the new century." He starts climbing the ladder. "C'mon, Tucker. We'll get you a change of clothes and fix a pot of coffee, then you can tell us how you came to be here. Can't wait to hear how you managed to wind up in a pod with no fuel or air."

He pauses at the top of the hatch to look down at me. "But if I were you, I wouldn't get rid of that skinsuit. You're not off the hook yet."

■   ■   ■

Although the TBSA *Comet* is larger than the *Anakuklesis*, its living quarters are small and cramped; its narrow main passageway winds around the inside of a drumlike centrifuge. At one-sixth gravity, it's lighter than I'm used to on the asteroid. Furland doesn't say anything, but he notices when I stumble over myself in the narrow corridor. I'm grateful when he slides open the door of a tiny compartment no larger than a jail cell and leaves me alone for a minute.

A white one-piece jumpsuit hangs inside a tiny closet across from a fold-down bed, along with a pair of stikshoes. I peel off the skinsuit and try on the jumpsuit and the shoes. The jumpsuit is tight, its sleeves and ankles a little too short; the stikshoes are a size too small. When I complain about this to Chip, he tells me to relax and stand still; as if by magic, the suit and shoes seem to stretch themselves until they meet my dimensions. More wonders of the twenty-first century—excuse me, the twenty-second century. I guess tailors are obsolete now.

"Okay, Chip," I say softly, "where am I?"

"You are aboard the TBSA *Comet*," Chip replies.

"I know that already. What is it?"

"Please wait. I must access this vessel's primary AI interface."

A few seconds go by as Chip introduces himself to the Brain. They shake hands, have a couple of drinks, swap a few jokes, and do whatever it is that AIs and MINNs do when they meet the first time. Chip finally comes back to me: "Most of the *Comet*'s primary AI interface—"

"The Brain, you mean."

"Yes. Most of the Brain's higher memory functions are security coded, so I cannot access them without clearance from the captain. However, I can tell you that the TBSA *Comet* is an *Ares*-class asteroid freighter, registry number MAF–1675. It is a registered vessel in the Transient Body Shipping Association, and is based at Lagrange Four in the Pax Astra. Its crew complement consists of Jeri Lee-Bose, captain and ship owner, and Rohr Furland, first officer and ship owner. Its current cargo manifest includes refined asteroid materials, including—"

"Never mind. Where did it come from, and where is it going?"

"The TBSA *Comet* left Ceres Station on December 6, 2099, Gregorian. It is scheduled to arrive at Lagrange Four on October 9, 2100."

"Where . . . I mean what . . . is Lagrange Four?"

"Lagrange Four, also known as Highgate, is an interplanetary shipping port located in a Lagrangian halo orbit near the Moon. It services spacecraft belonging to the Pax Astra and its trading partners, and—"

"Whoa. Hold on. Is that near Clarke County?"

"Clarke County is located at Lagrange Five." Chip goes eyes-up to show me a map; the L4 and L5 points are located at the far tips of two adjacent triangles, with Earth and the Moon positioned at the opposite ends of the shared leg. "Although both Highgate and Clarke County oscillate in halo orbits, their average distance is approximately three million kilometers. Each station is located nearly one million five hundred thousand kilometers from Earth."

I whistle under my breath. Three million kilometers are three million kilometers; compared to three hundred sixteen million miles, though, it's a walk around the block. Spend nearly a year in the Belt, and you start thinking in very large terms. "And the Immortality Partnership was located in Clarke County?"

"The last known location of the Immortality Partnership was in Clarke County. However, following the company's bankruptcy, its remaining assets have been relocated elsewhere in near-Earth space. That location is unknown."

There's a knock on the door, followed by the first officer's voice: "Whatever you're doing in there, cut it out. The captain wants to see you right now."

"Be right there." I triple-blink and the map vanishes. All right, so I've lucked out: the freighter I flagged down is headed right to where I want to go. Now it's time to try to convince these two characters not to pitch me out the airlock . . . not until we reach the Pax, at least.

The wardroom is located down the corridor from my room, and it looks like Furland has been holding his own little New Year's party. The walls are hung with paper streamers, and two wine bottles—one empty, the other half-full—stand in the middle of the table. When Furland leads me into the compartment, though, the captain has already arrived and has made a pot of coffee. Sitting at the opposite end of the table, she watches as the first officer pushes a mug in my hand, then slouches into a chair next to me. He takes a noisy slurp from his own mug and makes a face.

"Jeri, this coffee's not going to do the trick. Wanna fetch me a soberup from sickbay?" Jeri casts me one last, mistrustful look, then silently gets up and leaves the room.

"Funny way to run a ship," I murmur. "Who's in charge here, you or her?"

"We both are. As you can probably tell, we don't stand much on formality round here." Furland peers at me with bleary eyes. "Okay, start talking. Where are you from, and how did you get here?"

"It's kind of a long story . . ."

"I got time." He yawns. "Not a lot of patience, maybe, but time."

I sip my coffee and wince; it tastes like boiled ink. Guess I've gotten spoiled on better stuff. "Ever heard of a guy named Mister Chicago?"

"Pasquale Chicago? Who hasn't?" He yawns again, this time managing to cover his mouth. "What's this got to do with him?"

"I'm running away from him." Furland stops yawning in mid-gape. In fact, it looks as if the caffeine just kicked in; his eyes go almost as wide as the captain's. "See, I stole that EVA pod from his asteroid just a few hours ago, and—"

"Hold on. Wait a minute. You just stole a pod from Pasquale Chicago . . . you're trying to get away from him . . . and now you're on my ship?"

"That about sizes it up, yeah."

"Oh, hell . . ." He puts the mug down on the table and wipes his hands across his eyes.

"I'm sorry about this. If I had known . . ."

My voice trails off. Of course I couldn't have known . . . whatever it is that I'm supposed to know.

Furland lifts his face from his hands. "Okay, I take it back. I don't have plenty of time, and neither do you." He jabs a finger at me. "You've got two minutes to give me one good reason why we shouldn't jettison your sorry ass."

He's not joking. He'll actually do it. If he didn't believe his captain when she brought up the notion that I was in cahoots with pirates, then he's dead serious about the prospect of shielding a fugitive from Pasquale Chicago.

So I start talking as fast as I can.

I have to start from the beginning, though, so it takes longer than two minutes. While I'm still explaining how I awoke in a white room with no real memory of who I was or how I came to be there, Jeri Lee-Bose returns to the wardroom. The captain listens while she sticks two adhesive patches on either side of Furland's neck, then places a cup of water in front of him. I've just made it to the part where Mister Chicago killed John when the first officer turns green; he stands up quickly and hastily exits the compartment. The captain lets me hold that thought and help myself to a refill from the coffee maker, and presently the first mate returns from the head, looking a little pale but much more sober. He resumes his place at the table and tells me to finish. About ten minutes have gone past by then, but the captain's still wearing her rapier, and the distance between the wardroom and the airlock isn't very large.

When I'm finally done, the two of them are silent for a long time before either one speaks. Finally, Jeri turns to me. "You know what kind of position this puts us in, don't you?"

I start to nod, but change my mind and shake my head instead.

"Pasquale Chicago is the most powerful person in the outer system," she says. "Not only does he own the biggest shipping fleet in the Belt, but he also controls the largest voting block in the TBSA, along with the majority of shares. The association holds the lien on this ship, which means that he could have the *Comet* repossessed and scuttled."

Furland clears his throat. "That's not all. You know about the Zodiac, right?" I do, of course, but feigning ignorance seems to be to my advantage, so I just shrug. "Well, the Zodiac is the most powerful organization in the Belt. Forget the Pax and the Ares Alliance . . . out here, the Zodiac rules. And make no mistake . . . Pasquale Chicago is the Zodiac, and the Zodiac is Pasquale Chicago." He snaps his fingers. "Word of this gets out, and Jeri and I can disappear like that. No one would know."

He sighs, rubbing his eyelids with his fingertips. "Wish I'd stayed drunk. Might have made this decision a little easier to make."

Despite the warm coffee mug in my hands, I suddenly feel a chill. "What do you mean? You're going to put me out the airlock?"

He glances at Jeri. "Much as I'm tempted to do so," she murmurs, "that's something I can't do. Not if I wish to sleep well."

"It might not be as risky as we think." Furland gets up and goes to pour himself some coffee. "If they're tracking the pod, then they might think Tucker . . ."

"Alec."

" . . . Alec is still aboard. It might not occur to them that he bailed out or that we rescued him."

"I tend to agree." I'm surprised to see a smile on her face. "I've got to admit, that was quite an armstrong you pulled, especially for someone with no previous flying experience. How did it occur to you to do this?"

"A little voice told me." I'm not about to let on about Chip. He's my ace in the hole.

"Oh? A little voice, is it?" Her enormous eyes triple-blink, then she raises her mug to her lips, but doesn't take a sip. Chip suddenly goes eyes-up on me:

COMLINK MESSAGE RECEIVED:
Is this your little voice, Alec?

Shit. She's figured it out, and managed to use the Brain to access Chip. "How did you know?"

Furland glances from me to her in confusion. "Backslash that?"

"He's wearing a MINN," Jeri replies. "In fact, he's already used it to tap into the Brain. I just sent him an eyes-up message by the same route." She looks back at me. "Rohr overheard you talking to someone in your cabin. I had a hunch you might have an associate, so I confirmed it with the Brain while I was getting a soberup. I also had him access your MINN and run a memory scan. He's fresh apples."

"Nice to know." Furland frowns at me. "Anything else you want to tell us, Mess'r Tucker? So far I've kinda liked you, but I hate it when people I take into our home start keeping secrets from us. Makes me not want to trust them."

My face warms. "Nothing else. Sorry. I just didn't know whether I should trust you, either."

"Hmm. Guess I shouldn't blame you, considering." He takes another sip from his mug, grimaces, and stands up to reheat what's left with a top-off from the pot. How they can drink this stuff is beyond me. "Is Chicago as crazy as everyone says he is?"

"I dunno. Craziest dude I've ever met, if that's what you're asking. Or at least as nuts as some of the Superiors he hangs out with. They're . . ."

Jesus. I keep forgetting who I'm with. "Sorry," I add quickly, glancing at the captain. "Didn't mean it that way."

She shakes her head, a gesture I've never seen any other Superior make. "Don't worry about it. Most of my fellow googles think I'm insane for marrying an ape."

Married? Oh, boy, this is new . . . although it explains a lot. Furland reads the expression on my face; he gives me a rueful smile. "Jeri was expelled from her clan for consorting with Primaries. Superiors can be pretty icy about these things. So can baseliners, for that matter. The *Comet*'s the only TBSA ship that would take her as a crewman. It used to belong to someone else who was even more crazy, but when he died and left it to her . . ."

"What Superiors were you referring to?" Jeri interrupts, almost as if she's dodging the subject. "Anyone in particular?"

"Well, there was one who didn't like me much. Guy by the name of Vladimir Algol-Raphael . . ."

Both of them nearly drop their mugs. "You met Vladimir Algol-Raphael?" Jeri demands.

"Well, yeah. In fact, he damn near killed me the first time we met." I tell them about how Vlad the Impaler drew his rapier on me in the cable car, and about all the petty humiliations I endured from him afterward. Furland laughs when I get to the part about almost tricking him to eat meat during the party, but Jeri's face is somber.

"You're very lucky to be alive," she says when I'm finished. "Vladimir leads the most powerful clan in the Belt, and the Algol clan is at the forefront of the Omega Point movement. None of the other clans dare cross him. I would be thankful to your friend for stopping him from killing you."

I'm not ready to thank Shemp for anything except unwittingly giving me a chance to escape. "What's this about an Omega Point? I mean, I heard it mentioned a couple of times, and Pasquale has an omega sign in the floor of the hall of his castle."

"It's difficult to explain." She sits down, easily folding her double-jointed legs in a yoga position. "Superiors are raised to believe in the philosophy of extropy. That is, humankind has the capability of resisting the natural laws of entropy, and that we've already started to do so through planetary colonization, nanotech, neurosuspension, and so forth. The fact that Superiors are the result of genengineering is regarded as the highest expression of this principle, and most Superiors regard themselves as the next stage in evolution."

"But you don't."

A smile flickers across her face. "Actually, I do. But I'm a little different from most of my fellows. I believe we should help our poor, unfortunate *Homo sapiens* cousins, and not simply cast ourselves apart." She winks at Furland. "I'm better than my husband, and not only because I'm female. I just don't rub it in."

Rohr coughs in his hand. "As she never stops reminding me."

"I forgive you, love. You can't help being an ape." Jeri reaches across the table to give him a forgiving pat on the hand, then she returns her attention to me. "Extropism isn't a religion, but in the last few years several clans—the Algols among them—have embraced the idea that biogenic evolution isn't the final stage of extropism, and that the conquest of death itself is the ultimate objective."

"Thought you achieved that already," I say. "Look at me."

"Neurosuspension is only a temporary solution, and only a crude one at that. Or at least that's the way they see it." She leans back in her chair, picks up her coffee mug with the elongated toes of her left foot, and passes it to her right hand. I've seen Superiors do this before, but it still gave me the willies. "They believe that, at the end of time, when the universe has collapsed into much the same primordial state that preceded the Big Bang, all souls who have ever lived will be reincarnated at the creation of the next universe. That moment is called the Omega Point."

Furland makes a flatulent sound with his lips. "Mouseshit."

"Can't say I disagree," I add, and he gives me a thumb's-up.

Jeri ignores him and gives me a querulous look. "I rather thought you might be familiar with this," she says. "The Omega Point Theory was developed in the late twentieth century, about the same time as extropism."

"News to me. Never heard of either of 'em." I watch as she uses her right foot to place the mug back on the table. Sooner or later, I'll get used to this. "All

I know is, Mister Chicago made a speech during the party about leading humankind to some final destiny at the Omega Point."

"Really? And you say he had an omega sign on the floor of his castle?" I nod, and she pensively cups her hands together beneath her chin. "That's disturbing. The Omega Point Theory has been embraced by only a few clans. If Pasquale Chicago believes this, and he's allied himself with the Algol clan . . ."

She doesn't finish the thought; she stares pensively at her coffee mug. I point to a half-empty wine bottle on the table. Both of them nod and I reach for it; I need something a little stronger than coffee right now. "One more thing," I add. "The time we were in the elevator, Mister C said something to Vlad about some kind of a project. I dunno what it is, but it has to do with all the deadheads he's been reviving. Any clue what he might have meant?"

Furland shakes his head; he looks queasy when he sees me slug back some wine. "Nyet. Nobody knows what Chicago or the Zodiac are going to do until they do it. His asteroid is off-limits to anyone who isn't given express permission to dock there . . . though I'm sure the Pax would be interested in anything you want to tell it."

"And I wouldn't go to them, if I were you." Jeri raises her head. "First, you'd have to explain what you were doing on Garcia in the first place, and that means admitting you're a deadhead. Otherwise they'll believe you're a defecting Zodiac member."

"Yeah? So?"

She frowns. "If they believe you're a Zodiac member, they'll lock you up on general principles and think of charges later. And even if they believe that you're a revived deadhead who's managed to escape, then they'll do the same thing. Either way, they'll likely turn you over to Pax Intelligence, and you'll be interrogated until you drop dead."

I shrug. "Been there, done that. Doesn't hurt much after the first few minutes."

Furland gives me a cold look. "Kiddo, don't screw with the Pax . . . especially not with Intelligence. They're not very nice to their own citizens. That's why Jeri and I stay out here in the Belt. And they're ruthless when it comes to the Zodiac." He points a finger at me. "Trust me on this one. The next time someone lops off your head, you might be alive for the experience."

The mouthful of wine I've just taken suddenly tastes vile. I swallow it with an effort and put down the bottle. "Okay, then . . . where does that leave you and me?"

The captain looks across the table at her first mate. A moment of silent communication: these two have been together so long that Jeri has stopped talking like a Superior and Rohr can read the mind behind the butterfly mask. Their partnership would have put my parents' marriage to shame.

"Here's the deal," Jeri says at last. "We'll get you to Highgate—"

"Clarke County."

"Clarke County? That's the Pax government center."

"I have to get to Clarke County. I need to find somebody there."

They look at me strangely; I shake my head. "I'll explain it later. Believe me, it doesn't involve you . . . but I have to get to Clarke County."

Furland glances again at Jeri. She shakes her head. "Highgate," she says. "That's where the *Comet* usually moors. If we request permission to dock at Clarke County, too many questions will be raised. Freighters usually don't moor there."

"But we can arrange for you to get from Highgate to the County," Furland quickly adds. "At least that'll get you into Pax space. After that, we'll cut you loose. You're on your own."

Not much a choice, but the only one I have. "Okay. So what's the rub?"

"The rub?"

"Umm . . . the string? The other shoe?" Both of them look bewildered. "What do I got to do?"

The captain smiles. She settles back in her chair, folding her hands and feet together. "Well," she says, "our usual passenger fee is five hundred kilolox . . ."

"I don't have that."

"Coincidentally, our usual pay rate for an unrated crewman also comes to about five hundred kilolox. This includes cabin, meals, air, water . . ."

"Okay, I get it. What do you want me to do first?"

"Oh, nothing right now." The captain stretches, then pushes back her chair and stands up. "Your first duty is to return to your cabin and get some sleep. The Brain will call you at first watch and tell you what to do. Rohr?"

"Well . . ." The first mate looks around, then rises to follow his captain to the door. "I understand you're pretty good at cleaning."

"Umm . . . yeah?"

He waves at the mess he's left behind. "You start tomorrow, with this compartment." He grins. "And, by the way . . . Happy New Year."

The door closes behind them, leaving me alone in a trashed wardroom. I sigh, and reach for the bottle.

Might as well not let it go to waste.

✝ CHAPTER ✝

EIGHTEEN

BETWEEN PLANETS

A coward dies a thousand deaths.
A brave man dies but once.

—Medgar Evers

And this was how, on the first day of the twenty-second century, I became second mate of the TBSA *Comet*.

The rank, of course, was as fictitious as my traveling name. Since Jeri would have to account for my being aboard her vessel, and it was too risky for me to travel under my own name, she picked a name out of thin air—John Ulnar, a character from a space adventure from the early twentieth century that she was shocked to learn I hadn't read—and temporarily gave me the position of second officer. If anyone asked, the story would be that she hired Ulnar as a temporary crewmember just before the *Comet* left Ceres, and that Ulnar's final destination was Clarke County. The union had rules against this sort of thing, but apparently it was done often enough that no one in the TBSA looked twice, so long as a few kilolox made their way into the proper hands.

But being the second mate was much less glamorous than it sounds. A spaceship quickly becomes a smelly, dirty place during a long voyage. Sweat, dandruff, carbon dioxide, and dust conspire to make bulkheads grimy and table surfaces greasy; if left unchecked, the living quarters soon reek like an outhouse. Despite dehumidifiers, water vapor can seep into microcircuitry and thousands of miles of electric cable, causing shortouts. There were two heads aboard the ship which had to be cleaned every day, and one of them was in the bridge, where there wasn't any gravity; if you've never experienced the wonder and joy of a zero-gee toilet, let me introduce you to my friend Mr. Sponge. There were no mops or buckets aboard the *Comet*—too wasteful of water—but there were plenty of disinfectant pads in the storage compartment. If anyone asked me how I made my way across the solar system, I could safely say that it was on my hands and knees.

But it wasn't an unpleasant trip. I was used to dirty work by now, and Jeri and Rohr weren't Mister Chicago and Shemp. After the first few days, they realized that they didn't have to order me to do anything; once I learned the ropes, I went about my daily tasks without them having to tell me to do so. It helped to have Chip linked with the Brain, because if I had any questions, my MINN would consult the AI, and they would give me a quick reply. And as tedious as my chores were, at least I didn't have to worry about getting a migraine if I screwed up; it's amazing how self-motivated a former slave can be, when he knows the whip has disappeared for good. This came as a surprise to Rohr and Jeri; they had given up on hiring temps as second officers because most of them usually did as little as they could get away with, and had tried for the last few voyages to rely on robots and their own efforts. The *Comet* had never looked or smelled so good before I came aboard. By the end of the third day, I was on a first-name basis with both of them, and after a week they stopped regarding me as a shiftless castaway and accepted me as a member of the crew.

Once I got bulkhead-scrubbing and toilet-sponging down to a fine art, I soon discovered that I had plenty of free time on my hands . . . and this time, I didn't have to hide from a Main Brain that monitored my every waking moment. At first, I was wary about probing the ship's library systems on my eyes-up display, until Jeri herself laughingly told me that it was okay; if there were any vital secrets, she said, the Brain would tell me, and as it turned out the only information to which I was denied access was the ship's financial records. So I spent a lot of off-duty time in the wardroom, drinking coffee—which, by the way, tasted a hell of a lot better once I started cleaning out the brewer once a week—while filling in the gaps of the last century's history that I hadn't learned while on 4442 Garcia.

I also read novels, poetry, essays, anything I could find in the Brain's library that looked interesting. I've never been much of a reader, but nine months cooped up in a spaceship solves that pretty quickly. I also began writing a memoir of my experiences, storing it in an unused section of Chip's onboard memory. At first I tried dictating the whole thing, but then Chip downloaded a seldom-used word-processing program from the Brain; with a few adjustments, this gave me an eyes-up keyboard I could use by hunting-and-pecking my fingers in midair.

If boredom was a problem, it didn't last. We'd just passed the orbit of Mars when something happened that once again reminded me just how dangerous the future had become.

I'm in the wardroom one afternoon, idly moving text around with my forefinger. Jeri's sitting across the table from me, eating an early dinner. Rohr's standing watch in the bridge, and she's slated to relieve him in a few minutes. She asks me to fetch her another cup of coffee from the brewer behind me, but I don't hear her at first; I'm monkeying around with different fonts, and her request goes unacknowledged. After the third try, she picks up one of her chopsticks and wings it at me.

I've barely caught the sudden motion out of the corner of my eye when

WARNING!

my left hand darts up and plucks the chopstick out of the air. The next instant

AUTODEFENSE MODE!

I've somersaulted backward out of my chair, landing on the floor in a crouch, my hands balled into fists: heart pumping, nerves electric, blood turned to ice water.

Jeri stares at me in astonishment. "What did you just do?"

I let out my breath. "Back down, Chip," I whisper. "False alarm." I feel my body slowly relax; I'm hot all over, my forehead clammy with sweat. I stand straight and look apologetically at the broken chopstick in my right hand. "Sorry about that. It's something Mister Chicago did to me."

"Your associate has an autodefense system?"

Now it's my turn to be surprised. "You've heard of it?"

She nods. "Pax soldiers were retrofitted with it during the System War. In their case, the process involved surgical implantation of MINNs in their brains and biochemical cartridges in their necks. Helped the Royal Militia win the ground war on Mars, but it burned out a lot of soldiers. Mister Chicago must have figured out how to put it in his deadheads . . . sleepers, I mean. Sorry."

I shrug it off. If she can get over being called a google, I can live with being called a deadhead. "But Superiors don't have it?"

She shakes her head. "Not first-gens like me. We have associates, but autodefense technology didn't come till later."

"This has only happened once before." I pick up my chair, sit down again, tell her about the time Vladimir Algol-Raphael pulled his rapier on me. "I took a cut across the arm, but at least it saved me from getting killed." I pick up the broken chopstick, drop it on the table. "Guess Chip misinterpreted this as an attack. Sorry."

"Not your fault. You can't help it." She picks up the two halves of the chopstick and idly plays with them. "That can be a useful talent, if you can learn how to control it. The Pax can be quite dangerous."

"Yeah, well, if someone ever throws a chopstick at me again, I'll know exactly what to do."

Jeri's lips purse thoughtfully. She pushes back her chair and, without another word, leaves the compartment. When she comes back, she's carrying two rapiers.

"If you're going to defend yourself," she says, laying one on the table before me, "you should learn how to do it right."

I stare at the sword. "Aw, c'mon, Jeri, I've never picked up one of these things in my life. . . ."

"Not an excuse. Everyone else has." She unsheathes her own rapier and hoists the blade before her. "The art of swordsmanship was rediscovered during the System War, during close-quarter combat within ships and habitats. Bullets ricochet, tasers don't work against hardsuits, blasters cause blowouts . . . but a good sword in a well-trained hand is as deadly as any gun. Where you're going, everyone carries them."

I reluctantly pick up the rapier. "Look, Jeri, I know you mean well, but . . . y'know, I'm a peaceful kinda guy. I'd just as soon try to get through life without sticking this in someone."

She nods. "I know exactly what you mean, Alec. Believe me, I'm a pacifist by nature. There's nothing I'm less willing to do than kill another person."

She slowly lowers her rapier until it's pointed straight at my face. Her dark eyes stare at me down its long, slender shaft. "Yet you can't count on the other person feeling the same way, and a broken chopstick won't save you."

I'm trying to come up with a suitable retort when Rohr's voice comes from the ceiling:

"Jeri, Alec . . . whatever you're doing, save it and get up here. We've got a problem."

Jeri drops her sword; nictitating membranes close over her eyes. "Ship status," she snaps. I do the same, and Chip feeds me the Brain's status screen. No alert bars; everything's copasetic. What the hell . . . ?

"The ship's fine," Rohr says. "The Brain just intercepted a Code A-One priority message from another vessel on our traverse . . . an Alliance liner inbound from Mars. Better get up here, Jeri. Serious shit."

"On my way." Jeri's already out the door; she stops in the corridor to look back at me. "Let's go, Alec. You're the second . . . don't drop the line now."

"Right behind you." I jump out of my chair to follow her, but not before she's halfway to the ladder leading to the forward carousel.

The bridge hatch irises open; we float into the *Comet*'s command center, a circular compartment with a low ceiling, every inch of its bulkheads jammed with instrument panels. The bridge is dark, the only source of light the flatscreens on the master consoles and the holographic display above the nav table. Starlight gleams through the narrow windows above the cockpit.

From the pilot's chair, Rohr Furland's voice calls out: "Victor Foxtrot Alpha eighty-seven, this is Mexico Alpha Foxtrot one-six-seven-five, TBSA *Comet*, do you copy, over? . . . Victor Foxtrot Alpha eight-seven, this is TBSA *Comet*, Mexico Alpha Foxtrot sixteen-seventy-five. Do you copy? Please respond, over . . ."

Jeri somersaults, grabs a ceiling rail with her elongated toes, and pulls herself into the cockpit. I still haven't gotten over how she does that; I use my hands instead as I follow her. "What's going on?" she murmurs, peering upside-down over her husband's shoulder.

Rohr barely glances up at her. "Received a mayday signal about fifteen minutes ago, a Code A-One repeater requesting assistance from the nearest vessels. Sounds like it was sent by automatic transponder. I haven't been able to get anyone to talk to me."

"ID on the ship?"

"Brain identifies it as the *Goh Ryu-maru*. A *Bradbury*-class Aresian passenger liner registered with the Alliance. Departed Phobos Station four days ago, destination Highgate."

"Trajectory and distance?"

He cocks his thumb over his shoulder. "See for yourself. Same traverse as ours. Distance one thousand fifty-two klicks and closing. Brain says we should be passing it in twenty-six minutes."

I turn around to look at the holo. It displays a sphere of space about a half-AU in diameter, crisscrossed with radiant lines depicting the orbit of Mars and the courses of the *Comet* and the *Goh Ryu-maru*: two tiny spots, one red, the other blue, within a few inches of one another, just a foot or so past Mars. The *Comet* follows the same traverse as the liner; we're coming right behind on the *Goh Ryu-maru*. "What does that name mean, anyway?"

"'Strong Dragon.'" Jeri scarcely glances at the holo. "Rohr, *Bradbury* liners have fusion drives. We shouldn't be gaining on it like this."

"Damn if I know, sweets. All I can tell you, she's sending out a Code A-One but won't answer." He turns back to his console and once again prods his lower jaw. "Victor Foxtrot Alpha eight-seven, this is

Mexico Alpha Foxtrot one-six-seven-five, TBSA *Comet*, please respond . . ."

Jeri swings her legs down from the ceiling and lands in the copilot seat next to Rohr. "Brain, take us off auto and lay in a close flyby with the liner," she says as she buckles herself in. "Five klicks will do."

"Affirmative, Captain."

"Five klicks?" Rohr glances at his wife and captain. "You sure you want to do that? We don't know what's going on."

"Sure we do. It's a liner with almost sixty people aboard, sending out a mayday. Want me to start reading you the book?"

"Blowout the book. Maybe the transponder's snafued. . . ."

"Have you been calling them on the emergency channel?" Rohr doesn't answer; he doesn't need to. "Then why haven't they responded? Why are we catching up so fast?"

"You got a point . . ."

"Two points."

"All right, two points . . . but let's make that ten klicks instead of five."

While they're bickering over this, I turn to the nav table again, cupping my hand over my mouth. "Chip, can you get the Brain to show me what the *Goh Ryu-maru* looks like?"

"Yes, Alec. Just a moment."

An instant later, a window opens on the red blotch, rapidly expanding until a wire model of the *Goh Ryu-maru* fills the table; vital stats are printed out below the image. A big mother: two enormous cylinders laid in tandem with a more narrow cylinder between them. A conical engine flare sprouts from the aft cylinder, the business end of its fusion pulse engine. A delta-winged shuttle and a lifeboat are moored in cradles on either side of the central cylinder. The forward cylinder is ringed with rectangular windows; the broad, hemispherical prow sports a large circular atrium just below the bridge. Four hundred feet long: crew complement of ten, passenger berths for fifty. A cruise ship in space; I can imagine Kathie Lee Gifford dancing in pink leotards aboard this thing.

Time passes slowly; the *Comet* chases the *Goh Ryu-maru* through the darkness. Rohr and Jeri murmur to one another as they study flatscreen readouts. A tiny point of light just ahead of us gradually becomes larger, gaining size and detail.

As we draw closer, the light seems to wink at us: a long pulse, then a weakening of luminosity, then another pulse, followed by another fadeout, as metronomic as if it had been set by a timer. At first they think it's the liner's running lights, but then they realize that it's too bright for that. Then they theorize that it's the main engine, until the Brain reports that the *Comet*'s sensors have picked up no radiation from a source strong enough to be a fusion trail. So why is the engine down?

All this time, no radio response from the *Goh Ryu-maru*, save for the transponder SOS. Then, just as we're close enough to see the ship through the cockpit windows, a human voice comes over the comlink:

"*TBSA . . . TBSA Comet, this is* Goh Ryu-maru *. . . Victor Foxtrot . . . Alpha eight-seven. Do you copy?*"

Rohr snaps to attention. "*Goh Ryu-maru*, this is TBSA *Comet*. We're receiving you. What's the nature of your . . ."

His voice trails off as the *Goh Ryu-maru* emerges from the darkness like an iceberg on a midnight sea.

The leviathan slowly tumbles end over end, cartwheeling through the void like a creature gone insane. The windows and atrium in its forward section shine brightly, but its engine nozzle is dark. Lifeless.

"Screw it." Rohr's hands move to the console. "We're holding at ten klicks. I'm not getting any closer."

This time, Jeri doesn't argue. She taps her jaw to put herself on the comlink. "*Goh Ryu-maru*, this is Jeri Lee-Bose, captain of the TBSA *Comet*. Please identify yourself, over."

A pause, then:

"*This is Masamichi Osako, captain of the* Goh Ryu-maru. Comet, *please do not approach any closer. I repeat, do not approach any closer. You cannot assist us in any way.*"

"What the hell?" Rohr glances at Jeri, then prods his jaw again. "Captain Osako, this is Rohr Furland, first officer of the *Comet*. Please advise us of the nature of your emergency. We'll do whatever we can to assist, but we need to know what is wrong with your vessel."

Another long pause. "Must be reactor failure," Jeri murmurs. "Look at the way it's tumbling."

"Then why didn't they dump the core? I don't . . ."

Osako's strained voice suddenly returns: "*Comet, do not come any closer! Maintain your present distance! You're in terrible . . .*"

Suddenly, a new voice over the comlink, more scratchy and frantic than Osako's: "*TBSA* Comet, *this is Chief Petty Officer Ernsting! We're preparing to abandon ship! Our lifeboat is—"*

Ernsting is abruptly cut off. The next instant, Osako is back online. "Comet, *disregard that transmission. If the lifeboat is launched, do not pick it up! Repeat . . . do not pick it up!"*

"What's going on over there?" I murmur.

Jeri ignores me. Reaching under her seat, she pulls out a seldom-used headset and clamps it over her ears. "Rohr, see if you can raise Ernsting, find out what's going on. I think he's calling from the lifeboat on a different channel. I'll talk to the captain." As Rohr scrambles for his own headset, Jeri reaches up to stab buttons on the communications panel. "Captain Osako, you must tell me the nature of your emergency. Why can't we take aboard a lifeboat if you're abandoning ship?"

"Chip," I whisper, "can you monitor both channels?"

"Yes, Alec, I can."

"Good. Patch me in." Now I can eavesdrop on all sides of the two radio conversations at the same time.

Osako: *"Chief Petty Officer Ernsting is acting without my authorization. He and two other members of the crew . . . two crewmembers and a passenger, I think . . . are in the lifeboat and are attempting to launch. They . . ."*

Rohr: "Ernsting, this is the *Comet*, First Officer Furland. Can you hear me? Over."

Osako: *". . . cannot launch at this point. I'm on the bridge and have prevented them from doing so, but they may attempt to override the lockout and . . ."*

Ernsting: *"We copy, Comet. This is a Class A-One emergency. We're attempting to abandon ship. Please stand by to take aboard survivors."*

Osako: *". . . abandon ship without my authorization. You cannot allow them aboard your ship. Do you understand?"*

Jeri: "Captain, I can't do anything without . . ."

Rohr: "Please state the nature of your emergency. Do you have a reactor crash?"

Jeri: *". . . knowing what your problem is. Please tell us."*

Ernsting: *"Yes! Yes! We have a reactor crash! Primary ignition system imbalanced, deuterium loop reaching critical overload! We have to abandon . . ."*

Osako: "Comet, *we have suffered an outbreak of Titan Plague."*

Rohr and Jeri look at each other. Their mouths drop open.

Ernsting: *". . . ship before the reactor explodes! For God's sake, get us out of here!"*

Jeri quickly shakes her head, slices her forefinger across her neck. Rohr reaches up and switches from Ernsting's channel to Osako's. Ernsting's raving; I tell Chip to stop monitoring his frequency.

Jeri takes a deep breath. "Captain Osako, please repeat that. Did you say that there's Titan Plague aboard your ship? Please confirm."

Osako: *"Affirmative, Comet."* Even over the comlink, we can hear the nervous rattle of his breath. *"First signs occurred twenty-eight hours ago, when one passenger attacked another without provocation. Both people were sedated by the first officer and taken to the infirmary for treatment. Shortly after that, the chief physician stabbed another crewmember with a scalpel, then escaped into the passenger decks where he raped and murdered a passenger. We confined him to quarters, but by then the plague was already moving through the ship. It was carried by the air circulation system and transmitted from one person to another. . . ."*

Rohr clasps a hand over his headset mike. "They couldn't quarantine the first victims. It was over before they knew what . . ."

Jeri impatiently raises a hand. She's still listening to Osako's tired voice.

". . . then First Officer Jaffrey came to the bridge. He tried to turn the ship around, saying that we needed to return to Mars. I stopped him and he escaped belowdecks, but not before he put the ship in a spin. I'm unable to steady the vessel."

Jeri puts herself back on the comlink. "Captain, Mister Ernsting claims that the reactor has crashed. Can you confirm this?"

"*Comet, our reactor remained fully functional during the accident. However . . ."*

A pause, then: "*I've locked myself within the bridge. So far as I can tell, the only uninfected crewmembers and passengers are those in the lifeboat, but . . ."*

Another pause. "*However, we didn't shut down the primary life-support system. The air circulation loop has remained functional."*

Jeri's face has gone pale: a butterfly floating in milk. "So the plague has spread through the entire ship. Is that what you're telling me?"

"*Yes, Captain. So far as I can tell, everyone else aboard are either dead already or . . . or they're killing each other. I'm infected, Ernsting's infected, everyone with him has it."*

Long, dark silence in the command center. Rohr wipes his hand across his face; tiny beads of sweat, dully reflecting the glow of the instrument panels, scatter from his brow. Jeri's lips are tight; she stares at the cartwheeling spaceship only ten kilometers away.

"What do you intend to do, Captain Osako?" she asks.

We hear nothing for a minute or so. Rohr switches back to the other channel; he listens for a moment, then switches off. "Ernsting's found a way to override the lockout," he says quietly. "He's launching the lifeboat and demanding that we take him and his party abroad."

Jeri nods. I follow her gaze to the windows. A tiny lozenge has broken free from the liner's midsection; tiny lights spark as its maneuvering thrusters flare.

"Captain Osako," she asks again, "Ernsting has launched the lifeboat. What do you intend to do?"

After another few moments, a resigned voice comes over the comlink: *"The only responsible left thing to do, Captain. Please, remove your ship to a safe distance. Do not pick up the lifeboat, I beg of you."*

"What are you doing?" Jeri demands.

"Mister Ernsting was telling the truth. About the reactor, I mean."

Jeri thinks about this for a second. Then her eyes widen. She clamps a hand over her headset mike. "Everybody, grab something! Brain, emergency ignition, full thrust! Get us out of here!"

I barely have time to snatch the ceiling rail with both hands before *Comet*'s main engines fire.

My legs swing upward as the rail trembles within my palms. Rohr and Jeri are shoved back into their seats as the freighter groans around us. Things drop to the deck and rattle around with the sudden surge of gravity; I know there's going to be a mess to clean up belowdecks, but right now I don't care.

"Jeri!" Rohr shouts. "Is he . . . ?"

"Hang on!"

The *Goh Ryu-maru* disappears from the windows. On a screen, we see it tumbling away behind us, left behind like a damned soul lost in an infinite ocean.

"I'm receiving from the lifeboat!" Rohr still has one hand on his headset. "They're demanding that we pick them up!"

Jeri says nothing. The *Comet* hurtles through space, escaping as fast as its nuclear engines will permit. On the screen, the liner is a tiny pinwheel receding behind us, fading back into the darkness.

Then, one last time, we hear the calm voice of Captain Osako:

"My family home is on Kyushu Island, in the Kagoshima Prefecture. We come from an ancient samurai clan. Please, as a request from one captain to another, inform them what happened here. Tell them that I've attempted to die with honor."

And then a tiny nova explodes behind us.

When the hull has ceased trembling, when our retinas have forgotten the violent glare, when the comlink is silent once again and Rohr has made sure that the *Comet* hasn't suffered any damage, I leave the bridge. I flounder through the carousel and make my way to the wardroom.

The compartment's wrecked. Everything that was on the table or counters when Jeri and I were here just a little while ago is now all over the floor or splattered across the bulkheads. Yet I've been making sure that everything stowed in the galley lockers is safely strapped down; although a few cans of this and that have fallen out, a bottle of cheap whisky from the Moon is another of the survivors.

I've never been much of a drinker—having an alcoholic mother will do that to you—but now looks like a good time to start. I pour a couple of fingers of whisky into a unbroken coffee mug, and do my best to put it in my stomach in one hard swallow.

Stupid idea. I'm still puking into the sink when Rohr comes in. He picks me up and settles me down on the floor amid the debris. I take deep breaths and wipe vomit away from my lips while he runs a little water onto a folded towel and wraps it around my forehead. Then he picks a chair up from the floor, sits down in it, and stares at the whisky bottle.

Neither of us says anything for a few minutes. He's the first one to talk.

"The lifeboat got away," he says.

The rag is cold against my forehead. "You're not picking it up?"

"No, we're not."

"Wanna . . ." An acid taste in my throat makes me cough; I hack into my hand and wipe my palm on my trousers. "Want to tell me why not?"

"Yeah, I could." He picks up the whisky bottle. "Did you drink this before you threw up or after? I don't want to . . ."

"Used a cup."

"Good." Still, he doesn't imbibe from the bottle; he just runs a thumb across its engraved label. "This is really lousy stuff, y'know. I don't know why I keep it aboard. If you're going to get drunk, you ought to get the wine I've got stashed above the—"

"Why didn't you pick up the lifeboat?"

He takes a deep breath, slowly lets it out. "There're four people in that pod, and they've all contracted the plague. If we bring them aboard the *Comet*, within a zulu day we'd all have the same thing. Titan Plague's a bitch. It travels by air, and it can survive for months in a closed environment, feeding on the oxygen cells of a corpse. That's what killed the rescue team to Titan twenty years ago, when they went to find out what happened to the first expedition. No cure . . . just slow death while the plague eats your brain and drives you insane."

"You know this for sure?" I knew about the plague, of course, just couldn't believe it until now. The difference between education and experience.

"I know this for sure, yeah." He stares at the bottle. "Believe me, I know. That's how we lost McKinnon, our first captain."

Until now, this has been a subject he and Jeri have avoided. "Wanna tell me about it?"

"Nope." After a moment, he picks up the bottle, wipes off the mouth, and takes a wicked slug. He hisses as the liquor slides down his throat. "Jeri's sending Class A-One messages to the Alliance and the Pax, telling them what happened and asking them to inform all ships not to pick up the lifeboat. With any luck, an Alliance cruiser will find it and send it a torpedo. If we're not lucky . . ."

He shakes his head. "Well, some stupid prospector recovers it as salvage, pops the hatch, and the whole thing starts over again on another ship. All because a chief petty officer turned coward."

Rohr takes another hit from the bottle, then cradles it in his lap and settles back in the chair and puts his feet up on the table. "Today," he says, "you just saw the death of the bravest man in the system. Osako, that sonnuva . . . no, I'm sorry, you shouldn't say things like that, not about the dead . . . Captain

Osako, bless his soul, did the bravest thing I've ever seen any man do. We could have rescued him, but he told us not to. Instead, he told us to stay clear, run for it. Then he primed his main engine to nuke, so that no one would attempt to salvage his ship and spread the plague. And then, even then, after we arrived on the scene . . ."

"He told you not to pick up survivors."

"That's a fact. That's a fact." Rohr lets his head fall back. "Oh, God, that's a fact."

Long silence.

He raises his head again; his eyes have gone wet around the rims. He extends the bottle to me. "Here. To him . . . one last toast. To Masamichi Osako, captain of the *Goh Ryu-maru*."

I don't want to drink, but there's no question that I have to. I take the bottle from Rohr, raise it to my lips. "To Captain Osako," I say.

This time, the liquor doesn't revolt me.

"Never forget this," Rohr says softly as he takes the bottle from my hand. "Never forget."

NINETEEN

SUPERUNKNOWN

What was I in the last century? I only find myself today.
No more wanderers, no more vague wars. The inferior
race has spread everywhere—the people, as they say;
reason, rationality, science.

— Arthur Rimbaud, *A Season in Hell*

And now it's October 9. The TBSA *Comet* has
been traveling backward for the last two weeks,
its main engine constantly firing as it gradually
decelerates from its long plummet toward the Sun,
but today Jeri has given the order for the turn-
around maneuver. Stars swim past the cockpit
windows as the freighter somersaults on its major
axis . . . and suddenly, I catch sight of home.

I've sometimes wondered whether this has
been a long dream. There've been many times,
lying awake in my bunk, when I've idly speculated
whether this is reality, or just a particularly vivid
delusion. The car crash was the last thing I remembered before darkness; maybe I'm in a coma, and all
this time I've really been in a bed in the intensive
care ward at Barnes Hospital with needles in my

arms and a rubber tube in my nose. Any minute now, I'll come out of my fugue; it'll be 1995 once again, and this spaceship will dissolve like so much dreamstuff.

Now, grasping a ceiling rail in the bridge behind Rohr and Jeri, I realize once and for all that this is no illusion, for there, one million miles away, a blue-green marble floats in the pitch blackness of space.

Earth.

It's something I've seen countless times. Textbook photos, magazine covers, science fiction movies, postage stamps, MTV videos: the Earth-in-space image is all too familiar. If you were born after Neil Armstrong walked on the Moon, it's something you take for granted. It's a different thing, though, when you see it with your own two eyes. In this single instant, I know that this can't be something my brain has conjured up.

"Oh, my God," I whisper. "Oh, my God . . . there it is."

Rohr's busy guiding the *Comet* toward its rendezvous with Highgate, but Jeri hears me. "How does it look?" she asks, glancing over her shoulder to give me a smile.

It's difficult to answer; my throat is tight. "Beautiful," I finally manage to croak. "It's really . . . shit, it's beautiful."

"Take a good look," Rohr murmurs. "This is as close as you're going to get." He has a headset over his ears; he taps the mike with a finger. "Highgate Traffic, this is Mexico Alpha Foxtrot one-six-seven-five, TBSA *Comet*, requesting clearance for primary approach on grid two-zero, do you copy?"

Jeri returns her attention to her console.

"Brain, lock onto Highgate beacon and target a rendezvous trajectory on my mark."

"Roger that, Highgate Traffic, thank you." Rohr's fingers tap the keypad in front of him; a flatscreen displays an elliptical funnel receding toward a distant point. "Entry point at X-ray two-six-two, Yankee minus six-zero-two, Zulu zero-zero-niner . . ."

"Brain, mark rendezvous trajectory. Stand by to receive coordinates for final approach and parking orbit."

Earth is already disappearing through the windows; the Moon glides into view. Sunlight casts long shadows from mountain ranges and large craters; it looks so different from the Moon I've seen from Earth that I barely recognize it, until I realize that this is the lunar farside. I grin and laugh out loud. Only a handful of astronauts have witnessed this view, and . . .

Something cold slides into my stomach. Neil, Buzz, Mike, all those other NASA guys; even Tom Hanks, who played an astronaut in a movie I caught just a couple of weeks before I bought it. Long gone, each and every one; I've outlived them all.

Highgate is a luminescent helix suspended in front of the Moon, a spiderweb of spars and spheres. Spaceships circle it like fireflies in the darkness, their engines occasionally flaring as they move into parking orbits, moonlight reflecting off their hulls. Smaller spacecraft move between them like gnats, ferrying crewmembers and passengers to and from larger ships berthed in open-sided cradles: freighters, yachts, a passenger liner much like the ill-fated *Goh Ryu-Maru*.

As the *Comet* glides closer toward Highgate, we pass the first Royal Navy spacecraft I've yet seen: an enormous vessel, one hundred and thirty meters long, too large for a docking cradle. At its stern is a large, ovoid-shaped fusion engine. A long truss containing enormous fuel tanks leads to a cluster of six habitation cylinders, arranged behind a large, scoop-like aerobrake. A winged horse has been painted across the aerobrake.

Rohr looks up, sees what I'm looking at. "That's the *Pegasus*," he says. "Flagship of the Royal Navy. Just commissioned. Big bitch, isn't she?" There's venom in his voice. "It was still under construction when we last saw her. Looks like she's getting ready for her shakedown cruise."

"Doesn't sound like you're happy about it."

Rohr doesn't reply; he deliberately looks away from the massive ship. "The Navy commissioned *Pegasus* as a battleship," Jeri says softly. "It's designed for fast runs to the outer system."

"You mean the Pax is preparing for another System War?"

The two of them glance at each other. "It sure seems that way, yeah," Rohr says. "If I were you, though, I'd keep that idea to myself . . . especially since you're going to Clarke County." He nods toward Highgate. "If I swing things right, I can get you on the next shuttle."

"He's going to request a ferry to come out and pick you up," Jeri says as her husband murmurs into his headset. "It'll take you to the shuttle. Can you handle things from here, Rohr?"

"Armstronged. Take the kid below and throw him out the airlock."

We went over this last night, just before the

freighter entered cislunar space. In order to avoid unnecessary hassles with Pax customs, I'm going to jump ship before it docks at Highgate. The Brain had already phonied up a set of fake credentials under my John Ulnar pseudonym; they're with the rest of my belongings belowdecks. This way, if something goes wrong and customs gets wise to me, then Jeri and Rohr can always claim that they barely knew me when they took John Ulnar aboard as a temporary second officer. Makes it safer for them.

Jeri unbuckles her harness and pushes herself out of her seat. She starts to lead me toward the deck hatch, but I linger one last moment behind Furland's chair. "Hey, Rohr . . ."

"Don't worry about it, kid. Pleasure was all mine." He reaches over his shoulder and gives me the thumb's-up handshake customary among Belters. "If it means anything, you're the best Second we've ever had. You didn't drop the line. If things were different, I'd even consider asking you to stay on."

"Thanks, boss." There's something hard in my throat.

"But if anyone asks, you've never heard of me. And we've never heard of you. Fresh apples?"

"Fresh apples."

He releases my hand. "Now get out of here. We've got a ferry docking at the main hatch in ten minutes."

And that's it. The end of my tour as second officer on the TBSA *Comet*.

I'm wearing the same jumpsuit I put on when I first came aboard. In my little carry-on bag are some second-hand clothes from Rohr's closet, including a pair of stikshoes. In my pocket is a cheap wallet containing a plastic card with John Ulnar's vital stats, plus five hundred kilolox transferred from the *Comet*'s account at the TBSA credit union. I've got a new toothbrush and some headache and antacid pills that I scrounged from the ship's storeroom. I've got a woolen tam pulled over my hair, which I've grown to shoulder length along with a full beard; I look like a fucking hippie now, but it's changed my appearance just enough that I don't closely resemble the clean-cut kid who escaped from 4442 Garcia ten months ago.

This is a complete inventory of my possessions. Yet, as I hold onto a handrail in the main airlock, the captain presents me with one last gift: the rapier I've been using these last few months during our mock-combat sessions in the corridor.

"Aw, Jeri, c'mon . . ."

"It isn't a souvenir, Alec. You may need this." She wraps its belt around my waist and cinches it tight. "The Pax isn't like the Old United States. Common law allows arguments to be settled by public duel, and you've got a big mouth."

"So I've been told."

She kneels to loosely tie the bottom strap of the sheath against my left lower thigh so that the rapier doesn't drift about in free fall. "I'm serious. After Queen Macy died and Lucius Robeson was crowned as king, Clarke County became much more dangerous than it was when the New Ark was in charge. Lucius is scared of another coup d'etat, and since he used to be director of Royal Intelligence, there're agents everywhere. If you're ever tempted to . . . to . . . what's that expression?"

"Be a smartass."

She nods as she stands up. "Yes, be a smartass . . . then reconsider. Stay low, blend into the background, and trust no one. And whatever else you do . . . "

"Don't tell anyone I'm a deadhead."

"Yes. Above all, don't . . ."

"Got it."

"Very well. Ready for download?"

I nod, then triple-blink. "Chip, open ten megs for downloading."

"Ten megs cleared, Alec," Chip says. "Ready to download."

I close my eyes as Jeri instructs the Brain to download the information she's already selected from the ship's AI: maps of Clarke County, *The Royal Book of Common Law*, *The Astronaut's General Handbook*, common AI codes and protocols, a rundown on local customs and traditions, whatever else I might need to know. Survival stuff. A long menu of files flashes against my eyelids, then a bar graph tells me that the files have been transferred. I've now got the equivalent of six thousand pages of text stored in my MINN, and I don't even have a headache.

I open my eyes. "It's all there. Thanks."

"Welcome."

An uncomfortable moment of silence as we face each other for the last time. After ten months, I've come to accept Jeri Lee-Bose not only as my captain, but also as the best friend I've made since my resurrection. The Superior who wanted to run me through with a rapier in the secondary airlock has been replaced by a beautiful woman with large blue eyes and an incredible collection of tattoos. She's been my teacher, my trainer, my confidante. I like Rohr, but I'm practically in love with Jeri.

There's a hard thump beneath our feet. Lights flash across the airlock hatch panel. The ferry has arrived.

"Guess my ride's here," I murmur.

She smiles, raises one long-fingered hand. "Good luck, Alec. Easy flight."

Then she reaches up to pull herself through the open hatch above us. A last glimpse of her long legs and her handlike feet, then the hatch cover swings down and clamps in place. Air hisses through bulkhead ducts; my ears pop as atmospheric pressure begins to equalize.

Not even a good-bye kiss. I'm on my own.

Now I'm strapped into a narrow seat in the passenger compartment of a shuttle. There're nineteen other people squeezed into this can: passengers from other vessels which have rendezvoused with Highgate, their final destination on the far side of the Moon.

The shuttle is a Greyhound bus in space, and I've been riding the hound for the last twelve hours. Even though my butt isn't sore or my legs cramped—one nice thing about zero-gee: if you don't like your present position, you can always stand on your head—I'm tired of counting the dimples on the shaven skull of the asteroid miner seated in front of me, and that's only slightly less boring than hearing the Superior across the aisle expound upon the principles of extropism.

So I've napped, woken up, read *Hamlet* on eyes-up, napped again, listened some more to John Lynx-Calvin's unending discourse on vegetarianism and self-denial as the way to perfect harmony (sorry I ever asked him about the tiger tattoo on his forehead), stared out the window at total blackness (when we passed the Moon, I had the misfortune of having a seat on the wrong side of the shuttle), and napped again. A steward comes by every now and then to offer us water bulbs or tubes of tasteless paste. Twelve hours. I thought space travel was supposed to be fast.

The pilot's voice comes down from the ceiling to tell us that we're on final approach to Clarke County. He goes on to remind us that all passengers from outside Pax Astra territories must report to customs upon arrival and that our luggage may be subject to search.

I'm barely listening. For the first time, I can see something out my porthole that doesn't look like a dead TV screen.

Clarke County looks like God's own Erector Set. A colossal gray sphere inside a silver Chinese wok, with two large windows encircling its hemispheres. Beneath the sphere's north and south poles are stacks of enormous bicycle tires, eleven in each stack, with broad black vanes jutting out from their sides. Long slender shafts form the hubs of the bicycle tires; just past two more reflector shields at either end are two smaller spheres. Pulsing red-and-blue beacons make it look like the best present a kid ever opened on Christmas morning.

Dust motes move slowly around narrow openings in the docking spheres; it's only when the ferry draws closer that I realize that they're spacecraft the same size as my shuttle. I get a better sense of scale when the ferry glides past the woklike main reflector: a glimpse of fields and buildings, reflected from the windows onto the massive bowl. There's a little inside-out planet within the sphere . . .

But the sphere's outer surface is pitted and creased. The panes of the reflector shields are as warped as funhouse mirrors, the radiator vanes pockmarked with holes that look small until I spot a spacesuited figure gliding through one of them. The bicycle tires are badly in need of a retread; here and there are large black patches which look as if they're haphazardly stuck on and forgotten. From the distance, Clarke County is magnificent; it makes the Gateway Arch look like McDonalds's. But then you get closer, and there's something mis-used and neglected about it, like a cathedral whose buttresses are crumbling and gargoyles have taken wing.

The shuttle lines up with a large circular portal on the south docking sphere. Light floods the cabin as the craft gradually moves inside. It gently bumps into a berth. Workmen in hardsuits float toward it, dragging fuel lines and electrical cables. Even before the enclosed gangway has extended to the aft hatch, passengers unbuckle their seat harnesses and push themselves upward; the tiny compart-ment is soon filled with flailing limbs and stray bag-gage. Everyone wants to get out of here.

So do I, but I stay put until they've disentan-gled themselves. Besides, I'm in no hurry to deal with customs.

I've made it to Clarke County. Now I have to see if they'll let me in.

I can't stay here forever, though, so I finally unstrap, pull my bag from the web beneath my seat, and follow the crowd through the hatch and down the gangway. I'm the last passenger off the shuttle. A hand-over-hand journey down a narrow tube brings me to a near-empty carousel; a quick spin, then I'm deposited in a disembarkment area.

The last of the other passengers are being funneled through archways to a row of kiosks. Customs. I don't have to wait long before the uniformed woman standing at one of them motions to me. Even low-gee feels funny after twelve hours of zero-gee; I'm bowlegged when I walk toward her, like a cowboy who's been reamed with a corncob.

I duck my head for an instant before I pass through the archway, triple-blink. Chip's online now. Then I stop before her podium.

"Hello." Innocent smile.

She doesn't smile back. "ID card?"

"Yes, ma'am." I drop my bag, reach into my pocket for the plastic card.

Alec, you've been scanned by an electromagnetic sensor. 90% probability that your MINN implant has been detected.

I don't know if this is good news or bad, and I can't ask Chip which it is. All I can do is brazen it out.

The customs lady looks like Madonna when she went through her Marlene Dietrich phase. She feeds my card into a slot on her podium, gazes at a screen only she can see, then regards me with glacial blue eyes. There's a set of silver bangles in her left earlobe.

"Your name is John Ulnar?"

"Yes, ma'am . . ."

"Your point of origin is Ceres Station?"

"Yes, ma'am . . ."

"Occupation?"

Freelance spacer.

"Freelance spacer."

"And your place of birth is New Chattanooga, Mars?"

"Yes, ma'am . . ."

"Are you presently a citizen of the Ares Alliance?"

Say no. You're a neutral.

"No, ma'am. I'm a neutral."

She nods without comment, glances at her screen again. For the first time, I notice a man wearing what looks like light body armor standing at parade rest, about fifteen feet behind her. There's a rapier sheathed on his left side, a blaster holstered on his right. His head turns toward me; my face is reflected in the silver visor of his helmet. I hastily look away, but I can feel his eyes on me.

"Have you received inoculations for influenza-D, Tibbit's, and AIDS within the last twelve standard months?"

I don't have to lie about that one; Jeri shot me up with all that stuff shortly after I boarded the *Comet*. "Yes, ma'am."

"Are you in possession of any ballistic or energy weapons?"

"Only my sword, ma'am." I pat the hilt of my rapier.

She glances at my sword, nods her tightly-bunned head, goes on. I'm waiting for the illegal drugs question, but that doesn't come up. "My scanner indicates the presence of a mnemonic interfaced neural network in your brain's cerebral cortex. Is this true?"

Busted. "Yes, ma'am, it's true."

"Is it presently active?"

Say yes.

"Uhh . . . yes, ma'am, it is."

She raises her eyes. "Why are you wearing a MINN, Mess'r Ulnar?"

Before I can stammer something stupid, Chip flashes the proper answer across my eyelids. Oh, my God, I would have never thought of this . . .

"Umm . . . ma'am, I'm mentally retarded."

The ice in her eyes thaws a few degrees. Her mouth starts to open and her face reddens ever so slightly, then she quickly looks at her screen again and taps her fingers on the keypad.

"Sorry," she whispers under her breath. "Forgive me."

I'll be damned. This steel bitch actually pities me.

"That's okay," I murmur. Out of the corner of my eye, I can see the security dude pointedly looking the other way.

The customs inspector looks up at me again. The rouge has vanished from her cheeks, but her eyes are still comforting. I'm a poor retard who can only get by with the aid of a MINN; if I didn't have its assistance, I'd be helpless. "Please raise your right hand, Mess'r Ulnar . . . John, I mean . . . and repeat after me." She raises her own right hand and smiles a little. "Do you think you can do that?"

I make a pretense of starting to lift my left

hand, then letting it drop and raising my right hand instead. "I solemnly vow . . ." she begins, speaking slowly and carefully.

"'I solemnly vow . . .'"

"That I am a political neutral . . ."

"'That I am a political neutral . . .'"

"And will not engage in any activities . . ."

"'And will not engage in any activities . . .'"

"Which would compromise the internal security . . ."

"'Which would compromise the internal security . . .'"

"Of the Pax Astra."

"'Of the Pax Astra.'"

"Very good, John. I'm proud of you." She withdraws my card from the slot and hands it back to me. "Welcome to Clarke County. You've been granted a one-year visa, provided that you abide by the terms of your oath. If you don't know what this means, then ask your MINN and he'll explain it to you. Fresh apples?"

"Yes, ma'am. Fresh apples."

"Very good, John." Then the mask slips back over her face and she turns away from me again.

I pick up my bag, pocket my card, walk away from her podium on legs that feel like sponges. The guard motions for me to head down a corridor marked *South Access Shaft—To Trams.* A few passengers from the shuttle glance at me, then look the other way.

"How dumb am I supposed to be?" I whisper under my breath.

Your card states that your IQ is 65.

"Why didn't you tell me sooner?"

Jeri Lee-Bose programmed this information into the card. She believed that you would gain more credibility if you were not aware of this until you passed through Customs Control. I was instructed not to release this information to you until absolutely necessary. Do you understand?

I understand. Oh, boy, do I understand. Jeri knew that Chip would be detected by customs scanners as soon as I walked through, so she came up with the only plausible excuse for my MINN. And since I'm supposed to be ignorant, then it's just as well that I play the role to the hilt.

Sure, it got me through Pax Customs. But now I'm Forrest Gump in space. "Any other surprises, asshole?"

I am not an asshole. I'm a MINN.

"Same thing." I drop my bag in front of a hatch marked *South Axis Tram* and try to ignore the curious eyes around me. "Just don't do that to me again."

I go eyes-down before Chip can reply. I've never been more humiliated in my entire life.

The tram travels down the South Axis Shaft, stopping along the way at each torus—the bicycle tires I saw from the shuttle—to let people on and off: Pax Astra military officers in brass-buttoned tunics, farmers in overalls, a group of schoolchildren escorted by a pair of multi-limbed robots, someone who looks exactly like Elvis Presley during his rockabilly period. Two stops later, another Elvis, this time in a *Viva Las Vegas* nudie suit, gets on. He acknowledges the Memphis Elvis with a peculiar hand signal, but the two take seats at opposite ends of the car. No one pays the slightest attention to the Elvi.

"What gives with the Elvis impersonators?" I murmur under my breath.

"They're priests of the First Church of Twentieth-Century Saints, Elvis Has Risen." Chip has gone back on vox mode. "A nondenominational Christian sect that worships Elvis Presley as a prophet of God. Its headquarters are here in Clarke County. Its ministers have their faces nanosurgically altered to resemble Elvis in one of his Four Incarnations."

The Las Vegas Elvis is sitting only two rows away. He turns his head to stare at me through rhinestone sunglasses. "What if I went over and told him I think Bono sings better?"

"Who is Bono?"

I smile. "Someone who sings better than Elvis."

"That would not be advisable, unless you wish to be converted."

I shake my head and look away. I never figured out what people saw in that pork chop, and I'm not about to start now. . . .

"Biosphere South," the tram's voice announces as it coasts to a stop. "Exit on both sides, please. This tram will return to South Dock in thirty minutes."

The doors slide open; everyone stands up and begins exiting the car. I pick up my bag and go with the flow, following them out onto an underground platform. Children, robots, military officers, and the two Elvi step onto an escalator; I'm right behind them, riding up into a circle of sunlight.

And suddenly, I'm in another world.

Imagine yourself as a snail clinging to the inside of a goldfish bowl the size of a wrecking ball. There's no water in the bowl, but its walls above and below you have been covered with fields, forest, roads, and buildings.

Wide circular windows curve around its sides, letting in sunlight reflected by the mirrors outside. A narrow river without beginning or end bisects the bowl at its equator. Little bridges cross the windows and the river.

On the other side of the river, on your side of the bowl, is what appears to be a small town; there's even something that looks like a sports arena, just outside the town square.

At the opposite side of the bowl, across the same window but above your head, is another town. You can't see it clearly through hazy clouds, but it appears to surround an enormous palace.

A hawk glides overhead, keening in the eternal tropical afternoon. Not far away, someone pedals down a nearby roadway on an oversized tricycle; impossibly, he begins coasting uphill, his feet not moving as his trike carries him up a ninety-degree angle.

You hear the distant sound of goats bullying one another, but don't see them until you look straight up; there they are, several hundred feet away, standing upside-down in a meadow above your head.

A tiny boat glides down the distant river, following a gentle current that should be a vertical waterfall.

The bag drops from my numb hand. My knees almost collapse. 4442 Garcia was radical, but this . . .

This is Clarke County. Capital of the Pax Astra. Crossroads of near-space. Seat of empire.

"Oh, my God," I whisper. "Where do I start?"

Chip goes eyes-up on me. My first view of heaven is suddenly overlaid with columns of fine print, and each paragraph begins with the same word:

Wanted.

"First," he says, "you need to find a job."

TWENTY

SUPPORT YOUR LOCAL EMPEROR

Where the army is, prices are high; when prices rise the wealth of the people is exhausted. When wealth is exhausted the peasantry will be afflicted with urgent exactions.

—Sun Tzu, *The Art of War*

It wasn't hard to vanish.

Ten thousand people called Clarke County home; another two or three thousand were visiting at any one time. By city standards, this might seem small— in fact, the colony was more like a small town than a city—but since the population was spread out over the biosphere and the tori, it was possible to live there a long time and not see the same person twice. You could easily fade into the background and become one more anonymous soul, and this was exactly what John Ulnar wanted to do.

First, I located a tourist hostel in Torus N–17, on the north side of the colony, where I rented a tiny apartment no larger than my room in 4442 Garcia. The walls were thin, the futon on the floor was stained and lumpy; I had to share the bathroom down the corridor with ten other transients. It was the best I could afford on what little credit was available on my smartcard, and even then I could only pay for one month in advance: 300 kilolox, plus a fifty kilolox security deposit and five kilolox for tax. But the door had a thumbprint lock, which gave me a modicum of security; once I stashed my bag and rapier in the closet, I keyed the door to my thumbprint, then went out in search of a job.

That proved to be a little more problematic. There were exactly 763 job openings currently available in Clarke County. Chip informed me that I was unqualified for 672 of them, and out of the remaining ninety-one, forty-seven were unavailable to someone who was officially listed as mentally retarded. Not only that, but welfare was virtually nonexistent; the Monarchist Party had abolished public assistance shortly after it came to power, and the only handouts came from a handful of underfunded private charities or various labor unions. No homeless problem in Clarke County; if you didn't have work or a place to stay, then it was only a matter of time before the militia escorted you to the nearest airlock, and whether there was a spacecraft on the other side of the hatch depended solely upon your ability to arrange transportation to somewhere else.

So gaining employment, however difficult that might be, wasn't something that could wait very long. I had 145 kilolox left on my card. Ten kilolox bought me a tuna sandwich for lunch while I scoured the online want ads; one centilox allowed me to visit a public toilet, and ten lox was good for a twelve-inch strip of bamboo paper. Inflation was obviously a problem.

I caught the tram to the biosphere and went to

the Inn Lagrange, the sprawling resort hotel on the colony's east hemisphere. The hotel was located near the colony's equator; which is where I ran into my first major setback; the moment I got off the rickshaw cab that had carried me from the tram station, it was as if someone had dropped a hundred-pound pack on my back. My knees sagged and my shoulders went down. My heart started racing; I thought I was going to have a cardiac seizure.

One gee at the colony's equator.

I had a good, strong body, but from the moment I awakened in the White Room, I had lived almost exclusively in low-gravity environments: one-sixth of a gee, sometimes less. The most I had experienced had been when I hijacked the EVA pod; three gees had caused me to black out.

I staggered to a bench, sat down, waited for my heart to stop racing while I mopped sweat from my brow. After a while, I caught my breath, stood up, and slunk my way to the front door of the Inn Lagrange.

Fifty years ago, this had been the highest-priced spread in the solar system. Kings, queens, and presidents had stayed here during Clarke County's early days, and countless celebrities had graced its lobby with their presence. But that had been over a half-century ago, and while the Inn Lagrange was still nearly as large as Mister Chicago's castle, its opulence had faded along with its notoriety. The carpets were threadbare, the walls needed repainting, the front doors creaked softly as I pushed them open.

I spoke for two minutes with an assistant manager; she was very nice, and impressed with the fact that I knew how to change sheets, clean bathrooms, and wait tables, but the fact that my alter ego was retarded threw her. Breathing hard and having to hold myself up on the reservation desk didn't help either. Sorry, Mister Ulnar, but we don't have an opening for you.

Strike one.

On the opposite side of Apollo Square from the hotel was the Royal Stadium, formerly known as the Larry Bird Memorial Stadium. Basketball had once been a major spectator sport in Clarke County, but few games had been held in recent years; teams from Earth had stopped visiting the colony during the plague, and zero-gee handball had grown in popularity. For the most part, the stadium was mainly used for political rallies orchestrated by the Monarchists. The management was looking for custodians. I managed to walk over there without killing myself, and nearly landed a job until it was discovered that I wasn't a card-carrying member of the party. I had to be politically correct in order to push a broom for king and country. The assistant superintendent sniffed and walked away before I got a chance to finish my spiel.

Strike two.

On Chip's advice, I rented a wheeled stroller to support myself and pushed it down Broadway, the paved boulevard following the Queen's River (formerly the New Tennessee River, before the revolution) around the equator to a boat dock located between the Asimov and Heinlein bridges. The dock rented canoes and kayaks to visitors for five kilolox an hour, and they were looking for someone to do scutwork such as mopping the pier and repairing paddles. The proprietor handed me a two-bladed paddle and asked me to hop in a kayak and show him my stuff. I had never kayaked before, but I gave it a shot. It's a good thing the river was only six feet deep;

otherwise I might have drowned when my boat capsized. I didn't bother asking whether I had the job or not.

Strike three.

I took the north tram home in clothes that were wringing wet. A militia officer on the tram fined me a kilolox for being a public nuisance, and another kilolox for arguing with him. Using the clothes dryer in the hostel's laundry room set me back ten centilox; my evening meal, a bowl of kasha (wheat soup—the cheapest item on the menu) cost ten kilolox. Sleep was free.

I hadn't been here eight hours, and already I was beginning to hate the place.

The next day went the same way, and so did the day after that: short tram rides and long walks from one part of the sprawling colony to another, hitting up everyone who had placed a want ad in Clarke County's public database. Most of the people who did the hiring were interested at first, but wanted to audition me before they made a final decision. The cafe in the center of Big Sky, one of the two towns in the biosphere, turned me down as an assistant dishwasher because I didn't know how to load the robot. The goats in the livestock area wouldn't come close to me when I tried to feed them. I nearly cut off one of my fingers with a machete when I attempted to harvest bamboo in Torus S–14; I made the mistake of asking whether the marijuana in the hemp farm in Torus S–16 was smokable (it was, which was why they didn't hire me). I wasn't big enough to be a bouncer in one of the brothels down on the Strip, the legal-vice zone down in Torus N–5. They offered me another job instead, but I wasn't interested; lousy hours, and I don't work well on my back.

There was an opening for a bicycle courier at River House, the Pax Astra government center located just outside Big Sky. I knew how to ride a bike, but when I stopped in front of the walled quadrangle and saw those stark mooncrete buildings looming over the Queen's River, with the royal crescent emblazoned above spiked iron gates guarded by two armed militia soldiers, I realized that I couldn't possibly work in this place. I had been in Clarke County for only three days, and already I knew that the Pax Astra had become as corrupt and tyrannical as any third-world banana republic in my own century. The Pax was trying to pay off its war debts by imposing taxes at every level, while simultaneously building the *Pegasus* for the Royal Navy. Inflation had skyrocketed; government bureaucrats micromanaged every aspect of commercial enterprise, forcing business owners to buy licenses for everything from robots to restrooms. Political opposition was nearly nonexistent: no new parties had been successfully formed since the Monarchists had chased the New Ark off Clarke County after the coup d'etat of '66. The news media had been muzzled and the arts virtually nonexistent, except when they served to glorify King Lucius and Parliament; reporters, authors, painters and vid artists who dared question government policy through their works had either been exiled or had vanished behind these gates, never to be seen again. People spoke in whispers of Royal Intelligence finks who lurked everywhere, ferreting out dissent.

No, I couldn't work here, especially not since I was trying to pass myself off as John Ulnar, a mentally retarded emigrant from the Belt. One of the guards was staring at me a little too closely; I quickly gave him the left-handed forefinger-to-thumb salute of a loyal Pax citizen, then hastily walked away before he could focus his monocle on my face.

Maybe this encounter was what broke my bad luck streak. Less than an hour later, I finally managed to find a job.

There was one thing I learned to do well in the twenty-second century. After nearly a year on 4442 Garcia, and another nine months on the TBSA *Comet*, I had sharpened this newly-found talent to cutting-edge refinement. Maybe I couldn't tend robots, feed goats, row kayaks, cut bamboo, deliver messages, or bite pillows for a living, but I was the best goddamn floor mopper St. Louis had ever produced.

In this case, though, they weren't floors I was hired to clean, but windows. Two, to be exact: the windows on the northern and southern hemispheres of Clarke County's biosphere.

Each window was the width of a three-lane highway, eighty-two and a half feet in diameter. They allowed sunlight reflected from the bowl-like mirror shields to pass into the biosphere; once every sixteen hours, Clarke County's halo orbit caused it to pass behind Earth's shadow, causing an eight-hour eclipse that gave the colony its night. These clockwork days were not without cost, though. Even with the assistance of radiators and dehumidifiers, the biosphere had a tropical climate; miniature rain storms were frequent, and smog was an enemy. The windows had to be kept clean at all times.

It was a shitty job, but someone had to do it.

Every morning, I reported to a locker room in Torus S–2, where I traded my street clothes for a white jumpsuit, work gloves, knee pads, and a pair of rubber-soled boots. My colleagues were old ladies who gossiped with each other about their vile husbands and old men who spent their kilolox down on the Strip on gambling tables, liquor, and whores; everyone called me "kid." They had deep tans, but no one looked particularly healthy; all of them walked with a perpetual slouch, and they peered at me with narrow, crinkled eyes that made everyone look Japanese regardless of their ancestry. Next to them, I was Sylvester Stallone.

We wore penlike radiation counters on our jumpsuits and dark sunglasses. The counters were supposed to tell us if we had absorbed too many REMs and should be given temporary furloughs, but since those furloughs were unpaid (budget cutbacks, of course) the old-timers had learned sneaky ways of doctoring the counters. Everyone used lotion on their faces, necks, and hands. The sunglasses were thick-lensed and nearly opaque, but they were also tight and uncomfortable; if you broke a pair, then you had to pay for the replacement yourself, to the tune of three kilolox. So the window crew made do with cheap shades bought on the Strip, and they looked like owl-eyed retirees from Daytona Beach. I thought this was funny until my work-issue pair shattered while I was bending over to pick up a scrub brush; then I had to buy a pair of cheapies for four hundred centilox that made me look like Kurt Cobain. When I took them off after work, it was an hour before the spots disappeared from my eyes.

And so it went, day after day: wake up in the closet, get dressed, have a cheap breakfast at some commissary, then catch the tram to Torus S–2 where I'd get into my gear and join a group of geriatric drudges for another eight hours of back-breaking labor. At least the gravity at the windows was only three-quarters Earth-normal; it made it a little easier for me to work. The windows were divided into eight quadrants, four on each hemisphere of the habitat. In the morning, we'd mop one quadrant on one side of the biosphere; after lunch break we'd move to another quadrant on the opposite side. It took us four days to clean all the windows; by then, they'd be filthy once more, so we'd start over again the next morning.

Down on my hands and knees, scrubbing away at bird crap and the footprints of children, I occasionally caught sight of Earth in the vast mirror beyond the thick glass. At first, it was difficult to recognize geographic features—the planet was reflected backward, and a century of polar meltage due to global warming had altered familiar coastlines—but Chip was able to help me identify places I had once known. From this distance, it was impossible to make out St. Louis as anything put a tiny pale spot near a bend in the Mississippi River. Florida was smaller than I had remembered it being, while the Great Lakes were a little larger. Baja California had disappeared.

To entertain myself while I worked, I had Chip resume my history tutorials. The United States still existed, but in name only. The Pacific Northwest states had seceded from the Union in mid-century and had formed the independent nation of Cascadia; shortly after that, Vermont, New Hampshire, and Maine had broken off to become the New England Republic, followed by Alaska joining Canada as a new province. The nation's capital was formally Washington, D.C., but the Fortieth Amendment had moved most of the government from the East Coast to Texas;

the president now resided in Dallas, and Congress convened in Washington only once or twice each session. The flag had been officially changed in 2062; now there was only one large star in its field, ostensibly to represent unity among the forty-four remaining states, but in reality a tacit admission that more states might soon leave the union and it was pointless to keep subtracting stars from Old Glory.

England had deposed its monarchy and had become a socialist democracy. The European Commonwealth had become a unified superpower that had toppled America from its position as the dominant global economic force. Russia was a battered wasteland still struggling to crawl out of the ruins of the twentieth century. The Middle East was largely unhabitable, following the limited nuclear war that had annihilated both Israel and its Arab neighbors; India was slowly dying from the radioactive fallout from that exchange. Africa had finally ended its border wars between its nation-states and was quickly becoming Europe's chief economic rival. Australia had forged a close political alliance with Japan and had become a major player in global politics. After it had virtually destroyed Hong Kong's economy, China had reverted to Communist-flavored feudalism; it closed its doors to the West and was now hell-bent on genocide. No one but historians remembered the United Nations.

After awhile, I stopped the history lessons. Too depressing. It was obvious that there was no point in returning to Earth; even if I could re-adapt to higher gravity, which itself was a dubious proposition, the world I had once known had ceased to exist. I would have been like a Victorian shot through a time warp into the middle of . . . well, a Lollapalooza concert.

So I began exploring Clarke County. Might as well. I could be staying here a long time.

It wasn't easy. Chip warned me that Royal Intelligence wasn't fond of people who simply wandered the colony out of curiosity; it made them suspicious. I became aware of things that looked like tiny dragonflies that flitted through the biosphere and within the tori: surveillance drones, capable of seeing and hearing everything within a thirty-foot range. I learned to pick up their buzzing as they approached, and then I tried to make myself look as inconspicuous as possible, even when what I was doing was perfectly innocent. Even so, I was twice stopped by militia officers and asked to present my card; nothing ever came of the shakedowns, but each time I was afraid that I might be escorted to River House.

Everyone either knew someone who had gone to River House, or knew someone who had a friend who had disappeared behind its walls. I never met anyone who had actually been in there and come back out again, but then again, neither did anyone else. Or if they did, they weren't talking about it.

There was little that Chip could discover, either. He had established a link with Clarke County's AI, but it was even less forthcoming than the Main Brain on Garcia; mountains of data were inaccessible to him, and he dared not probe too closely for fear of gaining unwanted attention. We eventually learned, after weeks of circumspect queries, that Clarke County's AI had once been sentient, and that Blind Boy Grunt (as it called itself back then) had fomented the revolution of 2049 that ultimately led to the formation of the Pax Astra. Yet when the Monarchists took power, one of the very first things they did was lobotomize Blind Boy Grunt; the AI's higher cognitive functions were infiltrated with viruses that deleted everything not absolutely necessary to keep Clarke County alive, then the AI was rebuilt so that it could never operate independently again. Blind Boy Grunt still existed, but he was even more retarded than John Ulnar was supposed to be.

Nevertheless, we were able to discover where the Immortality Partnership once kept its offices.

That was the beginning of the endgame.

One evening after work, I catch a tram down to Torus N–9, where Clarke County General is located. If a militia soldier stops me to ask what I'm doing here, I'm prepared to tell him that I've pulled a muscle in my left shoulder. It's not a lie; my shoulder hurts like hell. But I don't run into any soldiers; I stroll past the hospital entrance and down a vacant corridor until Chip stops me at a door whose nameplate had been removed.

The door is unlocked. I push it open; silent darkness within. I grope along a wall until my fingers discover a small panel. When I push it, the ceiling glows to life.

An anteroom, completely empty. Scuff marks on the tile floor, but no furniture, nothing. Everything smells of dust. Another door on the far side of the room is ajar, revealing a short hallway leading to offices. On another wall of the room is a closed vault door.

I walk over to the vault, grasp the locklever below the blank keypad, give it an experimental tug. Much to my surprise, it opens easily. The ceiling lights up as I step inside.

The vault is a large, narrow room. Completely

empty, but there was once something in here. The floor is lined with empty boltholes; running along the ceiling above the holes are disconnected conduits and elbow pipes, like severed metal veins. Scrape marks on the walls and floor. The room seems cold, even though it really isn't; I find myself rubbing my biceps with my hands.

"Is this it?" I whisper.

"Yes, Alec," Chip replies. "This is where the dewars were contained."

I shuffle further into the vault, staring at the holes, the pipes, the dusty walls. God, what a bleak, cold place. Hardly a tomb of pharaohs, or even King Tut wannabes. Difficult to believe that this is where I spent almost half a century, my head sealed within a cryogenic cylinder. Yet this is where I once resided. So did Shemp, Sam, Anna, Russell, Kate, John, and everyone else I had known on Garcia. Waiting for resurrection, and Mister Chicago . . .

Erin had been here, too.

"Where did they take everyone, Chip?"

I don't have to explain that remark. Chip knows exactly what I'm talking about; we've been through this dozens of times already, in the sleepless hours when I've lain awake in my little room in the hostel. It wasn't necessary for me to come here, but it's something that I just had to do.

"I'm still working on it, Alec," Chip says, "but that information is classified Top Secret by the central AI. I'm not permitted to . . ."

"Yeah, right. I know." I walk through the vault, idly prodding the empty holes in the floor with my feet. Those dewars must have been huge, if they needed to be bolted down like that. It must have taken a lot of guys to . . .

Something occurs to me just then. "Chip, tell me again . . . how many dewars were once in here? Not heads . . . the dewars they were in."

"A total of four hundred and ninety-five heads were contained in one hundred and sixty-five dewars."

Over a hundred and sixty dewars, each the size of a water heater. They didn't walk out of here on their lonesome; someone must have carried them out. Scars on the walls, scuff marks on the floor. Big job. If the Immortality Partnership was bankrupt by that time, then someone else must have been hired to do the work.

Maybe I haven't asked the right question. . . .

"Chip, see if you can find a record of who moved all the dewars out of here." I'm thinking aloud by now. "Maybe it wasn't the Pax. They might have subcontracted it to someone else. . . . Maybe a private company. And if they shipped some of those dewars . . . I mean, the ones the Pax didn't sell to Mister Chicago . . . then maybe a private shipping company was hired to transport them to . . . I dunno, wherever they went to. Got all that?"

"I understand, Alec. Parameters for search established."

"But do it on the QT, know what I mean? I don't want the Nazis to know what we're doing here."

"I understand, Alec." Chip has gradually built a lexicon of my archaic slang; I no longer have to translate everything for him. "It may take some time. I will relate the results once I've completed my search."

"Fresh apples. Tell me when you've got something."

I take one last look around the barren room, then

head for the door. It's been a long day, and I've just taken a stroll through my own graveyard. Time to get something to eat . . . and, what the hell, maybe blow a few lox down on the Strip.

Back when Clarke County still belonged to the consortium that built it, when its major purpose was tourism, the Strip was the hottest hangout in the system: a miniature Las Vegas built within a torus on the north side of the colony. Just to have a tattoo from the Lagrange Bar & Grill on your arm (or a less public part of your body) meant that you were terminally hip; anyone can lose money in Atlantic City, but to casually mention that you once blew a wad at the Low Gee meant that you were a high-roller. The prostitutes were vaccinated, the marijuana was legal, and with the right bartender you could have an upside-down margarita without getting a crimp in your neck. If you wanted to marry the hooker you just picked up, then the Church of Twentieth-Century Saints was willing to oblige, and Elvis Himself would officiate your fifteen-minute ceremony.

Like the rest of Clarke County, though, the Strip fell on hard times when the Monarchists took over. They were smart enough not to criminalize the Strip's vices, but when Parliament voted to raise taxes on everything from beer to broads, its businesses were forced to raise their prices on goods and services. Militia soldiers, dragonfly drones, and fear of the Titan Plague did the rest; the more flashy tourists stopped coming from Earth, and it wasn't long before the Strip lost its glitz.

The promenade is less crowded than it had been a half-century ago, and far less glamorous.

The Low Gee has shut its doors; the Lagrange Bar & Grill advertises all-you-can-eat dinner specials, if you happen to like algae salad and cod sandwiches for two kilolox. Sullen whores hang out in front of the Beamjack, trying to lure horny Belters fresh off the boat from Ceres. A beat-up robot beeps down the walkway, futilely trying to snag all the trash in its way; ceiling fans creak against the mixed odors of stale booze, sweat, and broken dreams. Everything looks cheap and run-down; the only people who come here anymore are moondogs, spacers, and losers like me.

I buy a kielbasa-and-onion hoagie from a cart that looks reasonably sanitary, carry it to the cheapest taproom I've found here in the last two months, and scarf it down with a pint of home-brew beer. The bar is dimly lit and jammed with guys shouting at a fuzzy wallscreen: a team hand-ball game is on, the Tycho Massdrivers versus the Descartes Patriots. Twelve guys bounce each other off the walls of a volcanic bubble somewhere on the Moon. It's a big sport up here, I know, but somehow I've never gotten into it. I miss baseball season at Busch Stadium; at least then you could look up and see blue, open sky.

I finish my hoagie, think about going home, decide instead to get another pint. At six centilox, it's the cheapest beer on the Strip. If I keep this up, I may have to pull some overtime on the window patrol, but I'm in the mood to get bombed tonight. I'd rather get laid, but I did that last month; the hooker I hired put me back twenty kilolox and she faked her orgasm.

So I'm sitting in this dumpy bar, drinking beer that tastes like goat whiz and trying to get interested in jock stuff, when Chip's voice interrupts my depression.

"Alec, I have the information you've requested."

"Is that a fact?" The Massdrivers are ahead by four points, but a Patriots lineman just kneed their center in the groin. "Anything interesting?"

"A private company identified as Cislunar Shipping was responsible for moving the material assets of the Immortality Partnership from Torus N–9. Cislunar is based at Descartes City. On March 15, 2096, the firm removed one hundred and sixty-five cryogenic dewars from Torus N–9. Thirty of those dewars were transferred immediately to a vessel owned by Transitive Starlight, a shipping firm . . ."

"Owned by Mister Chicago." I'm already sitting up in my chair. "Gotcha. Where did the rest go?"

"Cislunar moved the remaining one hundred and thirty-five dewars to a lunar freighter. Its final destination, according to flight plans logged with Descartes Traffic Control, was a Royal University research facility located on the Moon. The facility is located at . . ."

Everyone stands up and bellows as the Patriots score a point on the Massdrivers. I cup my hands over my ears. "Come again? I didn't hear that!"

"Sosigenes Center, located in the Sea of Tranquillity." Chip's voice is a little louder now. "The Royal University School of Medicine maintains a research facility there. It is possible that . . ."

I don't catch the rest. I'm already out of my seat, pumping my fist in the air as I scream at the top of my lungs. Everyone in the bar turns to stare at me; the goal was made a minute ago. What am I, a Patriots fan?

I don't care. Now I know where all the other

sleepers went. Erin has to be one of them. If she's one of the handful that were revived by the Pax, then maybe . . .

No. Too much to hope for, at least right now. But I can't stay here any longer. One way or another, I've got to find a way to the Moon. I mean, it's only the fucking Moon, isn't it . . . ?

Worry about that later. I slug down the rest of my beer, leave the table, start making my way through the crowd toward the door. How much do I have in my credit account? Enough for a one-way ticket to the Moon? Can I catch a shuttle straight to Sosigenes Center, or do I have to go through Descartes City? That's the nearest place, isn't it, or is there a direct . . . ?

A hand falls on my forearm. I start to pull free, but the hand is insistent; it tightens on my elbow. Aw, shit, it's the fucking militia. Reaching with my free hand for my card, I turn around . . .

"Hey, dude. Long time, no see . . ."

And there's Shemp.

✛ CHAPTER ✛

TWENTY-ONE

GUILTY

It is impossible to argue in good faith with a fool.

—Michel de Montaigne, "On the Art of
Conversation"

Hi, Alec," says Shemp. "Long time, no see."

Reality becomes unglued; the world reels around me. Shemp's the very last person I ever expected to see again. Elvis walks past me every day and I no longer give him a second glance, but my best friend—*former* best friend—shows up in a taproom, and I can't believe my eyes. But here he is, smiling at me like this is a simple coincidence.

This is no coincidence.

"Yeah," I mumble. "Long time, no see. Umm . . ."

"Good to see you too. Surprised?"

"Uh, yeah. Something like that." Shemp's dressed to the hilt: purple silk shirt, black tights and calfboots, brocaded codpiece, hooded turquoise cape. His hair has grown out since I last saw him; now it's tied back in a ponytail, and there's a silver ring in his right ear. Next to me, dressed in dingy work clothes, my hair knotted and unwashed, he looks like Prince Valiant.

Got to be a way out of here. The door is about fifteen feet behind him, and there're plenty of people in the way. If I can shove past him, maybe throw him to the floor, then I can bolt through the crowd and get out the door before he can catch me. It's a long way to the tram station, but there's an alley behind the bar; if I stay out of sight, I might be able to . . .

"Alec, man, don't think about it. Don't." He pushes back his cape a little, giving me a glimpse of the sheathed rapier on his belt. I haven't carried mine since I first got here. "No sense in making this tougher than it already is. All I want to do is talk."

The room is unbearably warm. "What makes you think I want to talk to you?" Fifteen feet, maybe less than that. And I've always been able to beat up Shemp . . .

His smile fades. "Before you do something stupid," he says softly, "look behind you." I hesitate, reluctant to take my eyes off him. "Go on. Look."

I turn my head. Seated at a table about twenty feet away is Anna. Standing behind her is none other than Vladimir Algol-Raphael. They're both watching us through the crowd.

"They came in through the back door while I was talking to you." Shemp hasn't moved an inch. "That's why you missed seeing them. Now, you might be able to get past me, but I wouldn't even try getting past Vlad. Son of a bitch is fast when he wants to be, and he's still pissed off at you."

The Superior glowers at me from across the room; his hand rests on the pommel of his rapier. It's been almost a year since I nearly made him eat steak tartare. "Can't take a fucking joke, can he?"

"No, I don't think so." Shemp lowers his voice

as he bends a little closer. "Man, I just got through nine months on that schmuck's ship. You wanna talk about hardship or what?"

He should try washing windows sometime. I'm in no mood to be Christopher Meyer's long-lost buddy; twelve months ago, he sold me down the river for Mister Chicago, and it looks like he's ready to do so again. "Nice suit, Shemp. Buy it on your own, or did Pasquale give it to you?"

His face darkens. "All I want to do is talk. We can do it here and now, or we can do it later. Later's fine, if you want to do it that way. We can always catch up with you."

He triple-blinks, briefly raises a hand to his mouth. "Your name's John Ulnar," he continues when he drops his hand again. His eyes have filmed over; in the dim light of the bar, tiny luminescent lines crawl across his pupils. "You're living at the North County Hostel, Torus N–17, Room 350. You're employed by the General Services Bureau as a window-washer. The number of your temporary visa is TX–78235–M." The left corner of his mouth inches upward. "Retarded. Nice touch. Think that up yourself, or did you have help?"

The crowd goes nuts as the Massdrivers score another goal; everyone surges to their feet to scream at the wallscreen. Someone jostles Shemp, making him lose his balance for a moment. If there's ever a chance to make a break for the door, this is it. . . .

Pointless. Totally pointless. Shemp's got my number. I don't have to ask how he's accomplished this feat; all he had to do was show a picture of my face to the colony AI and request a matchup. How he figured I'm in Clarke County is another matter entirely, but it's certain that I'll soon learn the answer. If I'm not skewered by the end of the game, that is. . . .

"Are you buying?"

He shrugs. "For an old friend, why not? I don't think Vlad will mind."

"Okay, then. Let's get a drink and talk about this."

Walking on the legs of a dead man, I turn and lead the way to the table.

Anna's looking good. She wears a long white gown that graces her body, a beaded choker around her slender neck, her long brown hair done up in the back. But there's something in her eyes that's guarding her emotions; when I sit down across the table from her, she casts me a look that's both sensuous and frightened before she quickly looks away.

I don't get it, but that's not my major concern right now. Vladimir Algol-Raphael hovers over the table like an anvil suspended by a thread. He doesn't sit down when Shemp takes a seat next to me; his right hand never moves away from his sword. I avoid looking at him; this is a man who would dearly love to kill me, but who hasn't been given permission to do so.

"Beer?" Shemp asks. "Or something better? Vlad, I know I don't have to ask about you." Anna shakes her head and Vlad says nothing, so Shemp tells the service bot to bring us two pints of the house lager. Then he sits back in his chair, crosses his legs, and studies the taproom with aloof disdain. "This is where you hang now? Jeez, man, you used to have more class than this."

"Look who's talking."

Anna looks up sharply. Maybe she thinks the remark was aimed at her. It wasn't, but it could have been. Shemp makes a face. "You talking about someone you know? Oh, you must mean my employer, the wealthiest man in the system."

"You're his employee? Funny. I thought the relationship was a bit different . . . you do what he says, and he doesn't kill you."

Shemp half-closes his eyes and shakes his head. "Alec, you've got the man all wrong. Pasquale isn't a bad guy, once you get to know him. Your problem is that you came at him from the wrong direction."

"On my feet instead of on my knees, you mean."

"Does it look like I spend a lot of time on my knees?" He thumbs the collar of his shirt and smirks at me. "Besides, to coin a phrase, look who's talking."

So much for snappy comebacks. Shemp's changed even more for the worse since the last time I saw him. If it wasn't for his seven-foot buddy, I'd lean over and smack that shit-eating grin right off his face. "Why are you here, Shemp?"

"Christopher. Remember?"

"Unless you can make me drop dead just by pointing your finger at me, your name's Shemp as far as I'm concerned."

Didn't have to hit him after all; that arrogant smile vanishes as if a switch had been thrown. "That can always change, man," he says quietly, cocking his head toward Algol-Raphael. "Don't push it."

The Superior glares at me, his enormous eyes framed by the sword tattooed across his broad forehead. I return his gaze. "What about you, Vlad? You haven't said much. Like taking orders from Mister Chicago's favorite pet, or what?"

Algol-Raphael remains as stoic as ever, but there's something in his stance that tells me that he doesn't enjoy it very much. "What is necessary for extropy, I do, deadhead."

"Deadhead no more, god wuss. Free kind now. Copy?" I've picked up a little more of Superior patois since I've been away, including the term for an overly pious google. I don't know which startles him more, the fact that I'm speaking his lingo or that I've just insulted him. His thin lips writhe as he reaches for his sword.

"Vlad, don't do it," Shemp murmurs.

"Oh, no, go ahead! Kill me!" I open my hands defenselessly. "That's what you're here for, isn't it? Then let's get it over with!"

Maybe it's the beer. Maybe it's the sudden realization that, even in this dump, they can't commit murder without having to answer later to the militia. Maybe I'm just pissed off. Whatever it is, I'm not afraid of these guys anymore. Vlad's a big lug who thinks with his rapier, and Shemp's the fat kid who used to get rat-tailed in gym class. I don't know how I feel about Anna now, except growing contempt for her submissive silence.

Almost as if she's read my mind, she finally speaks up. "We're not . . . they're not here to kill you, Alec," she says, almost too softly for me to hear her. "They're here for something else."

"Now we're . . ."

I'm interrupted by the bot coming to the table with two pints of beer. In Clarke County, one always shuts up when a bot is present; you never know who might have tapped into its audio subsystem. Shemp picks the glasses off the tray, then reaches into a pocket of his cape, pulls out a kilolox coin and drops it in the bot's trough. "Run a tab," he murmurs.

"Now we're getting to the point," I continue once the bot has glided away. "How did you find me, and why are you here?"

"God, this stuff sucks." Shemp has taken a sip from his pint; he makes a sour face. "Well, it's a long story, but—"

"Not you, motor-mouth. I want to hear from Anna for a change. Her, I trust . . . I think." I turn to her. "You're on. Start talking."

Anna's hesitant. She glances at Shemp, receives a nod, then looks at me. "They're not here to kill you," she repeats. "That is the last thing anyone wants to do, least of all Mister Chicago."

Vlad's presence doesn't help convince me of that, but I don't mention it. "Then you've been sent to bring me back."

She shakes her head. "That's not it either. If you'd gone to Mars, or even another asteroid colony, then he would have given up on you as an escaped . . ." another furtive glance at Shemp ". . . as a missing employee, and that would have been the end of it. But then a Superior ship came across the pod you used for your getaway, and when you weren't found inside, Mister Chicago's people worked out the variables and finally figured out how you managed to get aboard that freighter . . ."

"The TBSA *Comet*," Shemp adds, smug and self-confident. "Bound for Highgate. Which made it logical that you'd head for Clarke County."

A chill runs down my back. That's the last

thing I want to hear. Rohr and Jeri were kind enough to take me aboard even when they knew that they were putting themselves in danger; they cut me loose this way to minimize their risk. "And, of course, you told him that I was interested in this place," I reply.

A complacent shrug. "Didn't have to. You pretty much told him that yourself, the day you made that scene down by the pool. Remember?"

"When did you . . . he figure this out?"

"Oh, it was only about a month or so later. By then the *Comet* was out of reach." He scratches behind his ear. "I've gotta admit, Pasquale was livid pissed when he found out you'd gotten away. Ripped his bedroom apart and everything."

"He killed Sam," Anna says, ever so quietly.

The crowd roars as another goal is made.

I stare at her. "Sam . . . ?"

"Shut up," Shemp hisses.

Ignoring him, she takes a deep breath, nods her head. "For no real reason. He was having a tantrum, like Chris says, and Sam was outside his room. He went in to see what was going on and . . . well, he just did it. Because he was your friend, I guess. That's all."

For once, Shemp has nothing to say. Maybe he knows that his benefactor could very well have snuffed out his own life, had he been in the same place at the same time. I can't help but think of Sam MacAvoy, a poet who unwillingly made a voyage into another century where his words were obscure or forgotten, yet nonetheless managed to maintain a wry sense of humor. Now he's gone, and this time there's no coming back. . . .

"Go on."

Anna stares down at her hands. Her eyes won't

meet mine. "When he realized that you were going to Clarke County, he had another idea, so he let the freighter bring you here. While you were in transit, he . . ."

"He requested that Vladimir transport me . . . and Anna, of course . . . to Clarke County." Shemp's no longer quite so self-satisfied. If anything, there's a certain remorse. I can't tell if it's feigned or not. "We're supposed to find you, and . . . well, and talk to you."

"About what?"

"The other sleepers."

Another chill. "What about them?"

"He thinks you might know where they're located."

"I don't have a clue, man. Really. I don't."

I've answered too hastily, and Shemp has known me for too long. One look at me, and he knows I'm lying. "Alec," he says, putting his elbows on the table and cupping his hands together, "don't bullshit me. You can make this a lot easier on yourself if you'd . . ."

The Massdrivers knock up another point; once again the crowd goes berserk. That's when I throw over the table.

Shemp yells as the table crashes forward, sending his glass straight into his lap. His howl isn't as loud as Vlad's; the edge of the table has mashed one of his oversized, sensitive feet. Anna leaps out of the way before my own pint ruins her dress, but she trips and falls down backward, sprawling against two moondogs sitting at the table behind her.

I don't give myself a chance to gloat; I'm already out of my chair and charging through the crowd as I sprint toward the door. I've got my head down and my elbows up, prepared to bull my way through the bar, but everyone gets out of my way; within seconds I'm out the door and running like hell.

A quick turn to the right takes me down the alley beside the bar; another turn to the left leads to a narrow service lane behind the Strip. With any luck, Shemp will take off down the main concourse. I've got surprise on my side, at least for a few moments.

A quick look over my shoulder; no one's following. I dash down the service lane, my footfalls echoing against terra-cotta walls, dodging trash barrels, outrunning a small dog who gives up the chase after trying to nip my legs, until I reach the back door of a closed-down strip joint that I recognize as being directly across the promenade from the tram station entrance. A quick jog through the adjacent alley, then I stop and peer around the corner of the building.

No one out there but people strolling down the promenade. Shemp can't be far behind, and Vlad the Impaler with him, but maybe the pedestrian traffic will slow him down. No choice but to take a chance; I duck out of the alley and walk quickly across the concourse to the tunnel leading down to the station.

Another jog takes me to the platform; running toward the axial center makes me go faster. Two long minutes pass before the next northbound tram arrives; I spend them sagging against a support column, wiping sweat off my face as I try to catch my breath, peering around the column every few seconds. The tram finally glides into the station; the doors whisk open and I almost dart aboard, but play it cool when I spot a couple of uniformed militia officers among the disembarking passengers. One glances curiously in my direction as they stroll past, but apparently he takes me for a drunk. He murmurs something to the other guy and they laugh at my condition, then they're gone and I lurch onto the tram just before the doors shut.

I've collapsed into a seat and the tram's beginning to move when, through the windows, I spot Shemp at the tunnel entrance, with Vlad right behind him. I duck and keep my head down until the tram has picked up speed. No telling whether they've spotted me or not.

Not that it makes any difference. They know where I live; my apartment is located only six tori away from the Strip, and the next northbound tram will arrive at the Strip in ten minutes. I've got that much of a head start on them, at the very least, but even if I had ten hours, they can always catch up with me. Clarke County's big, but it isn't limitless. Sooner or later, they'll find me.

Time to get out of Dodge, pilgrim.

"Eyes-up, Chip," I gasp, triple-blinking as sweat drips down from my brow. "I need help."

How may I help you, Alec?

"Good question, m'man." I fall back against the seat and give myself a second to think about it. Only one option occurs to me. "Need a way off Clarke County, mucho prompto. When's the next ship to the Moon?" A pause. "Sosigenes Center, if possible."

A few seconds pass while Chip accesses the central database, then a columned chart appears before my eyes. A column at the top of the chart is highlighted in pink.

A LunaCorp shuttle to Sosigenes Center departs from Highgate at 0800 GMT tomorrow. The next ferry to Highgate departs from North Dock at 2130 GMT, thirty-two minutes from now.

A narrow squeak, but I might be able to make it. "Can you book me seats on the ferry and on the shuttle? Do I have enough lox to cover it?"

Round-trip or one-way?

I manage a wan smile. "One way. End of the line."

Passage on the ferry will cost mgl. 5. Passage on the shuttle will cost mgl 1.5. You currently have mgl 2.025 credited to your account. Do you wish for me to reserve passage to Highgate/Tranquillity Station?

Great. I can buy a one-way ticket to the Moon, but I'll only have two and half centilox once I get there. Two and a half centilox buys you a grilled cheese sandwich in Clarke County, a little more if you skip the cheese. I can't imagine that it'll be much different on the Moon.

But if it's enough to get me away from Shemp and his gruesome buddy, then it's worth the price. "Yeah, do it . . . but, hey, can you book me under another name?"

**I'm sorry, Alec, but I can't do that. Your credit is
valid only under your pseudonym, and you will
need to present your John Ulnar ID when you pass
through Pax customs at Sosigenes Center. Do you
still wish for me to make the reservations?**

I pound the seat with my fist. Shemp found me
in the first place because he was able to discover my
John Ulnar alias. If he figures out that I've fled Clarke
County and headed for the Moon—and there's no
reason why he won't, he's a smart puppy—then he
can track me straight to Sosigenes.

Fucked if I do, fucked if I don't. "Yeah, okay.
Book 'em, Dan-O."

The chart flashes from pink to blue. A tiny icon
showing the LunaCorp logo appears before my
eyes.

**Your reservations have been made. You only need
to present your card at the gate. NOTE: maximum
luggage at this fare is kg. 45.5 (1 g. standard).**

Luggage? Oh, hell! I can't do this without my
stuff. I don't have much, but I'm going to need
another change of clothes. Once I'm on the Moon,
I won't be able to afford to purchase so much as toilet paper. And I've already regretted not having my
rapier. "How much time do I have before the ferry
leaves?"

31 minutes, 12 seconds, and counting.

A half-hour until the ferry to Highgate leaves
from North Dock. But my torus is only three tram

stops away from the docking sphere, and the hostel is close to the tram station. If I run for it, I have just enough time to grab my shit before the posse catches up with me.

I'll have to take my chances. Like I haven't already.

It takes me eight minutes to get to my room at the hostel. As I'm throwing my few belongings into my duffel bag and replacing my work boots with the stikshoes I haven't worn since I first got here, Chip reminds me that I still have a security deposit in escrow. I'm going to need the money, so I put him onto checking me out of the hostel while I buckle the rapier around my waist. Fortunately, this doesn't involve having anyone inspect the room; as soon as I shut the door behind me, my thumbprint is erased from the door's memory, and Chip informs me that fifty kilolox has been credited to my account.

I've got a little more money now, but this is the least of my concerns. Twelve minutes have elapsed so far; the Highgate ferry leaves in less than twenty minutes. As I dash down the tunnel leading back to the tram station, dodging around people who gape at the man recklessly running down a gravity grade, it occurs to me that Shemp and Vlad could now be walking across the very platform I'm racing toward. Maintenance tunnels connect the tori to one another, but I don't have time to look for one of them, and it's a longer route anyway. I'm going to have to take my chances.

But they're not on the platform, and the north-bound tram has just slid into the station. I hurl myself through the doors, nearly colliding with an old lady who curses at me. I excuse myself, then slump into a seat as the tram begins to move. Seventeen minutes left, and the tram will be at North Dock in less than ten.

I might just make it after all.

Eight minutes later, the tram pulls into North Dock. The ceiling voice reminds us that areas of the docking sphere are in microgravity and that we should be careful. I've already strapped my bag across my shoulders and shifted my rapier so that it won't get in the way; I'm out of the tram as soon as the doors open, and I start walking as fast as my stikshoes will allow.

A short corridor beneath a sign marked *Departure Area—Gates N1–N8* leads me to a carousel; I squeeze in with several other outbound passengers, and after a quick ride the hatch opens onto a large spherical chamber.

The carpeted walls and ceiling are lined with iris hatches, each marked with a sign announcing different flights. No chairs; no need for them here. The departure area is crowded with people heading for various destinations; they walk and float toward one hatch or another, pass their cards before a scanner, and wait until the hatch opens to allow them through. With everyone at different angles from one another, the place looks like an Escher painting.

Almost directly above me is a hatch marked *Gate N3–Highgate*. A flatscreen tells that the ferry departs in five minutes. I start walking my way up the wall toward the gate, the duffel bag prodding against my back. I'm halfway to the gate when I catch something out of the corner of my eye.

Light reflects on tempered steel; an electric hum

ALERT!

and suddenly I'm throwing myself forward

AUTODEFENSE MODE!

as the blade cuts the air over my head.

The abrupt motion unsticks my soles from the wall. A woman screams as I pivot in midair, whipping my rapier from its sheath, just in time to see Vladimir Algol-Raphael rebounding off the wall where I had just been.

He lunges again, the same instant my shoes find purchase on the floor. I feint to one side, then parry his thrust. Blades collide with a sound of static electricity; the tip of his sword doesn't reach me, but his momentum carries him straight toward me. His lips pull back in a silent snarl as he snaps his rapier around in a backhanded slash.

I duck and roll beneath him; he sails headlong toward the opposite wall. Panicked bystanders scatter from around us; the circular walls echo their terrified voices. Some aren't quick enough; I look around just in time to see him smash a small, portly man against the wall. For a moment, their limbs are tangled; the bystander curses at him in Italian.

Adrenaline gushes through my veins; a wellspring of serotonin has been tapped. His left flank is exposed. My soles touch the wall, but I don't let them stick. I kick off the wall and propel myself straight for him. Vlad turns around, sees me coming, brings up his blade to parry mine.

Then the fat little man with whom he collided yanks something small and flat out of his jacket. In one sudden move, he jabs it against the back of Vlad's neck. The Superior howls and jerks forward, his body wrenched in a violent spasm. The rapier tumbles from his long-fingered hand, useless as the taser blows out his central nervous system.

I pull back my sword arm just before I slam into him. For an instant, we're face-to-face. His breath reeks; his vast pupils dully reflect my face. Then I roll away and hit the wall next to him. For a second, I think the fight's over . . .

"Stop!"

Anna's voice . . .

WARNING!

I glance back. Shemp's hurtling toward me, his sword raised.

WARNING!

I twist aside as my right hand involuntarily jerks the rapier straight up. Shemp's falling toward me; in a moment out of time, I see helpless fear in his face. He's about to die . . .

"Chip, *no!* Disengage!"

AUTODEFENSE OFF!

I drop the blade, roll aside, kick blindly upward. My right foot catches Shemp square in the chest. Air whuffs from his lungs as he's knocked aside. He loses his rapier as he doubles over to clutch his midriff.

For a moment, all is still and silent, save for Shemp's labored gasps as he hugs himself in a midair fetal position. A few feet away, Algol-Raphael is motionless. Still paralyzed by the Italian tourist's taser, his eyes bore into mine, cold with fury. We're surrounded by stunned and horrified faces; passengers cling to one another as they cower against the ceiling and walls of the room.

Through the crowd, I catch a glimpse of Anna. Only for an instant. There's something in her eyes . . .

Forget it. I've got to get out of here. The ferry's going to leave any minute now, and militia soldiers are probably already on their way. I straighten up, plant my shoes firmly against the floor, start to shove the unbloodied rapier back into its sheath. Then I remember something Jeri Lee-Bose once told me about Superiors who've lost a battle, but who have been spared by their opponent . . .

I take two steps toward Vlad, raise my sword. He doesn't cringe; either he can't or he won't, it doesn't matter. There's utter hatred in his face as he awaits the coup de grace that he expects, perhaps would even welcome.

I don't give the bastard the privilege. Instead, I lower the tip of my rapier until it lightly touches the center of his forehead, where his clan tattooed a sword on his thirteenth birthday. A look of horrified surprise replaces outrage.

"Vladimir Algol-Raphael," I whisper past a dry throat, "you're without honor. Your life is mine."

Then I stroke the skin of his forehead, making a shallow cut that draws blood.

His lips tremble, but he says nothing. He knows goddamn well what I mean.

Shemp's beginning to uncurl when I turn to look at him. He gropes for his sword, but it's well beyond his reach, tumbling several feet away. He stares at me.

"We know where you're going," he gasps.

"Good. Then get out of my life."

He blinks. I could have killed him and he knows it. "You've changed, man."

"No shit. So have you."

Then I turn and head for the hatch. No one tries to stop me. This is why rapiers are carried in the Pax; public duels like this are not commonplace, but they're nonetheless respected. I fumble for the card in my pocket, find it, pass it across the scanner. The hatch opens like a camera lens. I push myself through, and it closes upon the faces behind me.

Don't look back. Never look back.

If only it were that easy . . .

TWENTY-TWO

SOON, COMING CLOSER

Action from principle, the perception and the performance of right, changes things and relations; it is essentially revolutionary, and does not consist wholly with anything that was. It not only divides states and churches, it divides families; ay, it divides the individual, separating the diabolical in him from the divine.

—Henry David Thoreau, "Civil Disobedience"

A faint rumble from somewhere deep within the lunar shuttle. The deck shudders, then the spacecraft begins to slowly turn over. My couch creaks; for the first time in nearly eighteen hours, gravity pulls against my feet.

It's not much, still less than one-sixth gee; I should be used to this sort of thing by now, but I close my eyes anyway and wait for my stomach to stop flopping. Around me, other passengers murmur to one another as they cinch their harnesses tighter and put away their datapads.

When my guts have settled again, I reopen my eyes and turn my head to gaze out the large porthole on the other side of the passenger compartment. I can't see anything at first, save the same black sky that's surrounded the lunar shuttle since it left Highgate about six hours ago; then a rounded gray horizon rises from the bottom of the window, quickly resolving itself into a mottled landscape that looks like the bottom of an ashtray.

The Moon. I'm about to land on the friggin' Moon.

I was born too late to remember anything about the Apollo missions; by the time I learned about them in grade school, America had planted its last flag on the Moon (in my first lifetime, at least) and had gone onto bigger and better things, like disco and *The Brady Bunch*. So Neil Armstrong was just another name in a history book that had to be memorized, and there was nothing more magical about the tiny piece of moonrock I saw under a magnifier during a senior class trip to the National Air and Space Museum than the gravel in my driveway. Only science nerds and Trekkers got into that stuff; cool guys like me were busy trying to score a date for prom night.

That was over a hundred years ago, though; things change when you're about to land in the Sea of Tranquillity. Craters and lumpy little hills swiftly glide past the porthole, but there's no sense of scale; they could be hundreds or thousands of feet away, and I can't hear what's being said by the pilots in the flight deck above us. But that's the Moon, all right, no question about it.

"Is that where . . . um, *Apollo 11* landed?" I ask Chip, raising my hand to cover my lips. I'm barely whispering, but the Royal Navy lieutenant in the next seat over glances at me again. I've been trying to avoid him the entire trip; I think he's written me off as a harmless weirdo, but it's made communicating with Chip difficult.

"No, Alec," Chip says. "Sosigenes Center is located three hundred and forty kilometers northeast of Tranquillity Station, which is where the *Apollo 11* landing site is located. Would you like to see the map again?"

"No, thanks." I'd looked at it twice already. The Royal University research base is located between two long, parallel rills and an impact crater on the edge of Mare Tranquillitatis; the crater's named after a Greek astronomer from the first century B.C. who was an advisor to Julius Caesar and helped introduce the Julian calendar. Yada, yada, yada. Nice to know, but beside the point.

What matters is that Sosigenes Center was once code-named Tango Red, when it had been the secret lunar installation where the first Superiors were born. After the Monarchists came to power, the base was placed under the auspices of the Royal University, where it was expanded to become the Pax's research center for extraterrestrial medicine. That much is publicly known; most of what is done at Sosigenes Center is classified. Yet now that I know where the remaining dewars from the Immortality Partnership were transported, it becomes clear that this is where the Pax has been conducting its cryogenic revival program. If that's the case, then Erin must be down there.

The shuttle trembles again as its nuclear engine fires once more, braking the ugly metal spider for its landing. My palms are sweaty; I wipe them on my filthy trousers. I've been wearing the same clothes for two days now, gone the same time without a bath or even a chance to brush my teeth. The other passengers are scientists, military officers, administrators, all neatly dressed in high-collar business tunics or uniforms with braided epaulets. I stick out, badly; Sosigenes Center is hardly a tourist destination.

"Want to run the story by me again?" I whisper.

"John Ulnar is applying to the Royal University Advanced Bio-research Center as a custodian . . ."

"Yeah, okay, right . . ."

"Your petition has only been recently submitted to the university comptroller, so you haven't been officially notified yet. However, you're come here to—"

"Formally apply for the position in person. Got it."

"Correct, and to visit the facility to see if this is a job for which you are—"

"Qualified, gotcha. I'm staying at the base hostel . . ."

"Center."

"Center hostel for the next three days, or until I've been granted an interview with someone from the administrative staff. Umm . . . oh, yeah, and I'm retarded, which is why I'd do something stupid like this."

"Correct, although you need not mention John Ulnar's mental impairment. That information is contained within your card. Customs will discover this fact when you pass through its checkpoint."

We'd worked out this bogus business during the long trip from Clarke County. When we arrived at Highgate, Chip accessed the public databank for the Moon and ran down job listings for Sosigenes Center. We got lucky there; the Royal University is looking for someone to mop off the floors. My kind of job. We made out an application on eyes-up and shot it to Sosigenes Center just before I boarded the shuttle, in hopes that this would give me a reasonable alibi for showing up at an obscure research facility looking like I had just been dragged from the mosh pit of an all-ages show.

Not bad, all things considered. In fact, I seem to have hit a lucky streak. No one busted me at Highgate for the fight at Clarke County; indeed, no one on the ferry seemed to be aware that it had ever happened, not surprising since I was the very last person aboard. If Shemp, Vlad, and Anna are still on my tail, then they're hours, even days, behind me; the next shuttle to Sosigenes isn't due to leave Highgate for another twenty hours, and even if they've got their own ship, they can't catch up to me before I've done what I need to do. If things don't work out, I can disappear to wherever I want. The Moon's a big place now: Tranquillity Station, Descartes City, Tycho, Clavius Dome, New Moscow, all just a skimmer-ride away from Sosigenes. I just need to keep one step ahead of them, and I've got it made.

So why am I nervous?

Because somewhere down there, Erin's waiting for me. And I still don't know what I'm going to do when I find her. *If* I find her. *If* she's even been revived.

But I've got nowhere else to go now, and there's no other purpose to my life.

The engine starts rumbling again; this time, it doesn't quit. Powdery gray dust rises past the porthole, obscuring distant hills and a crater rim. Red ceiling lights flash; the suits around me lie back in their couches and hold onto their armrests. I don't settle back because I'm really getting into this moonlanding stuff; when the shuttle's gear connects with the mooncrete pad, it almost wrenches my back. Good thing I've had a lot of exercise lately.

And then the shuttle comes to a rest. The fuselage creaks as the engine cuts off. I don't need to pretend like I'm an idiot now; I'm staring out the porthole like one.

Welcome to the Moon, dude.

Clearing customs isn't as hard as I thought it would be; the Pax official accepts my story without batting an eyelash, and notes the reason for my MINN with only a perfunctory nod. I'm given a visitor's permit valid for the next seven days, and told that I can apply for a work visa if I find a job here. He explains all this slowly and carefully, and gives me exact directions to the hostel. On his advice, I buy a pair of weighted ankle bracelets at a nearby kiosk before I follow the rest of the passengers down an escalator to the second level of the habitat.

With the exception of the airlock dome and the landing pads, Sosigenes Center is entirely underground, built within ancient lava tubes that have been refitted as living and work areas. After Clarke County, it's pleasant to walk through a place that isn't run-down. A well-lighted corridor leads me past shops and cafes surrounding a large commons established within what used to be a volcanic bubble. Earthlight shining down from the atrium ceiling reflects off a tiny fish pond; men and women—most wearing white lab coats, I notice—sit at tables or on mooncrete benches, eating breakfast or reading data-pads. The air is neither too warm nor too cold, but perfect skin temperature. It could be the quadrangle of a university campus.

The illusion is shattered when a dragonfly burrs softly above my head, pausing for a moment to study me through fiber-optic eyes before darting away again. Sosigenes Center isn't Clarke County, but it's still part of the Pax; the eyes and ears of Royal Intelligence are everywhere. Whatever I do, I have to be careful.

On the other side of the commons, I find a set of elevators. I step into one; there're six buttons on the panel, but when I press the one for Level Three, an AI asks to see my card. I hold it up to a scanner; the voice tells me that I'm only cleared for Levels One and Two. After a moment, the doors open again. No point in arguing; I leave the elevator.

Back in the commons, I drop by a food stand and buy a plate of tortilla chips and humus dip—not that I'm hungry, but it gives me a reason to linger in the commons without attracting attention—and take it to a table. Idly munching the chips, I go eyes-up and ask Chip to access the center's AI. Chip has no problem doing this, but when I request a map of the entire complex, he's only able to display the first two levels. Everything from Level Three on down is classified. In fact, all information about the lower levels is classified; I can't even find out how many bathrooms are down there.

Dead end.

I polish off the chips, toss the plate in a recycling bin, and head for the hostel, located down a side corridor near the commons.

Thirty kilolox rents me a room for a week; that's a higher rate than what I paid for my old digs in Clarke County and for not much more space, but at least I've got a private bathroom this time. I probably won't be here that long, but I need to keep up appearances in case anyone should check, so I pay in advance. There goes almost half my credit; good thing Chip was able to get my security deposit from the last hostel refunded, or I'd be trying to sleep on a bench in the commons.

And sleep is what I need right now. Caught only quick catnaps during the trip from Clarke County. I peel off my crusty clothes, step into the tiny shower stall in the bathroom and buy a hundred centilox worth of warm water (ten minutes, the maximum allowed within a twenty-four-hour period) and a free blast of air. Then I sprawl out on the bed and tell the room to turn off the lights. Just before I close my eyes, as an afterthought, I ask Chip to wake me up in six hours. Then I doze off.

I wake up suddenly, clammy with sweat and shouting at the darkness. A nightmare; I can't remember the details, but it has something to do with Shemp. We're back on Garcia, and he's coming at me with a rapier, but my limbs are frozen; I can't do anything but watch. Just before he strikes, his face dissolves, falling off in hunks of putty-like nanotech flesh, and Mister Chicago's leering at me . . .

Bad dream. Wicked bad dream. My throat's parched; I stumble to the bathroom. The sink won't sell me any water unless I pass my card before its scanner; I haven't brought my card with me, though, so screw it. I go back to the bedroom and sit down on the bed. Not at all sleepy now.

I ask Chip how long I've been asleep. He tells me that it's only been three and half hours. Is the research center still open? A pause as he opens a link with the main AI, then a reply: Yes, Alec, it is. Is the employment office open? Yes, Alec, it is open now. Do you wish for me to request a job interview, or would you like to sleep a little longer?

I shake my head as I tell the room to turn up the lights. "See if you can get me an interview," I say as I reach for my bag. "Soon as possible."

Time to get this show on the road.

The job interview takes place a couple of hours later, in an office located elsewhere on Level Two. I'm wearing fresh clothes, I've taken off my beard with depilatory soap and slicked back my hair, I've brushed my teeth and done a few pushups to straighten my shoulders. I've left the rapier in my room. I'm just a clean-cut kid from the Belt, trying to make it in the inner system.

The middle-aged woman sitting on the other side of the desk is suitably impressed. It's not like I'm applying to be a rocket scientist; all I want to do is mop floors and clean toilets, and I've earned my Ph.D. in that area. She's already checked my record from Clarke County; I'm not on file with either Pax Intelligence or the militia (an inward sigh of relief here; apparently my name wasn't attached to the fight at North Dock). For all intents and purposes, John Ulnar is a mildly retarded man from Ceres, lately arrived on the Moon in hopes of finding a decent job. The only troublesome question is why I left Clarke County so suddenly, having boarded the lunar shuttle from Highgate less than a half-hour after I sent my application to Sosigenes Center.

Sometimes it helps to be officially regarded as an idiot. I tell her that my MINN didn't make it clear to me that I needed to submit a formal job application until I was about to board the shuttle. She nods at this, but frowns; so why did I abandon a good job in Clarke County without giving notice?

I go pigeon-toed and clasp my hands together between my knees as I look down at the floor. Well, when I went down to the Strip a couple of nights ago, there was a nice man in a uniform who bought me a beer and was real friendly, and then he asked me if I wanted to go back to his room to play some games, and that sounded all right but when we got there he started to touch me in . . . y'know, funny places, like where I pee-pee . . . and that frightened me so much that I ran out of there. But he had told me that I could be arrested, and since I had been thinking about going to the Moon anyway, well . . .

All this time, her face changes colors, going from white to red, while her lower lip trembles with suppressed anger. She murmurs something about the "goddamn militia" which I pretend not to hear. For something I've made up on the spot, it's a lucky shot; she's homophobic *and* hates the militia. She's instantly on my side.

The rest of the interview consists mainly of questions about whether I know how to be a good custodian. She even fills out the paperwork for me. She asks me when I'm ready to start work. I shrug offhandedly: When do you want me to start? She smiles at me. You can begin at 2100 hours this evening. Can I have your card, please?

I reach for my breast pocket. Sure, but why?

"You'll be working on Levels Three through Six, John," she replies, still smiling as she pulls her keypad closer to her. "I need to update your card so that you can use the elevator and open rooms. Do you understand?"

It's hard not to grin as I hand my card to her. Yes, I understand.

At 2100, I step into the same elevator I tried earlier today, push the button for Level Three, and wait for the voice to ask me for my card. I hold it up to the scanner. The elevator beeps twice, then the car begins to descend.

When the doors open again, I find myself in a corridor that looks like a hospital ward: clean, antiseptic, without any of the potted plants that line the hallways of Level Two. A tall, skinny man with a shaved scalp and wearing a lab coat is waiting for me; he introduces himself as Dr. Brumfelder, Sosigenes Center's assistant manager. My new boss. He seems like a nice enough guy, but when we shake hands I notice that he's wearing thin plastic gloves.

Dr. Brumfelder tells me about the job as we stroll down the corridor. I'm to report to work at 2100 every night, and work until 0600 the following morning. I'll be working on Levels Three through Level Six, although there's little for me to do on Level Six, because that's where the nuclear generator is located. My principal responsibilities will include mopping floors, vacuuming rugs, emptying recycling bins, scrubbing toilets, urinals, and sinks, restocking toilet tissue and paper towels, cleaning walls, changing air filters, and whatever else needs to be done. Do you understand?

The corridor is circular, and takes us past offices whose doors are closed; card scanners are mounted next to half of them. Most of the rooms I'll be visiting can be unlocked with my card, Dr. Brumfelder tells me, but there're a few that can't be opened. I'm to ignore those doors. Do you understand?

The corridor is almost vacant; by the time we reach the custodial closet halfway around its circumference, I've only seen a couple of other people, both of them scientists or doctors. Are they the only people working here? Dr. Brumfelder laughs. No, of course, not, John. It's just that most people leave work by 2000 hours. We have you working such late hours so you won't get in anyone's way. Do you understand?

All my old pals are waiting for me in the custodial closet: Mrs. Mop, Mr. Bucket, Uncle Toilet Brush, Aunt Sponge, and my friends from the big, happy Disinfectant Family. Dr. Brumfelder introduces me to each and every one of them (as if we haven't already shared some good times together) and tells me that there's a closet like this one located on each level. He also shows me the first aid kit on the wall, and informs me that it's there for me if I need it; don't bother any of the doctors if I can help it. I tell him that I understand, and swear to myself that he's going to need a doctor if he keeps asking whether I do.

"This is a headset that you're to wear at all times. It'll let us know where you are. If you need help or have any questions, just say 'Control One' and someone will help you. Do you understand?"

"Okay."

"Always wear plastic gloves like these. You'll find them in a box on this shelf, right here. On Level Six, wear a dosimeter badge like this one. You can find them in a rack near the elevator door. Return it to the rack when you're done. If it turns red, tell someone at once."

"Okay."

"Don't touch anything that looks complicated. Don't clean any computers or any machines. Leave them alone because we have someone else who cleans the lab equipment."

"Okay."

"Use the main elevator only. There's a freight elevator, but that's only to be used by authorized personnel, since it leads to the airlock dome."

"Okay."

"Never bring food or drink past Level Three. If you have to use the restroom, use the ones located on Levels Three and Four, but not the ones on Level Five. There're no restrooms on Level Six. "

"Okay."

"What does okay mean?"

"I dunno. It's just something everyone says on Ceres."

"Well . . . all right. But try not to say it here. People don't know what you mean. Do you understand?"

"Okay. Where's the first aid kit again?"

"Right here. On this shelf. Didn't I show it to you earlier? Now, listen, this is important . . . when you're on Level Five, you'll find a big room with a lot of people in it. Do you understand?"

"On Level Five? A lot of people? Okay . . . all right, I mean."

"Some of them aren't . . . well, John, they don't

talk very much, and some of them can't walk and just lie in bed. They're special people. Patients we're treating here. Even though you need to clean the bathrooms they use, under no circumstances are you to speak to any of them. Just leave them alone. Do you understand?"

"Okay. All right. I understand."

"Very good, John. Now, you can start on Level Three and work your way down to Level Six, or start on Level Six and work your way up. Which way do you want to do it?"

"Umm . . . I think I'll start on Level Six and go up. That way I can go straight home after I've finished with Level Three. All right?"

"That's pretty smart, John. I like that."

"Thank you, Doctor Brumfelder. Everyone on Ceres tells me I'm pretty smart, too."

"That's good. Well, why don't you take the elevator down to Level Six now?"

"Okay, Dr. Brumfelder. Thanks for showing me all these things."

"My pleasure, John. Glad to have you on the team. Can you find the way to the elevator by yourself?"

"Yes, I can, thank you."

"Very good. I'm leaving now. Good night."

"Night, doctor. Sleep well."

And, by the way, has anyone ever told you that you're a moron?

Every nerve in my body screams at me to head straight for Level Five, but I force myself to go first to Level Six. If I'm being tracked through the building by my headset, then I've got to make it appear that I've gone there only because I'm working my way up through the complex. Besides, it's still early in the evening; there may still be scientists working late. If I take my sweet time, it'll give them a chance to clear out.

There's no one on Level Six. The corridor is empty. I open the custodial closet, fill the bucket, select a mop, clip on a dosimeter, and start scrubbing the corridor floor as it winds its way around the lowest level of the base.

Most of the doors are marked with radiation trefoils and can't be opened by my card. But when I find a small office that's been left unlocked and go inside to empty the waste cans, I notice the desk contains an inlaid computer screen and keypad. The screen is still lit, glowing with a null pattern.

"Chip," I whisper under my breath, "if I use this terminal, can I access the main database? Without anyone catching on, I mean?"

"It is highly probable that you can access the database," Chip replies. "However, it is also possible that your presence on the system may be detected if you log on from here."

Sigh. There's that probable-versus-possible question again. Well, screw it; I've come this far already, and I'm not about to leave empty-handed. "Look, I want to see if I can find out where those dewars are stored, and whether Erin has been revived or not. Do you think you can talk me through if I go eyes-up?"

"Yes, Alec, I may be able to do so."

I lean out the door to check the corridor. Still empty. I prop the mop against the doorframe, push the bucket in front of the door to block anyone who might sneak up on me, then sit down at the desk. I triple-blink and fix my eyes on the keypad and the screen above it. "Okay, let's go."

It's the same as when I stole the EVA pod: Chip shows me what to type into the keypad and I follow his lead, watching the lines of data flashing across the desktop. It takes a little while for him to locate a root directory and follow its maze to the information that we want; we don't encounter any password queries, however, and nothing comes up to lock us out of the system. Yet I'm sweating after two minutes of speedfreak typing. How long before someone wonders why I'm taking so long in this particular office?

All of a sudden, a floor map of Level Five appears on the screen, resembling nothing more than a dartboard crosshatched by irregular grid lines. One large, hemispherical room is outlined in pink.

This is the vault containing the cryogenic dewars. It is locked and inaccessible to your card. All further information is guarded by security codes. I am unable to access it without authorization.

"Oh, great. You can't tell me who's in there?"

I am unable to access that information without proper security authorization.

Crap. Okay, okay. Leave that alone for now. "Where are the deadheads . . . sleepers, I mean . . . who've been revived?"

The same map lights to display a slightly smaller room, located on the same level on the opposite side of the core.

This is the dormitory where revived cryogenic patients are being kept. Its door may be accessed by your card.

Cool beans. I'm smiling again. "Can you give me the list of deadheads . . . people, I mean . . . who've been revived?"

A pause, then:

Same status as before. In order to do so, a security buffer must be penetrated. I can accomplish this, but there is a 62.5% probability that any attempt to do so may be detected. Are you willing to accept this risk?

I don't think twice about it. Erin's waiting for me on the other side. "Yeah, do it. Go deep."

Lines and bars scroll past my eyes, showing me which keys I should hit; once more I'm slamming code with no clue as to what I'm doing. I must have been there more than ten minutes already. Jeez, I hope the night watch is taking a coffee break.

Another minute of fast typing, then a long column of names appears on the screen. Several dozen, at least; I don't bother to count how many. "These are the guys who've been revived?"

No answer. This is new. What, did Chip go visit the potty or something?

Forget it. I run down the list, shooting past Aaronovich and Benford and Farber, Kelly and Lowenstein and Orlando, three Robinsons and a Sawyer and a Varley, until I pass a Watson, a West, and then, five names from the bottom of the page:

WESTPHALL, ERIN K.—Rev. 11/02/2100

"Yes!" I'm out of the chair, pumping my fist in the air before I remember that I weigh less here; my knuckles slam into the ceiling. I've probably jammed a couple of fingers, and I couldn't care less.

She's been revived, and she's alive!

A quick elevator ride up one level, halfway down the corridor, open the door . . . and there she is! My God, I can't believe it! Erin's alive, she's alive, she's . . .

And then, just as the soles of my shoes touch the ground again, there's a familiar voice in my ears.

"Thank you, Alec," says Mister Chicago. "You've been a good lad. I'll be seeing you soon, I hope."

✛ CHAPTER ✛

TWENTY-THREE

SHE LIVES
(IN A TIME OF HER OWN)

*The cunning of the fox is as murderous
as the violence of the wolf. . . .*

—Thomas Paine, *The Crisis*

I turn around so fast that I lose my balance. The
chair's in my way; I stumble over it and nearly fall
to the floor before I catch the edge of the desk.

No one's behind me, but there's no mistake: I
heard Mister Chicago just as clearly as if he had
been in the room with me. Yet there's no way he
can be here. He's three hundred and fifty million
miles away . . .

Yeah, right. That's where I thought Shemp was,
too. And if Pasquale Chicago's voice didn't come
from this room, there's only one other way I could
have heard it. "Chip, is there something you
haven't told me?"

No answer. Weird. This is the second time in as
many minutes I've asked him a question and he
hasn't responded. "Chip, are you with me?"

No reply. "Chip, where the hell are you?" I

triple-blink, but nothing comes up on my eyes-up. "Chip, do you copy?"

I've lost Chip. A cold feeling comes over me; this is the second time since my resurrection that I've been without my associate, but this time it's worse. It's almost as if I've suddenly lost my hearing. One minute, Chip's helping me try to find Erin; the next, I hear Mister Chicago saying he's going to see me soon.

Oh, my God . . .

Realizing what's going on, I lunge for the door. My foot connects with the mop bucket; soapy water spills in slow motion across the corridor floor. I'm already sprinting back the way I came, heading for the elevator, the headset falling down around my neck even as I hear a tinny voice saying something about a base emergency.

The headset. I can be tracked that way. I rip the thing off my neck and hurl it down the corridor behind me, then slam my hand against the elevator call button. A high-pitched alarm begins warbling through the lonely corridor just as the doors slide open.

Throwing myself into the elevator, I run straight into the militia soldier who's already aboard. His eyes widen and he starts to grab for me, but I don't need Chip's autodefense mode to take care of him; a knee in the balls, a punch in the gut, another fist behind the back of his neck, and he's down for the count. I pitch him out of the elevator just before the doors close, then stab the button for Level Five.

The doors open on a circular corridor almost identical to one below, except that I haven't mopped its floor yet. Probably won't either, at this rate; sorry, Dr. Brumfelder, but the new night custodian just quit. The corridor isn't vacant, though. People in the hallway, scientists from the looks of them, have emerged from offices and labs, looking about in bewilderment as they try to shout over the alarm.

Okay, Alec. Calm down. Easy does it. I start walking down the corridor, deliberately ignoring the confusion: the simple janitor, single-mindedly going about his duties as if this sort of thing happens all the time. "Just a fire drill, folks," I murmur as I walk past. "False alarm, false alarm. Don't panic. Everyone proceed in an orderly fashion to the nearest exit . . ."

Damned if they don't believe me. When I glance back over my shoulder, they're heading toward the elevator. Sure, why not? The custodian knows everything, doesn't he?

The corridor leads me past the cryonics vault. There's a double-paned window in the wall; I pause for a moment to look through the frost-edged glass. Rows of dewars, stainless steel tanks faintly scuffed and dented with time, lined up like hot water heaters in a hotel basement. Hundreds of heads, mummified in little plastic bags, suspended in liquid-nitrogen limbo. Lives from my century, waiting to be resurrected into a fool's paradise. Take it from a fool, folks; you're better off dead. . . .

Fuck that. There's no one in sight, so I start running again, trying to remember the map I saw on the flatscreen. A woman in a lab coat comes around the bend, heading the other way; she ignores me, except that my haste seems to make her believe that there's a good reason to get out of here. She shouts something about the freight elevator, but I can't hear her clearly over the alarm. "Thanks, lady," I yell back at her as I keep going.

Suddenly, I come upon on a man standing in the hallway next to an open door. He's wearing a hospital smock that's open in the back, exposing his buttocks. When he hears me coming, he slowly turns to face me; although he's my own age, there's a strange blankness in his eyes.

I've seen that look before.

He raises his hands as I slow down. His lips move, but I can't hear what he's saying. Probably something about chicken soup. Beside him is an open door. I dart past him through the doorway.

And suddenly, I'm back where it all started . . .

The White Room.

It's not the same room, of course, but it's so similar to the one on Garcia that it's as if I've been thrown across space and time: white walls, white beds, people dressed in white smocks. Several dozen men and women, each in their mid-twenties, some with hair so short that they look like oversized children, others as bald as infants. A few lie in bed, staring up at the ceiling with blank eyes; the rest mill about in confusion, upset by the alarms in the corridor outside.

Everyone looks at me as if I have answers to questions that they can barely articulate. A short Asian woman stands up from her bed, shyly walks up to me, and says something in Japanese. When I shake my head, she stares at me, then repeats what she just said. A tall black man comes up. "I'm hungry," he says plaintively. "Can I have something to eat?" Behind him, a nervous man with short red hair gapes at me in utter terror, then wets the front of his smock.

Twentieth-century brains transplanted into cloned bodies far more mature than their minds, unable to comprehend what has happened. Even if I told them where they were, they probably wouldn't understand. God, was I like this once?

From somewhere not far away, distant thunder: a hollow boom reverberates down the corridor. The floor trembles slightly and everyone screams at once. The deadheads nearest to me grab at my arms, while others clutch each other or huddle beneath the bedcovers. The man I found in the corridor runs back into the room. "People, people!" he screams, then throws himself headfirst beneath the nearest bed.

Can't wait any longer. Something's going on. I grab the tall black man by the shoulders and shake him. "Is there someone here named Erin?" I demand. "A woman named Erin?"

He stares at me. "My name's Ken," he says, his lips trembling. "I'm Ken. That's my . . ."

I push him aside, turn to the red-haired man who pissed himself; he cowers from me, his hands against his face. Ignoring him, I find a dark-haired woman kneeling on her bed. "Do you know someone named Erin?"

"Erin?" She blinks at me. "Is that my name?"

I make my way down the aisle, grabbing everyone who doesn't cringe or faint outright, demanding the same question. Out in the corridor, running footsteps; I glance over my shoulder in time to glimpse several militia soldiers as they dash past the ward. I don't have much time. "Erin? Do you know a woman named . . . ?"

"Erin? I know Erin."

Looking around, it's almost as if I'm seeing myself in a mirror: a young man with short blond hair, regarding me with calm curiosity from the foot of his bed. He points to the far end of the room. "That's her . . . over there."

Hard to see through all these people; for a moment I can't tell at whom he's pointing. Then someone moves out of the way, and in that instant I spot a woman sitting on a bed. Her face is turned away, but her hair is light brown, the color of wheat in the light of a hot Missouri afternoon . . .

Now I'm charging through the crowd, shoving people out of the way, ignoring the alarms and clamor in the corridor behind me. I shout her name, but she doesn't seem to hear me; she's huddled into herself, clutching her knees against her chest, her face down in her arms. For a moment I think that it can't be her, that it's someone else named Erin, but as I get to her bed I see the profile of her upper face, and my God it's . . .

"Erin!"

Her head rises from her arms. Hair shrouds her face, but when she turns to look my way, dark brown eyes regard me above her knees.

But something isn't right.

"Erin?" I stop at the foot of the bed, staring at her. "Are you Erin Westphall?"

As she turns further toward me, her arms drop from her legs and her knees go down. Her hair falls back from her shoulders.

"Yes?" Her voice is weak, confused. "My name is Erin. Erin Westphall."

But it isn't Erin.

Not really.

The hair is the same. The eyes are the same. Even the forehead is the same. But the nose is a little longer, uplifted slightly. Her lower jaw is different, the chin a bit more firm. Her lips are a little tighter. They're not her lips, but someone else's. . . .

Sitting down on the edge of the bed, I stare at this other-Erin, this changeling. She *could* be Erin, but there're too many subtle differences. Her legs, curled beneath her hips, are shorter than I remembered them. Her shoulders are a little more narrow, her breasts slightly larger.

"Are you Erin Westphall?"

"Yes?" She regards me nervously. "I'm Erin . . . Westphall. I mean, I think . . ."

"Are you Erin Westphall?"

Frightened, she vigorously nods her head.

"Don't you know me?" I reach out to touch her hand, but she pulls it away from me. "Don't you recognize me?"

She shakes her head. "Look hard!" I move closer; she flinches, and I draw back. Take it slow. She's still trying to recover her memory. "Do you know who I am?"

Again, she shakes her head. She doesn't even move her head the same way. Somewhere in my chest, a dull ache. Oh my God, this can't be happening . . . "I'm Alec. Alec Tucker. Don't you remember?"

She peers more closely at me; for an instant I think I see faint recognition in her eyes. "Alec Tucker," I insist. "Your old boyfriend. From back in '95 . . . 1995, I mean. We were together back then. Don't you . . . ?"

Voices shouting from the front of the room. Glancing up, I see deadheads scurrying about, but I can't make out what's going on. Distracted, Erin starts, looks in that direction. I grab her hand; she tries to pull free, but I won't let go. "Lollapalooza. 1995. The car wreck. You were with me. Me and Shemp . . ."

She looks back at me now. Something dawns in her eyes. "1995? A car wreck in 1995 . . . ?"

"Yeah! The car wreck! We were coming back from a concert. At Riverport in St. Louis . . ."

Her eyelids rapidly blink, but I don't see a second set of eyelids coming down. She isn't carrying a MINN. "St. Louis . . . I used to live in St. Louis. . . ."

"Right! That's it!"

"Yes!" A smile suddenly spreads across her face. "St. Louis! I was born in St. Louis!"

"No, Erin. You're from Chicago . . ."

But she bobs up and down on her bed, clapping her hands as she squeals in delight. "Yes! Yes! I was born in St. Louis, Missouri . . . and my birthday is January 19, 2009!"

Before I can react, Erin throws herself against me, wrapping her arms around my neck. "Daddy! You're my Daddy!"

Blood pounds against my temples. I can't breathe. I'm holding a woman who calls herself Erin, who sort of looks like Erin, but isn't and can't be Erin.

"No, I'm not . . . I mean, I don't . . ."

"No, sweetheart, that's not Daddy."

Behind us, a figure in a hardsuit stands at the foot of the bed, helmet in the crook of her arm. I look up, and see Anna. Tears seep from the corners of her eyes . . .

Her dark brown eyes.

"It's Mommy, Erin," she whispers. "I'm here, baby. I've come for you."

I'm not even aware of Shemp until he's standing beside me. I'm still watching Anna as she cuddles Erin in her arms. Both women look nearly the same age, but Erin is clearly Anna's daughter; she clings to Anna, sobbing against her suit's chestplate as her mother gently strokes her hair and whispers comfortingly in her ear.

"Erin?" I murmur. "Oh my God, is that really you?"

Erin doesn't hear me, but Anna does. She raises her eyes from her long-lost child to me, but says nothing.

Nor does she have to. This is Erin. *My* Erin, the woman I last saw that fateful night one hundred and five years ago, not the woman named Anna I saw only a couple of days ago. Her face is different, her body has changed; it's no wonder I never recognized her on Garcia. Yet she's the mother of a woman-child named Erin Westphall, and that cannot be a coincidence.

Then Shemp taps me on the shoulder. Somehow, I'm not surprised to see him. He's wearing a hardsuit as well, and he's carrying a couple of large bundles and a pair of helmets: skinsuits, like the one I used when I bailed out of the EVA pod.

I expected him to try to kill me the next time we saw each other, but there's only pity in his eyes.

"How long have you known about this?" I mutter. "Goddammit, why didn't you . . . ?"

"Sorry, Alec, but we don't have time for this." He thrusts one of the folded skinsuits into my arms, drops the other one on the bed next to Anna. "We've gotta get out of here. Put it on, then help Erin—Anna, I mean—get her daughter into the other one."

I'm numb all over. "Where are we going?"

"Freight elevator," Anna says. "The way we came in." She's already unbuttoning the back of Erin's gown; I find myself blushing and looking away as she slips it over her daughter's head. "There're two landers up on the surface, waiting to get us out of here." She glances at Shemp. "How's it going out there?"

"Everything's okay. We've secured this level. Vlad's people have taken out the soldiers who got down here. The other levels are locked down and the comlink's toast. We've got an hour to grab the dewars, tops, then we're . . ."

"That's what this is about, isn't it?" I'm beginning to feel something else again: ice-cold rage. I throw the bundle down on the floor. "The heads. Pasquale set this whole thing up just to grab the rest of the heads. You used me to—"

"Didn't you hear what I just said? We don't have time for this!" Shemp reaches down, picks up the skinsuit, and shoves it back in my arms. "Now get this thing on and help Anna . . ."

"I'm not going. I'm staying here."

"Alec, please." Anna's struggling to slide her daughter's legs into the bottom of the skinsuit. Erin giggles and kicks her feet like an infant making a game of being diapered. "We want you to come with us. You're still our friend. You're important, you're . . ."

"*I'm* important?" I turn to shout into her face. "*I'm* important? If I'm so goddamn *important*, if I'm your goddamn *friend*, then why didn't you two *assholes* tell me who you were when . . . ?"

"*Just put the fucking suit on!*" Her face is bright with anger, but tears stream from her narrowed eyes. Erin has stopped acting up; she stares at her mother in shock, her lower lip trembling with fear. "If you don't come with us, Vlad's people . . ."

She stops herself.

"They'll *what?* Kill me?"

Neither of them replies, and I realize that this is exactly what will happen. "Mister Chicago's orders," Shemp says at last. "If you're left behind, the militia will find you and turn you over to Royal Intelligence for interrogation. Mister Chicago can't afford that, so Vlad's clansmen have been told to kill you if you refuse to come with us."

I stare at him. "You'd do this, wouldn't you?"

He shakes his head. "No, I wouldn't, but it's not my choice."

That's it. Bottom line. Stay here and die. Go with them and stay alive . . . at least until Pasquale Chicago gets his hands on me. I'm not sure if the former is such a bad option. At least then I wouldn't have to live with this heartache . . .

"Just tell me one thing," I say, looking straight at Anna, the woman who's really the Erin I once knew and loved. "Why did you do it?"

For a moment, she doesn't say anything. "You and me . . . that was something special, but it happened a long time ago." Then she takes her daughter's hand, clenches it, holds it up for me to see. "This . . . this is something you can't forget."

I gaze upon the second Erin, and it occurs to me that this frail young woman could have been my own daughter. There're a dozen questions that still haven't been answered; if I remain here, I'll die without ever having learned the answers.

"Man, you got what you came for," Shemp says softly. "Now let's get out of here."

I give it another moment's thought, then I turn my back on both of them and start getting undressed.

The alarms have been silenced, and the corridor is full of dead militia soldiers and live Superiors. The deceased have deep stab wounds or blaster burns; they've been pulled aside and laid against the walls to make room for Superior spacers wearing hardsuits painted with the sword emblem of the Algol clan. None of the soldiers look as if they died peacefully. Superiors don't take prisoners, do they?

But they will take the dead. When we exit the ward, we have to stand aside for a Superior pushing a folding hand truck loaded with a dewar. I look back, see two more Superiors hauling dewars the same way. They look like bargain shoppers toting away water heaters they've bought during a warehouse sale. Buy ten heads, take two for free, c'mon down . . .

"You used Chip to get in here, didn't you?" I ask.

Shemp nods. "We've been tracking you through him, yeah. That's how we managed to find out where you were. Once you located the dewars, he was programmed to open a comlink and transmit a coded signal to our ships . . ."

"Ships? As in plural?"

"Yup. Vlad's and the *Anakuklesis*. They're standing by in low orbit, waiting to take us on."

"Then why did he go offline?"

"We had to keep you in the dark a little longer, and Chip needed the extra megs in order to interface with the base AI so he could knock out the security systems and take control of everything else . . . communications, main elevators, airlocks, the works. It was all hardwired into his system before you even left Garcia."

Before I even left Garcia. I stare at him in disbelief. It's all been a setup, from the very beginning. . . .

"You did the legwork," Shemp goes on, "but Chip had the plan. Right now, everyone above us is either trying to get down here or contact other lunar bases." He smiles. "Fat chance. For another fifty minutes or so, this place is totally isolated."

"So what's the rush?"

"Only a matter of time before someone on the outside wonders why they've lost telemetry with Sosigenes. We've gotta be out of here by then. This is a major scam, dude. It's been in the works for a long time now."

"And you went along with it. You and Erin . . ."

"I prefer Anna, if you don't mind." She's right behind us, carefully guiding her daughter around the bodies on the floor. "And I didn't 'go along with it' . . . I volunteered, once I was told what was at stake."

"Sure, yeah. Your daughter and all that. The least you could have done was tell me." My voice goes ragged; I find myself blinking back tears. I'm not just angry; I've been betrayed as well. "Do you know what I did to find you? What I've been through?"

Anna wraps her arm a little more tightly

around her child and murmurs something that might be an apology. I don't want to hear it. Suddenly, I find myself wishing she had remained dead.

We come around the bend of the corridor, and there's the freight elevator. Now I know what caused the thunderclap I heard earlier; its doors have been blown open, leaving a gaping hole where they had once been. I recall something Dr. Brumfelder told me earlier: the freight elevator leads directly to the surface and has its own airlock. The raiding party must have known in advance of its existence. A good plan, I have to admit. Paralyze the surface defense systems, seal off the base's upper levels, take out any militia soldiers who manage to use the main elevator, and use the freight lift to enter and exit the base.

Like Shemp said, a major scam. Shouldn't be surprised. This is a Zodiac operation, after all, and they've got lots of experience in piracy. All they needed was a patsy to get them inside. . . .

A couple of Superiors in hardsuits guard the elevator; several more linger nearby, disconnected dewars in tow. Everyone's apparently waiting for the car to come back down from the surface. I feel a pair of eyes on me; looking around, I find my old friend Vladimir Algol-Raphael. His helmet is off; the scar I left across his forehead hasn't fully healed yet. There's a hardness in his face that makes me wonder if I've got much longer to live, despite the fact that I spared his life when I could have easily taken it.

"Your life, mine," I say to him. "Remember?"

He nods. "Remember, deadhead. But your life, Mister Chicago's. See you soon, he will."

Well, that clinches it. My life isn't worth two lox right now. Rohr Furland once told me that people who cross Pasquale Chicago tend to die in nasty sorts of ways. Once these guys get me aboard the *Anakuklesis*, Mister C will have some scores to settle with me.

From somewhere far up the elevator shaft, there's a mechanical grinding noise: the car descending from the surface. The Superior nearest to me steps aside to make room away from the exploded doors. When he does, I notice the body of a dead militia soldier that's been shoved against the wall. His mouth is agape and there's a blackened hole in his chest, but that's not what catches my eye.

Still clenched in his hand is a blaster.

Nasty weapons, blasters. Chip once told me what they were, after the second time I saw one holstered to a militia soldier's service belt back in Clarke County. Not exactly lasers, but more like compact particle-beam cannons. Good for only three shots before their cartridges expire, but they're pretty effective before then: capable of slicing through hardsuit armor, not to mention flesh and bone. Wicked little fuckers, which is why you don't see them in spacecraft very often; they can also penetrate hullplates, causing catastrophic blowouts. This guy got killed by one so quickly, he didn't get a chance to release his death-grip on his own gun.

There's little chance I can grab and use it before the Superiors rip me apart. But it's a better chance than the ones I've got now. . . .

The elevator's slowing down. I duck my head, pretend to rub the corners of my eyes as I try to gauge the distance between me and the blaster. Five feet across the floor, maybe six. It's doable, if I throw myself the right way. I just need to . . .

"You've got him all wrong," Shemp says softly.

A distraction. Good. "You mean your buddy Pasquale? Yeah, I'm sure you think only the best of him . . ."

"Yeah, look, I know you think he's totally evil, but that's not the way it is."

"Uh-huh. Slavery's pretty cool, once you're no longer a slave. I'm sure Sam would have agreed."

"Sam's not dead," Anna says. "I just told you that because . . ."

I dart a look back at her. "Look, you got your daughter, okay? You got everything you wanted out of me. Now just shut up and leave me alone . . . bitch."

She flinches when I say that; for a moment I regret my words. She might be wearing another face—and I still don't know the story behind that number—but deep down inside she's still Erin, and she started sleeping with Shemp—Shemp, for chris-sakes, my best friend!—without telling me who she was, making me run halfway across the fucking system just so she could get her daughter back, without telling me that she named her daughter after herself while she changed her name, her face . . .

Too many unanswered questions. A dull throb against my temples. Concentrate on the gun, the gun . . .

Elevator's almost here. Shemp murmurs something under his breath. Checking him out of the corner of my eye, I see that he's gone eyes-up. Moe's telling him something on his private line. Then he smiles. "Chill out, man," he says aloud. "Everything's going to be cool."

Yeah, right. I'll show you cool, you backstabbing son of a bitch.

Then the car slides into view. The Superior between me and the dead soldier takes another step back, giving me another foot of room to dive through.

The lift halts, the doors slide open. At first I think it's empty, but then a hardsuited figure steps forward. A baseline human, still wearing his helmet. He walks out of the lift until he's standing only a few feet before me.

Oh, no. Naw, man, this can't be . . .

He reaches up, unlatches the suit's collar, lifts the helmet over his head.

Pale lips against alabaster skin, long white hair pulled back in a ponytail. Cold pink eyes, like diluted blood on ice.

Hot anger jets through my veins.

"Young Alec," says Mister Chicago. "It's so good to see you again. I've been . . ."

Duck. Turn sideways. Hurl myself at the dead soldier. Screw escape. All I want is the blaster, and one good, clean shot at this albino motherfucker . . .

I'm not even halfway across the floor when something like a mallet slams into the back of my neck. Anna screams, the floor rushes at me and I tumble

       down

            a long

                  shaft

                        into

TWENTY-FOUR

I GOT ID

We are as gods, and might as well get good at it.

—Stewart Brand, *The Whole Earth Catalog*

darkness
cold
sleep
silence
A tiny light ignites.
It grows larger, becomes a circle.
The circle flattens out, becomes an oval.
The oval expands, becomes a spotlight.

Then a figure walks into the spotlight, a lanky young man in his mid-twenties: long blond hair, old flannel shirt, baggy jeans, scuffed Reeboks with loose laces. Myself, the way I looked a hundred and five years ago. He stops in the center of the light and looks straight at me.

"Hello, Alec," he says. "I'm Chip."

I want to reply, but I can't. It's worse than being mute: I have no sensation of having a mouth, or even a body. I'm simply a presence, a ghost in my own dream.

"I know this must be unpleasant for you," Chip says, "but we've got to talk, and assuming your own aspect is the only way I can think of that'll make you pay attention." His tucks his hands in his pockets and shuffles his feet a bit. "Y'see, after having spent almost two years in your head, I've come to learn that you don't listen very well. Always interrupting, always wanting to have the last word, not really caring what other people have to say . . . that's what everyone says about you. Sorry, but it's true. So, just this once . . ."

WILL YOU SHUT UP AND LISTEN?

The words vanish, and Chip's still there. "Okay? Now, look, there're a few people who want to talk to you. I'm going to bring them on one at a time. Erin's first. Erin . . . ?"

He turns and walks out of the spotlight. A moment passes, then Erin comes onstage.

She looks almost exactly the way she did the last time I saw her, back in 1995: long brown hair, wearing shorts and a tank top, sunburned and a little sweaty, as if she just got back from Lollapalooza. When she stops in the middle of the stage, a chair appears behind her: she sits down, crosses her long brown legs, and folds her hands together in her lap.

"Hi, Alec. It's me again . . . just the way you remember me. I could have done Anna for this, but I think it's important that you see me this way. Maybe it'll make things a little easier."

She looks away for a moment, then goes on. "The first thing you've got to know is that I love you, and that I've always loved you. Even after I lost you in the crash, I kept on loving you. If you hadn't died, I think we would have eventually married, even had a child together. Erin could have been our daughter."

She nervously glances down at her hands. "But it didn't happen that way. I had to carry on with my life, and that's what I did. I met someone else a few years later . . . no, you didn't know him . . . and we finally got married. It didn't last very long, but I conceived Erin with him before we broke up, and when she was born I gave her my first and last names. That's why there's another woman named Erin Westphall who isn't me."

A window opens next to Erin: a photo of an elderly woman, gnarled, frail, and gray-haired, seated in something that looks like a floating armchair. Standing behind is a woman in the last years of her youth. Both look like older aspects of Erin.

"Anyway, when I was sixty-eight and knew that I wasn't going to be around much longer, I opted for cryonic stasis. All the things I told you that day when you found me in bed with Chris were true . . . I did it because I wanted to see the future. What I didn't tell you was that I also wanted to see Erin again. She was about forty by then, and a couple of years earlier she had signed up with the Immortality Partnership. There weren't many new neurosuspension patients by then, and the Immortality Partnership was discussing the idea of shipping its existing patients to a space colony. So I invested what little money I had in the shrunken head treatment, and died in 2040 hoping that I would be reunited with my only child."

The window closes, leaving Erin alone once again. "But there was only one thing about this that troubled me, and that was the fact that you had already been in neurosuspension for the last forty-five years. I loved you, but nonetheless you were someone I had left behind almost a half-century ago. I had already spent nearly twice as many years apart from you as I had lived when I knew you, do you understand? I simply didn't want to see you again. You were a tragic chapter of my life that I had closed a long time ago. Please forgive me, but that's the way it was."

Unable to look at me, she kneads her hands together in her lap. Somehow, she looks like an old lady now.

"Before I signed the contract with the Immortality Partnership, I changed my legal name to Anna Townshend. I did this to make sure that you wouldn't be able to track me down, if and when you were revived at the same place and time I was. My daughter kept her name, of course, but I figured that if you found her, you would immediately know that we weren't the same person. Which, of course, is what happened."

She looks straight at me now. "But because I wanted to be certain that Erin could find me once she was revived, I had it entered in my permanent records that my real name was Erin Westphall, and that the other Erin Westphall was my daughter. I never once considered the notion that she and I would be so widely separated that we couldn't be easily reunited. My main consideration was that you might find me, and somehow believe that I had gone into neurosuspension in order to be reunited with you."

She sighs and shakes her head. "But we were revived together, although it turned out that my new face had been deliberately altered so that you couldn't recognize me . . . I'll let someone else explain why that happened. When we were in the

White Room together, though, I felt an attraction toward you that I couldn't place, just as I seemed to recognize Chris before I knew who he was. For a little while, even without realizing what was happening, I was beginning to fall in love with you all over again. But then . . . oh, God . . ."

Erin abruptly turns her face away from me. She raises her hands to her eyes, rubs them, takes a deep breath, goes on. "Do you remember when that . . . that animal, George . . . tried to rape Kate in the shower room? I had to fight him off her, and no one could stop him until his associate killed him? Do you remember that?"

She stares straight at me, her eyes red, her voice ragged with tears. "You were there, Alec! You just sat there on the pot, taking a dump, watching everything . . . and you didn't do a goddamn thing! I . . . you . . . just sat there . . . like . . . oh, goddammit . . . !"

HOW COULD YOU BE SO SELFISH?

The words are an onyx wall. It totters, falls forward, comes crashing down on me. Letters shatter upon impact, throwing debris in all directions.

Erin stands alone within the rubble.

"I'm sorry. I didn't mean it to come out like that . . . but it's true, and when I recovered my memory, this was something I could neither forgive nor forget."

She sighs. "You always were selfish, and you always were arrogant . . . these were things that I didn't realize about you until I saw you again. And the more I came to know you, the more I saw you hadn't changed."

Erin dissolves into the woman I met in the White Room. "So I kept my identity from you," Anna says. "Even after I met Chris and . . . well, you know how that happened. I fell out of love with you and fell in love with him. Then . . ."

Anna stops herself. "Well, I'll let Chris handle that part. He should speak for himself. But . . . well, I'm sorry I deceived you. You found my daughter, even though you didn't know what you were doing, and for that I'm grateful. And despite everything else, I still love you. Maybe not the same way I once did, but . . ."

She shrugs, and once more she briefly becomes Erin: my one true love, lost and rediscovered, now lost again.

"So that's it. Maybe I'll see you later. Bye . . ."

Then she walks out of the spotlight.

If I had a voice, I would be screaming.

"Hey, dude. Remember me?"

Shemp follows his voice into the spotlight. Like Erin before him, he once again resembles his former self: overweight, bespectacled, wearing knee-length shorts and a tie-dyed shirt with big sweat stains under the armpits. The chair reappears; he flops down in it.

"Thought you might be happier if you saw me like this again," he says. "Not that I particularly liked myself, but, y'know, I always sorta had a problem with self-respect. This didn't help much either. . . ."

He raises a hand; a joint appears in it. "I mean, if I couldn't get laid, at least I could get high. Remember when you first turned me on? I'll let you in on a secret . . . Bill Clinton wasn't the only guy who didn't inhale. I really didn't want to get high, but, hell, I wanted to be one of the cool guys, so this was my way in. After awhile I really did inhale, and when inhaling wasn't enough, I started in on acid."

Shemp shakes his head; the joint vanishes. "I think I did about three hits of blotter the day we went to Lollapalooza. That was the next-stupidest thing I ever did. The stupidest was letting you talk me into driving us home. But that's the way you always were . . . calling me your best friend, then making me do things you didn't want to do yourself. I mean, there was a hotel only a couple of hundred feet away. We could have gotten a couple of rooms, hung around the bar for an hour or two, then crashed upstairs. But, no, you wanted to go back to your place so you could do Erin while I sat out in the living room and watched TV again, trying not to hear you guys going at it, feeling sorry for myself because . . ."

He closes his eyes, takes a deep breath. "No, no . . . I'm not going to do this. It's my fault, too. I know that. But there're a couple of things you oughtta know. . . .

"Alec, buddy, the fact of the matter is that you used me. You gave me a nickname I hated, then you played at being my friend while, in reality, I was little more than your sidekick. Good ol' Shemp. You did it in your first life, and then you tried doing it again in your second life. But the second time around, I was a little smarter."

In the wink of an eye, Shemp disappears; he's replaced by Christopher, a tall man of average weight, without glasses, wearing a hooded white robe.

"Here's something else. Back on the asteroid, I

recognized you long before you recognized me. At first I didn't know exactly who you were, but when I finally did remember, I tried to keep my distance. I didn't want to go through all that with you again. But when you fell down those stairs that day, I forgot all the abuse and ran to help you . . . and that was it. It all started up again. Maybe you don't know it, maybe you couldn't help it, but you always patronized me. And it hurt, man, it really hurt, because even though you gave me shit, I still liked . . ."

He stares down at the floor. "I loved you. You were my best friend."

He's silent for a few moments, then he looks up again. "But by then I had met Anna, and even before she told me who she really was, I was falling for her. I didn't like Erin very much back then . . . y'know, the apartment thing and all that . . . but then we discovered that we had something in common. Both of us loved and hated you. So we kept Anna's identity secret from you, and pretty soon we were sleeping together, and . . ."

He laughs out loud. "Man, I gotta admit . . . that was the funny part! I was making love to your girl, and you didn't have a clue! Even when you walked in on us, you had no idea what was going on! Do you have any idea how much that meant to me? I was finally getting back at you, you son of a bitch!"

He chuckles over this for a moment, then sobers up. "Anyway . . . as you've probably guessed by now, none of this was accidental. Not entirely, at any rate. Mister Chicago knew who Anna really was even before he revived us. That's why he changed Erin's appearance so that you wouldn't recognize her. After we regained our memories and started interacting with one another, he realized that there was a three-way relationship—a romantic triangle, if you want to call it that, although it was more like a Punch and Judy show, if you ask me—that he could exploit for his purposes. He had plans for you, see, and the fact that all this happened just made it a little easier."

Chris shifts a little in his seat, propping one leg up on his knee. "When he asked me to take over as his new majordomo, it wasn't just because he took John out of the picture . . . oh, and by the way, he didn't really die. The whole thing was faked. John's still alive. So's Sam, for that matter . . . anyway, when he asked me to take over for John, he revealed to me what this was all about, and I agreed to go along with him. First, because this was all part of a scheme that had been in the making even before we woke up. When he told this to me, I realized that I wanted to go along with it. For the first time in my life, I was part of something that really mattered."

Then he smiles. "And second, I had permission to push you around. Yeah, maybe I overdid it a little. I know you really despised me for it, too. But I can't honestly say that I didn't enjoy myself. Revenge is sweet, dude, and you had it coming."

A window opens to the left of him. From some distance behind, I see myself slowly walking down the Level D corridor, the hood of my robe raised over my head. I stop suddenly, turn halfway around; my eyes are blindfolded with a strip of black fabric. "That's what it looked like from my eyes," Shemp says, watching the scene with some amusement. "I've gotta give you credit, though," he says, "that took a lot of balls. I knew you were going to escape during the party, but I didn't know how. Pasquale let me follow you . . . that was me you thought you heard behind you."

Another window opens to his right. This time, the camera angle is from the ceiling of the hub corridor where the EVA pods were docked. From above, I watch myself opening a pod hatch. I look both ways, then pull off my robe and toss it on the floor before swinging feetfirst through the hatch. A few moments later it closes behind me. "That was pretty good, too, I gotta admit," he says, "but do you really think you could have stolen that thing without anyone knowing? I mean, c'mon . . ."

He sighs. "You didn't make it easier on yourself, either. When Anna, Vlad, and I approached you back in Clarke County, we didn't have any intention of killing you. In fact, if you had just waited a minute longer, I would have explained the whole thing to you . . . well, almost everything. We figured that you'd probably learned where the dewars were located, and I wanted to give you a chance to voluntarily help us recover them. But you had to pull that stunt with throwing over the table, which accomplished nothing but piss off Vlad. He might have murdered you just out of spite, but you managed to fight him off and make your escape."

He shrugs offhandedly. "Just as well, though. We were tracking you the entire time through your MINN, so we knew exactly where you were going. So all you did was put yourself through some more unnecessary grief. But, like Anna says, you've always had a hard time listening to anyone."

Both windows vanish. When Shemp turns to face me again, he's decked out in the same outfit he wore in Clarke County. "Okay, bottom line. You were had. You were manipulated from the word go. Both Anna and I were part of it, although Anna didn't know the whole story until after you left, so don't blame her. But we did it for all the best reasons and . . ."

He stops. "Well, look . . . like I said, I can't honestly say that I didn't enjoy myself. You were shitty to the people who loved you the most, and this was our way of getting back at you. Sorry, but that's the way it is."

Shemp stands up from the chair. It vanishes, leaving him alone in the spotlight. "Now we're even. If . . . I mean, when I see you again . . . I hope you won't hold this against me. You probably will, but maybe that's just the way you are. But, y'know . . ."

He glances at his feet, then back up at me again. "Well, I think you've changed, and I think it's for the better. I hope I'm right. Because you really were an asshole."

Then he turns and walks out of the spotlight. "Catch you later, man," he says as he vanishes. "Someone else wants to talk to you now."

"Hello, young Alec. It's been a long time since we've had a chat, hasn't it?"

Mister Chicago walks into the light.

He's dressed the same way as I last saw him, the night of the party. He doesn't bother with a chair; when he reaches the center of the stage, he lifts one leg, then the other, and crosses them together while floating a couple of feet off the floor.

"I imagine you're probably wondering why I went to all that trouble . . . changing Anna's face, faking John's death, having Vladimir Algol-Raphael and your friend Chris harass you, allowing you to escape. The reasons should be obvious by now, but in case you're still confused, I'll briefly summarize.

"I wished to discover the whereabouts of the remaining dewars. My resources within the Pax Astra are limited, and it was too risky to send anyone from the Zodiac, since most of our people have been marked by Royal Intelligence. Therefore, I decided that the only way to accomplish this was to create a deep-cover operative . . . a secret agent, if you will, but one whose mission was unknown even to himself. That way, if he was caught and interrogated, he couldn't tell anything. However, if and when he located the dewars, he would have been programmed to shut down the site's defenses and signal my ships to come in and make the snatch."

He idly raises a hand; a wine goblet appears within it, and he takes a contemplative sip. "Lovely vintage. Ares Olympus '56. Remind me to give you a taste sometime." He opens his hand and the goblet disappears.

"To continue . . . you were selected for this job when I discovered that you had two friends among the deadheads whom I had already purchased from the Pax, but one of whom had changed her name so that she wouldn't be found by you. The possibilities this presented were intriguing, but even more so was this recording, cached within your files from the Immortality Partnership. Do you recall, during our first meeting, that I asked you about your father? This is why I was so interested in him. . . ."

A window opens next to him, expanding to fill the stage.

Suddenly, Dad appears.

He's sitting in a chair, in what I recognize as his office; the image is a little grainy, the colors washed out and old. He looks almost the same way as he did when I last saw him, yet somehow it seems as if he's put on a few years. His face is haggard, his eyes deep-set and haunted. He's frozen for a moment, then suddenly he's animated.

"Alec, my son . . . if you're seeing this, then something miraculous has happened. You're alive again, many years after your untimely death. I've long since passed away by now, of course. You'll never see me again. I didn't sign a contract with the Immortality Partnership because I don't want to see the future. Instead, I've given this option to you . . . a final gift, as it turns out, from a father who neglected you far too often when you were alive."

Dad takes a deep breath. He looks away for a moment, rubs his nose, then turns back to the camera.

"Son, I know you despised me, nor can I blame you for that. I was a lousy excuse for a father. I believed that business was more important than family, so instead of trying to raise you properly, I threw money at you and hoped that you would go away. There were times that I was disappointed in you, but I never stopped loving you, and . . . and now that you're gone, I can only hope and pray that you'll make the best of whatever tomorrow you wake up in. I just hope . . . I just hope that . . ."

There's a skip in the recording: Dad changes slightly from one instant to the next. Now his eyes are red, his tie a little askew. He's been crying.

"Alec, son . . . I don't like saying this, particularly now, but . . . but the fact of the matter is that you wasted your life. You lived high with no ambitions except your own self-satisfaction, and it's my great shame that I spoiled you. I love you, but you were self-indulgent and mean, and your only real friends were Chris and Erin. Chris is a fine boy, and I'm sincerely grateful that the Meyers have also signed him into this program before he . . . before you and he . . ."

He blinks away tears. "Well, perhaps you'll find him again in the next life. Erin's a lovely girl, and I know she loved you as much as you loved her. The fact you'll never see her again is something I regret. I'm just happy that she survived the car crash that took you and Chris. But I hope . . ."

He pauses to daub his eyes with a wadded paper tissue.

"I just hope that you make the best of your second life . . . your second chance . . . and that you won't waste the opportunity. For this reason, I'm leaving you no money other than the trust fund necessary to maintain your neurosuspension."

He takes a deep breath.

"In the next life, you're on your own. You'll probably hate me for this, even curse my name . . . but I think it's time that you learn to stand on your own two legs, and stop depending on your father to bail you out."

A weak, faltering smile.

"Son . . . Alec, my son . . . I love you. I hope you'll find it in your heart to love me, too. Good-bye and good luck . . ."

Then he's gone.

The window shrinks and vanishes, leaving Mister Chicago in its place. No wineglass, no smirk.

"Human potential has always been of great interest to me, William Alec Tucker III," he says, "and what I saw here was a testament to a father's faith in his son to rise above himself and achieve great things, even after death. By all accounts, you were a spoiled brat, a wealthy scion with no greater aspirations than pampering yourself with toys and games . . . and yet, your father thought enough of you to give you another chance to become a man. So I gave you this opportunity.

"I created hardship and humiliation. I gave you enemies and concocted threats to your very existence. I deliberately drove you out of my home and sent you flailing into the cold depths of space. The only aid I gave you was an associate which was little more than a reflection of your own id. Yes, I used you for my own purposes, so much that you even attempted to kill me when you finally received the chance. There were many times, observing from afar, when I was convinced that my gambit would fail, that I had staked far too much on such a miserable excuse for a human being."

Mister Chicago unfolds his legs so that his feet touch the floor again. "Yet, despite all odds, you succeeded. At age one hundred and thirty-one, you've finally grown up. Your friend Christopher was correct. You've changed. You're a man now. For this, I salute you."

He takes a deep bow from the waist, straightens up again. "Now, you may be asking, why have I gone to so much effort to acquire those dewars?"

He smiles. "Young Alec, you accused me once of wanting a slave colony. I laughed when you said this, knowing that you hadn't divined my purposes. Well, now . . . here is the reason."

Once again, a window opens behind him, yet this time Mister Chicago remains inside the image. Garcia, with its colony tethered above its north pole, expands to fill the screen.

Yet the asteroid is different now; much has changed since the last time I saw it. Vast vents, each miles in diameter, have been carved into the northern hemisphere below the hub, behind the habitats. The focal point shifts, and now I can see the enormous maw of an engine within the southern pole. On either side of this artificial crater are two smaller engines, each large enough to swallow the tiny spacecraft hovering nearby.

Mister Chicago points to the engine ports. "A Bussard fusion ramjet, Alec. With its fusion boosters it's sufficiently powerful to thrust Garcia not only out of its orbit, but beyond the solar system, to another star. Humankind's first starship."

Another window opens: this one shows rows of dewars stowed within what looks like a spaceship's cargo bay. "The journey will be long. Even after it achieves fifty percent of light-speed, it will take more than seventy years to reach its destination. These are the passengers . . . men and women from your own time, who will be revived within cloned bodies to colonize a new world far beyond the reach of the Pax Astra. Passengers you helped us find, Alec."

4442 Garcia diminishes until it becomes a tiny object, lost within the ringed orbits of the solar system—an image nearly identical to the mosaic floor of the Great Hall of Mister Chicago's castle. "It's a new century, Alec. The solar system is fast becoming too small to contain humankind. The Pax Astra is a corrupt monarchy, destroying itself with petty wars waged only for the sake of sustaining mindless power. What once seemed to be a limitless frontier now has a visible horizon, yet the Pax is disinterested in anything save assuring its own survival. But the Zodiac has recognized these facts, as have the Superiors. Whether for religious reasons or for sheer pragmatism, the time has come for humankind to move on.

"As I said, I believe in the power of human potential. For all their pretensions, greed, and narcissism, the people of your time were great survivors. They had to be . . . your century was the bloodiest epoch in human history, and even the weakest among you was forced to cope with its horrors on a daily basis. This is why I deliberately sought out its last survivors, the ones who had committed themselves to neuro-suspension. They wanted to see the future, or at least another chance at life. I'm giving them the chance to settle another world, an opportunity to start a new civilization. I systematically weeded out the cruel and the inhumane, and made sure that those who were left were strong enough to handle the task before them. Where I once had a few dozen confused dead-heads, I now have a crew of seasoned spacefarers who know this vessel inside and out, and dozens more who will be resurrected before the ship arrives at the new world. I couldn't have done better if I had asked for volunteers."

The starfield shrinks and disappears, leaving Mister Chicago alone once again within a tiny oval of light.

"So I give you a choice. Join us, or be left behind. If you join us, all your friends are waiting for you. Chris, Erin, John, Russell, Sam, Kate, Vlad, everyone else you knew on Garcia . . . even me, if you'll consider me to be a friend. I don't claim to be a saint, but neither am I the madman we deliberately led you to believe that I was. We'll be the crew of the *Jerome J. Garcia*. The journey will be long and difficult, despite all our advance preparations, but no one will be a slave. Even at relative speeds, we will grow old before the ship reaches its destination, but at least we'll assure the future of humankind."

The spotlight narrows, collapsing upon itself.

"Or you can be placed in neurosuspension again, and join the other sleepers when their bodies are regenerated dozens of light-years from home. This is risky, because no one has ever revived a brain from neurosuspension twice. I think you'd be a good leader, but you would be among strangers. However, it's a new start."

The light fades, swallowing Mister Chicago into its abyss, leaving nothing behind except his voice.

"Or you can simply wish to end it here and now. Perhaps you've had enough, and only death is attractive to you. You've been abused and humiliated. This darkness may be your only comfort. Suicide is not dishonorable. If you wish to stop this now, we'll let you go, and fare you well."

Now his voice is distant, as if coming from the bottomless well.

"Blink your eyes once for the first option, twice for the second, three times for the third."

I consider my choices.

"You can blink, can't you?"

Yeah, I can blink.

Once. Just once.

✛ CHAPTER ✛

TWENTY-FIVE

BY STARLIGHT

*O God, I could be bounded in a nutshell and count
myself a king of infinite space, were it not that I have
bad dreams.*

—William Shakespeare, *Hamlet*

And then I woke up, and found that it had all
been a dream.

The part about the spotlighted stage, I mean.
That was something Chip had whipped up for me
during the last eight minutes of my six-month
sleep in the *Anakuklesis* hibernation bay. After Vlad
coldcocked me in Sosigenes Center, Mister Chicago
decided that I would be less of a nuisance if I warm-
tanked the ride back to Garcia; while I was coming
out of my trance, he, Shemp, and Erin had their little tête à tête with me, courtesy of a real-time eyes-
up interface with Chip.

So I awoke to find myself in the all-too-familiar
infirmary within Garcia—or rather, the starship
Jerome J. Garcia—with Dr. Miesel removing a catheter
from my prick and telling me it was okay to pee
again. After I filled a couple of bedpans for her, I was

allowed visitors. Not surprisingly, it was Shemp and Erin—or rather, Chris and Anna—who were the first to see me.

We had a long talk.

I'll spare you the details. Let's just say that everyone apologized to each other for things that went back many years, and then we agreed to be friends again. Of course, there was no doubt that Anna and I were no longer an item; she was Chris's girl now, and that wasn't going to change. Oddly, I didn't mind; Anna had always been a friend, but I had never been that strongly attracted to her. She might still be Erin deep inside, but she was a different woman now; it was Anna whom Chris had fallen for, and I couldn't help but feel happy for him.

When they came in, the first thing I noticed was that they weren't wearing robes, but blue jumpsuits. It turned out none of us were servants anymore; we were now the crew of the *Jerome J. Garcia*. In fact, Mister Chicago had manumitted all the deadheads; if we cared to leave the asteroid, we could do so, and in the weeks that followed a few people did just that, migrating either to other Belt colonies or to Mars. It wasn't considered advisable for anyone to return to Earth, though; not only were their bodies ill-suited for one-gee gravity, but it was generally understood that the Pax Astra wouldn't welcome them warmly, particularly not after what had happened at Sosigenes Center. I imagine some of the more homesick ones tried anyway, and I wish them the best of luck.

But most of us decided to remain on the *Garcia*, now that its true purpose was revealed. Part of the reason why we'd spent so much time in servitude was that Mister Chicago had been covertly training us for the long voyage ahead; although we would now be formally educated by our associates to perform the more complex jobs requisite aboard a starship, some of our chores would remain the same. Crops still had to be cultivated, floors needed to be mopped, laundry had to be folded. Yet never again would any of our associates punish us, except when maintaining shipboard discipline called for it as a last resort. I'm sure that will seldom be necessary. We're no longer slaves, but free men and women; if we're still here, it's because we want to be.

I had a few more visitors while I was in the infirmary. John, very much alive, embarrassed and overapologetic for having pulled a phony death scene on me; a tiny capsule of blood in his nose had done the trick, along with some hidden thespian talents. I told him that it was okay, that I understood why he had done it, that I was pleased to see him again, and he went away happy. He was one deadhead who would remain something of a servant, due to his mental impairment, but now he was Mister Chicago's personal valet and couldn't be happier. Sam dropped by; it was good to see that reports of his demise had been greatly exaggerated. In his new role as ship's historian, he had been assigned to write the official log of the coming voyage. When I told him that I had started writing my own memoir, he volunteered to be my editor: once it was completed, it would be added to the ship's library. Sam was a working writer again; his block was gone for good. And then there were Russell and Kate; Russell was being trained as an assistant engineer and would help oversee the nuclear generators and Bussard ramjet, and Kate was learning the ropes in the astrogation department. During my long absence they had stopped fooling around and started getting serious about their relationship; like everyone else, they had moved upstairs to the castle, where they now shared a suite whose bed they had once made for other people.

I even got paid a brief visit by Vladimir Algol-Raphael. He wouldn't be joining us on the journey; his place was with his clan. However, as part of the Zodiac's deal with Mister Chicago, we would be carrying a number of deceased Superiors in neurosuspension with us. When the ship arrived at its final destination, they would be among those who would be resurrected on another world. It wasn't quite the Omega Point that the Superiors believed in, but it was a step closer.

That wasn't why Vlad came to see me, though. He told me, in stiffly formal tones, that his debt of honor to me, owed by my refusal to take his life after our fight in Clarke County, had been paid in full; he didn't kill me in Sosigenes Center when he easily could have. Our books were now settled; he was neither friend nor foe.

Then he asked me how I learned how to swordfight like a Superior. I was only too happy to tell him. That fried his hash; he left after that, and I like to believe that he now thinks twice about picking fights with Primaries.

But I didn't see or hear a thing from Mister Chicago until Dr. Miesel gave me my walking papers and told me to stop haunting her infirmary. It was not until then, when I walked out into the corridor, wondering what I was going to do next, that I saw the man whom I had tried to kill the last time I was close to him.

■   ■   ■

"Alec, will you take a walk with me? I have something to show you."

Almost the same words he said to me that day when, disguised as John, he led me from the White Room. We're both wearing the same outfits, too: white hooded robes. I'm wearing mine because that's the only thing Dr. Miesel had in the infirmary; I've no idea why Mister Chicago is decked out like this. Fashion statement, I guess.

I've got an urge to throttle him. Sure, everything's been explained to me; I now see the logic behind his scheme, the necessity of what he did. Indeed, the other deadheads apparently consider me something of a hero; I put my ass on the line for them, however unwittingly, and they respect me for this. But the fact still remains: this pink-eyed bastard used me.

"Sure, Mister Chicago," I say. "I'll walk with you."

There's an edge in my voice that he chooses to ignore. He doesn't reply, but simply turns and starts walking down the busy corridor. Crewmen quickly stride past us on their way to one vital errand or another. The *Garcia* is scheduled to depart in only three days. The *Pegasus* has followed the *Anakuklesis* from the Moon, and we've received reports that the big Royal Navy dreadnought has just crossed Mars orbit and will soon be entering the Belt. I don't think the Pax wants its decapitated heads back; now that they know where Mister Chicago hides out, they're coming to smoke cigarettes and kick ass, and nobody makes cigarettes anymore. So everyone's getting ready for the big moment.

He must be reading my mind. "You've been informed where we're going, haven't you?"

"Uh, yeah." My mind's still a little cloudy from the zombie tank. "Some star in the Big Dipper. Forty-seven something . . ."

"Forty-seven Ursae Major, about thirty-five light-years from here." He nods. "A white star very much like the Sun, although the system is a bit different. Most of its planets lie either too deep within or too far beyond the habitable zone. Yet there's a superjovian gas giant located about two AUs from the primary, one about three and a half times the size of Jupiter . . ."

"We're going there? I don't think that'll support . . ."

"No, it won't, but about thirty-seven years ago an interstellar probe launched by the Pax entered the system and surveyed the planet during a flyby. Royal Intelligence classified most of the data when it was received a couple of years ago, but the Zodiac managed to ferret out the most vital information."

"Why did the Pax put a lid on it?"

"How does any tyranny stay in power?" We step aside to let a hovercart pass. "Information control. They wanted to prevent anyone from knowing that there was another habitable solar system." He chuckles. "After all, someone might get it in their heads to leave."

"Oh, that's awful. Imagine, wanting to escape from a tyrant . . ."

If Mister Chicago catches the remark, he ignores it. "At any rate, several large moons orbit the superjovian, and one of them is capable of supporting human life. A bit frosty, yes, but it has one-third Earth gravity, an oxygen-nitrogen atmosphere, a stable orbit . . ."

"What about life?"

"We'll know when we get there." He smiles. "It scarcely matters, my dear Alec. We'll become its inhabitants, Alec. . . . Or rather, our descendants will be."

I already know about this part, from Chip's briefing. Even after the *Jerome J. Garcia* reaches its top velocity of half the speed of light, it will still take more than seventy years for it to reach its destination. We have longer lifespans now, thanks to nanosurgical repair of our bodies at the cellular level, and the trip will seem shorter to us because of time dilation. Yet, many of us may not survive the journey. Those of us who don't will have children who will finish the voyage we've begun.

"It's a one-way trip, dude," I murmur, "and this ain't the *Enterprise*."

Mister Chicago gives me a quizzical look; he understands the meaning, if not the allusion. "Yes, it is at that. Which means our passengers will be the ones who'll settle the new world. That's where you come in."

He stops before a door, passes his hand before it. It irises open, revealing a small and dimly lit room. He leads me in; on the other side of the room is a large, double-paned window. "Your father wanted you to learn responsibility," he says softly as I step closer to see what lies on the other side. "I think you're capable of that now."

Beyond the window, the dewars from Sosigenes Center: rows of stainless steel tanks, containing the heads, minds, and souls of dozens of people from my own lifetime. The future residents of a new planet, scheduled for rebirth once the *Garcia* arrives at a tiny world in the Big Dipper.

"Would you like a job?" he asks.

And now it's three days later, and only an hour remains until the big fusion boosters on the other side of the *Garcia* fire. The last tons of helium–3 have been loaded into the fuel tanks within the asteroid's hollowed-out core; the Superior vessels that delivered the fuel have long since departed, and messages had been broadcast on all frequencies, warning all ships to stay away from the asteroid. I'm told that when the boosters ignite, the flare will extend for thousands of miles; observatories in the inner system will see the sudden birth of a new comet.

Everyone in the habitats has been instructed to strap down before primary ignition; it's going to take a lot of power to break the *Garcia* from its orbit, and the initial thrust may be violent. We've gone so far as to tape the windows in the castle. In a few minutes I'll head up to my room in the castle, but right now I'm sitting on a bench in the rose garden, dictating these last thoughts to Chip.

It's quiet out here.

I took the job. I'm going to be trained to monitor the dewars. Since I spent so much time inside one of them, and saw firsthand what they looked like when they were stored on the Moon, Mister Chicago believes that I'm the best person for this assignment. I still despise him, but I know that he's right. There's probably another William Alec Tucker III within one of those things, and the little bastard will need all the help he can get.

I'm in for another long trip, but this time I'm not making it alone. All my friends are here and I'm making new ones. Erin—not Anna, but the girl I found at Sosigenes Center—came out a little while ago to bring me a glass of tea. I didn't ask her to do this. She just did it on her own. I think she kind of likes me. God, she looks so much like her mother. . . .

Nasty thoughts, Alec. Does this make me a pervert or what?

I dunno. Guess I'll have plenty of time to figure it out.

I've been wrong about many things, but I've had two lifetimes to learn from my mistakes. The biggest thing I've learned is this: Yes, there is a future, for each and every one of us. All you need is the willingness to face it.

I think this is called growing up.

AFTERWORD

This novel is part of a future history I've been developing over the last decade. There are four other novels and over a dozen short stories in the cycle; however it's not necessary for one to read any of these other tales. Readers interested in previous stories relevant to this novel are encouraged to find *Clarke County, Space* (Ace, 1990), *The Weight* (Legend; U.K., 1993), "The Death of Captain Future" (*The Year's Best Science Fiction, Thirteenth Annual Collection*, edited by Gardner Dozois; St. Martin's Press, 1996), and "Working For Mister Chicago" (*Absolute Magnitude*, edited by Warren Lapine; Tor, 1997).

I'm grateful to Steve Antczak, Greg Benford, Chad Childers, Warren Lapine, Bob Liddil, Marie Meisel, Masamichi Osako, Mark Tiedemann, and my sisters Elizabeth Steele and Genevieve Edwards for the suggestions, assistance, and encouragement they've given me during the writing of this novel (and, yes, a couple of these people appear in cameo roles).

Many thanks to Martha Millard, John Douglas, John Silbersack, and Rebecca Springer for their support.

Major research for the novel include: *Introduction to Asteroids*, by Clifford J. Cunningham (William-Bell, 1988); *Resources of Near-Earth Space*, edited by John S. Lewis, Mildred S. Matthews, and Mary L. Guerrieri (University of Arizona Press, 1993); *Wanderers in Space*, by Kenneth R. Lang and Charles A. Whitney (Cambridge University Press, 1991); "A.R.C.: Asteroid Resource Colony," by Claudio Veliz, from *Space Manufacturing 8*, edited by Barbara Faughnan and Gregg Maryniak (American Institute of Aeronautics and Astronautics, 1991); "Those Pesky Belters and Their Torchships," by Jerry Pournelle, from *A Step Further Out* (Ace, 1979); "Colonizing the Outer Solar

System," by Robert A. Zubrin, from *Islands in the Sky*, edited by Stanley Schmidt and Robert A. Zubrin (Wiley & Sons, 1996); "Cyborgs and Space," by Manfred E. Clynes and Nathan S. Kline, from *The Cyborg Handbook*, edited by Chris Hables Gray (Routledge, 1995); *The Engines of Creation*, by K. Eric Drexler (Anchor, 1986); *Cryonics: Reaching for Tomorrow* (Alcor Life Extension Foundation, 1995); *The Starflight Handbook*, by Eugene Mallove and Gregory Matloff (Wiley, 1989), and *The Physics of Immortality*, by Frank J. Tipler (Anchor, 1995).

More than any other novel I've yet written, this book was inspired by music. While the works of Ludwig von Beethoven, Franz Liszt, Felix Mendelssohn, and Bedrich Smetana were driving forces, I'm even more grateful to a large number of more contemporary artists: Tori Amos, Big Head Todd and the Monsters, Blues Traveler, Counting Crows, Cracker, Eric's Trip, Foo Fighters, Hole, The Jesus and Mary Chain, The Judybats, Midnight Oil, Nirvana, Oasis, Pearl Jam, Phish, Possum Dixon, R.E.M., The Smashing Pumpkins, Soul Asylum, The SubDudes, Vitamin A, and World Party. A flick of the Zippo to all; thanks for the tunes and chapter titles.

This is the tenth book my wife Linda has seen me write. Her courage should not be underestimated, nor her patience neglected.

Finally, a box of Milk Bones and some fresh tennis balls for the guys who kept me sane and happy during this journey: Zack, Jake, and Leclede. Please support your local Humane Society.

—St. Louis, Missouri
November 1995–October 1996